"FORGET ABOUT LAKE WOBEGONE. HANDS DOWN THE SMALL TOWN OF CHOICE IS TALL PINE."

—*Library Journal*

"Landvik has small town life down to a T.... [Her] strength has been in developing rich, unusual and memorable characters. This book is no exception.... Give *The Tall Pine Polka* a whirl."

—*Colorado Springs Gazette*

"Off-kilter characters with grit and humor populate this delightfully quirky novel.... So vivid and lively are Landvik's characters, readers will wish they could jump in the car and go find Cup O'Delight, settle in at the counter, and join a high-energy jam session. This is another down-home winner for Landvik."

—*Booklist*

"[A] swift-moving romp...Having previously created beguiling characters in *Patty Jane's House of Curl* and *Your Oasis on Flame Lake*, Landvik invites readers to belly up to the counter and join the regulars sipping coffee at the Cup O'Delight Cafe... [*The Tall Pine Polka*] is good-natured and zooms along, fueled by zany Minnesota energy."

—*Publishers Weekly*

Selected by the Literary Guild® and the Doubleday Book Club®

Also by Lorna Landvik

Patty Jane's House of Curl
Your Oasis on Flame Lake

The Tall
Pine Polka

—◆—

Lorna Landvik

Ballantine Books • New York

A Ballantine Book
Published by The Ballantine Publishing Group

www.randomhouse.com/BB/

This is a work of fiction. Names, characters, places, and incidents either are the product of the author's imagination or are used fictitiously.

Library of Congress Cataloging-in-Publication Data: 2001116595

ISBN 0-449-00370-1

Manufactured in the United States of America

First Hard Cover Edition: September 1999
First Trade Paperback Edition: June 2001

10   9   8   7   6   5   4   3   2   1

Prologue

There are four words Fenny Ness wished she had never spoken. These four words were not ones that cause obvious heartbreak like "We must operate immediately" or "I want a divorce," but because they were spoken, they nearly (literally) blew Fenny's chances for a normal life. Four innocent words addressed to a beefy teenager standing behind a counter patterned with smudges: "One Burrito Suprema, please."

Of course, nobody knew that *Ike and Inga* would become one of the top-grossing romantic comedies ever made. A bartender in Boston, after seeing the movie, was inspired to invent the "Ike & Inga Igloo," a blend of gin and shaved ice and peppermint schnapps, and within days the drink was being served in bars and lounges across America. Costumed *Ike and Inga* parties were held on college campuses and in singles apartment complexes. A production assistant wrote an account of the making of *Ike and Inga* and was a bestselling author two weeks after the book's publication. *Variety* called the movie "one of the biggest surprise hits in cinematic history." Harry Freed, the movie's producer, agreed completely with that assessment. His career had been based on pumping out low-budget B movies, and that one should actually become number one at the box office *and* receive critical praise was a likelihood he'd been too levelheaded to ever consider. Especially considering his nephew had so much to do with it.

"*Ike and Inga?*" Harry had said when his secretary brought him the script. "They did this a couple years ago—it was about that singer who wound up in jail, and his singer wife. The one with the muscles and the good legs."

"That was Ike and *Tina*," said his secretary. "Your nephew wrote this." She pointed to the bottom of the cover page, which read in fancy gold leaf, "Conceived and written by Christian Freed."

"That idiot," said Harry as he began kneading his temple with his fingers. Reading one of Christian's scripts was reminiscent of Harry's Golden Glove days in the ring with Hookie Turk: there was no way of escaping without a headache.

"It's actually kind of a cute story." Like all good secretaries, she read all of his correspondence before her boss did. "He's really come along since that one about the paid assassin/manicurist."

Harry rolled his eyes. "Then I'm presuming it's better than the one about the taxidermist who goes on a stuffing rampage at his high school reunion?"

"*Much* better. Really, Harry, this one's going to surprise you."

Harry sighed and sank into the cushions of his cracked leather chair. Drawing his knees to his chest, he wiggled his small feet at his secretary. She smiled at her employer of twenty-eight years, who in this position (one he assumed often) always reminded her of one of her grandchildren. But whereas grandchildren might want to be tickled or have their diapers changed, Harry Freed only wanted to be primed for work.

"You can't concentrate if your feet can't breathe," he told his secretary long ago.

Other secretaries might rebel against being asked to take off their boss's shoes, but Harry's secretary liked doing things for him. She had, after all, carried a torch for him for years, even though he wasn't interested in lighting it with his own.

She gently untied and pulled off her boss's wing tips and placed them in a wildly patterned bread box on top of his desk. Harry firmly believed in "a place for everything and everything in its place"—he simply chose to make use of things that, if used for their original intent, were useless to him.

"See," he explained to his secretary on her first day of work, "I get a lot of presents—people want to impress me, be my friend. So I get a god-awful hand-painted bread box from an actress who takes a couple of pop-art classes and suddenly thinks she's Andy Warhol. I'm supposed to put my bagels in that neon mess?" Harry paused, took a long drag of an unfiltered cigarette (he smoked in those days but quit when he started waking up to a cough instead of a clock alarm), and ashed it into a soap dish covered with pink porcelain cupids. Looking up at his new secretary, Harry had laughed at the confusion that lifted the penciled eyebrows on her young, pink face.

"Don't look so scared, honey. I've still got all my marbles. All tiger's eyes, too, I'll bet."

His secretary tried to smile and wished she had paid more attention to the "Staying Ahead of Your Boss" lecture that was given on Commencement Day at secretarial school.

Standing up behind his desk, Harry had spread his arms like a priest blessing the communion altar.

"Now, I don't want to hurt anyone's feelings—I'm a nice guy and you'll learn that soon enough—so I don't throw away any presents. Now, it stands to reason that I'll store my shoes in a hand-painted bread box, I'll ash my cigarette in a soap dish, and I'll give panhandlers movie passes instead of spare change. Y'understand?"

"Yes, Mr. Freed," lied his secretary. Her head bobbed up and down like a dashboard toy.

"Good," Harry had said. "Now go take a good long coffee break while I enjoy a little shut-eye."

And Harry's secretary had learned soon, just as he told her, that Harry was a nice guy. When her husband ran off with the girl who steam-pressed suits at the dry cleaner's, Harry's secretary thought she was finally free to love Harry and confessed this to him. Harry wiped away tears that began swimming in his dark brown eyes and took her hands.

"Just because I'm here," he said, "don't use me the way I use my bread box. There's got to be a better place for your lovely feelings."

Now Harry cleared his throat. "Save your trip to outer space for the weekend, honey."

Harry's secretary jumped so that her glasses, dangling on a silver chain around her neck, thwacked against her chest. It wasn't often Harry caught her meandering down Memory Lane.

"And pour me a nip, *por favor*."

His secretary opened the cabinet of the old teak grandfather clock and took out a bottle of brandy and a shot glass. She filled the glass and set it down on Harry's desk blotter, waiting for the words he always said.

"Now take the bottle, jazz up your coffee with it, and take a good long break." This was a treasured Thursday ritual. Back in her own office, she turned on the coffeemaker, instructed the switchboard to take all calls, put on her stereo headphones and a Nat King Cole album on the turntable. (She was never one to upgrade to tapes or CDs; she found the fuzzy hum of the needle against the record an integral part of her listening pleasure.)

An hour later, she had listened to both sides of the album, finished the shawl collar of a vest she was knitting for her son, and had a buzz on that would last the rest of the workday.

And Harry, who had finished reading *Ike and Inga*, sat facing the window, staring out past studio buildings the color of sand, past the line of brown smog smeared along the horizon. He rocked back and forth, unconsciously massaging his bald spot with the pads of his fingers.

"Well, well, well," he said aloud. His nephew, whose ambition had always outrun (by a great distance) his talent, had actually written a good script. Oh, sure, there were some lines that creaked like old floorboards, but on the whole, it was *good*. Harry checked the cover page to make sure it was his nephew's byline and then he called in his secretary to take a memo.

Harry Freed has told Fenny this story at least a dozen times.

"It's your beginnings," he explained. Although Harry is a worldly man, occasionally he suffers from the delusions of one who has spent his life making movies: that Hollywood, and not the equator, is the center of the earth. "The day I read Christian's script was the day you began your rendezvous with Fate."

"Fate had rendezvoused with me before, Harry."

"Well, sure," agreed Harry, "but not *Hollywood-style*."

Part One

Part One

Chapter 1

Two thousand miles from Hollywood, California, Fenny Ness would have preferred any sort of date with Destiny to the one she was on now.

She was ice-skating on the frozen surface of Tall Pine Lake with Craig Asper, who, when he wasn't falling, was trying to get Fenny to invest in his motivational tapes business.

"I get letters from guys who were on the brink of bankruptcy," he was saying, taking Fenny's arm as he wobbled on the ice. "Knowing that we helped them not only get back on their feet but *ignited their earning power* is really satisfying—makes you sort of understand how Albert Schweitzer and those other humanitarian guys felt."

It had taken Fenny a while to understand that the many stupid things Craig Asper said were *not* jokes; that he *did* think his "Strike While It's Hot and Earn!" tapes could perhaps save the world, or at least those interested in lighting a match to their earning power.

"Why do you make so many references to fire?" Fenny had asked earlier in the Northlands Inn dining room. This was a young man whose main interest, when she knew him at Bemidji State, had been beer, not blazes.

"Because fire is energy," said Craig, gazing into the table's candle flame with what Fenny thought was an interest bordering on pyromania. "Fire is power. The sun is a ball of fire and without the sun we'd die."

Fenny waited a moment for further elaboration, but there was none, and she made the first of many surreptitious glances at her wristwatch. Fortunately, she hadn't brought a swimsuit, so she had a good excuse for declining his invitation to take an after-dinner dip in the Jacuzzi and suggested they go ice-skating instead.

"You can rent skates from the hotel," she said.

"Great," said Craig, with none of his usual salesman's enthusiasm.

Right in the middle of his lecture on buying real estate with no money down, Craig took approximately his tenth fall.

"Enough of this Hans Brinker shit," he said, rubbing his tailbone. "Let's go back to the lodge and have a drink."

"Go ahead," said Fenny. "I'm just going to skate a little longer."

Craig Asper shrugged. "However you get your jollies."

Fenny watched as he stumbled in his skates up the wooden walkway to the small trailer the hotel had set up as a warming house and returned the wave he gave her just before he opened the door. Then, in the long clean strides she'd been unable to use while holding up the wobbly entrepreneur, she skated around the shoveled rink and then skated around it again, backward.

"She's fast," said a little boy, who on double-bladed training skates was making his way around the rink with his mother. He was right; Fenny was fast, and without the burden of Craig Asper on her arm, she felt she could almost fly.

The Rainy River cuts an aquatic border between Minnesota and Ontario, Canada, and situated on the south bank of this river was Tall Pine. It was an aptly named town, one that inspired tourists to remember poems they had memorized in junior high school ("This is the forest primeval . . .") and to send postcards with scribbled exclamations: "It's like Hal and I have been set down in the Christmas tree farm of Paul Bunyan!"

International Falls, at thirty miles to the east, and Baudette, at forty miles to the west, were the nearest metropolises, and it was there that the citizens of Tall Pine did their bulk supermarket and clothes shopping, where they got their driver's licenses renewed and their backs adjusted.

When Sigrid Ness's mother died, she and her husband, Wally, returned to Tall Pine for what they thought would be a two-week stay, long enough to bury Lena Nordstrom and take care of her affairs.

The couple hadn't been to their native Tall Pine since their wedding, having spent their entire married life in pursuit of international travel.

Sig was boxing up fishing lures in the general store/bait shop that had been in her family for over fifty years when Alma Forslund, a friend of her mother's, had come in and told Sig how happy she was to see Lena's daughter in the shop again and when was the blessed event?

"Blessed event?" said Sig, thinking for a moment that the woman was referring to the upcoming close-out sale.

Alma patted her own tummy. "It's sort of a sixth sense of mine. I can tell when an egg's incubating—even before the hen knows what hit her."

The doctor who had brought Sig into the world confirmed her pregnancy.

"I'd say you're about two months along."

Sig merely stared at him, as if she had just been told she'd won a lottery that she thought was no longer being held.

After sixteen years of a childless marriage, Sigrid and Wally Ness assumed it wasn't in their cards to bear fruit and multiply, and now, having conceived, they realized they were dealing from a whole new deck.

"So what about Belize?" Sig asked Wally, referring to the place that was next on their agenda.

"What about it?"

"Well, I know people have babies all over the world, but I'd like to have mine here."

Wally took his wife in his arms. "I am so glad you said that. I want to stay here and have the baby, too. I think it's time we settled down."

"You don't have to sound so apologetic," said Sig, laughing. "I think we should settle down, too."

Still holding one another, they laughed, in the delighted way of a long-married couple that finds they still can surprise one another.

Throughout Sig's pregnancy, she and Wally worked on reconfiguring Nordstrom's General Goods & Bait into two separate stores. They sold Lena's drafty Victorian house in town and moved into the log house that Wally had inherited from his long-dead parents.

"We're not settling down permanently," said Sig, who with an upside-down mop dusted years of cobwebs tatted into the corners of the ceilings.

"Absolutely not," said Wally. The couple felt a need to reassure one another that they weren't giving up adventure, only embarking on a slightly different kind.

"Birds' nest," said Sig resolutely. "But they still fly."

Wally nodded. "I don't see any clipped wings around here."

Fenny (her given name, Honoria, was dropped when as a toddler she had made her parents laugh and declared, "Me Fenny") was soon to experience her parents' wanderlust when at three weeks of age she was loaded up in the Dodge van and taken on a holiday trip through the Southwest. She spent her first Christmas at a campground outside Carlsbad, New Mexico, being rocked in front of an aspen-wood fire as a big-voiced woman from Tenafly led campers through peppy versions of "Good King Wenceslas" and "O Holy Night."

Sig and Wally were thrilled at her arrival, but they felt the major concession—staying in Tall Pine and giving their child stability—had been made and that few other concessions in their active lives were necessary. Conversely, Fenny was included in everything. As an infant, strapped onto her mother's back while Sig and Wally cross-country skied deep into the woods, she watched moonlight fall like blueing liquid across the snow; at six months of age, cradled in a life jacket between seats, she took her first boat ride.

The Ness family home was two miles outside Tall Pine proper, a log house whose front door faced a lake and whose back door was just yards away from a forest.

Fenny thrived there. By age six, she knew how to bait a hook and cast a fishing line, how to tie a slipknot, how to dive off the dock Wally had built. She could tell which trees belonged to the spruce family and which to the pine; she knew how to roll up a sleeping bag into a tight, neat cylinder and how to get her bearings by finding the North Star in a sky overwhelmed with pinpoints of light.

In the summer, the Ness family sat fishing until sunset striped the sky with colors, the water gently slapping the sides of the boat as orange darkened into red and red bled into dusk. In the spring, when the last of the ice gave way in big chunks, Fenny stood between her parents, watching vees of geese return from their winter vacations.

They roasted chestnuts and popped corn in campfires by Tall Pine Lake, they pitched tents in forest clearings, they carried lanterns through a frosty night to rescue a baby wolf trapped in the burlap sacks that covered the tomato plants.

When marooned inside, the Nesses' idea of entertainment was not sitting in front of a television set (which they did not own) but holding contests in birdcalling (Sig always won—she could give a lonely loon hope), knot tying, and target practice. Sig and Wally were not hunters, both disliking the taste of game; target practice for them was more a test of skill and hand-eye coordination.

Once Lars Larson, a hunting and fishing guide and their nearest neighbor, stopped by to find Wally, Sig, and Fenny perched in three corners of the living room, casting fishing lines at a Maxwell House coffee can in the middle of the room.

"Anything biting?" he asked, scratching the back of his broad, blond head.

The Nesses had kept the bait part of Nordstrom's General Goods & Bait and expanded on it, turning it into Wally's Bait & Camp. It smelled of fish and worms, the hardware of new rods and reels, tent canvas and the sweat and funk of canoeists who had stopped by to share their stories after weeks spent exploring Lake of the Woods or Rainy Lake or any of the other dozens nearby.

In the summer, for fifty cents per fish, Wally cleaned the catches of neophyte fishermen and -women whom he had, hours earlier, outfitted with bait and bobs and advice on where to find biting northern and walleye pike. It was a profitable sideline, and Fenny was often called upon to help; she could scale and gut a five-pound muskie in under two minutes.

On the other side of the thick wallboard that separated the two stores was Sig's Place, home to the craftwork of northern artisans. There were crocheted tablecloths; agate earrings; hand-knit sweaters patterned with reindeer and snowflakes; jars of potpourri, their fragrances dark and smelling of lake country; butter-soft moccasins, tanned, beaded, and stitched by Mae Little Feather (the most talented of her contributors but also the crabbiest); framed needlepoint samplers, their stitches immeasurably tiny; wool blankets; and patchwork quilts.

The only thing that wobbled the integrity of Sig's Place, as far as its proprietor was concerned, was a table in the northwest corner on which perched handiwork of the church circle women. Sig had been loath to open the shop to amateurs, but she grew tired of the pressure from Benevolent Father's Lutheran Church (known locally as B.F.), of which she was a member.

"Surely you're aware of the reservoir of talent in our congregation," said Gloria Murch, wife of the pastor.

Sig said no, she wasn't aware of any such reservoir, but when Gloria had an idea, she held on to it like a pit bull and soon Sig was besieged by doodads and gimcracks and ornaments that oozed driblets of hard and opaque Elmer's glue.

Serious customers ignored what Sig referred to as the Junk Table, but the churchwomen bought each other's handiwork, so Sig could be certain that even a Nativity scene made of dyed Q-Tips or the bas-relief map of Minnesota constructed of multicolored macaroni shells would eventually sell.

Running their own businesses, which they did with Fenny's help (it was she who made the stores' bank deposits, who washed the windows until they shone, who dusted and arranged merchandise, swept and waxed floors; she who double-checked invoices, who knew when to order rods and reels, and how to bargain with Mae Little Feather without losing her shirt), engaged the Nesses, but certainly not like their passion: travel. They indulged this passion domestically (they didn't consider Canada, right across the river, a foreign country) throughout Fenny's childhood, taking yearly trips to far-off states during the winter, and countless weekend camping trips throughout the year.

Fenny was a cheerful and able camper until homesickness set in and she'd begin to worry if their backyard bird feeders were empty or if Sig and Wally had remembered to put the canoe in the boathouse.

Even as a small child, nothing pleased her more about their travels than the ride home, when she began to recognize the landscape around Tall Pine.

"Twees!" she'd cry excitedly, and as she got older that exclamation gave way to ones like, "Oh, it's so beautiful here!" or "I am so happy to be home!" When she got into high school, she began making excuses why she couldn't join them on a canoe or camping trip: "I've got homework" or "It's Homecoming weekend" or "I've got a date."

Sig and Wally expected a child of theirs to inherit *certain* qualities, and she had; she was naturally easygoing like Wally, but when pushed, could be as feisty as her mother. ("If everyone stood up for themselves," Sig counseled Fenny, "bullies would be out of business.") Like both of them, she had a sly sense of humor, was an excellent sportswoman and a lover of the great outdoors (particularly the outdoors surrounding Tall Pine), but as yet, she felt no compulsion to backpack through Europe, to sign on as a cruise ship dishwasher and visit different ports, to ride crowded, tilting buses up into the thin altitudes of the Andes; to do what Sig and Wally had themselves done.

This is what baffled them: How had they spawned someone who hadn't inherited their *defining* trait, their spirit of adventure? How had their daughter become—it was hard for them to even say it—a *homebody*?

They came to the sad conclusion that Fenny didn't answer to the call of the wild, but as Sig once said, "the purr of the tame."

They talked over this genetic mystery as seriously as musical parents discuss an offspring's inability to carry a tune, or athletic parents puzzle over their child's inability to carry a ball.

"Maybe it's something she'll grow out of," Wally said hopefully.

"I don't know," said Sig, shaking her head. "The older she gets, it seems the more she's set in her ways."

The Nesses had planned on resuming their journeys abroad after retirement; until then, they were content to live vicariously through their daughter's daring and exotic travels—the only hitch being their daughter didn't seem interested in daring and exotic travels.

After high school graduation, Fenny rebelled further against her parents' wishes by enrolling in a state college close enough to commute to. She paid her tuition with a partial scholarship and money she had earned working in the shops; money Sig and Wally had hoped she would spend on airfares and youth hostel bills and tips doled out to rickshaw drivers and camel guides.

"It's not that I don't want to see the world," she told her parents. "I just want to see it educated."

"That sounds like an excuse to me," said Sig.

Wally nodded. "You can read a book anywhere."

They supposed they were impressed enough over Fenny's good grades and constant appearance on the dean's list, but still, at the price of shaming her Viking heritage?

By the end of Fenny's freshman year, when she still had no plans to drop out and book passage to Jakarta or Marrakech, Sig and Wally decided their own 'tch for international travel was something they finally had to scr ch by themselves.

"We're going to Belize," they announced casually one night at dinner.

"Belize. said Fenny. "Where's Belize?"

"It's the country we were headed to right before we found out I was pregnant with you," said Sig.

"It's in Central America," added Wally. "It faces the Caribbean."

"We're trading in our cross-country skis for surfboards."

"Our snow shovels for snorkels."

"How long will you be gone?" asked Fenny.

Sig and Wally looked at one another, laughed, and then said in unison, "Who knows?"

The answer, tragically, turned out to be "forever."

Fenny received a package from a place called Monkey River Town and the enclosed note read, "These are courage beads. Local legend has it that while wearing them, a person's natural bravery and thirst for adventure comes out. Guess who we thought could use them? Love, Sig and Wally."

Fenny laughed as she picked up the string of amber glass beads— she was willing to bet that her parents had created the necklace's "legend"—but no sooner had she opened the clasp than it broke, the beads skittering across the floor like tossed marbles.

On same day that Fenny crawled across the living room on her hands and knees collecting beads, her parents were riding a rented tandem bicycle down a coastal road, enjoying the sun on their backs and a discussion of the man who had let the room next to theirs. They were in their true element—a new place—and their senses reveled in the smell of the sea, the almost surreal tropical vegetation, the raucous cries of jungle birds.

"He's either a drug dealer or a spy," said Sig. "Anyone who wears a panama hat that *big* is hiding something."

Wally shook his head. "Have you seen his eyes?"

"How can I? His hat covers up half his face!"

"Well, take a peek at them sometime. They're the saddest eyes I've ever seen. I'd say the guy's had some bad luck in the love department."

"Not like us," said Sig.

"No, not like us."

Sig leaned back slightly, lips puckered. Wally, seated behind her, leaned forward to meet her kiss, and in their repositioning, the tandem bicycle swerved.

It was a swerve that met another swerve, a truck's swerve, caused by its driver, who, while tearing open a snack bag with his teeth, let go of the steering wheel to scoop up the cascade of corn chips that spilled onto his lap and the floor of his cab. His annoyance turned in a flash to terror as he heard a smack against his truck and then felt a bump. He saw an arc in his peripheral eyesight and realized it was a flying body.

He scrambled out of the cab of his truck, praying that it had been a dog or a goat he had hit, but then he saw the mangled bicycle mashed against his fender and, knowing that the arm that lay under his front wheel belonged to no bicycle-riding dog or goat, he fell to his knees.

The sounds the truck driver made matched those of Fenny when she got a telephone call from the American Consulate telling her Wallace and Sigrid Ness were dead.

Lars Larson, who was dumping a load of gravel onto the driveway he had agreed to resurface for Wally, heard Fenny scream.

"I can't get that scream out of my head," he told his wife Trude when she found him pacing in the rec room at three o'clock in the morning. "It sounded like the end of the world."

It *was* the end of the world, at least the world as Fenny knew it.

The gale force of her parents' deaths knocked her flat, and when she was finally ready to stand up again—to do something as simple as leave the house and go into town—she had the odd sensation of still being flat, of lacking dimension.

It was as if her spirit, her joy, her easy laughter—all those buoyant things that had shaped her—had deflated. She was only nineteen years old when she was orphaned, but felt at least fifty years older, and so it seemed only fitting that she should settle into Tall Pine like a retiree, following little superstitions she was convinced helped her get through the day, working odd hours at the shops, and hanging out with people twice and three times her age at a coffee shop counter.

Building up speed, Fenny jumped gracefully over the small border of snow, off the shoveled rink, and onto the lake. About two inches of snow covered it, but the blades of her skates cut through it cleanly and she zipped along the lake's edge, was skating fast, one arm behind her back, leaning over like a speed skater. The only sounds to break through the night air were those made by her blades on the ice and her breath: steady, even inhales and exhales.

Craig Asper was a guy who turned negatives into positives; if Fenny wanted to stand him up, that was her loss. By the time he had finished his second White Russian and was lecturing a very attractive bar waitress on her need to ignite her earning power, Fenny had skated several miles and was nearly home.

Chapter 2

Lee O'Leary was an heiress, but not the sort *Town & Country* featured on its cover. She was *large*, for one thing, with the kind of body romantics call "voluptuous" and those less romantic call "fat," and her auburn hair, shiny as a new copper pan, reached all the way to her waist. She wore it in old-fashioned coronet braids and had it trimmed every few months, never wanting her hair to be so long she could sit on it.

"I will not subject something I love to that particular indignity," she once explained to the barber.

She headed no foundation that bore the family name, she did not shop seasonally for clothes in Paris or New York, and her social circle was wide open to anyone, regardless of bloodlines or tax brackets. What Lee invested most of her time and a lot her money into was the Cup O'Delight and its patrons.

She had gotten into the restaurant business almost three years ago when the question, "What am I going to do with my life?" converged with a northern Minnesota retreat and a For Sale sign hanging in the window of the Red Dot Cafe. The restaurant was part of a sandstone building on Main Street that included Bick's Hardware on its left and Osterberg Accounting on its right, and other than memories of leathery burgers and the occasional bug crawling across the wedge of iceberg lettuce that constituted a house salad, all that remained of the Red Dot Cafe was its curious bit of fifties decor. Metallic red disks in various sizes had been attached to the wall facing the counter in a pattern as random as tossed marbles. It would have been easier to take them down instead of washing off years of grease, but Lee felt protective of their ugly uselessness.

She *had* taken down the yellowed canvas shades and replaced them with blue and white gingham curtains that matched, somewhat, the worn checkerboard tile floor. The leather banquettes and counter stools were bright red on their gathered edges, the color less vivid on pressure points. The white Formica counter was flecked with silver and gashed with tiny black craters from cigarettes that had fallen off their ashtray perch. The top edges of the jukebox were also marred with burn marks from all the cigarettes that sat smoldering there while a song was being chosen. One of Lee's first tasks was to initiate a nonsmoking policy, which would have banished the Red Dot's owners, a married couple who were dedicated fans of Lucky Strikes and responsible for many of the counter's burn marks. She also installed her piano along the back wall; it was too big to get up the narrow stairway that led to the two upstairs apartments that were included in the real estate deal.

Sunrise was just breaking through the winter morning as Lee made her first breakfast of the day. A long rectangle of hash browns was preheating next to rows of puckering bacon. She cracked two eggs and broke, unintentionally, both yolks.

"Sorry, Pete," she said to the man at the counter. "Looks like it's over hard this morning."

"Fine," said Pete. Anything Lee did or said was just fine.

Lee's customers paid for her mistakes; she didn't believe in throwing food out—"wrong orders or not."

Her customers accepted this provision; after all, Lee O'Leary was a good breakfast cook and her mistakes were tasty enough, and besides, who wanted to pick a fight with a five-foot-eleven, two-hundred-ten-pound redhead?

Sighing, Lee ground the heel of her hand into the small of her back. She had slept poorly the night before, owing in large part to her ex-husband's phone call. Every now and then, Marshall Stouffer (she had kept her own last name, a real coup, considering Marsh had tried to abscond with everything else of hers) called her up in the middle of the night, asking for money or forgiveness, making threats or excuses, and vowing to love her always or strike her down before her fortieth birthday (which was less than a year away). The contents of the conversation varied according to how much Marsh had drunk, but they always unsettled Lee and made it hard for her to sleep afterward. Time and again, she implored her ex-husband to reach out and touch someone else.

Stifling a yawn, Lee loaded Pete's plate with extra hash browns and set it in front of him.

"Looks swell," said Pete gamely, poking at yolks cooked to rubber.

Taking a cinnamon roll from under the plastic display case, Lee set it on a plate and spun it toward Pete.

"It's on me," she said. She hated to waste food, but she also believed in rewarding good sportsmanship.

The door opened and a gust of cold air scurried in like a winter gnome.

"Hey, Fenny," said Lee, slapping the edge of her spatula on the grill. "How'd your date go?"

"My date?" said Fenny, unwinding her scarf. "Oh, you mean my private seminar on how to ignite my earning power?"

"What?" asked Lee.

"Don't ask." Fenny sat down on the stool next to Pete's.

"Did you go someplace nice?" asked Pete.

"We had dinner at the Northlands, and then we went ice-skating."

"Ice-skating?" said Lee, who had been thrilled that Fenny opened the door of her social life, however briefly. "That sounds fun."

"It was, once he went to the bar."

"What do you mean?"

Fenny shrugged. "Well, he went to the bar, and I skated . . . home."

"Oh, Fenny," said Lee, exasperated, "what am I going to do with you?"

It was a question Lee often asked her friend.

Progress had been made in the three years that the two women had known each other; the grief that had swirled around Fenny like her own private atmospheric condition had lifted, leaving a residual melancholia that varied in degree, but had yet to completely disappear. Fenny seemed to genuinely enjoy her friends at the Cup O'Delight. (It did trouble Lee that she didn't seem interested in people her own age, but as Fenny pointed out, "No one my age stays in Tall Pine!") Still, Lee wished the young woman would assume a less passive role in her life and "attack" it more.

"I don't necessarily think life should be 'attacked,' " said Fenny when Lee gave her this particular piece of advice. "I mean, it's not supposed to be the enemy, is it?"

That Fenny had managed to retain a sense of humor (however black at times) gave Lee hope.

This humor, however, was not as valued by Gloria Murch, who in her role as town crier had been the first one to tell Fenny's sad story to Lee.

"Sig and Wally—her parents, God rest their souls—they had that same sense of humor—I think it's a Norwegian thing—they always had a smart remark. Anyhow, I guess Fenny's keeping up the tradition, because she's always making her little jokes." Gloria Murch raised her overplucked eyebrows. "*I* think it's what she hides behind. You know, the 'laughing on the outside, crying on the inside'–type deal." The pastor's wife had taken a psychology course at Bemidji State to better assist her in her role as church youth leader, and she was quite proud of her insight. "She dropped out of college—our Cynthia's on full scholarship at the University of Iowa, by the way—and now she lives like an old hermit—Fenny, that is, not Cynthia." She took a quick breath. "She only comes into town to work in her parents'—God rest their souls—stores; otherwise she's out at the ol' homestead, doing heaven knows what."

Then and there Lee had vowed to befriend her, and if the force of her personality wasn't enough to lure Fenny into her circle, then Lee would just have to bring out her secret weapon.

It was what Fenny, holding up her coffee cup, was asking for now.

The food at the Cup O'Delight was tasty—homemade and hearty—but what entered the realm of the remarkable was the coffee, which had given the restaurant its name. Its secret ingredient was known only to Lee O'Leary; Fenny had watched her carefully and knew that while she most often ground expensive Jamaican beans, she was open to Brazilian or Puerto Rican blends. She knew that once the coffee was brewed, Lee poured it into insulated pitchers, believing overheated coffee to be a sign of a lazy America in decline. Fenny thought of herself as an astute person, yet she never saw evidence of the magic elixir that changed Lee O'Leary's coffee from simply good to sublime.

Once a tourist sampling the coffee for the first time (these people were called virgins about to get "O'Delighted") put down his cup and sighed. "If heaven came in a cup," he said to his wife, "it would taste like this."

Lee concocted her special blend every morning before opening and filled a canister with it; she even had a reserve in case she ran out. Lee was crafty, all right.

"How's the shoe business, Pete?" asked Fenny.

"Slow," said Pete, smiling at the setup. "Course, I'm such a loafer." Modestly, he patted his oiled head of hair (only his sideburns were spared the Brylcreem) as Lee and Fenny laughed at a joke they had heard at least a dozen times. As the owner of Pete's Shoe Shack, Pete spent a lot of time thinking up shoe puns, but there were only so many to go around.

Lee poured Fenny a cup of coffee. Fragrant spirals of steam rose from the white ceramic mug and Fenny put her nose into them, sniffing deeply.

"Don't burn yourself," said Lee, smiling.

The door that led to the back room swung open and from behind it stepped a tall, bony man with a shock of white hair and thick black caterpillar eyebrows. He carried an empty bus tub, and when he saw Fenny, he dropped it. He had seen her the day before, but Slim believed in big welcomes.

"Hey, Slim," said Fenny.

He answered her with a bark.

"How've you been?"

Slim whined like a dog wanting a scratch on its belly.

"You keep up this canine business much longer and I'm going to take you to the vet's," said Lee, taking Slim's gaunt face in her hands. "I'll have you put to sleep and put us both out of our misery."

Slim growled, and one could hear the sarcasm in it. He shook off

Lee's hands, picked up the bus tub, and put it under the counter. He barked again, two short yaps.

"Well, thanks," said Fenny. "It's good to be back."

Slim was a deadly mimic who delighted listeners with impressions of Elvis Presley and Richard Nixon and Cary Grant, as well as more obscure salutes to people ranging from the singer Lulu to Chuck Connors as the Rifleman. When he felt constricted within the confines of the English language, however, he would imitate animals, with a strong partiality to dogs. Weeks could go by without a single yap from Slim, and then he might bark for days at a time.

Gloria Murch wondered if he wouldn't be better off in a mental institution.

"Not until he starts biting." Personally, Lee wouldn't be averse to Gloria getting bitten, and by something with sharper teeth than Slim.

In 1966, Slim Knutson was the crew chief in a UH-34D Sikorsky helicopter that went down in a place called Quang Tri. In his waking hours, he had learned how to distract himself from the memories, but occasionally in his dreams he revisited, in detail, that day: those sounds, those smells, those screams.

He thought the only disability he returned to the States with was a gash in his leg that, despite his scrupulous care, got infected over and over. Some people assumed his prematurely white hair (it had been leeched of its color by the time he was thirty) had something to do with Vietnam, but it was an inheritance from his mother's side of the family, and not from the war. He had finished his degree in forestry and worked for the DNR, but instead of time healing his real wounds—his psychic wounds—each year seemed to increase his despair, and when his second wife divorced him, he sank into an immobilizing depression and then into what Lee called "a really *post*-post-traumatic shock syndrome."

Slim didn't exactly remember how he wound up in Tall Pine, but he did, and over a cup of the best coffee he had ever drunk, he had told Lee a small part of his story, but it was enough for Lee to know he needed help, and by his third refill she had offered him both gainful employment and lodging in the efficiency apartment next to hers.

Slim contributed even more than Marshall Stouffer to Lee's late-night disease, albeit intentionally. At least twice a month, around the time "The Gerry Dale Show" would roll its final credits, Slim would begin screaming.

"Over here, Benson! Stay by me! Stay by me! Fucking VC! Someone help me!"

Lee O'Leary, rattled awake, her heart near fibrillation, would rush to Slim's room across the hall and climb into his bed, holding him until the terror that shook his body calmed and he fell asleep from exhaustion. Lee had taken him to therapists and doctors in Minneapolis, but they only filled out prescriptions that Slim refused to take.

"So he's shell-shocked and barks a little," said Lee. "Does that mean he's supposed to be tranked up the rest of his life?"

"How about some blueberry pancakes?" asked Lee. "I thawed a bunch of berries from the batch we picked last summer."

"Sure," said Fenny.

Slim took the *Minneapolis Star Tribune* Lee subscribed to and tucked it under his arm, giving a short bark as he went back into the kitchen.

"Leave the crossword alone," called Lee after him. "It's my turn."

Pete didn't dislike Slim, but he could only take so much of his "shenanigans." He respected his war service—he himself had had a blessedly high draft number—but he found it pretty pathetic that a grown man should have to bark like a dog to get attention.

Setting the two quarters he always left for a tip next to his coffee cup, Pete stood up. "I hate to be a heel," he said, "but I'd better get to work."

Lee served Fenny her pancakes as the door opened and the other early risers of Tall Pine came in for their breakfasts.

After his first and only visit to his sister's restaurant, Gerald O'Leary asked Lee why she enjoyed playing nursemaid to a bunch of lunatics.

"I'll hold up my lunatics to your lunatics any day," she answered.

Lee preferred to think of her friends as Tall Pine's more colorful citizens and was happy that the Cup O'Delight served as a club-house of sorts for them.

"This might not be the Ritz," Lee told her brother, "but believe me"—she slapped the countertop for emphasis—"this is where the elite come to meet."

The Dog Haus, with its liquor license, its smoked-glass mirrors, and its eleven varieties of sausage, attracted the town's business-people, and the fast-food franchises that rose like plastic pimples on the rustic complexion of small-town America took a good share of the town's teenagers and young families in a hurry. The Cup O'De-light, Lee liked to think, served the three very important F's—food, friendship, and fun.

The grill sizzled with orders and the counter was abuzz with the conversation of its regulars.

"Says here the president's on his way to Colombia."

"Good. I hope he stays there."

"Heine, you're just sore because you've never been able to put one of them Peace and Jokester candidates in office."

"That's Peace and *Justice*, Mayor, and pass me the pepper."

Miss Penk folded a section of the paper to the obituaries. "Hey, Reverend Wendy died."

"No."

"She sure did. It says so right here. Fifty-five years old."

"Zat old bag was at least seventy."

"Katte."

"Well, she gave me za willies," said Frau Katte. Her Swiss accent had been tamed by years of living in America, although her *th* always came out *z*. "Always singing off-key and asking zose poor tele-vision viewers to send money for her Prayer Power band."

"Mayor, weren't you a big contributor of Reverend Wendy's?"

Laughter ran down the counter like a current.

"Oh, sure. I was just about to sign over my bonds when they caught her in that motel room with the Prayer Power trombonist."

Along with Fenny, Mayor Lambordeaux, Heine Osterberg, Miss Penk, and Frau Katte sat at the counter on the same regular basis that students sit at their desks. When one didn't show up, telephone calls were made to his/her home to make sure the truant was okay, that no one was having chest pains or lying prostrate from a stroke.

Miss Penk and Frau Katte kept especially close tabs on one another; they were Tall Pine's only lesbian couple ("Well," explained Frau Katte, "we're za only ones who admit it. I still say za librarian and Arvid Nelson's nurse have somezing going") and didn't care who knew it. They never introduced themselves as cousins and didn't live a secret life behind shaded windows; they were openly affectionate with one another and often held hands while walking to the bank or to the Cup O'Delight, and whoever was bothered by it had to face Frau Katte's wrath.

Miss Penk, who also bore the distinction of being the town's only black citizen, had parents who'd given their children titles as first names, thinking it would "distinguish them in life"—she had a brother named Regent and another named Prince.

"Zose sexists," complained Katte. "Zey give za boys royal titles and you just a measly 'Miss.' " For solidarity, Katte (whose name was short for Katherine and pronounced Kah-tee) added a "Frau" in front of her name, "even zo technically I'm a Fraulein."

Miss Penk's hair, which she insisted was not a wig, was an elaborate tower of cream-colored swirls. At sixty-two years old, she was still shapely and showed off her figure in angora knit sweaters and jeans she ordered from the Spiegel catalog.

Short and squat Frau Katte (who more than once in her life had been described as "homely") was less a slave to clothes, her one consistent fashion statement being the green wool fez she always wore, making her look like a Tyrolean Shriner.

She now flicked the newspaper with the back of her hand.

"So, Fenny, what do you zink of this mini-mall thing they want to put up?"

"River Street's over a hundred years old," said Fenny. "It's a historical landmark." The saying "If it ain't broke, don't fix it" was one Fenny took to heart.

("You're the youngest of all of us," Lee had told her when they had known each other long enough to let truth override politeness, "and yet you're the one who thinks like a little old lady.")

("The world would be a better place if more people thought like a 'little old lady,' " said Fenny before accusing Lee of ageism.)

"Oh, Katte," said Miss Penk, "what's so bad about a mini-mall? We could use a good shopping district." (No one could ever accuse

Miss Penk of thinking like a little old lady, and if they did, she'd probably wallop them with a move she had learned in Bud Glatte's karate class.)

"Just what I want to do," said Frau Katte, "shop more."

"Well, now, I don't know," said Heine. "You got to admit it's pretty hard to get over to International Falls or Baudette in the winter. I wouldn't mind the convenience."

"Or the income," said Mayor Lambordeaux, always on the job. "A town's got to look forward."

"Come on, Mayor. Looking forward doesn't always mean looking for za dollar signs."

"Progress is a train," said a high-pitched voice. "Sometimes it travels swiftly, other times it derails."

A collective sigh lifted the shoulders of those at the counter as Mary Gore sat down.

"Come on, sweetheart," said Frau Katte to Miss Penk. "We've got zose contest forms to fill out."

"Yup," said Heine, rising. "And I'd better get back to my letter-writing."

"What's it this time?" asked Fenny.

Now that his son had taken over the majority of his accounting business, Heine was semi-retired, which gave him more time to keep up his weekly letter-writing campaign to his congresspeople and senators.

"Gun control," he said. "They're so durned stubborn on gun control."

"Oh, stay," coaxed Lee, afraid everyone would desert her and leave her alone with Mary. "I'll brew another pot O'Delight."

Slim came out of the back room, but, seeing Mary, he stopped, growled deeply, and walked backward through the swinging door.

"The usual?" asked Lee, holding up the coffeepot.

The curled ends of Mary Gore's flip swayed as she shook her head. With her sixties hairdo and eager, fresh-scrubbed face she looked like a faded deb, but instead of complementing this look with pearls and sweater sets, she wore "expressive" clothing that even a bohemian would pass up as weird.

She helped her elderly father run Gore Printing; her bread and butter was in wedding invitations and graduation announcements, but, as she told people, her soul food came from Yes! Publishing, a company she had started to "further the artistic expression of the North Woods."

"I'd like to furzer artistic expression," Frau Katte once said, "by kicking her right in za fanny."

"I can't stay," said Mary, and those at the counter visibly perked up. "I just wanted to drop off the latest *Angel Motors*." She set three small booklets on the counter and opened a cigar box that read, "Donations to the Cause of Art." "Hot off the presses."

Every month Mary Gore published *Angel Motors*, a collection of poetry, drawings, and stories, most of which she penned and all of which were reviled and made fun of by anyone unlucky enough to be given a copy.

After she had collected a dollar and forty-two cents in contributions, Mary left, muttering about how a society that fails to support its art is a doomed one.

"What on earth *is* this?" asked Miss Penk, peering at the booklet's cover. She was too vain to put on her reading glasses in public.

Mayor Lambordeaux studied it for a moment. He had excellent vision but hadn't a clue as to what he was looking at. "Looks like a mule jumping off a cliff."

"No, it doesn't," said Lee O'Leary. "It's a nude woman ringing a bell."

"Call Sheriff Gibbs in here," said Heine as he pushed the booklet off the counter edge to the floor. "I want that woman arrested."

"On what charge?" asked Fenny.

Heine shrugged. "I don't know—isn't there something like 'aggravated annoyance'?"

"Listen to this," said Lee. She cleared her throat.

" 'Dusty Roads' by Mary Gore:

> "Dusty, dangerous roads, all leading to the acrid
> vicinity of my heart,
> my pump of blood and love.
> Who will pause to sweep the bi-ways,
> to heighten visibility, to aid any and all traffic
> that wishes to stop and gas?"

"Zat woman's a psychopaz," said Frau Katte.

Slim's face appeared in the window of the swinging door and, seeing that Mary was gone, his eyebrows lifted in pleasure. He set a new supply of bleached rags in the bucket in the sink and then noticed the copy of *Angel Motors* Heine had pushed off the counter. His lips curled in a sneer and he crooked his leg and raised it, the booklet his fire hydrant.

"Slim," warned Lee, "we all feel the same way, but use the facilities anyway."

Fenny left the warmth of the Cup O'Delight, shivering in the wind that left Tall Pine's one stoplight swaying above Main Street. She dawdled, inspecting the shovels for sale in the rack outside the hardware store and reading the front page of the weekly *Tall Pine Register* through the glass of a corner newspaper stand. She stood at the post office window staring at the display of new stamps, until finally she turned and began walking toward Sig's Place. Gloria Murch was coming by with "some real cute stuff," an event that would leave Fenny stranded in sadness, missing her parents and the jokes they would have shared over the latest church circle abominations.

Chapter 3

Spring was a slow season to start up in northern Minnesota. There were at least a half dozen tentative thaws before the one came that would melt down winter once and for all. It was on the first day of the presumed true thaw that a red Alfa Romeo sped into town, slush flying in gray arcs from under its churning wheels.

Corby Deele looked out the window of his barbershop, diverting his attention from the precision trim he had been performing on the dyed and dwindling hairs of Heine Osterberg.

"Californians," he said, noting the license plates. He shook his head and snipped the air with his barber shears.

The sports car braked to a halt in front of Sig's Place and from its low-slung doors emerged Christian Freed and a young man who worked for the Minnesota Film Board and occasionally doubled as a location scout.

Christian slammed the car door with the confident grace of a young hotshot but immediately did the quick-footed hop/dance of someone who realizes his brand-new Italian loafers are submerged in three inches of melting snow. His tirade lasted almost a minute and contained an average of one expletive per two seconds.

Having seen many such tirades, the location scout rolled his eyes.

Christian's tantrum ended when it was replaced by a revelation.

"Boots," he said, the way a thirsty man would say "water." "I need boots."

He had studied the *Farmer's Almanac* and the weather forecasts in *USA Today* and since arriving in Minnesota had worn carefully selected layers of wool and goose down that made him look fifteen pounds heavier and would have kept him cozy on an expedition to the Arctic Circle. The problem was, he hadn't remembered his feet.

Christian looked up and down the sleepy avenue of shops. "Ever hear of a frickin' Italian shoe store?" he asked no one in particular.

"Pete's Shoe Shack."

"What?"

The scout pointed toward the end of the commercial district. "Pete's Shoe Shack. Down the street there."

They traversed the short block to the store, Christian swearing every time he jumped over a puddle and failed to clear it.

Taped to the door window of the Shoe Shack was a sign that read, "Gone to Lunch."

"Good idea," said Christian, stomping his wet feet. "Now, why don't you be a good little scout and find us a restaurant."

The young man rolled his eyes again. The novelty of showing his state to someone from Hollywood had ended somewhere between Minneapolis and St. Cloud, just about the time Christian asked him why he lived in Minnesota: "Are you afraid of the big time or do you like living in the boonies?"

There wasn't much of a lunch crowd at the Cup O'Delight, owing to the O'Daily Special. Occasionally, Lee O'Leary was moved to honor her Irish heritage by serving corned beef and cabbage, despite the fact that most of the regulars shared a dislike of the dish.

"What are you all?" Lee asked. "Anti-Irish?"

"Anti-*cabbage*," explained the mayor.

"Anti-*cooked* cabbage," amended Heine.

"P.U.," said Christian as they entered the restaurant. "Something's rank."

"Not so loud," said the scout, who knew it was bad manners to correct a client, but enough was enough.

They hung up their outerwear on the coatrack by the door and sat at the counter, next to a woman who wore a patchwork caftan covered with tiny reflective disks.

"Greetings," she said over her coffee cup.

The scout nodded at her, opening the menu.

Mary cleared her throat.

"Love is a penny," she began, reading from a pamphlet next to her pie plate. "Tossed aside or stored in the dark confines of a wallet's pocket with currency much easier to spend. Dimes of sexual gratification. Quarters of material security. How can the penny not get lost amidst all this shiny stuff?"

Christian and the scout looked at one another, neither having any sort of rebuttal.

Mary smiled her benevolent artist-to-peons smile. "That, gentlemen, is just a taste of the delicious artistic smorgasbord you'll find here in the Great North Woods."

The scout adjusted one of his contact lenses. Christian inspected his fingernails. They both knew the rule of not making eye contact with crazy people.

"Say no more," said Mary, reaching into the large shopping bag at her feet. "Two copies of *Angel Motors* on the house. Talk about your lucky days."

The swinging door banged open, Lee O'Leary emerging behind it.

Immediately she saw the two strangers sitting at the counter, their faces a combination of perplexity and annoyance.

"Mary," she warned, narrowing her eyes. "Quit pestering my customers."

The woman leaned forward and stage-whispered, "Lee would consider Shakespeare a pest if he happened to recite a sonnet to someone sitting at her counter." She rose and, after adjusting the shoulder pads of her caftan, slid her check back toward the napkin dispenser. "Put it on my tab, okay, love?"

"Okay, *love*," said Lee.

"Hi," said Lee, her hands on the pillowy cushions of her hips. "You boys ready to order?"

"I'll take a Caesar salad," said Christian.

"We have chef salads," offered Lee.

"Whatever," said Christian. There was a gruffness in his voice; he had no tolerance for fat people, especially ones who could be pretty. Hadn't this woman heard of liquid diets/Weight Watchers/liposuction?

After the location scout ordered a hamburger, Lee went over to the coffee machine.

At this point Frau Katte and Miss Penk entered the cafe and, seeing the strange men, they sat down at the end of the counter, eager to witness a special event.

Lee set the coffee in front of the men.

"We didn't order that," said Christian. "The fact is, I'd like a latté."

"Latté, schmatte," said Lee. "Now, hush up and try it."

The scout stifled his urge to hold up his cup in salute. He had been driving around Minnesota with Christian for two days and was weary from the strain of it. He gave Lee a coconspiratorial smile and sipped at his coffee. The pleasure center in his brain stood on alert. He took another sip.

Both Frau Katte and Miss Penk stopped unzipping their matching parkas and watched him as carefully as Jane Goodall watched apes.

The scout was unaware of his rapt audience, his concentration directed solely at the taste in his mouth. Endorphins, like soldiers of hedonism, marched through his body.

"Good, ya?" asked Frau Katte, nodding so that the cord of her fez bobbed up and down.

"Just about the best coffee in the entire known universe," added Miss Penk.

Get a load of Muff and Jeff, thought Christian, chuckling at his wicked wit.

Christian wasn't positive, but he trusted his first impulses enough to know that this small town, however bad its cafe was, had definite possibilities. They had driven (Christian had flown in but had hired a driver in Los Angeles to bring his Alfa Romeo to Minneapolis; he wasn't about to drive around in some shabby rental) hundreds of miles through small-town and rural Minnesota and nothing had said, "This is Ike and Inga country," as loud as this place had.

He hadn't yet been disappointed in the physical charm of the town, which fit the description he'd written in his script, "full of pine trees with quaintness up the yazoo," but he was underwhelmed by the locals—a crazy woman reciting poetry, if that's what it was; a fat and presumptive waitress who pushed coffee on unwilling customers; and elderly lesbians who had nothing better to do than stare at anybody who wasn't a part of their warped homosphere.

"Do you have decaffeinated?" asked Christian, pushing his untouched coffee aside.

"Don't believe in the stuff," said Lee.

"Christian, you've got to try this," said the scout, a little breathless.

"No, thanks." When Christian made a point, he wasn't one to dull it with compromise. "I'll have water. You do have plain water, don't you?"

Lee smiled sweetly. "Let me just draw it up from the well."

She served the men their food and gave Frau Katte and Miss Penk the piece of apple pie à la mode they liked to share in the afternoon.

"So, who are zose guys?" asked Frau Katte in a whisper that could be heard throughout the restaurant.

"Oh, excuse me," said the polite scout, wiping his mouth with a paper napkin. "My name is Jeff Welles and this is Christian Freed."

"We're filmmakers," said Christian, unable to resist defining himself by his occupation, which was how introductions were made in L.A. "Well, at least I am. I'm from the West Coast."

He waited for the fawning interest this statement usually inspired.

"Is that so," said Miss Penk, stirring a packet of sugar into Frau Katte's coffee. "Gets hot there, doesn't it?"

"Sometimes," said Christian, wanting to add, *you moron.*

"We made a film, too," said Frau Katte. "Last year. We were all in it."

Lee O'Leary laughed and gestured toward the piano. "Sometimes we put on little shows in here. I taped one and sent it to my brother in New York. He already thinks I'm crazy for leaving the family business, and I like adding fuel to his fire."

Christian drummed his fingers impatiently, wondering why this waitress thought he might be interested in her life story.

"We were in the Big Apple last year," said Miss Penk. "We saw three Broadway shows."

"We won a contest," said Frau Katte.

The pair were inveterate contest entrants and had won everything from a year's supply of car wax to an all-expenses-paid trip to New York City to their latest prize, a speedboat.

"It was the easiest contest we ever won," said Miss Penk. "For the hard ones you usually have to write a twenty-five-words-or-less essay.

All's we had to do was send in three proof-of-purchases and the name of the composer of 'New York, New York.'"

Christian put his thumb and middle finger into the corners of his eyes and squeezed, hoping these two old hags would read his body language and shut up. He hated when conversation deteriorated into the banal (i.e., away from himself); it was a waste of his precious time.

"The movie we'd be making up here would be a *real* movie," he said, pushing aside the half-eaten salad that could have used some cilantro and winding his watch that told time in five different zones. "A film *I* scripted."

"When are you planning to do this?" asked Lee O'Leary, taking his plate and putting it in the bus tub.

"I don't know, could be summer . . . could be fall," said Christian, smiling at her eagerness. No one was immune to the excitement of moviemaking.

"Forget about the summer," said Miss Penk. "Have you seen the size of our horseflies?"

"Zis big," said Frau Katte, holding her hands as if measuring a walleye.

"I sincerely doubt horseflies could close down a movie production," said Christian with the grimace/smile that was becoming his signature expression.

"Our horseflies could close down whatever they darn well please," said Lee.

"Really?" said Christian, and the only thing that prevented him from passing out from boredom was the vision of a white-haired bag of bones rattling by, carrying a stack of porcelain dinner plates.

Jesus, this place, thought Christian, feeling the goose pimples rise under his long underwear and two flannel shirts. Full of weirdos and spooks and interracial dykes.

The sound of a sick wolf howling filled Christian's ears, and he gripped the edge of the counter as if in the presence of an alien being. He stared at its source, stared until the sound of laughter broke the spell.

"That's Slim," explained Lee. "He's just letting me know he's through for the day."

"You get so you understand him," explained Miss Penk. "It's all a question of listening to his tone and emphasis."

Frau Katte nodded. "Ya, I had a harder time learning English."

Slim howled again.

"So go," Lee told him. "Punch out."

Christian looked to the scout for some wink of acknowledgment—what kind of nutso world had they stumbled into?—but the man was sipping his coffee as if in a trance.

"Greg," he said, pushing the check toward him. "Let's blow."

"Hmmm?"

"I said, 'Greg, let's blow.' "

"It's Jeff."

"Whatever," said Christian. "Come on, let's get out of here."

They left the restaurant to Lee's invitation, "Come back anytime, boys!" and passed the proprietor of the Shoe Shack on the sidewalk (Pete always ate at home on Corned Beef O'Cabbage days).

But even had they recognized Pete, Christian had no intention of browsing in his shop for boots now; he wanted to get back to his hotel in International Falls, make a few calls (he had forgotten to charge up his cell phone and the inconvenience was driving him crazy), take a long bath, and read a couple pages of the paperback he had brought along (a TV critic's thumbnail reviews of all movies available on videocassette). He had had his daily quota of small-town rubes and their small-town rubbishness. Next time, he vowed, he'd write a screenplay that took place in Monte Carlo or Shanghai, someplace where the natives at least had some élan.

"Guy oughta be committed," he said, walking as if he were late for something.

"What?" said the scout, who was wondering if maybe it was a trace of caramel he had tasted in the coffee.

"That howling freak of a busboy they've got over there. That dog guy."

The scout chuckled. "Oh, him."

Near the car, Christian miscalculated his jump off the curb and immersed his Italian-loafered feet all over again in the wet slush.

"Three hundred dollars," he said. "These shoes cost three frickin' hundred dollars!"

As soon as he got back to his hotel room, he'd call his Uncle Harry and tell him maybe they might want to rethink this North Woods location crap and shoot on the back lot, but as he reared back his leg to kick a pile of slush aside, he lifted his head and saw, in the window of Sig's Place, Inga, the heroine of *Ike and Inga*.

Not knowing she was being watched by anyone, let alone a Hollywood scriptwriter, Fenny sneezed, spattering the windowsill with tiny droplets, which she rubbed away with her dust rag.

Chapter 4

When Christian Freed saw Fenny, he stood still, holding the car keys in the lock, his face drained of color, his mouth hanging open. What the scout didn't know was that Christian was muttering, "Inga, Inga"; to him it was as if the guy were in the throes of a petit-mal seizure. He had a cousin who was epileptic, and when his seizures came ("unbidden time-outs," his cousin called them), he looked much as Christian did now.

"You all right?" asked the scout.

Christian's lips moved faster and the scout was about to punch 911 on his cell phone when Christian pushed himself away from the car and dashed into the shop called Sig's Place.

The scout chased after him, hoping whoever was in the store knew some sort of first aid.

Fenny had just finished dusting the woodwork when the door crashed open, the bell above it jangling like an alarm. Someone was either very anxious to buy something or she was about to be robbed; either way, Fenny pushed her spine against the wall, her arms spread out for support.

"You!" said Christian, racing toward Fenny, knocking into a mannequin who modeled one of Mae Little Feather's leather jackets.

"What?" cried Fenny.

Christian raced toward her, and Fenny, her reflexes sharp, grabbed what was closest to her on the Junk Table—in this case a miniature model of Benevolent Father's Lutheran Church, made out of Popsicle sticks and thread spools—and threw it at her quickly approaching attacker.

Christian yelped, more from surprise than any pain, as the little church collapsed upon impact with his collarbone. He brushed the remains of the razed building off his jacket and with true surprise asked, "What'd you do that for?"

Fenny picked up a piggy bank made out of a plastic Hilex bottle. She waved it menacingly. "What do you want?"

"Yeah," said the scout. "What *do* you want?"

"It's Inga," said Christian, losing his patience. "Can't you see I've found my Inga?"

Fenny was not even close to understanding what the guy was talking about. Her eyes darted around the shop, looking for this Inga woman she hadn't seen come in.

The scout put his hands on Christian's shoulders and spoke into his ear. "Calm down, buddy, you're scaring the poor girl." He patted Christian's shoulders and then introduced himself and Christian to the young and flushed woman.

"You see, Mr. Freed wrote a screenplay and, from what I'm gathering—he's found his leading lady in you."

A framed needlepoint sampler of Minnesota's state motto (*"L'étoile du Nord"*) was digging into her back, and Fenny readjusted her position against the wall. She carefully surveyed the men before her.

The one guy looked safe enough, but the other one—well, he was shorter than her and skinny underneath all those clothes (wasn't he hot?), but she knew the little wiry ones were the ones to watch, the ones likeliest to fly off the handle because they had so much to prove.

"Let me see some I.D."

"What?" said Christian.

"She wants to see some I.D.," said the scout, pulling out his wallet from his back pocket. "Show the lady some I.D."

Christian held out his driver's license as if it were an FBI badge.

Fenny shook her head. "I mean I.D. that says you make movies."

Christian laughed. "There's no I.D. like that." He stepped toward her. "What, do you think you go down to the Beverly Hills Chamber of Commerce, pay a fee, and pick up your laminated producer's card?" What a naïf, he thought, what a beautiful naïf.

"Not one step closer," said Fenny, waving the plastic bank.

Christian stepped closer, smiling his confident, I'll-handle-this smile.

Fwwhhap. The Hilex pig made contact with his forehead. Fenny grabbed a handful of refrigerator magnets made of polymerized bread dough.

"These'll hurt," she warned.

"Show her your guild card," said the scout through clenched teeth.

Christian fumbled through the plastic windows of his alligator wallet.

"See," he said, showing the card he had earned writing several episodes of "Perky the Puppy," consistently the lowest-rated Saturday morning cartoon. "See, it says right here that I am a current, dues-paying member of the Writers' Guild."

"Never heard of it," said Fenny.

"And here's my card," said the scout, carefully watching her hand that held the bread dough pellets. "See, I'm with the Minnesota Film Board. I work down in Minneapolis." He cleared his throat. "Believe me, it's legitimate."

Fenny stepped closer until she could see for sure they weren't holding up book club membership cards or charge-a-plates.

"Okay," she said finally, releasing her handful of magnets. "So why are you calling me Inga?"

Christian had wanted to give Fenny the part the moment he saw her, and as much as he liked to throw his weight around, he knew he couldn't offer a big movie role to some salesgirl peddling knick-knacks in the northland boondocks. He knew that breach of protocol would send him straight to the minor leagues, right back to his "Perky the Puppy" desk (if they'd even have him back). He did tell Fenny that he'd get in touch with her as soon as he spoke to the movie's producer, and might she consider coming to L.A. for a screen test?

Harry had been bemused by Christian's announcement that he had found Inga. That Christian had written a good script seemed a fluke; surely he couldn't get lucky again with his casting abilities. Still, Harry thought, why not indulge the boy on this one, since he wasn't having much luck in L.A.?

And he wasn't. Along with Malcolm Edgely, who was signed to direct, and Emma Tuttle, Hollywood's premier casting agent for the kind of B movies Harry made, he had been looking at ingenues as well as actresses who explained that just because they no longer looked like ingenues didn't mean they couldn't act like them.

"True." Harry would nod. "Very true." He'd love to hire Paula Dunn, a thirty-five-year-old who made him cry in the last picture he had seen her in, but the sorry truth was that nobody would believe she was the twenty-one-year-old, fresh-faced Norwegian immigrant mail-order bride.

They had seen dozens of European actresses whose accents worked and dozens of American actresses whose accents didn't. No one had come close to doing what they wanted most: no one had dazzled them.

And so Harry agreed to offer the girl from Minnesota a screen test, for he had a curious philosophy guiding him on this picture, one that could be summed up by the words *What the hell.*

Chapter 5

Bets were placed throughout the town of Tall Pine (Sheriff Gibbs's and Mayor Lambordeaux's fifty-dollar one being the highest) as to whether Fenny would take or reject the offer of a Hollywood screen test.

"Screen test," complained Fenny to Lee. "Why is everyone making such a big deal about a screen test, anyway?" She was sitting at the empty counter, knocking the salt and pepper shakers together.

"Come on, Fenny. It's the *movies*. Being in the movies is the American Dream—right up there with being the president or owning your own home."

"It's not my dream."

"What *is*?" Lee asked, genuinely curious.

Fenny sat for a moment, studying the red and white shakers Lee had recently found in a cupboard—a holdover from the cafe's Red Dot days.

"I don't know," she said finally. "I don't know that I have one."

"Fenny," said Lee, her voice like a teacher whose prize student has given her a wrong answer. "Everybody has a dream."

Leaning back on her stool, her fingertips on the counter edge, Fenny began swiveling back and forth. "So what's yours?"

"I'm living my dream." Lee gestured with her hands. "Peace and quiet up in the north woods, plus I've got my own restaurant." She crossed her arms over her chest. "But we were talking about *you*, remember?"

"It's just . . ." There was a little catch in Fenny's voice. "It's just so *weird*. This whole thing's thrown me for a loop . . . and I don't like being thrown for a loop."

"When life throws you a loop, make a bow out of it."

"Gee, that's *deep*," said Fenny sarcastically. "Why don't you cross-stitch it on a pot holder and I'll sell it over at Sig's?"

"Maybe I will. So when are you supposed to let them know?"

"Tomorrow."

If Fenny had been shocked by Harry Freed's telephone call offering her a screen test (it had been several weeks since Christian's visit; long enough for her to think nothing was going to come of it), then Harry was equally shocked by Fenny's wish to "think it over." Screen tests were manna, answered prayers to legions of actors, and this unknown civilian wanted to *think it over*?

Fenny banged the salt and pepper shakers together like an arrhythmic castanets player.

"Stop," said Lee, cupping her hand over the tops of the shakers. "You're giving me a headache."

She dumped out Fenny's cooled coffee (ignoring a cup O'Delight was a sure sign of mental distress), walked around the counter, and sat down next to her friend.

"Come on, Fen, you're not being asked to give up a kidney. It's just a screen test. Granted, it's not within the day-to-day experience of most people, but so what? Carpe diem."

"Carpe diem yourself."

Lee scraped a drop of dried syrup off the counter with her thumbnail. "Look, Fenny," she said, exasperation creeping into her voice. "What's the worst that could happen?"

Fenny looked at Lee, her eyes wide with alarm. "Are you kidding? A million things—the plane could crash, I could get raped in the hotel room, I could get robbed and beaten, carjacked, there could be an earthquake, a sniper shooting from the freeway—"

"Okay, say you survived all that stuff," said Lee dryly. "But as far as the screen test goes—what's the worst thing that could happen?"

"I could make a fool out of myself?"

"Bingo," said Lee. "That's really it, isn't it?"

"No, it's actually the plane, or the hotel rape, or—"

Lee forged on. "Everyone's afraid of making a fool out of themselves. But you know what? Sometimes we have to. It's good for the system. So come on, Fenny, go out there. It'll only be a day or two. Big deal. And let's take this thing further—say you got the part—

which is a long shot, if you want to talk turkey—but *if* you did, they want to make the movie up here anyway, so you wouldn't be taken away from your precious Tall Pine." Lee put a little nod of emphasis at the end of her argument.

"But . . . what about my routine? I was looking forward to—"

"Fenny, you're twenty-two years old. That's too young to have a routine. Sheesh. You sound like a little old lady."

"Why do you always tell me that as if it's a big insult? I do not think sounding like a little old lady is an insult!"

"You don't have to yell." Lee took her hand. "Fenny, I'm going to ask you something and I don't want you to get mad at me, okay?"

The wall clock ticked away its seconds.

"*Okay?*" Lee said again.

Fenny shrugged her shoulders. "Okay, okay."

"What do you suppose Sig and Wally would want you to do?"

"Oh, Lee," said Fenny, pulling her hand away. "That's not fair—they . . . they—"

"Took chances?" suggested Lee. "Embraced adventure? Said yes to things?"

Fenny looked stricken, as if she had been slapped across the face.

"And they died!" she sobbed, burying her head in her arms.

"Fenny, you're not going to die," said Lee, rubbing her friend's back. "Of course, I can't say that for certain—no one can—but there's a good likelihood that you won't. I mean, not in the near future." She shook her head. "Geez, listen to me blather. What I'm trying to say is that your parents . . . well, you've told me yourself about how they were all about travel and adventure—"

"They thought of themselves as modern-day Vikings!" wailed Fenny.

"Exactly. And Vikings explore new things because . . ." Lee thought for a moment. "Because exploring new things is fun."

Fenny raised her head from the cradle her arms made and peered at Lee with one eye.

"Is that it?" she asked. "Is that your argument? 'Vikings explore new things because exploring new things is fun'?"

Lee blushed. "So I wasn't on the debate team. At least I made my point."

"You sure did. Now I know what motivated Erik the Red."

"Oh, Fenny," said Lee crossly. She stood up and went behind the counter. "I was just trying to say that you . . . that you might think about what your parents wanted for you. That for your own good, you might want to honor that spirit of theirs and try something new."

Fenny sniffed deeply and fixed her gaze on the red metallic disks hanging above the grill. Lee dumped the coffee filter in the trash. Fenny pushed down her cuticles with a spoon edge. Lee rinsed out a coffeepot. Fenny coughed. Lee wiped down the counter.

Finally, hitting the countertop with her fist, Fenny said in a tremulous octogenarian's voice, "All right. All right, dadgummit, I'll do it."

Lee gasped. "You mean it?"

At Fenny's nod, Lee leaned over the counter to hug her friend.

Fenny's knuckles were bulging white ridges; every time the plane rumbled through turbulence, she gripped the armrests of her seat and squeezed her knees together as if performing an isometrics routine.

The flight attendant advised her to think of turbulence as "potholes in the sky," but the analogy did little to assuage Fenny's belief that she was a dead duck. She had never flown by herself, and if she got out of this flight alive, she vowed she never would again. She had in her pocket the item she carried with her every day—a courage bead from the broken necklace that had been her parents' last gift to her—and she hoped it would serve, along with the tiny pinecone she picked up in her front yard, as sort of a lucky talisman. Mechanically she ate her honey-roasted peanuts (which could very well be her last meal) as she stared out upon the treacherous blue highway that needed major road repair.

When the ride calmed, Fenny didn't follow suit. She tried to decode every bell tone that was played over the PA system—did one mean an engine had failed? Did two mean there were problems with the hydraulics? She felt breathless and light-headed and signaled for the flight attendant, asking her if there was sufficient oxygen for such a full plane.

"There's plenty," the attendant assured her.

When the plane landed, she opened her eyes and stifled an urge to applaud.

In the airport terminal, a man in a suit stood at the gate, holding a sign that read, "Miss Femmy Ness." Approaching him shyly (it was strange to see someone advertising her), Fenny stood several feet away from him and waved her fingers.

The man pushed up a lens of his aviator glasses. "Miss Femmy Ness?"

"Yes. Well, actually, it's Fenny. Fenny Ness. But it's close enough."

The man turned over the sign and studied it. "I don't get paid extra to spell right." He gave her a gruff once-over. "Got any luggage?"

Fenny shook her head and held up a carry-on bag. "Just this."

"Bless you," said the man, taking her bag and starting to walk at a furious clip. "I hate luggage. People pack up their whole lives and expect me to carry it to the car."

Fenny was openmouthed during the drive; she thought she'd seen heavy traffic in International Falls during Crazy Days, but it was a trickle compared to this blurring rush of vehicles.

As they drove on La Brea Avenue, the driver offered a running monologue on the crime that plagued the city, interrupting it only to give brief descriptions of areas—"Inglewood, home of the Lakers and the Kings—and heinous crime . . . the Wilshire District, it's one of the least exciting parts of L.A., but it's still got plenty of heinous crime . . . Hollywood, well, what kind of heinous crime isn't committed in Hollywood?"

Oddly, Fenny wasn't frightened by the driver's bleak commentary. She heard his voice, but his words didn't mean much to her, intent as she was at looking at everything. Maybe it was that she had survived a plane ride *and* she was riding in the back seat of a limousine. Maybe it was that in Tall Pine that morning it had been twenty-eight degrees and here people walked around in shorts and skimpy tops. Maybe it was the man who stood selling oranges on the corner; there were no street vendors back home selling indigenous fruits, and if there were, what would they sell—gooseberries?

It was all so foreign to her. Palm trees, like telephone poles wearing fright wigs, grew out of pavement boulevards, and houses on stilts peered over the edges of brown hillsides. They drove down Sunset Boulevard and the billboards crowding each other for space had no back-home counterpart; neither did the gated mansions she saw once they were in Beverly Hills, unless of course you counted the Tall Pine Lodge, which had closed down the year before because of termites.

As the driver pulled up in front of her hotel, he warned her that just because they were in Beverly Hills didn't mean there weren't heinous criminals. "They just dress better."

They opened their car doors at the same time, meeting on the sidewalk.

"Hey," he said, "I was going to get that for you."

"Huh?" Fenny asked before realizing what he meant. "Oh, the door. I guess I'm not used to people wanting to open my door."

"Always expect people to do things for you in L.A.," he advised. "Attitude is *very* important here."

"Okay," said Fenny, not exactly understanding what he was saying but figuring she needed to respond. "Oh," she said, unzipping her fanny pack. "I should give you a tip, right?"

"It's been taken care of," said the driver.

"Okay," said Fenny, closing the zipper.

"Of course, if you want to add a little bonus, it's up to you."

The zipper was opened again. "What would be a little bonus?"

The driver looked to the sky. "Once James Coco tipped me a hundred bucks."

"Oh," said Fenny. She had brought only fifty dollars and had felt extravagant at that. After all, she was only going to be gone a day and a half.

"I wouldn't say no to a fiver," offered the driver.

"Okay." Fenny rummaged in her wallet and found a bill. "Here you go."

The driver accepted the money, tipping his hat. "Now remember what I told you — it's all attitude . . . and stay away from the heinous crime."

In her room, which smelled like refrigerated flowers, Fenny opened the envelope that had been given her at the front desk.

"Dear Miss Ness," it read, "I look forward with great pleasure to our meeting tomorrow. Christian has told me so much about you. A driver will pick you up in front of the hotel at 2:00. Enjoy our town. Until then I am, Sincerely, Harry Freed."

Fenny helped herself to an orange from an elaborate fruit basket whose card said was "compliments of the management." Free

Sample Day at the grocery store in Baudette thrilled her; a whole fruit basket she didn't have to pay for just about sent her over the top.

She checked the closet, the shower, and under the bed and, finding no hotel rapist, felt comfortable enough to adjust the pillows and pick up the folded paper triangle that listed the television stations.

"Twenty-four channels," she said, reading the guide. "Wow."

She called Lee, but the phone rang without an answer and then Fenny remembered Lee had agreed to help rice potatoes for the lefse that was a tradition at every Benevolent Father's potluck.

Too shy and too frugal to order from room service, Fenny helped herself to a banana and what might have been a mango or a papaya. She turned on the TV and spent the evening giving halfhearted concentration to its twenty-four channels and the *People* magazine Lee had given her at the Grand Forks airport. ("It'll get you in the mood," she said.) She didn't know when she fell asleep, but when she woke up at six-thirty, the television was still on and she was eased into consciousness by a former pro tennis player who was promising a studio audience whiter teeth and more confidence in just thirty days.

Fenny showered and then towel-dried her hair while a morning news show host interviewed a lottery winner who planned on spending her money on her favorite charity.

"Which one is that?" asked the host, the lines of his face furrowed in sincerity.

"The Me, Myself, and I Foundation," said the winner gleefully. "It's the most deserving one I can think of."

A game show (Fenny didn't think of turning off the TV; it seemed part of the hotel room ambience) pitted two hyperventilating contestants in a bidding war as Fenny dressed and put on the minimal makeup that was reserved for, if not special, then unusual, occasions.

Leaving her bed a snarl of sheets and blankets made her feel unfinished, but she was savvy enough to know that if she made it, the maid would just have to remake it. She stuck a few more pieces of fruit in her fanny pack and then closed the door on the still air of her room, oblivious to the TV pitch man who, dressed in ruffles and tight pants, danced the flamenco around a can of pork and beans.

In the lobby, two bellmen pushed pyramids of luggage behind a woman who was carrying on a spirited conversation with the two dogs she carried under her arms like furry footballs. At the bell captain's desk, a deliveryman deposited a four-foot-high floral arrangement whose banner read "Boffo B.O." Fenny had no idea what the message meant: all she knew was that B.O. was short for body odor and she knew one didn't receive flowers for it, boffo or not.

Outside, the air smelled as if something had burned, and Fenny blinked back tears.

"Is something on fire?" she asked the doorman.

He wiped a line of sweat off his upper lip with a gloved hand.

"No, miss. It's just the smog is pretty bad today."

According to the small map she had found next to the cable guide (which seemed to have taken the place of the Gideon Bible), she was only a few blocks from downtown Beverly Hills. She walked toward it, on a boulevard called Little Santa Monica, which was directly parallel to a boulevard called Santa Monica. Rust-free cars sped down both streets. Flowers, their colors and shapes wildly tropical (show-offs compared to the tulips and lilacs of Tall Pine), bloomed from bushes and vines and in plots surrounding trees. They astonished Fenny, these profuse blossoms; in air that had the weight of smoke, how could anything like that grow?

She entered a crosswalk and the yellow light changed to red. Still, the drivers who seemed so aggressive out in traffic waited patiently until she had crossed to the curb.

Rodeo Drive, the map said, made for the best shopping in the world. Fenny thought that was a claim open to wide dispute: the stores she passed mostly sold clothes, sometimes jewelry or luggage. Where were the grocery and hardware stores? The appliance outlet? Tall Pine's Main Street had more variety than this.

She walked into a store whose name was etched into a grand facade and immediately a woman in a black suit appeared at her side.

"Do you have an appointment?"

"An appointment?" asked Fenny. "Isn't this a clothing store?"

The woman, whose features were made slightly Oriental by the severity with which her white-blond hair was pulled back, attempted a smile.

"We sell statements here," she explained. "Not clothes."

The door opened and a couple entered arm-in-arm. They were

dressed like futuristic bikers in pieces of leather and pounded gold, and the tight-faced woman risked a fissure by smiling wide.

"Yves! Angelique!" She leaned toward them, her kisses an inch off their cheeks. The saleswoman dismissed Fenny with a wave of her pale white hand as she directed her preferred clientele toward a rack of statements.

Fenny window-shopped for a while, but it was boring. Looking in one window full of Lucite blocks and neon zigzags, she tried to figure out exactly what the store sold. When a policeman passed her, she half expected him to stop and inform her that window-shopping was against the law; either you bought it or you beat it.

She walked out of the commercial district and into the residential, what the map called the flats of Beverly Hills. The streets were lined with the trees they'd been named after, and one was as deserted as the next. It was as if shades had been drawn around each neighborhood.

There was, however, activity going on in the yards. Gardeners modeling a variety of straw hats trimmed shrubs whose edges were even as a ruler, and pruned bushes ripe with camellias. One yard, blasphemous with weeds, posted a sign that read, "Conserve Now — Don't Water Your Lawn," but it was ignored by dozens of sprinklers that buzzed and flitted like industrious insects.

A black Porsche, pulling out of a driveway, blocked Fenny's path and the driver, rolling down the window, asked, "May I help you?"

"No, thanks," said Fenny. "I'm just walking."

"Why?" asked the driver, but he had rolled up his window and accelerated into the street before Fenny could answer.

Around noon, Fenny took an apple out of her fanny pack and ate it. It did little to assuage her hunger, however, and she decided to splurge and buy some lunch. She had followed Sunset Boulevard east out of Beverly Hills and turned right on La Cienega, which her "This is L.A.!" packet said was the city's "Restaurant Row."

Near Third Street, between one restaurant that looked like an antebellum mansion and another that looked like a pink stucco bunker, a small shack squatted defiantly. It was called Señor Loco's, and it was there Fenny decided to have her lunch.

Chapter 6

As she sat in the limousine, Fenny was surprised to discover her knees were knocking. Daze, like an analgesic, had coated most of her emotions since she found herself in L.A., and she had mistaken it for calm. Everything had seemed like a game, but now it was as if the game board had been slapped shut by an intimidating reality and her old familiar companion, fear. She put her hands on her kneecaps; it felt as if she were trying to still timers that had just gone off.

Yesterday's driver was positively garrulous next to the one now driving; he answered Fenny's hello with a nod, and his muted conversation was directed only at drivers, calling them either "stupid idiot" or "stupid moron."

Why did I ever agree to come? wondered Fenny. And why'd I eat that burrito? It had tasted nothing like those at the so-called Mexican restaurant the Ness family had long ago eaten on trips to Fargo; this one was packed with spicy flavors she had never tasted before. Her stomach shuddered and quaked like the plates under the San Andreas Fault.

The driver pulled into an ornate gate topped with the words "World Star Pictures." A guard pointed past several low, rectangular buildings and the driver followed the path this finger had routed. When he opened the door for Fenny, she remained seated, absolutely still except for her knees, which continued their cha-cha.

"You coming?" asked the driver.

Fenny found enough saliva in her mouth to swallow, and with great effort pushed herself out of the dark leather interior of the limousine. She staggered outside the car, as if her legs couldn't bear her weight.

The driver, suddenly Sir Lancelot, took Fenny's arm and led her into the reception area of a dun-colored bungalow. Fenny clung to him as if he were a mortician leading her to the casket of her beloved.

"She's here to see Mr. Freed," he said to a woman dressed like a police officer.

"Sign in," said the woman, slathering hand lotion up her arms. She flared her nostrils and nodded toward a clipboard.

The driver handed Fenny the pen.

"Can you sign in all right, honey?" he asked. "Can you sign your name?"

"Say, what's going on?" asked the woman behind the desk, suspecting drug use by another screwed-up actor. "Is she all right?" She snapped her gum and the noise sounded like a cap pistol firing.

"She's fine," said the driver, and then, softer, he asked Fenny, "Aren't you?"

Beads of sweat dotted her upper lip. She took a deep breath and, nodding, signed her name. If she had stopped to examine her handwriting, she would have noticed it didn't resemble hers in the slightest (it was like a bad electrocardiogram reading), but she was too distracted by her sense of doom . . . and her cramping stomach.

"Uh, where's Mr. Freed's office?" asked the driver, seeing that Fenny didn't seem inclined to move away from the reception desk.

"Through the doors, top of the stairs, corner office." The guard pushed a button, setting off a buzzer on the door.

The driver gently disentangled himself from the hand Fenny had clamped on his arm. "Well, go on," he said. "It's all right."

Fenny looked at the kind driver whom she would have married out of gratitude, and tried to smile. To the driver, her face held the grimace of someone fighting the G force in a wind tunnel.

"You'll be fine," said the driver, gesturing toward the door. "Piece of cake."

"Thanks," whispered Fenny, and then, like a virgin facing a volcano, she squared her shoulders and walked through the buzzing doors. She tried to remember the words to the song Anna the schoolteacher from *The King and I* sang whenever she was afraid, but her mind couldn't conjure up any lyrics but "whistle" and "trick."

When she reached the top of the stairs her stomach was burning and her wobbly knees felt as if they might disintegrate altogether. After lapping up water from a drinking fountain, a man appeared at the end of the hallway and asked, "Fenny? Fenny Ness? It's me, Harry Freed." His arm whirled around, motioning her forward.

Fenny hesitated a moment, but then, smoothing the jacket that covered her roiling stomach, she breathed deeply and walked to the end of the hall, to the door that was marked "Freed Productions."

"Come in, come in," said the man. He moved his arms as if he were guiding a taxiing plane. He put a hand on her back, and she jumped as a static shock rose.

"Sorry," he said, guiding her past a woman knitting at her desk. "I give off shocks all the time. It's from running around stocking-footed. Oh," he added by way of introduction, "my secretary."

By the time Fenny turned to say hello, they were already in his office.

"Well," he said, moving around his desk—he was a whirlwind of motion—"my nephew Christian was sent away on business, but he sends his regards and I'll certainly tell him you're as pretty as he reported."

"Thank—"

"Sort of an Ann Sheridan type. Especially in that getup." He looked Fenny up and down, smiling. "Actually, I think I saw Ann Sheridan wearing that very same suit."

"I got it at a used-clothing store," said Fenny, who had no idea who Ann Sheridan was.

Fenny wasn't much of a fashion trendsetter. Any special-occasion clothes she needed were bought at the Take A Second Look consignment store in Baudette. The suit she now wore was maroon, its skirt mid-calf-length, its jacket decorated with a peplum and padded shoulders.

"Of course, good looks aren't anything so special here in Hollywood," continued Harry, who had a speech to make. "I mean, they're sort of mandatory, a requirement for citizenship. Unless you're a character actor . . . or a producer." He moved past a grandfather clock and toward a suit of armor on whose arms a trench coat hung.

"Yuh, Hollywood's about the only industry who can refuse to hire someone with the excuse 'she's not good-looking enough' and still get away with it. Not that I think sexual-harassment claims don't have their place. Say, you look a little pale, why don't you sit down."

He used his aircraft-guiding motion again, directing her to a couch full of pillows decorated with needlepoint messages.

Half of the hotel room fruit basket, one Burrito Suprema, and a clammy fear were busy at work in Fenny's digestive tract. Feeling hot and light-headed, she walked very carefully to the couch, reassuring herself that she felt fine, just fine.

"Mr. Freed," she said in a weak voice as she sat down.

"Call me Harry. I never could stand to be called Mr. Freed; makes me sound like someone I'm not. I don't know why it is that people get a certain age and think that being called by their first name is a show of disrespect—hell, that's their name—"

"Mr. Freed—"

"Now, what did I just say?" he asked, moving toward the window. "It's Harry, Harry, Harry, Harry." He flipped the blinds open and shut in time with his words. "Not the greatest moniker, but it's mine. I thought about changing it years and years ago when everyone was Rock or Tab or Troy, but what was I supposed to change it to? I'm a producer, not an actor. I don't have to sell myself in all those stupid ways. No offense—of course, it remains to be seen whether you're an actor or not."

"Harry—"

"But I guess we should read through some of the script and find that out, won't we?"

"Harry," said Fenny, her voice frantic, realizing the cramps in her stomach signaled an immediate need for release. Desperately she tried to contract her sphincter muscle, realizing she was going to—

"Harry!"

The producer turned from the window, puzzled at the urgency in Fenny's voice. Didn't she know the importance of small talk? It was the mainstay of Hollywood conversation. He was about to tease her that overeagerness was the sign of an amateur, but when he saw her face, the words dried in his mouth. The pretty face of the young woman was now a mask of pure, pale mortification.

Fenny bolted up and then, her voice as anguished as someone

who'd just stumbled out of a car wreck, she cried, "Harry, I think I . . . I . . . I pooped in my pants!"

There was a blip in time—it stood perfectly still and all sensations of sound and movement stopped with it.

In his office, a director had once threatened Harry with a saber (it was a movie prop, but still, it was sharp); an actress had opened her mangy rabbit coat to reveal her naked and rouged body underneath; a mobster offered him a kilo of cocaine; several process-servers had presented him with summonses; and a lion tamer, auditioning for Harry's *Jungle Coup* picture, had once paraded three Bengal tigers past his desk. A lot of people had done a lot of things in his office, but no one had ever, *ever* pooped in their pants.

Harry jumped into action. Dashing across the dark green carpet, his stockinged feet raising sparks, he opened a mahogany door.

"My private bathroom." Once again he waved his arms like an airfield director. "Please."

Harry was a producer; he knew how to get things done. After Fenny had closed the door to the bathroom (running hunched over, her arms clasped at her waist), he got his secretary on the phone and, cupping his hand over his mouth, he whispered, "Run down to Wardrobe and get me a complete set of clothes from shoes to underwear, size . . . oh, make it an eight."

"Any particular—"

"I need them now. Go. The clock's running."

He broke the connection and began to pace around his desk, his feet sparking.

Moving around his desk, he couldn't help sneaking a look at where Fenny had sat. He wondered if he'd have to call in an upholstery cleaner—Jesus, had she really shit in her pants? No, no, *pooped. I pooped in my pants.*

A snicker erupted from Harry's throat; he couldn't help himself.

I pooped in my pants. He took a few tentative steps and, stretching his neck, looked at the couch cushion, but there was no stain, nothing on the stupid needlepoint message pillows actresses gave him but the same old shit. He slapped his hand over his mouth, trying to seal in the laughter that rose in appreciation of his joke. Christ, I hope she didn't hear me, Harry thought. I don't want her to think I'm laughing at her. *I pooped in my pants.* Poor kid, what a child's confession. Of course, how *did* an adult announce something like that? Immediately, a line from one of his movies sprang to his mind: "Avast, matey—I've opened the hatch a wee bit early."

In the bathroom, Fenny sat on the toilet, completing the job she had prematurely started. Her body's betrayal had sent her into a stupor of shock and she stared at the small frosted glass window, wondering if she could fit through it and jump to the ground below. Since she was on the second story, she knew she'd probably injure herself, but surely a broken tibia or fractured elbow was less punishment than facing Mr. Harry Freed.

When his secretary knocked, Harry raced to the door, opening it a crack.

"Thanks, honey," he said, taking the clothes as surreptitiously as a prohibition bouncer accepting bootleg. His secretary pushed her face into the door opening, her eyes wide behind her glasses, trying to get a better view.

"*Thank you,*" said Harry, pressing the door shut with his hip.

He tiptoed over to the mahogany door and heard the sound of water running. Taking a breath, he rapped on the door with his middle knuckle.

"I'm leaving some things you might need right outside the door. I myself have an errand to run, but I'll be back in the office"—he looked at his watch—"in five minutes." He waited a moment for her response, and when there was none he left his office, slamming the door as loudly as possible.

Harry's secretary jumped, dropping the jelly doughnut she had been eating.

"Honestly, Harry," she said, "what on earth is going on?" She groaned then, seeing that the doughnut had fallen jelly-side down on her knitting.

Harry glanced back at the door he'd just slammed and tiptoed toward the desk of his secretary.

"Wardrobe give you any trouble?"

"Of course not, Harry. Lou and I have lunch practically every day."

"Lou? That old battle-ax still runs Wardrobe?"

"Yes, Harry," said his secretary crisply. "That old battle-ax still runs Wardrobe." She dipped a corner of tissue into her coffee and with it rubbed the jelly off what was to become a sweater cuff. "Now, do you mind telling me what's going on?"

Harry leaned toward her, and his secretary quickly grabbed her coffee cup before it was knocked over. Harry looked at the door again.

"Keep a secret?"

His secretary smirked. Harry knew that she was probably the only person in Hollywood who could.

"Okay, okay," said Harry. He picked a paper clip out of its holder and cleaned his thumbnail with it.

Harry's secretary crossed her arms in front of her chest, waiting patiently. A good portion of Harry's pictures had been murder mysteries and spy thrillers; he therefore thought of himself as the Master of Suspense, capable of wringing high drama out of any moment. He held the paper clip up to the light.

"Brilliant piece of design, this twisted piece of metal."

"*Harry.*"

"All right, all right." He leaned forward, his tie folding softly as it touched the desk blotter. He mouthed several words.

"What?"

Harry rolled his eyes and raised his voice to a whisper. "She pooped in her pants!"

"She *pooped* in her pants?"

"Shhhh!" Harry's head jerked toward the door.

"Oh, my heavens," said his secretary, standing up. "I'd better see if she needs any help."

"Don't go in there!" said Harry, shaking his head so vigorously that his jowls jiggled. "It's a secret between her and me. Got it?"

Harry's secretary sat. "Of course I've got it." She then busied herself with cleaning her desk. "My sister has the same thing."

"The same thing?" said Harry.

"It's a syndrome," said his secretary, nodding. "Her doctor calls it the 'After-Dinner-and-Coffee-Syndrome.'"

"What on earth are you talking about?"

"Some people have very sensitive gastrointestinal tracts. My sister is one of those people."

"Sensitive gastrointestinal tracts?"

"It's not that uncommon. My sister's doctor has a very chichi Beverly Hills practice and he told her he sees this sort of thing all the time."

"The After-Dinner-and-Coffee-Syndrome?" Harry said again, as if he hadn't heard correctly.

"He named it after female patients who are so excited to go out to dinner; you know, they've probably been ignored all week by their work-obsessed husbands and then they're excited and eat too much rich food and have coffee afterwards and, well, it's like a fast-working laxative."

"You have got to be kidding."

Harry's secretary shook her head. "There are different scenarios, of course. My sister's problem can occur anytime, anywhere. We had lunch in La Jolla last weekend, and boom—she had to get to a bathroom *immediately*."

"Good Lord," said Harry.

He knocked on his own office door—he'd given the girl ten minutes—before entering.

Fenny stood looking at the suit of armor, still wearing, Harry noticed, her Ann Sheridan suit.

"Makes a nice coatrack, doesn't it?" he asked. "A Polish count gave it to me."

"I . . . I didn't need all of these clothes," said Fenny, gesturing to the clothes she had draped over the back of the couch. "It really wasn't . . . it was just a little, it, it wasn't as bad as I thought." She squeezed her eyes shut, humiliated but feeling it necessary to give a damage assessment. "I'll return everything"—she stammered here—"everything I borrowed."

Harry knew "everything" was a pair of underpants. He held his arms above his head and grasped his hands, pulling them back until he heard his back crack.

"What I need," he said, "is an hour or so on the massage table." He then made two fists and cracked his thumb knuckles. Awkwardness was as palpable as a drop in temperature.

"Fenny," said Harry finally, "please. Sit down."

"I'd rather just go," said Fenny softly. She swallowed and scratched her earlobe. "Course, I guess I already did."

Harry reared up like a horse who'd just nudged against an electric fence. He looked at Fenny to make sure she'd said what he thought she'd said. She had. There was a smile on her face (a smile weighted with embarrassment, but still, her lips were pointing north). She had made a joke.

"Of course you already did!" said Harry, jubilant, and he began to laugh and so did Fenny, because it sure beat breaking down.

Harry opened a bottle of champagne he kept in the grandfather clock. He preferred to toast to whiskey, but he realized the celebratory symbolism of champagne and he popped the cork like a showman, making sure that a festive stream escaped.

"To Inga!" he said, holding his glass out in a salute.

Fenny looked at Harry as if he were speaking Bantu.

Harry clinked his glass against hers. "The part's yours," he said, a smile cutting across his three o'clock shadow. "If you want it."

Harry had known, that quickly, that Fenny would be starring in his next motion picture. He didn't care if it turned out she couldn't act (he'd worked with enough actors who couldn't); he didn't care if she was too tall (the leading man in his last picture wouldn't work with any actress over five-foot-three); he didn't care about any of the Hollywood criteria that had discolored too many of his decisions. What he cared about was a girl who could *poop* in her pants and then have the grace to joke about it.

"I don't know what to say," said Fenny.

"That's what we have scripts for," said Harry as he walked to the couch. "Now shit."

A blush flooded Fenny's face.

"I mean *sit*." Harry shook his head. "Bad joke. Sorry."

Fenny sat down. "Not as sorry as I am."

Harry splashed more champagne into their glasses and gently asked her if she had "that syndrome."

"What?"

Harry explained what he had just learned from his secretary.

Wide-eyed, Fenny said, "Well, I was nervous and I had all that fruit and Mexican food . . . but I don't think I have *syndrome*. I mean, nothing like that has ever happened to me before." She took a sip of champagne, shuddered, and peered at him over her glass. "You won't tell anyone, will you?"

"The media's been alerted." He smiled when she looked at him wild-eyed. "Kidding. I'm only kidding. The thing is, it's not so much what you do in Hollywood as how what you do is perceived. I mean, if we played this thing up right, it could all become part of your lore. Part of the Fenny Ness legend."

"The real poop on Fenny Ness?"

Harry laughed, liking her even more. "Something like that."

"No, thanks," said Fenny. "I'd like the legend to end right here."

Harry held out his hand and Fenny shook it. "But I'm warning you, I'm not going to stand for any more of those kind of party tricks."

As the champagne and the smoggy, but still golden, California afternoon slid by, Harry told Fenny how as a boy growing up in Flatbush, Brooklyn, he had skipped school to take the subway into Manhattan and sneak into movie theaters.

"No stickball, no ring-a-levio, no kick the can . . . none of the usual kid stuff for me. I was a movie buff by the age of nine. People like Gable and Garbo—I thought they were from another planet."

Fenny told Harry about Slim and the day he spent in the box elder tree in the park, pretending he was an ape. "Lee put a ladder up and brought him lunch and dinner."

Harry showed Fenny a yellowed and creased photograph he kept in his wallet, a picture he rarely showed anyone, of his wife Freesia, who had died of food poisoning at the age of twenty-one.

"We were only married sixteen months," said Harry. "But I've never been able to love another woman the way I loved her."

Fenny told Harry about her parents. "The thing is, I was going to surprise them. They always teased me about never leaving Tall Pine, but I was really thinking about calling a travel agent about getting a ticket to South America." She sniffed. "I was going to knock on their hotel door and say, 'Anyone up for a walk through the rain forest?' " She bowed her head, tears stinging her eyes.

After a respectful moment of silence, Harry raised his glass. "To Sig and Wally."

Fenny raised her glass and they clinked them together.

"What do you think they'd think of their daughter getting a job in the movies?"

"First they'd have to get over their shock that I actually came to Los Angeles myself," said Fenny. "Then they'd think it was pretty exciting, I guess."

"Do you think it's exciting?"

Fenny shrugged again. "Maybe . . . maybe I will, when things sink in. Right now I can't tell if this whole trip seems like a dream . . . or a nightmare."

Harry leaned his head back against the couch cushion. "I'll let you in on a secret, Fenny. In Hollywood, they can be one and the same."

Chapter 7

The potluck supper at Benevolent Father's Lutheran Church had been successfully combining food and fellowship until the fuse blew during Pastor Murch's remembrance of Thora Kemp, who had died two weeks earlier.

"We'll miss you, Thora, and those special caramel bars you brought to every potluck," said the pastor while several parishioners nudged each other, remembering how more than one crown or filling had been unhinged by the sticky caramel whose adhesive quality should have been patented. When Pastor Murch had asked for a moment of silence there was a faint buzz and then the lights went out.

Several people made noises of surprise and several other of the more pious church members shushed them, as if they were dishonoring Thora's memory, and then a shushee told a shusher to "lighten up," and the shusher said, "No one is going to tell me what to do," and then Pastor Murch, fearing an uprising, asked first for calm and second for a volunteer to go with him to the fuse box.

When the lights finally came back on, everyone, fearful of that glimpse at an uglier side of themselves, made an extra effort to be friendly, and when Coralee Glatte won the raffle (a set of Ginsu kitchen knives) they applauded like crazy, even though they might privately grouse later that it was not fair, she had won the lazy Susan at the raffle just two years ago.

Lee O'Leary had helped out making lefse only because she was allowed to take some home. She loved lefse—a Norwegian tortilla, only made with riced potatoes and served rolled up with butter and brown sugar—and hadn't mastered the making of it on her own.

She would shamelessly volunteer to help out whenever the church ladies at B.F. made it and then take her stash, leaving before the main event at which the lefse would be served.

"Just because you're not a Lutheran doesn't mean God doesn't love you," Gloria Murch had once told her in her relentlessly chipper voice as she snuck out before a Fellowship Tea.

"*That's* reassuring," Lee answered back.

Inwardly, she scoffed; just because she was lapsed didn't mean she was ready to run over to the heretical *Lutheran* side. She still felt a loyalty toward the Catholic Church, but she had a hard time forgiving the parish priest in Chicago who advised her to stay with Marsh, even though he beat her.

"You need to find a way to resolve this problem within the framework of your marriage," he had told her.

Lee was stung by this comment; where was the "we" in this? And yet, she rationalized, he was a priest and it was indoctrinated in him to try and avoid divorce at all costs.

But as she sat across from the man who continued to rub his hands as if all the grime of the conversation had settled there; as his counsel continued to urge her to forgive her husband, she had the odd but keen sensation of shrinking, until she felt she was nothing but a speck on the slippery maroon leather wing chair.

She had left the meeting thinking that any place that made her feel as small as a speck wasn't the place for her, and she went home to her penthouse apartment on Lake Shore Drive and enlisted the help of her maid Bianca to pack two suitcases full of clothing.

"I will miss you," said the El Salvadoran maid, who was taking real estate courses at night school, "but you are doing the right thing."

"I'll give you excellent references," said Lee, touched by her maid's support. "I can even make a couple calls before I go to see if any of my friends need help."

Bianca shook her head. "Don't worry about me. I was getting tired of the maid's life anyway. I will watch my cousin's children until I get my license." She made a gesture with her hands. "By next year, I will be buying and selling places like this."

Lee gave her an additional two weeks' pay and the women hugged goodbye in the marble-floored foyer.

"Don't change your mind," said Bianca, looking sternly into her former employer's eyes. "You leave that man for good."

When the taxicab pulled up in the apartment building driveway, Lee was giddy that her escape plan was going without a hitch, but as she pushed open the lobby door, suitcases in hand, she froze.

Marsh had pulled up behind the taxi, in the Jaguar he had bought to replace the BMW he had totaled on his way from a bar on Wabash to one on Wacker. Lee tried to turn around, but fear had disabled the part of her brain that sent signals to her legs and she stood there like a cow about to enter the slaughter chute.

Marsh had come home early, having argued with an idiotic client who was trying to undercut his commission, and he was in no mood to find his fat wife standing there under the apartment building canopy, holding two suitcases. The bitch had threatened to leave him before, but he never thought she'd ever get off her fat ass and actually do it.

He jammed the stick shift into park and jumped out of the car. His movement finally inspired some in Lee. She trotted over to the curbside taxi, her head down, afraid to make eye contact with him.

The taxi driver had just stepped out of the car and was going to help his passenger put her bags in the trunk when he found himself playing interference.

"I'll take those," said Marshall Stouffer, lunging toward Lee and her luggage.

"No, you won't," said Lee, holding on to the handle of her Mark Cross bags as Marsh tried to jerk them away.

"Please," said Lee to the driver, "help me!"

Lucky for Lee and unlucky for Marsh, the taxi driver coached boxing every other evening at the Boys' Club. He was powerfully built and not about to let some rich guy in a suit mess with his fare.

"*I'll* take these," he said, reaching for the bags with his well-muscled arms.

"Stay out of this, dickhead," said Marsh, and with a quick tug, he jerked one of Lee's bags out of her hands.

"No, *you* stay out of this!" said Lee.

"I think I'll side with the lady on this one," said the taxi driver. He grabbed Marsh's arm and squeezed as hard as he could, which was pretty hard.

"Eeee-yow!" hollered Marsh, dropping the suitcase.

Lee grabbed it, but not before Marsh, still in the taxi driver's vise grip, kicked her hard and fast, below her knee.

"You won't get away with this, bitch!" he screamed.

"And you won't get away with that," said the driver, who threw him to the ground like the trash he was. "Get in the car!" he instructed Lee, and she did, scrambling into the back seat and locking the door.

Marsh had hardly spent a second on the ground before he was up again, but he heeded the driver's warning, "Don't make me really hurt you." He stood there, his fists clenched, his silk tie hanging crooked from its knot.

As the driver backed away toward his taxi and opened the driver's door, Marsh yelled, "You'll never get away with this, Lee!"

He ran to the taxi, but the driver had already started it up and Marsh got in only one kick to the fender before it sped down Lake Shore Drive.

Lee flew to New York and stayed with her brother Gerald, but he, like the priest, voted for reconciliation instead of separation.

"Gerry," said Lee, "he beat me! Not once, not twice, but more times than I can count!"

"You're a big woman, Lee," said Gerald. "How much damage could he do?"

"I don't know why I expected comfort from you," she said. "You've always been on Marsh's side more than mine."

"Well, it's easy to side with the guy—I mean, come on—Harvard-educated, brilliant career in finance—"

"You should hear the way he talks to me, Gerald, the names he calls me—"

"—family's been here since the American Revolution, father an ambassador—I mean, those aren't exactly credentials you can blow off—"

"Maybe you're not hearing me," said Lee, wishing desperately that were the case, that maybe she was speaking too softly or that Gerald was going deaf. She raised her voice. "What has the

American Revolution got to do with anything? The man spends all my money, he's an alcoholic, *and he beats me.*"

She wondered what twisted fraternity both her priest and her brother belonged to that they would support the bad guy over the good woman. And she *was* good; she had convinced herself of that, despite the thing so many people thought made her bad, weak, disgusting: her weight.

She had met Marshall Stouffer at the one point in her life when a diet had been successful; she in fact had starved herself down to a weight she couldn't remember ever being. She struggled mightily to stay thin during their first two years of marriage, but the day she got a telephone call advising her of an affair between Marsh and the anonymous caller was the day she pulled up a chair to the refrigerator door and worked her way down its shelves. That was also the day Marsh, after she confronted him, beat her up so bad that she had to drive herself down to Cook County Emergency and have her lip stitched up and her broken wrist set. There were more confessions from guilty and/or vengeful anonymous phone callers, more sessions in front of the refrigerator, more beatings.

The bigger she got, the more Marsh told her it was her fault that he had to seek solace in the arms of other women — "How's a man supposed to get hard with a fat pig like you laying next to him?" — and the rational part of her knew he was wrong, knew he was bad. But the irrational part of her agreed with him; of course it was her fault, of course.

"All I'm saying, Lee," said Gerald, "is I think you were pretty lucky to snare a guy like Marshall in the first place. Give him up and you might just wind up alone the rest of your life."

She left Gerald's Trump Tower apartment in short order and spent a half day wandering around JFK, hoping to find inspiration in the eavesdropped conversation of travelers on where to go to start a new life. But no one, it seemed, was going anywhere they really wanted to go; most of the people she listened to were on business, going to destinations that offered not sanctuary but sales opportunity.

What did I expect? Lee asked herself, miffed that she had to seek ideas from strangers because she had no good ones of her own.

She considered going to Dublin but felt too much would be expected of her there. Even though Gerald ran the company from New York, the factories and warehouses of O'Leary Exports were located there and Lee didn't want to live under the burden of her name.

She was at a vending machine in the United terminal, pulling the lever that would release a Nestlés Crunch Bar, when a picture flashed into her mind. It was a moment of "Eureka!" and she was so excited she almost forgot (but didn't) to grab her candy bar before running to the nearest ticket counter.

Her destination was a section of northern Minnesota, which, the ticket agent explained, would involve a flight to Minneapolis, a connecting flight to Grand Forks—and "then you're on your own."

The picture in her mind that had spurred the ticket purchase was of the bucolic Camp Waganotoshi, where she had spent the happiest summer of her life, away from battling parents, her teasing brother, and the pressures of being a rich, lonely, *overweight* little girl.

She had spent six weeks canoeing and swimming, hiking and honing her never-before-realized archery skills. The girls in the Minnehaha Cabin became her dearest friends, and with them she short-sheeted the beds of girls in the Nokomis Cabin, sang endless versions of "Great Big Gobs of Greasy Grimy Gopher Guts," and learned how to swear in Dutch, courtesy of her cabin mate Ruutsie, a North Dakota farm girl.

At the closing campfire ceremony, she was awarded the "All Around Camp Waganotoshi Girl" pin (one that still had a place of honor in a jewelry box brimming with gold and pearls and diamonds) and wondered if life could get any better than it was that star-filled night that smelled of the lake and the incinerating hot dogs that Debbie Rolandelli kept throwing like darts into the fire.

And so Lee decided that a place where she had felt well liked and strong and useful would be a good place to begin her new life.

In Grand Forks, she bought a car, a huge fifteen-year-old mustard yellow Bonneville, and cackled as she drove it out of the car lot, feeling as if she were at the helm of a riverboat. She was more resigned than disappointed to find Camp Waganotoshi gone, the victim of developers who had razed the dozen cabins and lodge in favor of lakeside homes for rich owners who used them several weekends each year.

In truth, she was embarrassed that she had come to Camp Waganotoshi at all; if it was still standing, what would she have done? Applied for work as a counselor? Volunteered her services as camp cook? Polished her archery?

Lee drove north, along a road flanked by tall dark pine trees through which the spring sun occasionally found space to send down a sparkling ray. She had no idea where she was going now, but there were worse things, she knew, than driving in a car that felt like a boat, through the North Woods of Minnesota.

"Sure beats a sock in the eye," she said out loud, and said it again, because it was so true.

Frau Katte and Miss Penk sat at the counter of the Cup O'Delight, listening to Lee and Slim sing the Sinatra duet "Something Stupid." At the piano bench, Slim was a different man, his head cocked toward Lee not in a canine pose, but in one of concentration. Lee played by ear, and well, and at these evening get-togethers, she would oblige a wide range of requests.

Tonight her repertoire was limited in that there were fewer people to make requests, Heine Osterberg and Mayor Lambordeaux having been, as they told Lee, "bamboozled into going to the church potluck by the wives." Mary Gore never let the lack of an invitation stop her from coming, but she was otherwise engaged that evening, driving down to Bemidji to listen to a concert sung by Bulgarian monks. Pete had shown up once, but his invalid sister with whom he lived didn't like being alone at night, and besides, as much as he adored Lee, he was too shy to sit with a group of people without the comforting business of eating breakfast or lunch.

There was a moment of silence after their last blended note and then Slim lifted his chin and howled.

"I know how you feel," said Frau Katte. "Sometimes I get embarrassed by beauty, too."

"I make her blush all the time," said Miss Penk, fluttering her eyelashes.

Lee patted Slim's thigh. "Frank and Nancy had nothing on us."

Slim shrugged and went behind the counter, where he got a wedge of carrot cake out of the pie case.

"Good idea," said Lee. "Let's eat."

Dessert was always a part of their after-hours get-togethers, as was a pot O'Delight, which seemed decadent, brewed as it was after restaurant hours.

"Anyone heard from Fenny?" asked Frau Katte, helping herself to Miss Penk's frosting, which the latter never touched.

"She only left yesterday," said Lee.

"Ya, but you know Fenny. She gets homesick crossing za county line."

"Just think," said Miss Penk, her eyes dreamy. "Hollywood. I always thought I might have had some luck there."

"I'll bet you could have given Lena Horne a run for her money," said Lee.

"Oh, she didn't want to be an actress," said Frau Katte, touching her companion's cheek, "alzo she certainly is pretty enough for zat."

"Stunt work," said Miss Penk. "I was such a daredevil in my youth—and you know how athletic I am."

It was true: Miss Penk might qualify for senior discounts, but she was in excellent shape. Not only was she Bud Glatte's most disciplined karate student, she also drove to International Falls once a week to participate in a fencing club composed of seven people, all of whom were younger than her. She skated on Tall Pine Lake in the winter and swam in it in the summer, enjoying the looks of surprised admiration she got while wearing a bathing suit that, while not as skimpy as a bikini, was at least a two-piece.

"From looking at us, everyone zinks I'm za butch one and she's za fem," Frau Katte once told Lee, "but really, she could take me wiz one arm tied behind her back." Her eyebrows waggled, Groucho-like. "Not zat I would mind."

"I hope she doesn't get it," said Slim, and everyone sat up in their chairs, ready to listen.

The man would go for days without speaking—at least in a human language—and then when he did, it was with such calm and good sense that Lee had to think sanity was his prevailing state of mind and that his Old Yeller imitations were more for his own amusement rather than a definite nod toward craziness.

"Why do you hope zat, Slim?" asked Frau Katte.

The man's knobby shoulders moved up in a shrug, and he was silent for so long that Lee thought, That's it, he's used up his word quota for the month.

"Well, I miss her," he said finally, his eyes on his long fingers. "But more importantly, I don't think she's ready for that kind of life . . . or wants it."

Lee's delight over Slim's loquaciousness was tempered by impatience. "What does 'that kind of life' mean, Slim? She auditions for a movie and suddenly everyone has her jumping into some wild Hollywood life."

"I just don't think a person should do anything that goes against their basic personality."

"You mean away from her fear and worry?" Lee shook her head. "I'd think you'd *want* her to do anything that moves her away from that."

"Hey," said Frau Katte defensively, "zere's a lot more to Fenny zan fear and worry—"

"Yes," interjected Miss Penk, "Fenny's got a lovely personality."

"I'm not saying Fenny doesn't have a good personality," said Lee with a sigh. "I'm just saying it certainly can't hurt her to try something new."

Their debate on the state of Fenny's personality was interrupted by a strange voice asking, "You open?"

The group turned toward the door, where a man wearing a backpack stood.

"He was *huge*," Lee later told Fenny. "At least six-foot-five, and his shoulders were as wide as the door frame."

"Sounds like you like him," said Fenny.

"What makes you say that?"

Fenny clasped her hands under her chin and in a high voice tittered, " 'Six-foot-five and his shoulders were as wide as the door frame.' "

Lee blushed, just as she had when she first spoke to the man.

"Not for business," she had said, feeling as if the temperature in the room had just shot up. "This is just sort of a get-together."

"Oh," said the man. He ran a hand through his long black hair and turned slightly, as if to go. Then, changing his mind, he turned back.

"Is there any way I could get a cup of coffee at this get-together?"

There was no way the group could deny a man his O'Delight, or the pleasure they would get watching him drink it.

"Sure," said Lee, acknowledging Frau Katte's wink by raising her eyebrows. "Sure, come on over and have a seat."

The man did, and after he took his first sip, he fell off his stool to the floor.

"Wow," he said, staring up at the ceiling.

Lee and the others in the cafe laughed; they were used to strong reactions, but not quite this strong.

"That is some *good* coffee," said the man, still on the floor.

"Thanks," said Lee.

He stood up. "You're responsible for it?" he asked, and when she nodded, he asked, "Will you marry me, then?"

"Oh, good!" said Frau Katte. "Lee's getting married!"

"I don't even know your name," said Lee, still laughing.

"Bill," said the man, and before sitting on the counter stool, he shook hands with the three women and Slim. "Most people call me Big Bill, for obvious reasons, I guess."

You guessed right, thought Lee, looking at his hands, which were as big as skillets.

Half Polynesian and half Chippewa Indian, Big Bill had grown up in Honolulu and gone to the University of Hawaii on a football scholarship. Any hopes of a career in the NFL, however, ended when he blew out his knee in his first season.

"I'm glad it happened," he said, "because really, I never cared much for the sport. It lacks finesse, in my mind—just a bunch of big guys knocking each other over. And I *hated* being tackled."

He spent most of his twenties as a musician, his last professional gig alternating as keyboardist and guitarist in a trio that played cover tunes in the TikiTiki Lounge at the Royal Lei Hotel.

When he could no longer stand one more tourist request for "Hawaiian Wedding Song" or "Blue Hawaii"; when he knew for sure he'd punch the face of the next wise guy who asked him if the "Royal Lei" was really the place to get one; when he could no longer fasten any more buttons on his hotel-issued Hawaiian shirts—that was when he knew it was time to move on.

He spent several years crisscrossing the mainland; he was a museum guard in L.A., he sold tires in Trenton, stationery supplies in Dallas, and cordless phones in Cleveland. He was a bouncer in a Baton Rouge bar and a barker for a San Francisco nightclub. He picked garlic in Gilroy, corn in Nebraska, and grapefruit in Florida.

"Then it hit me," he told his rapt audience at the Cup O'Delight. "I was bagging jelly beans in this candy factory in St. Louis—that was a sweet job—no pun intended—because I *love* candy—and I thought, isn't it about time you looked up your father's people? See, I never met the guy—he left my mother months before I was born, and then she'd heard he died on a construction site in Lanai. But I knew he was from northern Minnesota, so I collected my paycheck, accepted a couple pounds of candy as a parting gift, and hitched on up here."

"So have you found anyone?" asked Lee. "I mean, anyone you're related to?"

Big Bill nodded. "I asked around at the reservation in Red Lake. A bunch of people there knew my dad. They told me his aunt lives up here."

"Mae Little Feather?" asked Miss Penk.

"That's her name. You know her?"

"Everyone knows Mae," said Frau Katte. "And everyone's afraid of her."

"She makes beautiful clothes and jewelry," said Lee. "She sells a lot of her work down the street, at Sig's Place. Fenny—she's my friend who runs the shop—she says she can hardly put Mae's stuff out before it's bought."

"Ya, she is talented," said Frau Katte. "But mean. I'd watch myself if I were you."

Suddenly Heine Osterberg rapped on the large picture window and after he was introduced to Big Bill, he sat at the counter, his hands around a cup O'Delight, and told them all about the church power failure and how fisticuffs almost broke out.

"And now the wife's mad at me, too," he said, shaking his head.

"Why's that?" asked Lee, filling his coffee cup.

"She wanted to cap off the evening at Rolly's, but I told her I was too tired to two-step." He shook his head again. "She really blew her stack at that one. She hates any reminder that I'm getting older."

"Well, she is, too, Heine," said Miss Penk.

"You'd best keep that observation to yourself," Heine advised.

"You should have brought her along to polka with us," said Lee.

"Irene doesn't understand our kind of dance."

"What kind of dance is your kind of dance?" asked Big Bill.

"Well," said Lee, "it's kind of hard to explain, but if you stick around for a while, you'll find out."

They didn't give Mary Gore credit for much, but it was she who inspired the description of what it was they did at the Cup O'Delight in general and at their after-hours (usually on, but not confined to, Friday night) get-togethers in particular. Inspiration had come to her after an evening that had featured a spirited debate on computer technology (Fenny griping that more than information, computers dispensed alienation); Frau Katte reciting "The Raven" in German; Slim and Lee singing an oddly compelling medley of the Kinks *and* Cole Porter songs as Heine joined in on accordion; and finally, a defensive karate demonstration put on by Miss Penk, with the mayor acting as "the assailant."

As they sat down to incomparable coffee and pecan pie, Mary rambled on about the joys of "this certain synergy we have, this unity of spirit, this mutual desire for ideas exchanged, talent exposed, songs sung, and bread broken.

"Why," she continued, her face flushed with excitement, "if life is but a dance, then we're all a small group linked in an exquisite North Woods ballet!"

Eyes rolled in their collective sockets and no one tried to dissuade Mary when she said she had to go home and work on her poetry; her muse was getting hungry and she had to serve it.

They waited until they heard her fire up the Gore Printing van she drove and then they burst into laughter.

"She should starve zat muse of hers," said Frau Katte.

"Or serve it strychnine," said Fenny.

"You guys are terrible," Lee said, laughing.

Slim began to lope across the room flailing his arms. Miss Penk followed, imitating his motions. Heine grabbed his accordion, and then everyone was up and dancing, first in a strange leaping conga line and then with partners.

"Ah," said Fenny, trying to follow the mayor's lead, "feel this *synergy*, this *unity of spirit*?"

"If life is but a dance," said Heine in a falsetto voice, "then we're all doing an exquisite North Woods ballet!"

"I'd say it's more a polka," said Lee, and then there was a change of partners and she found herself high-stepping with Slim, who barked several times and then, acting as his own translator, explained, "It's the Tall Pine Polka."

Big Bill had fit right in, thought Lee, looking out at the dark waters of Tall Pine Lake. She was smiling, feeling like the hostess whose usual good party had been enlivened by a handsome mystery guest—a handsome mystery guest who was now sitting next to her on the park bench.

When she had learned Bill didn't have a car, she asked him if he'd like a ride home.

"Nope, I like the walk," he said, "but if you'd like to show me Tall Pine by night, I wouldn't mind."

And so by the weak light of a spring moon, Lee had. They walked down Main Street toward the lake, with Lee giving commentary on the businesses they passed.

"Osterberg Accounting—that's Heine's—you met him tonight. He'll do your taxes, but he's more interested in getting you to sign a petition to send big industry polluters to jail."

They crossed the street.

"Sunstrom Sundries—for all your drugstore needs. We were all afraid the new Walgreens up in International Falls was going to take away some of their business, but so far they're hanging in there."

"Sundries," said Bill. "Sounds like what they sell is slightly illegal."

Lee laughed. "Martin Sunstrom? Pastor Murch looks to *him* for moral guidance. I'd doubt he even sells condoms, on principle alone." Lee was glad for the darkness, blushing as she did over having said *anything* that had to do with sex. She thought the atmosphere surrounding herself and Bill was charged enough already.

"And there's Denton's Grocery," said Lee, quickly. "It's got a great candy counter."

"Speaking of candy," said Bill, plucking two cellophane-wrapped jawbreakers out of his pocket. "Care for some?"

Lee accepted, and she and Bill walked on, soundlessly sucking on their candy. Occasionally Lee looked at Bill, his cheek distorted by the bulge the jawbreaker made. She felt as giddy as a schoolgirl being walked home by the cutest guy in the eighth grade.

Once they got to the lake, Lee suggested they take in the view from one of the park benches the city council had bought the previous year for Tall Pine's Downtown Renovation campaign. (They also okayed funds to plant a bed of petunias in front of the mayor's office and to sandblast the old stone facade of the library.)

"What a pretty town," said Bill, looking out over the water, and Lee found herself wishing he'd put his arm on the back of the bench so she could rest her head against it.

"It is," said Lee, feeling obliged to make conversation even though she would have preferred to use her mouth for other purposes. She stifled a giggle — what had gotten into her? — and cleared her throat. "It feels like home to me more than Chicago ever did."

"I like that saying about home being wherever you hang your hat," said Bill.

"Is that how you feel?" asked Lee.

Bill pondered this question for a while, and Lee tried to follow his gaze out at the lake, but found herself drawn to looking at him instead. The lines of his face were so straight and strong, and she wondered what he would do if she touched them with her fingertips. She folded her hands in her lap, restraining them.

"I'd like to," Bill said presently. "I think it would be a comfort to feel you belong anyplace you go in this big wide world. But I don't know — I do love the ocean and I don't know if a lake or a river can ever mean as much. And there's nothing like the smell of the tropics." He sniffed deeply. "But lilacs — lilacs do have their appeal."

Lee was censoring every sentence that popped up in her head before it came out of her mouth, so that *You have your appeal, too,* came out as, "Yes, I only wish their season lasted longer."

For the next half hour, she sat on that bench with Big Bill, holding up her end of the conversation while not saying one word of what she wanted to shout, and when Big Bill said he'd walk her back to the Cup O'Delight because it was time for him to get moving, Lee nodded and said, "Okay," instead of, *Kiss me now until the sun rises!*

Chapter 8

The next morning, Fenny, wearing a calico dress and a bonnet, stood in front of a camera on a chilly soundstage.

"She sure is cute," whispered Emma Tuttle, the casting director, whose dream of discovering the next big star had not yet been realized, although she had brought La Fluffee to the nation's consciousness. Still, she aimed higher than finding the perfect cat to star in litter box commercials; she wanted to discover the next Ava Gardner or Tyrone Power. They were her ideals, and while some might mock their acting abilities, no one could deny they had *it*, that indefinable thing that blared, "Movie star!"

Malcolm Edgely, on the other hand, did not believe in *it*. Stars were made, not born; they did not have an undefinable quality, they had a good part in a good story, and above all, a great director. In fact, if everyone responsible for an actor's stardom lined up in order of importance, the actor would come in about fifth, behind the director, writer, cinematographer, costumer, and makeup person.

Malcolm likened Hollywood to a big vat of brine that soured and pickled artistry, his own included. In his heart, he knew he had sold out big-time, but, he reasoned, if one is going to sell out, why not make it big-time? And his house perched on a cliff overlooking the Pacific, his Manhattan pied-à-terre, his fleet of foreign cars, his clothes custom-made by a London tailor, and recognition by the Hollywood elite was *big* big time.

He had come to California twenty-five years earlier, a fresh-scrubbed graduate from the University of Winnipeg, raring to change the world through film. His first effort, a movie about a young Canadian college student's search for himself, won rave reviews and several awards, as did his second and third films, but then he was wounded in love and tried to stanch his pain with fifths of Scotch, ultimately screwing up his personal *and* professional life.

When Harry Freed threw him a script about a homicidal substitute teacher, he knew it was the only bone he was about to be offered and so he grudgingly fetched it. It was a huge drive-in success, and in counting up the box office receipts, Malcolm began to forget exactly how or why he had wanted to change the world.

That he had lost his passion for moviemaking and now directed by rote was a truth that bothered him only on those nights when the bottle of wine he drank at dinner hadn't sufficiently anesthetized him and he lay awake listening to the roll of the waves and staring out the wall-sized window of his bedroom at the phosphorous surf.

He had come to the screen test only because he had an appointment nearby with his accountant. This would be the ninth movie he made with Harry Freed, and while neither man could claim respect for the other, they understood one another. Hollywood was a factory and they were on the assembly line, cranking out product.

"Are you ready, Stan?" he asked, and when the cameraman nodded, Malcolm called for action and Fenny stepped to the X she'd been shown, swallowing a lump in her throat as big and hard as a walnut.

The courage bead and pinecone she had stuck in her bra—the dress had no pockets—dug into her breast. She tried to clear her throat of the walnut, and then, gazing over the heads of those watching her, Fenny began the speech she had memorized the night before in the refrigerated chill of her hotel room.

She didn't say her first words as much as she squeaked them, and Malcolm Edgely leaned toward Harry and whispered, "It's Minnie Mouse!"

Emma Tuttle shook her head sympathetically; it was always painful to watch the unraveling of an actor, but Harry, ever faithful, ignored the snide and fretful reactions of his seat mates and thought, Just wait, you just wait. He didn't know why or how Fenny Ness was going to bowl them over, he only knew that she would.

Harry felt a flicker of guilt. He had sent Christian away to a "Writing Dialogue for Cartoon Characters" seminar in Santa Barbara advertised in the back of a trade paper.

"Why do I need to go to a seminar like that?" Christian had asked. "I write for the movies now!"

"Christian, I don't think you should ever turn your back on cartoons. Your screenwriting career isn't guaranteed, you know."

"But Uncle Harry!" Christian had whined. "I want to be in on this whole thing! I want to see Fenny's screen test!"

Christian went, pouting the entire way, and when a cute coed from USC asked if he might help her on a "Bruce the Silly Goose" episode, he had to admit the weekend might just work out after all.

Before he met Fenny, Harry had prepared himself for her to be a dud and the screen test to be a disaster, and perhaps unconsciously he wanted to spare the boy public humiliation. But obviously, Christian was on a roll; first he had done the unthinkable, which was to write a good script, and now he had exhibited a keen casting eye.

Malcolm Edgely shifted slightly in his chair, and out of the corner of his eye Harry could see Emma Tuttle's large chest expand and then stop.

That's it exactly, thought Harry, smiling. She takes your breath away.

"Ike Forrest, I did not travel over one deep ocean, two tall mountain ranges, and across Indian Country to be told I am not what you expected. Why did you presume to expect anything, sir? A man who needs to find his mate by mail is surely a man who has more a right to what he gets than what he expects!"

Even though Fenny found the writing a tad florid, she was speaking it the way her high school speech teacher advised—that is, to "believe what you say." She *was* Inga Anderson, an 1898 mail-order bride giving her intended the what-for.

Fenny had no idea she was mesmerizing her audience; she had no acting motivation other than a desire to get the speech over with and go home.

When she was finished, Emma Tuttle swiped a tear forging a path down her greasy foundation and Malcolm Edgely rubbed his chin, his world-weary version of *Bravo!*

Harry, whose smile was a constant throughout Fenny's monologue, now stood, applauding, even before Malcolm ordered, "Cut."

"What do you say we celebrate our finding Inga over lunch at Musso & Frank?" Harry was a traditionalist who eschewed the

French, the fatuous, and the flashy for the pleasures of the old Hollywood Boulevard restaurant.

Everyone agreed that was an excellent suggestion, except Malcolm, who had his meeting with his accountant to attend; a finance meeting that, in its own way, was a Hollywood celebration.

Fenny called Lee from LAX.

"Shouldn't you be on an airplane about now?" asked Lee.

"I will be in five minutes," said Fenny. "But I couldn't wait to tell you the news." She drew in a sharp breath. "Ma'am, the results of the screen test are in. And they're positive."

Fenny had to hold the receiver away so Lee's squeal wouldn't puncture her eardrum.

"Oh, Fenny, that's great! Unbelievable! Congratulations! How do you feel? When did they tell you? What was the screen test like? Was that little icky Christian guy there?"

"I'll tell you all about it when I get home. Just make sure you've got the O'Delight on."

"Honey, now that you're a movie star, I'll give you the recipe."

There was no ticker-tape parade to announce Fenny's return to Tall Pine, although Miss Penk and Frau Katte threw rice at her as she entered the Cup O'Delight.

"I didn't get married," she protested, surprised at how the pelted rice stung her face.

"You did better zan zat," said Frau Katte. "You got a part in a movie!"

Fenny recounted the story for the crew assembled. She thought for a moment that she might tell them about her "little accident"—after all, they were her closest friends—but then a self-protecting censoring mechanism kicked in and she decided some things, particularly a confession to pooping in her pants, were better left unsaid.

"My stars," said Heine when she had finished, "and I get to say I knew you when."

"When what?" asked Frau Katte.

"Honestly," said Miss Penk. "When she was a nobody."

"Nobody's a nobody," said Slim, who, leaning against the sink behind the counter, had listened intently to her whole story, his long arms folded across his chest.

"Oh, Slim," explained Miss Penk. "We just mean a . . . a regular person as opposed to a movie star."

"Movie stars are regular people," said Slim. "People just get a kick out of believing they're not." He growled then, for emphasis, and retreated into the kitchen.

"It's probably jealousy," said Mary Gore. "Some people can't stand to see the artistic success of others."

Nobody said anything; sometimes the things Mary said weren't worth any kind of response.

"When's the flick going to start rolling?" asked the mayor, proud of his savvy Hollywood lingo.

"They're thinking right after Labor Day," said Fenny. "They figure the weather'll be better then and not so many tourists—and then they hope to be done by November."

"Zere's no nudity, is zere?" said Frau Katte. "We don't want you to have to be bare-naked in your first motion picture."

"No," said Fenny, blushing at the very thought. "I'm sure there's no nudity."

"You don't sound so sure," said Miss Penk. "Couldn't you tell from the script?"

The rose pink that colored Fenny's face deepened. "Actually, I . . . uh . . . haven't read the script."

"Haven't read the script!" said the mayor. "Why, everybody knows you read the script before you sign a contract!"

"An artist must always know what's demanded of her and whether or not she and her art can comply to those demands," said Mary.

"What if it's a slasher movie?" asked Heine. "You know how I feel about gratuitous violence. I've written to several of my representatives about our need to—"

"Ya, ya, we know all zat," said Frau Katte, cutting him off. She waved her finger in front of Fenny. "You just make sure zat if you take your clothes off, so does your leading man."

"Fair is fair," concurred Miss Penk.

Fenny stuck around after everyone left, splitting the last piece of French silk pie.

"Well," said Lee, after her tongue had made one final swipe around her lips for any errant whipped cream. "You did it."

"Yes, but the way I did—"

"I am so proud of you. You jumped right in and did it."

"Lee, remember when you asked what the worst that could happen was? Well, I only got the part because—"

"I'm not listening to any excuses, Fenny. Your modesty can get a little tiresome, you know."

"Okay," said Fenny, shrugging. She had been so close to telling Lee exactly how she made her mark in Hollywood, but if she didn't want to listen . . .

"So do you have any other exciting things to tell me?"

"No."

"Good," said Lee. "Because I want to tell you all about Big Bill."

The kitchen door swung open and Slim emerged, his arms full of racks of clean cups.

"Why don't you call it a day, Slim," said Lee. "You look bushed. I'll finish cleaning up."

Slim nodded and shuffled to the far end of the counter. On some days he could start the morning doing one-armed push-ups; on other days, he felt he could barely stand up for all that pressed down on him. As he placed the racks in slots under the counter, he looked at Lee and Fenny. They were laughing and whispering like young girls, huddled together so close their heads touched. A wide beam of afternoon sunshine stretched across the floor and over them, and in that light Lee's hair shone like copper and Fenny's like gold.

You look like autumn fairies, thought Slim, or queens of the harvest, and he leaned into the rack of cups, wanting to tell them that and so much more. But, knowing his words were trite vehicles for his feelings, he did what he did when he had a lot to say and nothing to say at all; he whimpered like the sad old dog he was.

Chapter 9

Christian Freed felt an odd mix of victory and humiliation. By casting Fenny, Uncle Harry had welcomed him to the team, but by freezing him out of the process, he had benched him before the first play. Adding to his agitation was the memory of the instructor at the cartoon-writing seminar, citing his own series, "Perky the Puppy," as a perfect example of "strained didacticism."

He complained loudly about both subjects to his uncle while the two men were breakfasting at Canter's Deli.

"I mean, is this just a preview of what's to come? A little 'show-Christian-who's-boss' play? 'Now that we've got the story, let's ace out the writer'?"

"Christian, I thought you'd be thrilled we hired Fenny," said Harry. He pointed to the saucer of cream cheese. "Are you going to eat all that?"

"I *am* thrilled," said Christian, pushing the dish across the table, "but still, don't you think you struck a low blow in not having me at the screen test?"

"Christian," said Harry, slathering cream cheese on his own bagel, "I want you to look at Hollywood as a kingdom. The Kingdom of Hollywood, got it?"

Christian nodded.

"Now. Who do you suppose the king is?"

Christian thought for a moment. "The director?"

Harry snorted. "He'd like to think so, but the king is the person who runs everything, the producer. The person who *pays* for every-thing. The director is the prince, maybe even the heir to the throne, but never, never the king."

"Well, what are stars, then?"

"Same thing," said Harry. "Princes and princesses, although they'll never be in line for the crown."

"And the writer?"

Harry shook his head. "Not even a duke."

Christian gasped, as if he had just heard heresy. "Not even a duke?" he asked. "The writer is *not even a duke?*"

"All right," said Harry, trying to catch his waitress's attention. "All right, maybe a duke. But not a very important one."

"Uncle Harry, I am shocked," said Christian. "Deeply, truly shocked that you should hold the real creators of Hollywood in such poor regard. You of anybody should know that we're at least princes. *At least.*"

"Christian, I'm not going to waste your time or mine," he said, signaling for the check by making a scrawling motion in the air. "You've got to face facts. A good script is important, but it's just the beginning: now it's got to be produced and directed. It's like you've brought a cloth to me and Malcolm and now we're going to turn that cloth into something—say, a three-piece suit, maybe even a tuxedo."

Harry was pleased with himself, thinking maybe he should write that analogy down and use it in the speech he had been asked to give at an AFI dinner.

"So now you're comparing me to a *cloth maker?*" Christian asked. "I can't believe this. A cloth maker's even worse than a duke!"

"Thanks, dear," said Harry when the waitress set down the check. He took out his wallet. "I'm assuming I'm paying for this?"

"Why not?" grumbled Christian. "After all, you *are* the king."

Boyd Burch, who had been cast as "Ike Forrest, the sensitive, yet hard lumberjack," was also in a complaining mood.

"My leading lady is someone who's never acted before!"

His agent, as was her usual procedure, was both reassuring him and fueling his insecurities—making her position to him seem all the more important.

Mimi Schoals had made a small fortune off Boyd Burch, but as far as she was concerned, every nickel of her commission was hard-earned. Not only was she his agent, she was his teacher ("He's a fox," she told her friends, "but no Einstein"), schooling the big hayseed on manners and wardrobe and grammar and countless other things he hadn't bothered with on his way from a Montana cattle ranch to the top of the Hollywood heap.

"Harry says she's fantastic," she said, twisting a little in her chair, testing the fit of her waistband. Why, it actually did feel looser—maybe the Encino Diet was really working; it should, after all the guava juice and chickpeas she had to eat. "He says she's a real natural."

"But we didn't even test together. What if she ain't so natural with me?"

" 'Ain't' ain't a word, dear, and don't worry your pretty little head about it. You pay me to do the worrying, remember?" The agent made a mental note to supplement her diet regime with a personal trainer workout and then turned her full attention to the good-looking yahoo that was going to make her rich.

She surreptitiously looked down at an actor/model's eight-by-ten glossy she had opened in her morning's mail. This one was handsome enough to call in for an interview. Or maybe lunch. "*Nothing* to worry about, Boyd," she said, looking up, remembering she had a pep talk to conduct. "You're riding a rocket to the top, remember?"

"But what if we don't get along?" said Boyd. "You know Vivien Leigh couldn't stand kissing Clark Gable—"

"Boyd, please, I'm not in the mood for any of your quaint old Hollywood stories, okay? Now come on," she said, regaining her train of throught, "you'd have chemistry with a eunuch!"

The actor blinked. "What does that mean?"

Mimi sighed. "I mean you're so sexy it doesn't matter who your leading lady is because everyone's going to be watching you anyway."

Boyd smiled and his bleached teeth gleamed like high-gloss enamel. "Aw, you're just saying that."

"Because it's true," said Mimi, holding out her arms. "Now come here, cowboy."

Boyd slunk toward his agent, whose take, she bragged to her friends, was "ten percent and all the free nookie I want."

———

Fenny's problems had to do with work, too, but not Hollywood work. Jeremy Ericsson, who had worked in the Bait & Camp in the summers, had taken a job in Baudette as a veterinarian's assistant.

"It's my big opportunity," he said shyly. "I love animals."

Fenny didn't want to stand in the way of anyone's big opportunity, even though she knew she couldn't handle the upcoming tourist season alone.

Gloria Murch helped out at Sig's Place, but the pastor's wife had a worm phobia that precluded her entry into the Bait & Camp. "Just pray for Jeremy's replacement," she advised. "He'll show up."

Gloria was right; Jeremy Ericsson's replacement appeared one morning in late May, setting an armload of Mae Little Feather's leather vests on the glass jewelry counter.

"So you're Big Bill," said Fenny.

"So I am," said the man agreeably. "How did you know?"

"Lee O'Leary told me about you," said Fenny. "Lee from the Cup O'Delight?" Lee in fact had been disappointed that Big Bill had never returned after his first visit.

"I've been dreaming about that coffee all month."

"You don't have to dream about it," said Fenny. "The Cup O'Delight's open every day—well, except Sunday."

"I was up in Canada," said Bill conversationally. "With my new great-aunt. Well, newly found. She took me up to meet some of my other relatives. Man, it was a three-week party."

"Mae does such beautiful work," said Fenny, who had begun to hang up the vests. She looked at one made of deerskin, hand-stitched and embroidered with black and red glass beads.

"Her work's nothing like her personality."

"I wasn't going to say anything," said Fenny, laughing. "But now that you have . . . yes, I've worked with easier people."

"She admits it herself. She says, 'I'm nothing but an old crab.' She won't even let me sleep in the house."

"You're kidding." Fenny hung another vest, this one fringed and beaded cowhide, on the circular rack.

"No, she told me she's been on her own for so long, she can't stand to have anyone in the house. Although I am allowed in for meals."

"Where do you sleep?"

"In her backyard. In my tent. I can't say I'm looking forward to this winter."

"So you're staying for a while?"

Big Bill shrugged. "I'm sort of . . . *planless* at the moment." He looked around the store. "Nice place."

"Thanks," said Fenny. "It's my mom's." She nodded toward a wall. "Wally's Bait & Camp—next door? That's my dad's."

Big Bill nodded as he wandered around the shop. "Are they around?"

Fenny gasped, startled. "My mom and dad? They're—they . . . died."

"I'm so sorry," said Big Bill, and after a pause he added, "It's just that you . . . well, you used the present tense."

Fenny's voice was shaky. "I do that sometimes."

Big Bill wandered around the shop, finally stopping at the Junk Table.

"Good God," he said, holding up a slotted cube decorated with pink and blue pom-poms. "What is this?"

"It's a decorative tissue box. You know, to put your Kleenex in."

"But Kleenex already come in a box," said Big Bill.

"Don't ask me to explain anything on that table," said Fenny. "It'd be too hard."

Just as an idea bloomed in Fenny's head, Big Bill asked, "Are you the person that hires, then?"

"*What?*" said Fenny.

"Sorry," Bill said, confused at the tone of Fenny's voice. "I just thought that if your parents were . . . gone now, you might be the one to talk to about a job."

"You're not going to believe this," said Fenny, "but I was just thinking of offering you a job."

"You were? No kidding."

"Yeah. That's why I sounded so shocked when you asked about me being the person who hires. I need someone to help out at the Bait & Camp next door."

"I could do that," said Big Bill. "I've only fished twice in my life—once for marlin and the other for mahimahi—but I know a lot about camping. Hell, I live in a tent."

"I don't see that I'd need any more qualifications than that," said

Fenny, walking to the back room that led to the bait store. "You're hired."

Lee was tickled when Fenny brought her new employee over for a midmorning cup O'Delight.

"I thought you had taken off for parts unknown," she said.

"Nah," said Big Bill, "I think I'll stick around here for a while." He smiled at Lee and said, "I like the people."

"And I'm sure the people like you," said Lee, smiling back.

The first of the summer tourists arrived and Fenny's days were consumed by them. In the morning, she worked at Sig's Place, selling agate jewelry and pine-scented sachets and Mae Little Feather's leather goods; in the afternoons, she took small fishing parties out on the boat, to the good spot on the other side of the lake where the walleyes were cooperative. She showed a banker from Terre Haute how to take a fish off a hook, rescued an eight-year-old who had the confidence but not the skill to swim past the diving raft, and fended off a half dozen invitations to "take in a movie," "take a spin in the boat," or "take a ride," usually offered by men twice her age, with wives at home or, sometimes, waiting in an idling car in front of Sig's Place.

Big Bill didn't have the breadth of knowledge Wally had regarding nearby campgrounds or what the portages were like in Voyageurs National Park, or even what kind of bait a sunny prefers; but he was friendly and certainly seemed to attract more female tourists than Wally ever had.

"I like those exotic types," Fenny heard one woman tell another. "He's so big and *shiny*-looking. "

Fenny knew what she meant; there was something seal-like about the man; his black hair was shiny, his teeth were white and shiny, his dark brown eyes were shiny.

He fit easily into the social circle at the Cup O'Delight, even winning Pete's affection by giving him a new shoe pun. (In response to one of Pete's jokes, Bill had laughed and said, "Now, that's a real upper.") At thirty-four, he was younger than the other men (Pete was forty-eight on his last birthday, Slim was somewhere in his fifties, Heine had just retired, and no one knew how old the mayor was, only that he'd been mayor for over thirty years) and his relative youth stirred up the testosterone level, which had been sluggish at best. At least that's how Lee saw it. Heine and the mayor now engaged in arm-wrestling competitions and silly little tests of strength, and even Slim seemed to carry higher stacks of dishes and extra racks of cups from the back room. It seemed as if they all had a need to impress Big Bill in some way, to make sure he knew that he was among equals. It touched Lee, the little boys in all these men.

Fenny had asked the Cup O'Delight crew not to mention the upcoming movie to anyone, or if they did, not to mention her participation in it.

"But, Fenny," pleaded the mayor, "think of what that kind of publicity will do for the town!"

While it was hard not to let the occasional comment to a stranger slip—"Would you pass the ketchup, please, and say, did you know they're making a movie up here?"—the regulars obliged Fenny's request and did not point her out as Hollywood's next big star.

"Who knows if the movie will even happen?" she said.

Fenny had embraced the Norwegian philosophy that advised one not to count her chickens before they hatched, because who knew if the eggs were fertilized or not? As days passed, it was easy to think of the movie in the abstract, that her whole Los Angeles experience had been nothing more than a dream, a fantasy, but then the script arrived, in an envelope marked "Urgent."

"Looks like it's something important," said Monte Barsch, Tall Pine's mailman.

"Sure does," said Fenny, and ignoring his eager expression that asked, *Aren't you going to open that in front of me?* she thanked him for the delivery and promptly shut the door.

Fenny had to lie down after reading it, light-headed as she was with relief. There was no nudity. There was only one love scene, and it took place on top of a logjam, of all places, but the instructions "fade out" appeared right after the stage directions, which read, "While perched precariously on the logs, the couple is kissing passionately and Ike unties Inga's bonnet . . ."

If asked an opinion of the script, Fenny would be hard-pressed to give one; the dialogue occasionally was on the stilted side and the scenes moved so fast, but then again, what did Fenny know? She'd never read a screenplay in her life. The fact that it contained no nudity, however, moved it up several notches on her critic's barometer.

She put the script in her nightstand drawer and it became her bedtime reading. In five days, she had memorized the entire thing.

A surprise heat wave (heat waves were always more surprising in the far north than their more common counterpart, the cold snap) descended upon Tall Pine in mid-June. It was a muggy heat wave, too, the kind that overtaxed the region's power plant, causing two blackouts: the kind that caused big rings of perspiration to darken everyone's shirts (if they were wearing shirts); the kind that put the phrase "I feel like a wet noodle" into the general lexicon. The tourists that crowded into Tall Pine didn't seem to mind the heat—it gave them an excuse to wear less and less clothing. Lee O'Leary strictly enforced her "No Shoes, No Shirts, No Service" rule, turning away bare-chested, beer-bellied men and their barefoot, halter-topped wives who wanted to battle the regulars for counter space.

Every business increased its sales by wild percentages, except for Pete's Shoe Shack. ("Not much call for flip-flops or sandals repair," he reasoned.)

People swarmed into Sig's Place and Wally's Bait & Camp, buying everything from needlepoint pillows and woven wall hangings to nightcrawlers and fishing licenses.

"Boy, I think this is our busiest June yet," said Fenny one evening, tallying up the day's receipts. "Someone even bought the crocheted toaster cover. The one shaped like a loon." She shook her head. "There's no accounting for taste."

"Especially tourists' taste," said Big Bill. "They don't think their trip's a success unless they come home with some little souvenir of the place they visited."

"Yeah, but a crocheted toaster cover shaped like a loon?" asked

Fenny. "How is something that ugly supposed to bring back memories of the North Woods?"

"The same way hand-painted coconut shells remind people of Hawaii," said Big Bill.

After bagging up stacks of money in an old gray bank deposit sack, they locked up the stores.

"So remember, I'll be late tomorrow morning."

"Oh, yeah," said Big Bill. "Tomorrow's the big luau."

"Right," said Fenny, laughing. "The big Scandinavian luau."

For years, Tall Pine had hosted a Midsommer's Eve party. The original goal had been to introduce Scandinavian traditions to those unfamiliar with them ("Most everybody," Wally once pointed out), and it held to that goal, although there was always a contingent whose only interest was getting as drunk as possible.

What slight trouble there might be was always caused by tourists; if it had been up to Fenny, the whole celebration would be closed to anyone but those residents of Tall Pine who had some Nordic blood chilling their veins. She made exceptions for people like Lee O'Leary, Frau Katte, Miss Penk, and now Big Bill; to her they had earned honorary Scandinavian status by virtue of being her friends.

A clan of women who could trace their ancestry back to Trondheim, Norway, or Uddevalla, Sweden, or Helsingor, Denmark, had been getting together for weeks to plan the big affair. Wally and Mayor Lambordeaux (who claimed Finnish ancestry on his mother's side) had always been in charge of constructing the maypole; since Wally's death, Lars Larson had been recruited.

In decorating, they veered away from tradition; the maypole was decorated not only with entwined flowers and ribbons, but also with the lures and fishing bobs Wally had liked to add to it. Mayor Lambordeaux, always Tall Pine's biggest promoter, made sure the town's flag (a pine tree surrounded by a circle of blue) hung from the top. It was a colorful maypole, and in a good breeze, a percussive one, the lures and bobbers clinking and clattering like chimes.

Dawn broke on the day of the Midsommer's Eve party at sixty-five degrees and was ninety-four degrees by noon. The humidity, not content to be outdone by the temperature, checked in at ninety-five percent. A visiting couple from Tucson complained bitterly about the weather, vowing never to return.

"We could've saved ourselves the airfare and sat in the club's steam room for the same effect," the husband said at least a half dozen times until his wife snapped and told him she was going to push him off the fishing dock if he didn't shut up.

Fenny had spent the early morning at B.F., helping to prepare a menu that included finger sandwiches, boiled crayfish, Swedish meatballs, herring in mustard sauce, dilled salads, boiled new potatoes with sour cream, pickled red cabbage, and white cake with strawberries, and then ran over to Sig's Place, where she worked until three.

"Just what *is* Midsommer's Eve, anyway?" drawled her last customer, a tourist who introduced herself as Nanette from Blytheville, Arkansas, "and why do y'all have a party for it?"

Fenny carefully wrapped the tourist's purchase—a necklace made of polished rocks that came from the shores of Tall Pine Lake and a centerpiece made of pinecones and various nuts.

"It's the longest day of the year," Fenny said, her voice slipping into the monotone of a tour guide who's given one too many tours. Sig had always been immeasurably patient, explaining to the tourists that the Scandinavian winters are so long and dark that when summer finally comes, people want to celebrate. She quoted Strindberg, too, who described the season as a time when, "in all the countries of the North, the earth is a bride and the ground is full of gladness."

"Why're we all supposed to wear white?" asked Nanette. "I don't know if I have any white. White shows the dirt, you know."

Fenny smiled, and her jaws ached from a day full of insincere smiles.

"It's part of the tradition. People dress in white to celebrate the light."

"Well, I don't know," said Nanette, taking her purchase, "it doesn't sound as fun as Razorback Days."

By six o'clock the temperature had slid down to the mid-eighties, but the humidity had not budged and so the net gain was minimal.

Despite the heat, nearly two hundred tourists and townspeople had assembled in the park at the end of Main Street, whose low sloping hill led to Tall Pine Lake. Tiny white Christmas lights were strung across the trees, ready to be turned on at dusk, and even though there was a slight list to the maypole, it stood gaily and proudly by the bandstand. There was not one person who rebelled against the all-white dress code, and Fenny felt the flare of gratitude and affection a host feels for guests who've agreed to follow party orders they might not even understand.

"I told my husband this was silly," said Nanette, who had waved down Fenny. "But Lester says if y'all can't beat 'em, join 'em."

"We got these fancy duds at the Inn," said Lester. "They were havin' a big ol' white sale."

"A white sale," said Nanette, nudging her husband. "Why, you just made a little joke, hon."

Every year, B.F. managed to collect a supply of used white clothing (which they of course carefully laundered and bleached) for the vulgarians who came to the north shore with no idea of what constituted appropriate clothing for a Midsommer's Eve party. They usually sold out, too, selling the sundresses, outgrown shorts, and worn-out Sunday shirts the townsfolk donated. The proceeds made from this selective clothing sale always went to Will and Marion Shriever, who had been missionaries in Ghana for the past five years. In her letters to the church, Marion, the family scribe, always begged for cash so "we can feed our flock's tummies as well as their souls."

"Well, you two look great," said Fenny. It never failed; as curmudgeonly and possessive as she felt about the party, she never failed to be touched by the tourists who gamely put on hand-me-down white clothes, some of which she recognized from their former owners. (The polyester slacks Nanette wore were, in fact, half of the uniform Dolly Lambordeaux had worn to the annual picnic and softball game the mayor hosted for the town council, and still bore the faint traces of grass stain on the seat, acquired when Dolly had tried, unsuccessfully, to slide home.)

"Y'all should talk," said Nanette. "You look like Miss America."

"Better'n a Miss America," groused Lester. "Nowadays Miss Americas are more the scholarship types than beauty queens."

"You are way off on that one, Lester."

Fenny thanked the couple, and as they began arguing about the state of the Miss Americas' pulchritude, she made her way to the buffet table.

There would be no argument from anyone as to Fenny's beauty. She wore a white organza prom gown she had found at Take A Second Look in Baudette. Its skirt was made full by a slightly ripped net petticoat and there was faint discoloration under the cap sleeves, but it was perfect for Midsommer's Eve. Against the contrast of the white fabric, her skin looked even tanner and her eyes a deeper hazel. Her honey-blond hair was crowned in a wreath of wild-flowers, worn as an homage to Sig, who had always made sure that Fenny not only wore a wreath, but also completed the ritual by tucking wildflowers under her bed that night.

Norse legend had it that with these wildflowers under the pillow, the young woman whose head rested over them would dream of the man she was destined for.

"Did you ever dream of Dad?" she once asked her mother.

"You bet," Sig had said, winking at Wally.

The banquet had just been laid out and Fenny joined the other townspeople, who knew that those first in the food line got the best pickings.

"Fenny, if I were twenty years younger I'd ask you out for a date," said Heine, spearing a forkful of herring and putting it on his plate.

"Heine," said his wife Irene, who was more amused than per-turbed by Heine's vision of himself as a ladies' man, "if you were twenty years younger, you'd still be way too old for her." She pressed her shoulder into Fenny's. "You do look lovely, though, Fenny. Like one of those Breck Girls you used to see in the magazines."

Fenny mumbled a thank-you. She was happy enough with her looks but thought they were more an incidental part of her than a major one and felt awkward whenever anybody made a fuss over them.

She had just finished loading up her plate when the mayor, with the help of a megaphone borrowed from Sheriff Gibbs, announced, "Food!" The call had a similar effect to the one, *Fire!*

"Watch out for the stampede," said Heine as the crowd surged toward them like a herd of white, hungry cows.

Joined by Miss Penk and Frau Katte (who had traded her green fez for a white bowler hat), Fenny and the Osterbergs ate under an oak tree that had been split by lightning but that was so massive it still stood, albeit forked, forty years after the strike.

Frau Katte sucked the meat out of a crayfish shell. "I'm glad I only have to eat zese once a year."

Fenny laughed. "Just be glad there's no lutefisk."

When the line at the buffet table dwindled down to its last tourists, the mayor, Lars Larson, and his three sons acted as waiters, offering everyone a shot glass of aquavit.

"What is this stuff?" asked a pharmaceutical salesman from Salt Lake City.

"It's Scandinavia distilled in a glass," said the mayor, brandishing the tray.

"It's one-hundred-proof liquor," translated Pastor Murch as he helped himself to a glass. "Although that could be a low estimate."

When everyone of age had been served, the mayor instructed them to raise their glasses in a group toast.

"Skoal!" he said, and like eager language students, the group parroted him. Then, with a variety of grimaces, shudders, and face-making, the revelers drank their aquavit and the thought that they all might be unwilling participants in a group poisoning did pass the mind of an impressionable student from Brookings, South Dakota, who'd had to be deprogrammed from a cult in her sophomore year.

"That," said Mary Gore, who had joined Fenny's table, "is thunder in a bottle."

For once, everyone agreed with Mary.

"I could see why zis brought down za Viking Empire," said Frau Katte.

"Did it?" asked Miss Penk, who always deferred to Frau Katte's broad grasp of history.

Frau Katte shrugged. "I'm not saying it *did*, I'm saying it *could*."

In years past the aquavit had flowed freely, but people had gotten too drunk too fast. No one thought that stepping over puddles of vomit or passed-out tourists added much to a party atmosphere, and so there was now only one ceremonial toast. However, Lonnie's Bar & Tap contributed several kegs of beer (Lonnie didn't have a drop of Scandinavian in him, but he loved a party), so if it was a person's aim to get sloshed, it was an easy enough task to accomplish. And a fair amount of people, both tourists and townies, seemed to hold that as their goal.

"While I appreciate the diversity of being a Heinz 57, I do wish I could claim allegiance to one specific clan," said Mary Gore. "But who do I pay homage to? My brooding Scottish side, my practical German side, my hedonistic Italian side—"

"How about your blabbermouth American side?" croaked Mr. Gore, who was a little more blunt in his efforts to shut Mary up.

"Dad, I was only just saying—"

"You're always 'only just saying,' " said Mr. Gore. "Now, pipe down so I can hear the ladies sing."

As Mary pressed her lips together like the chastised daughter she was, everyone looked out to the lake.

In a variation of another Midsommer's Eve tradition, a group of women, all of them members of B.F.'s choir (except for Lee O'Leary, who was recruited because her loud and pretty soprano was needed to offset a majority of altos), rowed twenty feet offshore, singing Swedish songs that Alma Forslund, the old choir director, had taught them.

Every year in the *Tall Pine Register* there was a protest letter from Dag Hansum asking why "them singing ladies didn't ever sing any Norwegian songs," to which Alma always responded in writing, "I don't know any Norwegian songs, but if you do, please come down to church to teach us some." He never did, and Alma never expected him to. Dag was interested only in public criticism of her; fifty years earlier Alma had denied his wedding proposal to accept Stein Forslund's and Dag had been stewing in unwanted bachelorhood ever since.

The boatful of singers sang a hymn now and it seemed as if both the water's reflection and the rapture of the music transformed their faces. They looked years younger, even Alma Forslund, who thought of people in their sixties as "youngsters."

Lee O'Leary's copper red coronet of braids caught the light and seemed almost pink. As she began her solo, to the ladies' quiet humming, she stood in profile at the boat's prow, like a Valkyrie.

"Härlig är jorden, härlig är Guds himmel,
skön är själarnas pilgrimsgång.

Genom de fagra riken på jorden
gå vi till paradis med sång."

"In Scandinavia, the boat carrying the singing women takes them to church services," the mayor explained to a table of tourists. "Our gals like to paddle to shore after their concert and join in on the festivities."

"Sometimes you just have to break with tradition," added Lars Larson, whose three shots of aquavit were beginning to loosen up his normally tight lip.

"Tidevarv komma, tidevar försvinna,
släkten följa släktens gång.
Aldrig förstummas tonen från himlen
i själens glada pilgrimssång."

Tears welled up in Fenny's eyes as she watched the dozen women dressed in white rowing a boat across the blue and gold waters of Tall Pine Lake. That a concentrate of beauty had converged upon this small northern town was not an unknown feeling to her. Right now the heat was forgotten, the aftertaste of herring that rose in her throat in a burp ignored; it was a perfect moment, one Fenny was savoring with all her being, until a wolf's howl shattered the air.

The crowd, which had been watching the boat of singing ladies with a reverence that matched Fenny's, was suddenly full of words and motion.

"What was that?" they asked, turning away from the lake.

Another howl rode over their worried questions and a semiprofessional baseball player from St. Paul wondered if he should jog over to his pickup truck and get Lil' Lucy, the pearl-handled revolver he kept hidden under his front seat.

"Aaaarrrrrooooooooooo!"

Just as the crowd was ready to run for cover, to seek shelter from this wolf bold enough to crash a Midsommer's Eve party, Slim emerged from behind the bandstand, dressed in black. He was followed by Big Bill, who despite the heat wore a black rain poncho.

"Aaaarrroooo?" Slim howled, this time more a question than a warning.

"Who the hell is that?" asked the baseball player. "And why aren't they wearing white?" He was the type of person who took great offense at anyone who wasn't a team player.

"It's Slim," explained a chorus of townspeople. "And that's Big Bill."

"Okay, everyone, nothing to get excited about," said the mayor over the megaphone. "Let's just get back to our party."

This was the correct command to give to a group assembled for fun, and most turned back to the lake to enjoy the rest of the boat ladies' concert. Trouble was, the boat ladies had lost their lead singer, Lee O'Leary having ordered them to row ashore so she could tend to Slim.

"Oh, honestly," said Gloria Murch. "It's just crazy old Slim trying to get a rise out of everyone."

"Well, he succeeded," said Lee. "Now row faster."

When the boat got to shallow water, Lee disembarked, lifting the hem of her white dress in one great bunch above her knees.

As she ran across the rocky beach and up the low-grade hill, Gloria asked Alma Forslund just what exactly they should do now.

"One more verse of 'Härlig är jorden'!" instructed the old choir director, and they complied, but the sourness of their mood—of being upstaged by crazy old Slim, of losing their lead singer—bled into their music and they all silently agreed that the show was over, and when Alma beckoned Lars Larson and his sons to help pull the boat in, no one protested.

"Slim, you violated dress code," said Lee, finding him and her friends huddled at the base of the statue honoring Tall Pine's founder, Pierre LeFleque. She looked at Big Bill. "So did you."

"I thought he could use a sidekick," said Big Bill. "It's less lonely that way. Right, Slim?"

In answer, Slim shivered.

"He won't tell us what's za matter," said Frau Katte. "He just sits zere and shivers."

Lee sat down, wincing a little as her backside made contact with Pierre LeFleque's foot. She put her arm around him and sat holding him at the base of the pitted concrete statue.

"Slim, I thought we agreed you should stay home tonight."

Fear flashed in Slim's eyes and he shrugged, unable to even muster a growl.

Lee looked at her friends. "It's an anniversary Slim has trouble with."

Big Bill nodded. "He told me all about it." He looked down at Slim, feeling sort of silly talking about the man as if he weren't there. Which, in a way, thought Big Bill, he wasn't. Still, he wanted to make sure he wasn't betraying the first confidence Slim had shared with him.

Fenny nodded, remembering. "Oh, yes. It's the anniversary of his friends' death."

Slim had survived the downing of his helicopter and so had two of his two crewmates, but just barely, both men expiring from their wounds the next day in a mobile hospital.

Last year Lee had called Fenny, telling her to get over to her apartment quick—she was afraid Slim was going to hurt himself. Fenny found Lee trying to talk Slim into opening the locked bathroom door.

"Why shouldn't I join them?" he had asked. "Why should I be the one who got to live?"

Like Lee, Fenny thought of Slim as more idiosyncratic than mentally ill, but during times like these she remembered that the damage done to him was real and his mind and heart had sustained injury.

"Fenny, why don't you come with me?" asked Big Bill.

They rounded the statue and headed back toward the crowd.

"Where are we going?"

"Hunting."

"Hunting for what?"

"For something to make Slim feel better." He stepped back as a line of young children snaked past them. "Man, am I glad I missed that war."

"What war *wouldn't* you want to miss?"

"Good point. Aha," he said, taking several filled shot glasses off a tray on a picnic table. "These should do the trick."

"Bill, that's aquavit," said Fenny. "That's capable of a lot more than tricks."

"In that case," he said, putting the drinks back and lifting up the whole tray, "I'll take the whole thing."

"Aren't you hot in that thing?" Fenny asked as they made their way back toward the statue.

"Boiling. By the way, it's from the Bait & Camp. I didn't have anything black to wear, and we were right by the store—"

"The tag's still on the sleeve," said Fenny. "But I guess I don't get why you're wearing it in the first place."

A passing tourist reached out for a drink.

"Help yourself," said Big Bill amicably. "Well, like I said, it was too lonely for Slim to be mourning them all by himself."

"You're a nice man, Bill," she said, and added a teasing "But now we're going to have to sell that poncho as used."

Big Bill laughed. "Tell you what—I'll buy it. I need a good raincoat anyway."

"Here, Slim," said Fenny when they got back to the statue. She took a shot glass off the tray Big Bill held and handed it to Slim.

Slim looked up at her with something like gratitude in his eyes, while Lee's look was one of disapproval.

"Fenny, I don't really think Slim needs to medicate—"

Slim tossed back the drink. "I *do* need to medicate," he said, exhausted by the emotion of the day, "and medicate good."

The party was in full swing. Heine was on the bandstand, playing his accordion, drowning out Corby Deele and his violin.

Holding hands, children danced around the maypole, while adults partner-danced on the portable floor that had been set up. Heine liked to keep a fast, if not always consistent, rhythm, which left Corby Deele in midbar, his bow frozen above its strings, giving Heine the dirtiest looks a violinist ever gave a fellow musician.

"Slim," said Pastor Murch, "glad you could join us!"

"At least on the negative you guys'll show up wearing the right color," said the mayor, snapping Slim's picture. On special occasions—town celebrations, church socials, city council meetings—Mayor Lambordeaux doubled as photographer for the *Register*.

Slim and Bill did stand out among the sea of white, but neither seemed to be bothered by the inappropriateness of his attire. In fact, neither seemed bothered by much of anything.

"Whooo!" Big Bill had cried after his first taste of aquavit, and Slim the mimic downed his shot glass and repeated, "Whooo!"

This led to an improvised chorus of train whistles after every sip, of which there were plenty. It also led to the departure of Lee, Fenny, Miss Penk, and Frau Katte, who weren't as entertained by two men screaming, "Whooo! whooo! whooo!" as the two men doing the screaming were.

"You fellas are on your way to one big headache tomorrow morning," said Frau Katte as she followed the other women to the bandstand.

When there was nothing left in the shot glasses, the men decided it was time to join the party.

"Oh, man," said Big Bill as he stood up, "the ground seems to be shifting."

Slim laughed. "Something's shifting, but it's not the ground."

Big Bill stumbled after Slim, who walked as straight as the soldier he used to be. When Slim neared the dance floor, he grabbed Miss Penk by the hand and together they box-stepped through the crowd and up to the lip of the stage.

"Way to go, Slim!" shouted Heine, who believed so strongly in the restorative powers of accordion music that he had sent letters to nursing home directors with the idea of "playing live and recorded accordion music at least two hours a day—I can guarantee even your biggest sad sacks will perk right up."

"I'd ask you to dance," Big Bill said to Lee, "but I think any more movement might cause me to . . . puke."

"I appreciate you helping Slim out," said Lee, her arms folded over her ample chest, "but I don't think you needed to get both of you drunk to do it."

"Drunk?" said Big Bill. "Who's drunk?" He looked out at Slim and Miss Penk on the dance floor. "Does he look drunk?"

"He's right," said Fenny, who watched Slim's and Miss Penk's fancy footwork with resigned envy. Fenny felt ballroom dancing was just another bit of class denied her generation; the slow dances she had done with boys at school had been nothing but standing hugs broken by an occasional sway. "Slim sure doesn't look drunk."

"Well, he is," said Lee to Big Bill, "and so are you."

With this, she turned and walked back toward the picnic tables.

"What'd I do?" asked Big Bill, holding his hands up.

"Lee's ex-husband was a drinker," said Fenny. "The *mean* kind."

"I'm not a drinker. I'm just a little drunk, is all—a one-shot deal." Bill laughed at his unintentional pun and then said, "I'm going to go find her."

The humidity hadn't let up at all; the low-slung clouds now bulged with it.

"I hope we don't get rained on," said Fenny as the mayor pulled her onto the dance floor.

"No one can rain on this parade."

"Mayor, I can't dance," protested Fenny, and the third time she stepped on his foot, the mayor agreed.

"Just relax and feel the rhythm."

"I am relaxed," snapped Fenny. "It's just that I've never been taught to dance."

"It's just moving to the music," advised Miss Penk, floating by in Slim's arms.

"I know what it is," said Fenny, but she was relieved of any more advice and humiliation when Dolly Lambordeaux tapped her on the shoulder, telling her to "vamoose, kiddo, and let me dance with the best-looking man here."

"Okay," shouted Heine from the bandstand, "everyone around the maypole—guys on the outside, gals on the inside."

A low rumble rose from the horizon across the lake.

"Where's Big Bill?" asked Lee, sidling up to Fenny.

"He went looking for you," she said, taking Lee's hand and the hand of the tourist next to her.

Thunder sounded again.

Heine and Corby Deele lit into a Scandinavian pub song. The men on the outside circle began moving in one direction, the women on the inside circle the other direction.

"Oh, Fenny, I hope he's not a drinker," Lee said, a little breathless as the circle picked up speed. "I couldn't stand it if he were a drinker."

"Bill?" Fenny shook her head. "Like he said, Lee; I think he's just a little drunk." She looked around. "A lot of people are."

As the night wore on, the dazzling whiteness of the crowd had been diminished by sweat and food and drink spills. Over a dozen tourists had already crossed the line from entertainingly tipsy to obnoxiously drunk; one of these people, a landscaper from Milwaukee, under the mistaken impression that Fenny would be flattered by his touch, grabbed at her from the outside circle and tried to kiss her.

"Hands off!" barked Lee, always willing to stop a bully, as she herself was the victim of one for so long.

"Oh, don't worry," he said. "I wasn't gonna touch *you*. I'm not attracted to fat broads."

The circles moved around in a complete rotation before Fenny could stand up for her friend.

"Well, we're not attracted to stupid jerks like you."

"Huh?" said the landscaper, who was getting dizzy. "Who're you calling a stupid jerk?"

"Yeah!" said his friend, skipping drunkenly next to him.

"Oh, shut up," said Lee, which was the wrong thing to say to a man who did not take well to "bossy bitches."

"If I weren't a gentleman, I'd kick your teeth in," he hollered.

Heine and Corby liked to change the tempo of the music so those dancing around the maypole would have to speed up or slow down. Now they played fast and furious, and the crowd, laughing, twirled around. It didn't take long for Fenny and Lee to meet up again with the two drunks.

Thunder boomed across the lake and the air was charged with the electricity of the upcoming storm.

"Let's make up," said the landscaper.

"Yeah, how's about a kiss?" asked his friend, breaking free of the circle and lunging at Fenny.

"Get off me!" shouted Fenny, pushing him so that he stumbled to the ground.

The music was now going at a frantic pace, and Heine was singing along, "Stomachs growling / Thirst is howling / Pour one more / Like before!"

The landscaper, not appreciating his friend being pushed, lunged at Lee, and in the space of seconds, to the music of a cranked-up violin and accordion, all hell broke loose.

Slim picked the man who had knocked Lee down and flung him away from the circle. Miss Penk, fortifying herself with a Rebel yell, struck a karate pose and stood over the man who'd attempted to kiss Fenny. A tourist from St. Louis took a swing at a tourist from Salt Lake City. Martin Sunstrom's fifteen-year-old son shoved his best friend, Aaron, who he thought was paying a little too close attention to Belinda Bjornstrom, the girl *he* was trying to impress.

The circles broke up, and those not fighting spilled down the hill to watch those who were. Heine and Corby kept up their fevered playing until, not wanting to miss any of the action, they jumped off the stage.

"Show 'em what you got, Miss Penk!" said Bud Glatte, as she kicked the air by the drunk's face. He was pleased that his star karate pupil had a chance to strut her stuff.

"I don't even want you looking at her!" yelled Martin Sunstrom's son to Aaron, who had no idea why his best friend had turned on him, but decided it was time to slug him in the stomach anyway.

"What's your problem?" shouted the Salt Lake City tourist to his assailant.

Suddenly the hairs on everyone's arms stood up and a bluish light flashed. With a noise that sounded like a prelude to Armageddon, a bolt of lightning struck the old oak tree, splitting it for the second time in its career as the biggest provider of shade in downtown Tall Pine.

There was a suspended moment when all eyes focused on the flame of blue cutting through the tree as cleanly as a saw. And then Sheriff Gibbs, who was just about to break up the fight, used the authority his badge gave him to instead holler, "Run!"

It was, however, too late an order to be followed; the part of the tree ripped from its mooring came crashing down so quickly that if one were in its way, running wouldn't help. The maypole and the band shell were the only obstacles in its path, and the severed tree knocked over the former and smashed through the latter's roof, coming to rest in a puff of pulverized leaves, splinters, and crushed fishing lures. It came to rest in the same space where, minutes ago, Corby Deele had been trying to keep up with Heine's hyperkinetic version of "Akvavit!"

Fortunately, the fight had lured the musicians and the dancers away from the band shell and the maypole, and so what could have been a human tragedy was simply a headache that would plague the town council; i.e., should repair dollars come from the City Improvement Fund or the Parks and Recreation's one?

In fact, a slogan of sorts arose out of the debate: "Who Should Pay for What the Oak Broke?" but then Mary Gore had to dedicate an entire issue of *Angel Motors* to the whole discussion, taking all the fun out of it.

"As much as I would have liked to defend your honor, I'm glad I wasn't able to," Big Bill told Lee and Fenny later. He had missed all the action, holed up as he was in the portable bathroom. "If I've learned one lesson, it's that being drunk and big is a bad combination. Someone always gets more hurt than they were supposed to." He shook his head, remembering not past fights, but the potency of the Midsommer's Eve liquor that had prevented him from getting into another one. "I'm going to have to get you back for that aquavit stuff—it's not fit for human consumption." His face brightened. "I know—poi."

Frau Katte, who wasn't necessarily superstitious but knew a good omen when she saw it, confided to Miss Penk that in her Swiss village, legend had it that trees felled by lightning foretold of mayhem to come.

"There's always mayhem to come," answered Miss Penk. "That's life."

Chapter 10

So awful was Lee's marriage to Marshall Stouffer that she thought her escape from it was enough; her prayer for survival had been answered and she'd better not burden God with further requests, since He'd already taken care of the big one.

When she first married Marshall, Lee, who more than anything wanted to be a mother, prayed fervently that they would conceive a child, but after experiencing Marsh's violence, she was glad the prayer had been answered with a no. It was bad enough that he hurt her; there was no way she'd let him hurt a child.

Lee had an active prayer life, and often got down on her hands and knees, placing the palms of her hands together like a child, or a model in an old painting.

No one would have suspected Lee of talking to God; in fact, Gloria Murch thought she might even be an agnostic.

"How can she be an agnostic," asked her husband, the pastor, "when she just sang hymns with you at the Midsommer's Eve party?"

"Those were *Swedish* hymns," said Gloria. "She had no idea what she was singing."

Lee herself had a hard time justifying her dislike of religion with her love of God; the little girl who sought approval thought she was "bad" and might go to hell for turning her back on the church, while the adult reminded herself that she didn't believe in hell and God knew what Lee O'Leary was about even if a priest didn't.

Her prayers lately had been filled with gratitude over her new life: her new self-confidence, her new friends, her business, and for new peace, interrupted only sporadically by Marsh's phone calls.

Now a new prayer had entered her repertoire, one she had honestly felt she'd never be given cause or opportunity to use; a prayer of thanks for love found.

Lee's brother Gerald had asked her if she intended to live the life of a "spinster" (spitting out the word as if it tasted bad), and Lee said, "It beats the life of an abuse victim." This self-description always infuriated Gerald, who inevitably called her "overdramatic" and ended the conversation with the remembrance of a pressing engagement.

But now Big Bill had entered her life. He was what the best surprises are: unexpected and much better than she could ever have imagined. She had felt herself sliding down the precipice of love-at-first-sight the moment he had walked into her cafe. She didn't know if he felt the same way, but she had an idea he did. Big Bill was easy and flirtatious with everyone, but to Lee it seemed his flirtation, when directed at her, had a little more oomph. But she was careful; not wanting to move too suddenly and scare him off, she settled into a friendship with him, confiding her feelings only to God . . . and Fenny.

"Isn't he dreamy?" she asked.

"Yes, Barbie, like I was saying to Midge the other day, 'That Ken sure is dreamy.' Just a real doll."

Lee laughed and shoved sand at Fenny with the heel of her hand.

Having fulfilled their business obligations, they were lying on the only sand beach Tall Pine Lake offered, enjoying the late afternoon sun.

The Cup O'Delight, Sig's Place, and Wally's Bait & Camp all closed at three, and when Fenny didn't have any fishing parties to escort, she joined Lee and Big Bill after work. They took hikes and boat rides and swam, enjoying the all-too-brief summer.

Lee smoothed the bumps of sand underneath the beach blanket. She wore an old-fashioned swimsuit with a built-in chassis; wires and stays and elastic panels lifted and separated her. She was big but well proportioned, and her red hair, released from its coronet braids, fell over her shoulders in ripples.

"You know, Lee," said Fenny, regarding her friend, "you don't look like a Barbie doll."

"*Duh.*"

Fenny laughed. "I was going to say you look like a pinup girl."

"Oh, Fenny—you don't know what moral courage it takes for me to get into a swimsuit."

"It shouldn't. Really, you look good. You've got such a small waist."

"Comparatively speaking," said Lee with a sigh. She looked out at the lake where Bill swam. "But let's not talk about me. Let's talk about Big Bill."

"Well, he sure is popular at the bait store. He's got time for everybody—even for old Mr. Sunstrom, who comes in practically every day for a game of checkers. And Bill always pretends he doesn't see the old cheater cheat."

Lee nodded and played with the sand at the edge of the blanket for a moment. "For a long time, I thought that because I was able to once love a man like Marsh, something must be wrong with me—you know, maybe I was attracted to mean, violent men. But then Bill comes along and he's nice and kind—what a concept! Plus those shoulders."

Fenny smiled. "And . . . ?"

"And I like those bold gestures he makes—remember how I told you he fell off the stool the first time he tasted some O'Delight? And when he dances with someone on Polka Night, he'll bow to them afterwards like it was an honor to have them for a partner. And he even dances with Mary Gore! You couldn't *pay* Slim to dance with Mary."

"So, big shoulders and old-fashioned manners and no one's a wallflower when he's around—"

"I like how he kind of gets those dimple things under his eyes when he laughs. And his voice! It's so deep and rich—it's the kind that breaks out in songs about toting that barge and lifting that bale."

Fenny jerked her arm as if she were cracking a whip, an old high school gesture.

"Someday I hope to have his baby."

Fenny drew in her breath. "Oh, Lee. You really *are* whipped."

Lee sighed. "He's the whole package: everything I want in a man. Everything I'd want the father of my child to be."

"*Lee*," said Fenny, surprised at the depth of her friend's feelings. "Have you told him this?"

"Oh, sure," said Lee with a little snort. "If being with Marsh taught me anything, it's to be cautious. I'm going slow on this one." She smoothed the sand in front of her with her hand. "Right now we're in the friends stage. In a while, we'll progress to the more-than-friends stage. It'll happen," she said quietly. "There's no doubt in my mind that it will happen."

The two women lay on their stomachs, looking out at the lake as Big Bill, swimming in from the diving raft, stood up in waist-high water.

"And then there's his nose," said Lee. "His finely shaped nose."

Fenny nodded. "He does have a nice nose. Although if there were an all-around 'best nose' prize, it'd have to go to the mayor."

"The mayor?" said Lee, laughing. "You've got to be kidding. His nose looks like someone pinched it."

"You don't know a delicate nose when you see it."

"Maybe not. But I know a pinched one."

A teenage girl being chased by a teenage boy ran by, both of them kicking up little tufts of sand.

"Now, Slim," said Fenny. "Slim's got the best chin."

"Great jawline. And Pete's got the best hair."

"The best hair! It's all combed up in that Brylcreem junk."

"Still, there's a lot of it," said Lee. "But I change my vote anyway. Bill's got the best hair."

Big Bill's hair, now wet, lay slicked against his neck and down his shoulders. He ran up to the two women and, standing over them, shook his hands, sprinkling them with water.

"I figured out what your lake's missing," he said as he sat down on the blanket next to Lee. "Waves."

"We were just judging a body parts contest," said Lee.

"Really?" said Big Bill. "I thought only us crude, shallow men did that." He squirted a swirl of suntan lotion on his palm. "So how'd I do?"

"You didn't place," said Fenny sadly.

"Although we did give your elbows serious consideration," said Lee.

"I'll give you an elbow," said Bill, jabbing his crooked arm in the air before settling himself on the beach blanket.

"Hey, Bill—got any candy?" asked Fenny.

"When do I not have candy?" The answer was never; Big Bill carried candy as conscientiously as a smoker carries cigarettes. "It's in my backpack. Help yourself."

Fenny took out a crumpled paper sack that held as big a variety as a Halloween trick-or-treater's bag. She helped herself to a miniature Caravelle bar and some English toffees.

"Anybody else?" she asked, but by this time Bill had noticed Lee's peeling shoulders and was applying suntan lotion to them, and Lee, lying on the blanket, her eyes closed and her lips parted in a smile, was enjoying an altogether different kind of sugar.

In late August, the Cup O'Delight regulars piled into the Gore Printing van and made their pilgrimage to the State Fair.

"You mean they still have them?" said Big Bill, whose only familiarity with a state fair came from watching the Pat Boone/Ann-Margret movie once on cable.

Frau Katte giggled. "Oh, you just wait. You'll have more fun zan you can shake a stick at."

The drive to St. Paul took nearly five hours and the group had been on the road since seven-thirty A.M. The sun was high in the sky when Slim found a parking spot.

Inside the gate, the group held a conference and decided to split into groups and meet later for supper. Heine and the mayor headed off to Machinery Hill to sit on the tractors and the snowmobiles. Mary Gore went to see a troupe of cloggers in the band shell. Slim, Frau Katte, and Miss Penk decided to look at the paintings and photographs in the Fine Arts Building, stopping first to see a Police Canine Corps demonstration. After much debate, Lee, Big Bill, and Fenny chose as their first destination the swine barn.

They chose an ambling route, stopping often at what to many were the fair's biggest attractions: its many food stands. Grease was a main ingredient in many of their samplings: in the hot and sugared Tom Thumb mini-doughnuts, in the batter-fried cheese curds, in the pronto pups. They supplemented these empty calories with even emptier ones found in cotton candy, caramel apples, and four different flavors of fudge. That they shared everything instead of getting their own serving helped somewhat, but still, by the time they got to the swine barn, they felt more of an affinity toward the porkers than they would have had on empty stomachs.

They walked past rows of pens—some decorated with blue ribbons—in which all makes and models of swine slept, snorted, and rooted.

Lee wrinkled her nose, but Fenny loved the brown smell of the animal barns; their dung and hay and feed.

"Oh, my gosh, look at this," said Lee, wedging herself into a crowd that had surrounded a pen.

Fenny gasped and Big Bill whistled as they looked down upon a gray spotted pig, a prizewinning boar whose name was Homer and who weighed, according to his stats card, 1,016 pounds. He was a behemoth, ancient-looking, and lying on his side like a jackknifed truck.

"Euew, Mommy, what are those?" asked a small girl whose mother promptly pulled her away from the pen.

"Let's go see the ponies," said the mother, pushing her daughter toward the exit.

Fenny moved closer to the pen and saw a view that the man in front of her had been blocking: the boar's testicles, as cracked as elephant hide, big as volleyballs.

"Oh, man," said Big Bill. "The poor guy needs a truss."

The trio toured the 4-H building and watched a fashion show in progress, cheering loudly when an ecology-minded teenager from Wilmar won first prize for a prom dress she made out of black plastic garbage bags. In the Creative Arts Building, they looked at prizewinning pies, cakes, jams, jellies, pickles, peppers, and relish, and hand-stitched quilts that put the usual patchworks to shame.

In the Empire building, they saw portraits and still lifes made from varieties of seeds.

"Look at that Bob Dylan," said Lee, pointing to a picture made of flax, sunflower, and apple seeds. "It looks just like him."

"So does Muhammad Ali," said Lee. "If you squint you can't tell he's made of seeds at all."

They watched as the reigning Princess Kay of the Milky Way posed for a sculptor. Both artist and model were dressed in winter jackets, since they were sitting in a refrigerated room so that the sculptor's medium, which was butter, wouldn't melt. Finished busts (affectionately known as butter heads) of Princess Kay's attending princesses, all of whom were daughters of dairy farmers, were displayed on a ledge.

"What do they do with that butter afterwards?" asked Big Bill.

"I don't know," said Lee. "Maybe they serve it at a banquet at the end of the fair or something."

"That's right," said a woman standing nearby. "They usually throw a corn roast and everybody who helped them win their title is invited." She pointed to a butter head. "That's my niece right there."

"It'd be weird having people roll a cob of corn on your head," said Fenny.

"It's not weird at all," said the woman briskly. "It's part of the tradition."

The group reconnoitered for supper at a beer garden and then, after touring a roomful of classic cars and watching the beginning of a veterinarian exhibit (this didn't last long; the vet was spaying a beagle and few of the group could stomach the proceedings), they entered the gaudy netherworld of the midway.

It was almost dusk and the air was charged with the energy of teenage boys and girls on the lookout for one another. Heavy metal music blared from the rides, their bass lines thumping like bad heartbeats.

Along with the smells of pizza, french fries, and popcorn were the smells of cap guns ("Step right up, right up here, hit the moving target and win a teddy bear for your lady"), generators, hair spray, and smoke from the cigarettes that dangled from the mouths of the ride operators like obscene gestures. Underneath them all was the vague smell of vomit.

Fenny felt a thrill of excitement walking down the midway; it was the bad side of the fair, the overheated rumpus room, the place where the police were called to.

"When I was a girl, they used to have a freak show here," said Mary Gore. "In fact, the very first poem I wrote was after I saw the 'Tiniest Woman in the World.' Her eyes glassed over as they often did when she recited. " 'When she cries, are her tears the same size? / If she's doll-sized, are her feelings too? / Or does she hurt like me and you?' "

With a self-satisfied smile, Mary looked to see what reaction her poem was getting from her friends.

"Hey, you guys," she said, seeing them slipping through the crowd. "Wait up!"

The lines to the rides were too long, so the group decided to leave the midway and go on Ye Olde Mill, one of the oldest rides at the fair and a respite from all the other rides that tossed and twirled passengers until they were dizzy or threw up.

They passed the band shell, where the nightly talent show was in progress. A troupe of eight-year-old jazz dancers, in high-cut leotards, were gyrating to music like strippers.

"Whatever happened to little girls tap-dancing to 'You Are My Sunshine'?" asked Miss Penk wistfully.

Ye Olde Mill was a slow, languid ride, taken in old wooden boats through dark tunnels. It was popular among older fairgoers and those young people savvy enough to recognize a good Lover's Lane.

Slim, Lee, Fenny, and Big Bill got into the last boat and as soon as they left the open boarding area and entered the tunnel, Slim knew he was in trouble. The dank-smelling tunnel wasn't just black, it took that extra step into claustrophobic *pitch*-blackness. He had never had to flush out VC snipers in underground tunnels, but all the stories he'd heard from those who had suddenly filled his head.

"Lee?" came Slim's voice, small as a child's. "Lee, I need to get out of here."

In the narrow waterway, the boat thumped against the wall.

"Lee!"

"It's all right, Slim," said Lee. "We're coming to some light now. Look."

They passed a display window of what looked like lawn ornaments dressed in cheesy fairy-tale costumes, but soon were plunged into darkness again.

The boat rocked.

"Really, Lee, I've got to get out. I can't breathe."

Fenny wanted nothing more than to get out of the boat herself. She reached into her pocket and touched her courage bead with one hand and then she told Slim to hold her other hand, as much to comfort her friend as herself.

The boat rocked again.

"I'm going to get out."

"Slim, you can't get out," said Big Bill. "There's nowhere to go."

"You can't see anything," said Lee. "You'd get hurt."

Slim began to moan softly.

"Squeeze my hand," said Fenny, and when he did, she couldn't help but yelp.

"Sorry," said Slim before moaning again.

"We've got to distract him," whispered Lee to Bill.

"Slim," said Big Bill, "what's your favorite song?"

"What?"

"I'm taking requests. Tell me your favorite song."

"I just want to get out of this boat," whined Slim.

"I don't know that one," said Big Bill. "But I can fake it.

" 'I just want to get out of this boat,' " he sang, his deep baritone bouncing off the walls of the tunnel. " 'Even though it's solid and, uh . . . surely can float.' "

"Hey," said Lee, chuckling. "You're good."

The boat banged against the wall.

" 'I don't want a new car or a stock quote; no, I just want to get out of this boat.' " His voice soared into falsetto for the last note. Those serenaded laughed, except for Slim, and then the boat banged against a wall again and suddenly they were in the loading area and could see once more.

"Wasn't zat fun?" asked Frau Katte, waiting for them at the exit. "We smooched za whole time!"

It didn't take long for everyone except Fenny and Big Bill, whose coffee cups were perched on the console in the front seat, to fall asleep.

Heine and Mary Gore were out before the van got out of St. Paul, and at short intervals new snores would be added, so that by the time they reached Sauk Rapids, the van sounded like the inner workings of a clock, full of ticks and shudders and rhythmic whirs.

"Well," said Big Bill, "I survived phase one of my Minnesota Experience, now let's see if I survive phase two."

The next morning, Lars Larson was taking Bill on a two-week canoe trip through the Boundary Waters.

Fenny laughed. "It'll be a cinch, Bill. Although Lars is kind of a taskmaster. My parents and I went on a camping trip with him once and it's sort of like camping with a drill sergeant."

Big Bill sighed. "Why did I say yes?"

There were few cars on the highway and the dashboard lights glowed softly.

"Do you want to drive?" asked Fenny. He hadn't driven on the way down, and Fenny didn't want to hog the wheel on the way up, too.

"Why, are you getting tired?"

"No, I just thought you might like to drive."

"I don't drive."

Fenny looked at him. "You don't drive? At all?"

"Nope."

"Why?"

"Would you believe I was in a bad wreck?"

"Really?"

Bill scratched his chin. "No."

"No, what?"

"No, I wasn't in a bad wreck. I just asked if you'd believe I was."

"I don't follow you, Bill," said Fenny, and she passed a truck, watching in the rearview mirror as the driver flashed his lights at her, signaling that it was okay for her to get back into the lane. She signaled back, thanking him. She loved the Morse code of the open road.

Bill threaded his fingers together and held his arms out in a stretch.

"I've never been in a car accident, Fenny. I've never even been in a fender bender. Sometimes I wish I had—just so I had an excuse for why I'm so afraid to drive."

"You're afraid to drive?" said Fenny. This big strong man was afraid to *drive?*

"Yeah. Stupid, isn't it?" Big Bill flicked the top of the ashtray up and down. "It came on me just like that." He snapped his fingers. "I had just gotten to the mainland and I was visiting this friend of mine, driving his big old Impala into L.A., when all of a sudden— wham—I freak out. I can't breathe, I can't talk, I think I'm having a heart attack or something, and my friend's yelling at me to move. 'Move,' he says. 'Move! Someone's going to smash into us! Move!'

See, Fenny, I had stopped right in the middle of the Ventura Freeway. I was paralyzed. *Paralyzed.*"

"When was that?" asked Fenny.

"About five years ago."

"And you haven't driven since?"

Bill shook his head. "I've tried, but every time I get behind the wheel I feel like I'm going to die. That reunion up in Canada when I first got to Tall Pine? The one Mae wanted me to go to? She had to drive the whole way."

"You're kidding."

"She probably wouldn't have let me anyway—she says she never lets anyone drive her car—but still, I could have made the offer."

"Five years without driving," said Fenny, "I just can't believe it."

"Well, it's not that big a deal. I mean, there are other ways of getting around, you know."

"True," said Fenny, hearing the defensiveness in his voice. "I know—why don't you sing about it? Make up a little song to help you the way you helped Slim in the boat."

"Thanks," said Bill curtly. "But I think this is going to take more than a song."

Fenny didn't say anything, but Bill assumed her silence was judgmental. The only sound in the car for several minutes was the clicking noise Bill was making with his tongue, and then he said, "There are weirder things, you know."

They were about to find that out when Fenny pulled into a gas station in Bemidji. She filled up the gas tank and then stood under the plastic canopy in the eerie fluorescent light, scraping bugs off the windshield with a squeegee.

"I filled up the thermos," said Bill, appearing at her side.

Fenny couldn't remember if it was she who put down the squeegee first, or Bill who set the thermos on the top of the van, but it seemed at exactly the same time their arms were free and then, suddenly, were around each other and Fenny's lips met Big Bill's as if their rendezvous had long been planned.

Fenny found herself melting into that kiss, the bones of her legs and back seemed made less of calcium and marrow than they did a warm liquid, and she was glad Bill's arms were tight around her because otherwise she would have fallen backward onto the oil-stained concrete.

As easily as they had been drawn to one another, they pulled apart at the same time, and Fenny thought in that moment when they stood looking at each other that all breath had been sucked out of her.

Suddenly, picking up the squeegee seemed to be the most important business at hand, and she returned it to its bucket while Bill polished the thermos with his shirttail, as if he were trying to get a reflective shine.

Frau Katte, who had woken up and lifted her head to get her bearings, did so at the exact moment of Fenny and Big Bill's kiss; for a moment she thought she was dreaming. Didn't Lee have a thing for Bill? Of course she did, but Lee was sleeping next to her, her soft snore accented by a little hum.

She cast a pitying look at the snoring/humming Lee, and slipped her hand in the crooked arm of her own beloved, to whom she couldn't wait to tell this piece of news. She closed her eyes and smiled. She and Miss Penk loved tales of romantic intrigue, their own and everyone else's.

Labor Day blew the whistle on summer—it was an official end to the North Woods vacation season, as the few remaining families packed up their cartop carriers and hustled south, hurrying back to get the kids home in time for the first day of school.

The town breathed a collective sigh of relief; as much as they relied on the income the tourists generated, Tall Piners always looked forward to resuming their normal (and much slower) pace.

Big Bill had left with Lars Larson early in the morning, so Fenny didn't have a chance to talk to him about the kiss under the plastic overhang of the Conoco station (the rest of the ride home, post-kiss, was a strained one, with staticky radio music filling the huge gaps in their polite conversation; finally Big Bill leaned against the door frame and pretended to fall asleep) and what exactly it was supposed to mean. She knew she was thinking of Bill a lot—and in different ways than she had thought of him before—but Lee loved

him, and what right had she to horn in on Lee's (claimed but unsettled) territory?

While she was worrying about the kiss's implications, a phone
call from Christian Freed gave her more to worry about.

"Inga, baby, Christian here!"

"Christian?"

"So how's it going up there in Dinky Town? Ready for the cameras to roll?"

"I guess—"

"Because we're on our way! Harry says he's never seen a movie
come together so fast. I told him, 'Hey, Unc, what'd you expect?
You're working from the script of the century, heh, heh, heh.' "

"Heh, heh, heh," said Fenny.

"So, listen, we'll get in on the seventh and we'll have a nice long
talk then, okay?"

"Okay, but—"

"Ciao, baby!"

An involuntary shudder rippled down Fenny's back. Life felt too
big for her; it was as if the coat she had been wearing had suddenly
stretched out and she shivered in its baggy depths.

They came into Tall Pine like lumbering beasts; a convoy of semi-
trailer trucks that sat at the town's one stoplight, rumbling with
indigestion.

No one at the Cup O'Delight sat at the counter; they were all
pressed against the plate-glass window, watching the parade from
Hollywood roll by.

"Good night," exclaimed Heine, "what do they need all those vehicles for?"

"Hollywood," said Slim, and growled.

"My niece works over to the Northlands Inn," said the mayor.
"She says they had to put in a water bed and one of them shower
things that changes the pressure. Bunch a room alterations for that
Boyd Burch guy."

"We saw him in zat minizeries—what was it, Miss?"

" 'Blood of the Honeysuckle,' " said Miss Penk. "He played a Con-
federate soldier who'd lost his legs. He was quite convincing."

"Pish," said Frau Katte. "How hard is it to play an amputee? All you do is sit on your legs in a wheelchair."

"The wife and I saw that," said Heine. "It *was* dumb."

In a swirl of fabric, Mary Gore suddenly appeared on the other side of the window, waving furiously.

"Look what the special effects crew brought in," said the mayor.

Mary burst through the door like a firefighter coming through a smoky entrance.

"Well, break za door down, crying out lout."

"You'll never believe it," said Mary Gore, clasping her hands to her chest.

"*Angel Motors* won a Pulitzer prize," guessed Heine.

Mary smiled, as if considering the possibility. "Noooo," she said. "Say, where's Lee?"

"Right here." Lee pushed her way through the swinging door. She held a pot of peeled potatoes. "I decided to do my KP while everyone was watching the Hollywood parade."

"Isn't it fantastic?" said Mary, and she spun around so that the yards of her fringed and beaded skirt fanned out.

"What?" asked Lee, in spite of the group that stood at the window, shaking their heads and mouthing, *Don't ask.*

Mary jumped (and rather high, too, thought Frau Katte, considering her low and wide center of gravity). "I'm going to be in the movie!" She flapped her arms and hopped around like a bird on dewy grass. "Can you believe it, I'm going to be in the movie!"

Nudges were sent through the group. Lee poured herself a cup of coffee and leaned against the counter edge.

"Well, give us a few details, Mary. As if you weren't planning to."

Mary's smile was beatific; it wasn't often she was asked to elaborate.

"Okay." She took a dramatic breath and pulled a folded newspaper from her velveteen shoulder bag. "It's right here in the *Tall Pine Register*. 'Extras wanted for Hollywood motion picture, all types needed. Please apply in person Friday at the Banquet Hall in the Northlands Inn.'" Mary smiled in the way that never invited a smile back. "Maybe Fenny won't be the only one who gets discovered."

———

Boyd Burch was the first movie star to ever step inside Pete's Shoe Shack. Not that Pete was aware of this thrilling event; the last movie he had seen in a theater was *If It's Tuesday, This Must Be Belgium* back in the sixties, before his sister's accident. Going out to see a movie had been replaced by staying in and watching them on TV, or at least sitting with Phyllis as she watched miniseries and movies about murderous mistresses and alien landings. Pete never really paid attention to what was on-screen, preferring to work on his shoes.

Pete was a trained shoe repairman but a born shoemaker who had a flourishing mail-order business. Customers sent in an outline of their feet on brown paper and a one-paragraph description of themselves and Pete would handcraft the most durable and beautiful shoes they had ever owned. No one in Tall Pine had any idea he was, as one East Coast client called him, the "Wizard of Shoes," no one knew of the stacks of letters he had from delighted shoe owners, no one knew that he made quite a good living making these shoes.

"I don't know why you keep it such a big secret," said Phyllis. "You could make a lot more money if you made shoes for the locals."

This suggestion always caused a shiver of fear to zig down Pete's back and he became his most stern.

"Please, Phyllis. I don't want to make shoes for anyone in Tall Pine. I make enough money as it is."

The reason he had mail-order customers submit a paragraph describing themselves was so that he could design a shoe that fit their personalities, and the thought of designing shoes for people he knew mortified him. It was too personal, too private, and his comfort level with his friends in Tall Pine demanded that he only resole and repair their shoes, not make them. He had made one exception, however; ever since Lee O'Leary came to town and he realized that she was his ideal woman, he had been making her shoes. He had made nearly a dozen pairs of size tens, in leather he ordered from Brazil, in colors he had specially dyed, in styles he had fashioned himself. Pumps, oxfords, loafers—an entire wardrobe of the most beautiful shoes Lee had ever seen, had she been allowed to see them. Because they revealed too much of himself and his love for her, they were stored away in cheesecloth bags in his bedroom closet. These shoes were his secret valentines, his love sonnets, and he was working up the courage to give them to her; either when he finished the twelfth pair, or on the day when Lee confessed to loving him, whatever came first.

But now his attention was focused on the man in the cowboy hat who was inquiring about shoe lifts.

"I need to add two inches," he said, hoisting his leg up and resting a booted foot on the counter. "Six-four is a good height for a man."

When it seemed as if he were waiting for a response, Pete agreed. "Six-four's a good height."

"I'm already tall—especially for Hollywood—but I want to be in the 'Six-four Club,'" said the young man, with his leg still up on the counter. "Along with Jimmy Stewart, Henry Fonda, Gregory Peck, Clint Eastwood, and, of course, the club president, John Wayne. Although he cheated a little, too. I don't know how big them lifts of his were, but I heard he wore 'em."

Pete had nothing to say to that, so he took out his order pad from under the counter.

"Your name?" he asked, pencil poised.

"You playin' with me?" said the actor, who was used to being recognized.

Pete shook his head, wondering what he'd be playing. "Uh . . . your name?"

"Boyd Burch," said the actor carefully, as if he were making an announcement. "B-u-r-c-h. Like the tree."

Pete scratched a sideburn. "Okay, Mr. Burch, leave your boots here and I'll have them ready by tomorrow."

"Much obliged," said Boyd, who occasionally fell back on the rural western parlance his agent desperately tried to rid him of. ("You think it's sexy talking like Gabby Hayes?") "How about these, too?" He lifted a large leather bag, set it on the counter, and unzipped it. Inside were three more pairs of boots, but where the ones he wore were modern and zippered, these were old-fashioned lace-ups, their stitching wide and obvious. "These are for the movie. Why should the costume department know every single piece of my business? Next thing you know, you're seeing yourself in the tabloids."

Pete rubbed his jaw and his left sideburn. He had figured out that this man was in Fenny's movie and he wanted to be taller than he was, but other than that, the man was jabbering in a way Pete could hardly understand.

"I can have these done by Thursday," he said, getting back to business, a safe territory, conversationally speaking.

The man doffed his hat, revealing shiny blond hair underneath. "I thank ye kindly."

"Uh . . . ye are welcome," mumbled Pete.

The cowboy unzipped his boots, pulled off his socks, and then, digging in his bag once more, took a glossy eight-by-ten photograph from a leather portfolio. He used the pen on the counter to write something on it and then, flashing a smile whose cosmetic dentistry and orthodontics added up to equal the yearly income of an elementary school teacher, handed the photograph proudly to Pete.

"For your wall," he said. "With my compliments."

"Thanks," said Pete, and then, watching the barefoot man leave the store, he said softly, "It'll give me a real *lift*."

Chapter 11

On the first day of shooting, Fenny decided she didn't want to be in the movie after all. It wasn't the best of timing, she readily admitted to Miss Penk and Frau Katte, but she had made her decision and she felt good about it.

"It's important to feel good about a decision," said Miss Penk, giving Fenny a hand as the young woman climbed into their speedboat.

They had found Fenny on the narrow island in the center of Tall Pine Lake, sitting on a rock shaped like a recliner.

It was a place Fenny had shown them once when they were out fishing.

"See that chair right under that spruce? That stone La-Z-Boy? Sig and Wally used to call it my office. It's where I used to go whenever I needed to be alone."

It was where the two women thought immediately to look when Christian had barged into the Cup O'Delight, demanding to know, "Just where the hell is my leading lady?"

After Fenny was in the boat, Frau Katte leveled her no-nonsense stare at her.

"Fenny, you can't let zose people down. You gave zem your word."

"Katte, I thought we had agreed that Fenny didn't need any lectures."

"I agreed to nozzing of za kind. If she needs anyzing, it's a lecture."

"Katte," warned Miss Penk as she pulled off her terry-cloth sundress. She turned to Fenny, adjusting the top of her lemon-yellow swimsuit. "If you're not in any big hurry, do you mind taking me for a little spin?"

"No," said Fenny, surprised.

"Good heavens, now is not za time to water-ski."

But Miss Penk had already rolled over the side of the boat.

"Now let Fenny drive," she said to Frau Katte. "You always get to."

After she put her skis on in the water, Miss Penk took the tow rope.

"All right," she said, with a forceful nod. "Let 'er rip."

Fenny pushed in the throttle and the boat zipped past the island.

"It's not like I'm holding up the production," she told Frau Katte, feeling the older woman's stare on her. It was true, they were just shooting exteriors, but Christian had invited Fenny to watch, thinking it advantageous for a newcomer to immerse herself in as much of the filmmaking as possible. "I realize that when I *do* quit, I might hold up the production, but I'm not holding it up today because I'm not in any of the scenes. . . ."

"So zis is just sort of a practice quit, hmmm? *Mein Gott*, Fenny, I zought you were made of stronger stuff zan zat."

"I can't hear you," said Fenny, pretending the roar of the motor was more powerful than it was.

"Of course you can," snapped Frau Katte. "Don't be such a baby."

Fenny looked back at Miss Penk, whose hair flew behind her like a blond wind sock. The skier smiled and waved grandly.

"I'm not being a baby," said Fenny. "I'm only stopping myself from making a big mistake."

"Baby, baby, baby," taunted Frau Katte. "Just like a baby, you're only zinking of yourself. Just like a baby, you don't care who you inconvenience, as long as you get what you want. Wah, wah, wah."

Fenny gritted her teeth and concentrated on her driving. Other than several fishing boats out near the north shore, they had the whole lake to themselves. On the water's surface, the late morning sun doled out its sunshine in sparkles that would leap up as the nose of the boat drove through them. Fenny would have been having a great time if she weren't so miserable.

After a while, Miss Penk motioned that she was finished, and when Fenny circled the boat around to pick her up, Miss Penk suggested that it was her turn. Fenny agreed readily, happy to get out of the boat and away from the crying-baby noises Frau Katte interrupted her angry silence with.

In her T-shirt and cutoffs, Fenny skied. She was good, but not as fancy as Miss Penk, who liked to bend to the side until her head almost touched the water or do 360-degree turns. The sensation of speed, freedom, and excitement—and all while standing up on water—was just the release Fenny needed, and she began laughing. She skied and laughed until she let herself collapse into the water, exhausted.

"That was quite a ride," said Miss Penk, bringing the boat close. "You want more, or are you done?"

"Done," panted Fenny.

"I figure we've only got a week or two left of skiing weather," said Miss Penk as Fenny boosted herself into the boat. "The water's already a little nippy, don't you think?"

"Yeah, I do," said Fenny, rubbing her legs, which were dotted with goose bumps. She snuck a look at Frau Katte, who sat looking forward, her arms folded over her chest.

Miss Penk steered the boat back to the island, where Fenny's canoe was tied up.

"What time is it?" asked Fenny, and when Miss Penk told her, she nodded. "I suppose I still have time to get to the set."

"Yes, the faster you give them your resignation, the faster they can hire someone."

"Oh, I probably won't quit."

"What'd you say?" said Frau Katte, turning around.

"I said I probably won't quit. I think I'd be a lot better off if I did, but I guess they're counting on me."

"That's no small thing," said Miss Penk, "having people count on you."

"Zat's right," said Frau Katte, nodding. "In fact, it's a big zing."

As Fenny began rowing in the direction of her house, Miss Penk circled the island and floored it. Neither of their smiles diminished on the ride home, for both women were certain that their particular brand of therapy had been just what Fenny needed.

"You see, Katte, exercise makes a person think more clearly, especially waterskiing, what with its speed and—"

"All I know is, she was listening awfully close to what I had to say about keeping your word."

"When the body's moving, the mind is free to—"

"I zink it really hit home when I started making zose crying-baby noises—"

The two women laughed then, as the boat they had won in a contest skipped over the blue waters of Tall Pine Lake, willing to concede, as people who love each other are, that they were probably both right.

"Cut!" ordered Malcolm Edgely. The director sat back in his canvas chair and bent his thumb back and forth, studying it with great absorption as everyone on the set fidgeted in the uneasy silence.

They were shooting in an abandoned farmhouse four miles outside of Tall Pine; one that the production crew had refurbished, repainted, and redecorated so that now in stepping through the door, a person stepped back in time and into the turn-of-the-century home of Ike Forrest and his mother.

Fenny dug her little finger under the edge of her wig—it felt like a miniature furnace on her head—and scratched her scalp. She hoped this gesture wouldn't incite the fury of her director; equally innocent gestures had.

"What . . . exactly . . . do . . . you . . . think . . . you're . . . doing?" he had asked earlier that morning, in a voice that seemed barely able to cap a bubbling anger.

A frightened smile darted across the face of Grace Aisles, the woman playing Ike Forrest's mother, as she pressed her finger to her chest and asked, "Me?"

"Yes, dear. *You.* Do you think you're capable of finding your mark—or should I position a midget under your skirt to escort you?"

"You can save yourself the cost of a midget," said Grace in a tight voice. "I can find my mark."

Ten minutes later the propmaster was yelled at for placing a vase of flowers on the wrong side of the table and screwing up the continuity.

"This is the first shot," Fenny heard the man mumble as he pushed the vase to the other side. "So what's the dif?"

"Perhaps you care to address your comments to me?" asked the director.

"Perhaps not," mumbled the propmaster, but more clearly he asked, "This better?"

And now Malcolm Edgely was watching the fascinating show his bending and unbending thumb provided him as cast and crew members prayed they were not the cause of whatever impropriety inspired his latest rage.

Finally he grabbed his thumb with his other hand and clutched it against himself as if it were wounded. He rose and said to the air above him, "Five-minute break, everyone!"

"Take five, people," shouted the first assistant.

"For those of curious mind who wonder why we're taking the un-scheduled break," said the director, still to the ceiling, "I'll offer you this much." He looked at the actors and smiled. "I realize I'm not in company of the Redgraves"—his smile suddenly disappeared and his voice became harsh—"but can you at least pretend that good acting is something you might aspire to? Or is any kind of acting—even mediocre—simply beyond your ken?"

The director shook his head as if he were sickened by them all, and then stormed off to his trailer.

After an awkward silence, most of the cast and crew walked off the set, deciding how best to use their unscheduled break. Boyd Burch went to his trailer to do push-ups. Doug Woo, the cinematographer, and the propmaster went out on the front lawn to play croquet with the gaffer and the soundman. Bonnie Price took out her notebook and started working on the screenplay she was writing.

Fenny stood for a while in the bright farm kitchen, not knowing what to do. It was a state of being she was getting used to.

In less than a week, Fenny's life had been taken over by people she didn't know, people whose mission was to turn her into a fictional character. She spent her days having people put on her makeup in a half-hour procedure (in response to her query as to why a pioneer woman needs cosmetics, the makeup artist said, "A true natural look takes artifice"); having people lasso her into a corset until her waist measured an unnatural number; having more people dress her in floor-length calico dresses and then arrange a bonnet over a wig whose color made a canary look pale.

"Come on," said Grace, her co-star, "let's take a load off."

Lifting their skirts up as they stepped over swirls of cables, they walked outside the ring of lights to a grouping of chairs on the back porch.

As soon as they sat down in the canvas chairs that had their names on them, a production assistant appeared, asking if they wanted anything to drink.

"I'll take a coffee," said Grace. "And find me a cigarette, could you, please?"

"Menthol or regular?" asked the p.a., obliging as a butler.

"Regular."

"You want any coffee, Miss Ness? A soda, maybe?"

"Sure, David, coffee'd be great. But it's Fenny, remember?"

"Right," said the p.a. with a little salute.

Fenny was having a hard time dealing with being treated as if she were a queen of some oil-rich country. Production assistants hovered near, ready to run for whatever she wanted.

The p.a. returned with his booty and stood around until Grace stuck the cigarette into the side of her mouth, and then he lit it for her.

"Thanks, Davey," she said, blowing a plume of smoke out of her mouth.

"You're welcome," he said, and then he was gone so quick it seemed a magician's trick.

"Malcolm seems to be a little—"

"Don't even worry about it," broke in Grace. "The asshole's not worth it."

"Something really seems to be bothering him," said Fenny, trying again.

Grace inhaled deeply and Fenny heard a tiny "wahhh" coming from deep within her chest.

"Really," she said, and smoke spilled over her words, "*don't* worry about it. The guy's an asshole, he will always be an asshole, and trying to figure him out will not make him less of an asshole."

The fear that had almost made Fenny quit was so potent on her first day of shooting that her knees bobbed in their sockets and her hands shook as if she'd just come off a bender. But day by day she found comfort in the fact that everyone was afraid—afraid of Malcolm Edgely—and that common fear lessened her own.

"I worked with him a long time ago," continued Grace. "In *Sea Trolls*—did you ever see it? It's not too bad, for its genre, which is soft-focus-lovely-women-who-are-imperiled-by-monsters. The video's real popular in Japan, I hear."

"What was he like back then?"

"An *asshole*," said Grace. "Almost as bad as he is now. I wasn't going to take this part when I heard who was directing—I mean, you can only take so much—but then again, people aren't exactly knocking down the doors of us women of a certain age, if you know what I mean."

"How old are you?" asked Fenny.

"Forty-three," said Grace. "Ancient, huh?" She took a sip of coffee and stared out at the woods beyond the porch. "About all they have for me now is mother roles. I've played mothers to men who are older than me, if you can believe that shit. It's a rotten business, Fenny, but at least it's a rotten business that pays good."

David the p.a. appeared, as if he'd been zapped onstage by the wave of a wand.

"Malcolm needs you back on the set now," he said.

"Thanks," said Grace. She dropped her cigarette into her coffee cup and it hissed like a cat's warning.

As they walked back into the lodge, she took Fenny's arm, drawing her close, and whispered, "If he yells at you, don't take it personally. Number one, he doesn't know what he wants and that makes him mad, and number two, he's an asshole."

The propmaster stepped to the side as they passed.

"So, Gracie," he whispered, "I've got a special prop I'd like to show you tonight."

The gesture Grace made with her tongue was all the more lewd in contrast to her pioneer-woman clothes. "Can't wait," she said, and then turning to Fenny she asked, "How come all men think their props are so special?"

Over the next two days, Malcolm grew hoarse from screaming at people. He threatened to file a complaint to his union against the propmaster and asked Bonnie Price, the script supervisor, if she was dyslexic. Several times he asked Grace Aisles to tone down her sexuality. "I know you're afraid of getting older, Grace, but playing every part 'come-hither' doesn't make you any younger." He also was partial to phrases directed at the entire group: "Can we *pretend* we're making a movie and not dreck?" and "Are you trying to kill me by ineptitude or just plain spite?"

"Either one, we don't care," Grace whispered to Fenny.

It was the sixth day of shooting and to Fenny it seemed as if she had been working on the movie for months. Dressing up like a pioneer and saying lines like "Excuse me, Mr. Forrest, but sometimes a man gets too big for his britches and a woman's got to take in the seams" tended to do funny things to time, tended to make a minute seem like a day.

Not having coffee with her friends at the Cup O'Delight changed the tone of her day; she felt odd and unfinished, as if she'd forgotten to brush her teeth or comb her hair. Bill was still exploring nature with Lars Larson, and she missed him, more than she thought she would. She longed to see his face, hear his laugh, watch him dig in his pockets for candy.

Malcolm Edgely, dressed in his Cecil B. DeMille safari suit, was as tightly wound as ever, yelling over the most minor of infractions as if they were hell-bound sins.

Fenny had escaped his wrath until that morning, when she had the temerity to make a suggestion.

"What did you say?" he asked, his voice pleasant, if one ignored the current of disdain underneath it.

Fenny took the bait, not knowing she was committing a *big* sin in the Kingdom of Hollywood, and that was to question the director. She was merely feeling comfortable enough to cheerfully pitch in and offer help where she saw it was needed.

"Well, I don't really think Inga would be very happy about this. I mean, Ike promised to take her to the dance and now he tells her he's got to take the saloon owner's daughter."

Malcolm's thin lips moved like something slow and dangerous: the Edgely smile. "The saloon owner is also the mayor," he said.

"I know," said Fenny.

"And Ike wants to get in good with the mayor."

"I know," said Fenny again, "but Inga's a mail-order bride who's just come all the way from Norway to marry this guy—at his request—and then she gets stood up. I'm sure she doesn't like it."

The director went so far in his smile as to actually let his teeth show. He looked around the silent set, wanting to share this joke with his lackeys.

"Did everyone hear? She *doesn't like it.*" He turned to Fenny. "Now tell me how you arrived at that brilliant character analysis. Are you a student of psychology? Or perhaps it is you who wrote the script? Christian," he yelled at the screenwriter, who stood next to the key grip. "Christian, I know your name's on the script, but I believe our lovely little friend here thinks she wrote it."

Christian sank his hands as deep as they would go in the pockets of his tight black jeans and laughed a dry laugh.

"Shithead," muttered the key grip, and Christian wondered if he was talking about him or the director. Either way, he laughed again, nervously. Christian had been on the set every day, and even though it was hard to recognize his own kind, Malcolm *was* a shithead. Christian had made himself a bargain; he would tolerate the man's bad behavior (he had the elevated reverence for directors that most of Hollywood had) as long as Malcolm didn't screw up his movie.

Fenny stared at Christian, and if looks could kill, he would be writhing on the floor, begging for an antidote. She could have looked at anyone with contempt—she had no allies against Malcolm on the set (off the set, they were a united band of anti-Malcolmites); no one dared stand up for her.

Reminding herself that her little courage bead was in her bra, next to her heart, Fenny turned to the director, who had lit up one of his thin brown cigarettes.

"Malcolm," she said, "could I have a word with you?"

"A word with me?" asked Malcolm. He sat down in his canvas chair and exhaled a fat smoke ring. "Well, certainly, Professor Ness. Shoot."

"In private?"

The director's face contorted into a look of great surprise. "Why, Fenny," he said, and he held his arms out. "Whatever you need to say can be said in front of everybody. Isn't that right, Doug?"

Doug Woo looked at the floor, miserable. He shrugged his shoulders.

"See?" said Malcolm. "Now come on, Fenny, what's on your busy little mind? We're all friends here."

Fenny had been wondering if she should drop the whole thing and return to her mark near the woodstove, but he pressed a button that said *Fire!* when he asked what was on her "busy little mind."

"All right," she said, her voice well modulated even as she felt enough air wasn't getting into her lungs. "All right." She cleared her throat. "What I wanted to tell you was that I don't think you were considering Inga's point of view." She cleared her throat again. "I'm wondering if you ever stop to consider anyone's point of view."

"I don't have to," said Malcolm, wagging his head slightly. "I'm the director."

"I didn't know the word was synonymous with 'tyrant.' "

There was an almost imperceptible gasp on the set, but Fenny heard it, and it gave her confidence. "I mean, if you looked up 'director' in the dictionary, I don't think you'd see Mussolini's picture there."

Malcolm exhaled a plume of smoke.

"Mussolini, hmmmm? My, my, don't we have far-reaching references for such a young person."

Fenny felt her blood begin to boil—at least she felt her skin warm as if the blood underneath were heating it up. Her fight-or-flee instinct was revved up—and she wanted to do both.

"What's the matter?" prodded Malcolm. "Cat got your tongue? Now, please, you have the floor. Let's hear it."

Fenny saw herself being stripped of her bonnet and banished from the set, but she could hardly stop now that she'd been invited.

She sighed and then asked, "Do you have to make everyone feel like such a big jerk?"

"A big jerk? I've always believed we're responsible for our own emotions, Fenny. If you feel like a 'big jerk,' it's your fault, not mine." He smiled his cold smile and Fenny could see how he was enjoying this, the way some people enjoyed the taste of buttermilk.

"I just don't see why you have to make such a big deal out of every little thing."

"Fenny, my dear, it's 'every little thing'—the details—that makes up a good picture."

"Well, I think a good picture could be made without hurting everyone's feelings."

Malcolm fingered the button on his breast pocket. "Do me a favor, Fenny: Don't think."

Fenny breathed faster. She felt as if she were on fire with anger, and tried to contain her impulse to burst into tears.

"And do me a favor, Malcolm," she said, her voice wavering. "Don't be . . ." Her mind scrambled to come up with the perfect insult. "Don't be such a Malcolm."

She ran off the set, and there was an ashamed silence until Steve the key grip and Doug the cinematographer and David the p.a. began to clap. Soon everyone on the set was applauding, and while Christian didn't exactly bring his hands together, he did keep a vague rhythm by drumming his fingers against his thighs. It was a unified show of support, and Malcolm rose from his director's chair as if he had nothing more on his mind than getting a bottle of the lime mineral water he favored.

"It's a wrap," he said, and walked off the set to his trailer, where he'd call in the masseur he had written into his contract and instruct him not to "mince moves."

"Wild rhinos and elephants. Herds running. Grass trampled into green pulp. The village eyebrow rises and shoulders twitch at the possibility of releasing the bow and watching the poison arrow land."

Silence rolled over the counter; if someone had walked into the Cup O'Delight at that time, that person would have assumed some bad news had just been delivered.

Mary Gore smiled the humble smile of an artiste who knows her work is touched by the gods.

"Hollywood," she said, "is ripe fodder for the writer."

"So that's what that was about," said Lee, walking the length of the counter, refilling coffee cups. "That village eyebrow stuff threw me off."

Arranging the bright folds of her cape and skirt around her, Mary sat at the end counter stool. Creative souls were few and far between in the North Woods, but she would spread her vision to the ignorant masses if it killed her.

"*Un café, s'il vous plaît*," she said, holding her cup out to Lee with one hand. With the other, she opened her donations box and then passed a stack of *Angel Motors* to Pete.

Pete took one off the top and passed the stack, with a look of apology.

"Thanks *so* much, Pete," said Miss Penk.

"Ya, Pete," whispered Frau Katte, "what's za big idea peddling zis trash?"

Pete clenched his teeth, straining to say something clever, but he knew the perfect remark would come later, back in his shop, while he was filing down a heel or sewing an upper. Pete's wit was on a three-hour delay, so he settled for rolling his eyes instead.

"Be sure to check out the drawing on page two," said Mary. "It might remind you of Dante's version of hell, but it's what I imagine the soul of Hollywood to look like."

"Oh, well," whispered Heine as he accepted a copy from Frau Katte. "I was planning to reline my gerbil cage anyway."

"Why are you down on Hollywood all of a sudden?" asked Lee. "You were the one who was so excited about being an extra."

Mary twirled her finger in the tube of her flipped hairstyle. "Oh, Lee, just because I'm 'so excited' doesn't mean I don't see Hollywood for what it is."

When she had collected her donations (smiling sourly when the mayor put in two pennies— "My two cents' worth," he said), Mary gathered up her cape and sailed toward the door like a ship plowing through rough seas. She promptly ran into Big Bill.

"For what ails you," she said, thrusting a copy of *Angel Motors* at him.

"Nothing's ailing me at the moment," said Bill as he picked up some of the change that fell out of Mary's donations box. "But I appreciate the gesture."

"And I know you'll appreciate the art," she said, and then, raising her voice, she added, "unlike the rest of these heathens."

"Heathens?" said Big Bill, and looking toward the counter, he raised his arm. "My people!"

"Write a poem about your canoe trip," said Mary, as if she were presenting Bill with an offer he couldn't refuse, "and I'll publish it in the next issue."

When she left, Bill stood in the center of the room, his arms still raised.

"Canoe," he said. "Long, pointed, streaks through water. Water, cold, wet, holds up canoe. Rock. Big, sharp, bumps canoe. Canoe get owie. Canoe go down."

A chorus of bravos rewarded his effort.

"Thank you, thank you," he said, sitting at the counter. "But in all modesty, it's nothing compared to my opus, 'Paddle.' "

"You should recite it at tonight's Polka," said Miss Penk.

"Ya, and I'll do an interpretive dance," added Frau Katte.

"Hi, Bill," said Lee, and Frau Katte nudged Miss Penk, wondering if she heard the adoration in Lee's voice, too.

"Hey, Lee. I'd sure like some of that coffee. Lars Larson makes his strong, but not good."

Checking first at the window of the swinging door to make sure Mary Gore was gone, Slim entered the cafe and, seeing Bill, gave a perky bark.

"Right back at you, Slim. How's tricks?"

Slim scratched one of his bony elbows. "Tricky. The movie started, you know. Things are going crazy."

"Fenny's movie started? How's she doing?"

"We never see her," said Frau Katte. "Zey've got her going all day long out at za old Heneghan farmhouse."

"Some of us are going to be extras," the mayor informed him.

"I would think she'd be here tonight," said Miss Penk. "I can't see her missing the first Polka Night of the season."

The get-togethers tapered off in the busy summer, only to resume a more regular schedule in the fall.

"I can't see me missing it, either," said Big Bill.

Pete, watching Lee's face and listening quietly to everything, wished Bill would.

The heat from the campfire was stingy; Fenny drew her knees to her chest and sat as close as she could to the little tepee of burning logs.

The wind off the river was cold and the September night was dense and black, even as it was punctured by a million stars.

She shifted her position on the ground and looked over the flames at Big Bill.

He pushed marshmallows onto two sticks and handed one to Fenny.

"All the campfires I had with Lars Larson and we never once roasted marshmallows."

"Lars doesn't believe in any modern conveniences on camping trips."

"Yeah, but I didn't think that applied to food! We were eating berries off bushes. And pemmican! If I never have another bite of pemmican, it'll be too soon for me." Bill looked at Fenny's stick. "Hey, you're burning yours."

"I like them that way," said Fenny. She blew the flame that incinerated her marshmallows and then pulled the black cap of carbon off the top one, revealing its gooey white center. "Umm, umm, umm," she said, eating it.

Bill pulled off his own perfectly toasted marshmallows, and after he ate them, he set down his stick and went over to Fenny. No sooner had he sat down than they were in each other's arms. It was a position they had both wanted to be in all evening.

It had been a festive Polka Night. Fenny regaled everyone with tales of the movie set and the horrors of Malcolm Edgely; Bill, with tales of the Boundary Waters and the horrors of Lars Larson.

Slim had been in fine form, doing his Mick Jagger impersonation as he sang "Brown Sugar" to Heine's accordion accompaniment. Miss Penk taught everyone a line dance (everyone except Fenny, who just couldn't catch on to the steps) and the mayor read his first campaign speech (his wife Dolly had found it while cleaning out his office):

"In the words of our town founder, Pierre LeFleque, we must 'press on, people, press on.' The future is among these tall pines, and we must look upward to greet it."

"Not bad," came Frau Katte's critique. "A little on za schmaltzy side, but on za whole, not bad."

Lee and Bill played a few duets on the piano, and when their arms occasionally touched, Lee had to restrain herself from crying out, or laughing, or both. She loved sitting next to him and inhaling his smell; he smelled of lake water, of wood smoke from campfires. Her ex-husband had been meticulous in his hygiene and a fan of expensive colognes, but he had never smelled as good as Big Bill smelled now.

Frau Katte kept a cool eye on the complex geometry of this romantic triangle; although Big Bill danced with Lee and not with Fenny (who had to be in the mood to embarrass herself on the dance floor), although he was equally attentive to both, it appeared to the Swiss woman that when Bill and Fenny were close to one another, the air was charged, as if even the atoms and molecules spun with the giddiness of their attraction.

"Don't you feel zat sexual heat zey're zrowing off?" she whispered to Miss Penk.

"No," said Miss Penk. "No, I don't feel anything. If you ask me, it's Lee Bill's attracted to."

"What about zat kiss I told you about?"

Miss Penk rubbed her shoulder. It was finally cool enough to wear one of her angora sweaters, and she found herself constantly petting her arms. "Maybe it was just that, Katte. Just a kiss."

"Oh, pish. When is a kiss *just* a kiss?"

At the end of the evening, Lee offered to give Bill a ride home, but Fenny said not to bother, she had to pass Mae Little Feather's house on her way home anyway and she'd give Bill a ride.

Lee said, "Fine," in that way that didn't mean fine at all, but she brightened when Bill kissed her hand and told her to make sure she had plenty of pancake batter because he'd be in early for breakfast.

Eventually, the embraced couple moved from sitting to lying. Fenny's senses were having a field day; she could smell the pine needles underneath her and the nearby river, could taste marshmallows on Bill's lips, could hear an owl hoot, see the light of the campfire play on Bill's face, and most of all, felt Bill, felt his broad strong back underneath her hands, felt his soft lips on hers, his teeth, his tongue.

They lay kissing for a quarter of an hour.

"I'd invite you into my tent," said Big Bill, coming up for air, "but it's so nice out here. Unless you're cold?"

"I'm not cold," said Fenny. "Boy, am I not cold." As much as she didn't want to, she asked, "Bill, what about Lee?"

"Is this really the time to talk about Lee?" Sighing, he got up and threw another log onto the fire.

"I . . . I don't know when the time to talk about Lee is," said Fenny. "All I know is I feel guilty. She loves you, Bill."

Big Bill stood there, looking at the jumping flames.

"I can't help that, Fenny. I mean, I love Lee, too—as a friend—but I'm not going to feel guilty because I don't love her the way she loves me. And I don't think you should, either."

"How can I not? She's my best friend. I'm taking the one thing she really wants away from her."

"Fenny, you can't take something away from Lee that she doesn't have." He sat down again next to her and took her hand. "Now, I'm sorry that I can't return Lee's feelings, but not sorry enough to stop returning yours. Okay?" He kissed her.

Fenny was about to tell him okay when she came up for air, but she was interrupted by a voice yelling, "Be-yill!"

She started. Who could be out in the woods in the middle of the night calling for "Be-yill"?

"It's my aunt," he reminded her, laughing.

Mae Little Feather's house sat on a ridge overlooking the river, about two hundred feet from where Bill had pitched his tent.

"Yes, Mae?" Bill shouted.

"Get me some Chum Gum when you're in town tomorrow. And some Dr Pepper!"

"Okay, Mae. Goodnight."

There was no further response other than a door slamming shut.

"Thank God we're blocked by all these trees." Bill kissed her forehead. "At least I hope we're blocked by all these trees. If Mae sees you, she's liable to come out here with a shotgun."

"Bill, you're thirty-four years old. You're old enough to have company."

"Yeah, but not *white* company."

Fenny sat up. "Bill, I do business with Mae all the time. She *likes* me."

"She *tolerates* you . . . in your shop. But on her land, well, she'd look at you as an interloper. A *white* interloper."

"You make her sound like a racist."

"She *is* a racist. She's never forgiven the white man for what they did to her people."

Fenny stood up and brushed pine needles off the back of her jeans.

"Okay, that's it. I'm going."

Laughing, Bill took her hand. "Stay. I'll protect you. We'll go in the tent."

"I can't now. I'm too afraid."

"Of Mae? I was just kidding, Fenny. She wouldn't really hurt you. At least not *bad*."

"That's a comfort," said Fenny. "But really, Bill, I've got to get up early tomorrow. Goodnight."

She kissed him chastely, and before he could issue another protest, she ran to her car, which, parked on the old dirt road by the river, was hidden from Mae's house by more pine trees. The cold night air felt good in her lungs. She ran faster, feeling like she was escaping, and not from Mae. She was glad he hadn't made her answer his question of what she was afraid of, because her answer would have been, *You.*

Chapter 12

When Fenny arrived on the set the next day, she smiled and looked straight into Malcolm's eyes, saying hello, hoping that things might start fresh between them, but Malcolm was the type who not only held a grudge but embraced it, squeezed it, bear-hugged it.

"My, my, aren't we in a chipper mood today. Did we get lucky last night?"

Fenny felt the burn of embarrassment on her cheeks, but she took a breath that lifted her chest and straightened her spine.

"I hope we can do some good work today," she said, and, not waiting for Malcolm's snide response, she turned and walked away.

In the makeup trailer, Grace asked Fenny where she got the courage to take on Malcolm. "I mean, no offense, but I thought you were as chicken as the rest of us. Even more so."

Fenny shrugged. "Sig—my mom—didn't believe that customer-is-always-right business. She said she was willing to give them the benefit of the doubt, but sometimes they were just plain wrong."

"Okay," said Grace after a pause. "So what does that have to do with what we were talking about?"

"Well, she meant if they were too demanding or bad-mannered, you didn't have to take it. She said you should call them on it because taking abuse should not be part of the sale."

"Smart woman," said Grace, to whom Fenny had told her tragic story during one long break in filming.

"She was." Fenny nodded and then, surprised, she realized that she had just told a story about Sig without tearing up.

"Yes," pointed out Sharen, the makeup artist, "but Malcolm's not a customer. He's your *director*."

"Does that mean he can get away with treating people so bad?" asked Fenny.

"Yes!" said Grace and Sharen in unison.

Fenny laughed. "Are all directors like Malcolm?"

"The insecure ones are," said Grace. "And I'd say at least half of them are insecure."

"I'd say three-quarters," said Sharen, sharpening an eyebrow pencil.

"Well, then are most of the writers like Christian? And most of the actors like Boyd Burch?" (He exercised fanatically during lunch breaks because, as he told Fenny, "there's always another guy with better abs waiting to take your place.") "Is everybody insecure?"

Grace and Sharen looked at one another in the mirror.

"Uh-huh," said the makeup artist.

"Absolutely," said the movie veteran.

"Insecure because they don't want to lose what they finally got," said Sharen.

"Or totally spoiled—as in 'rotted' spoiled—by what they had to do to get that job in the first place," said Grace.

"What do you mean?"

"Fenny, yours is kind of a Lana Turner story—I don't know if even Lana Turner had your kind of Lana Turner story. I mean, you were *discovered*. You didn't do one thing to further your Hollywood career other than to be seen standing in a curio shop."

"A curio shop?" said Fenny. " 'Sig's Place' isn't a curio shop."

"I don't care if it's a sex-toy emporium," said Grace impatiently. "The point is, you didn't work for it. You didn't spend years pounding the pavement, visiting agents whose receptionists tell you not to come around anymore, sucking up to creeps who might give you one line in a TV movie, having casting agents tell you you're too old or too fat—"

"Hey, I didn't ask for this, it came to me. I didn't come to it."

Grace sighed and looked at Sharen in the mirror. "Unlike us poor schmucks who chased after it our whole lives."

"Right," said the makeup artist, rubbing a wedge of sponge into foundation. "Us poor slobs who had to *work* to get where we are."

"You guys!" protested Fenny. "All I'm saying is—"

"And all we're saying is, *that's* why so many people in Hollywood are so insecure. They know what they had to do to get a job and they *never* want to do it again."

"Now shut your eyes and shut your mouth," said Sharen. "I've got to put your face on."

The scene to be shot involved the Widow Forrest and Inga setting the kitchen table. The Widow Forrest counsels her future daughter-in-law on how to please a man, especially a "rapscallion, trouble-seeking, fun-loving billy goat like my son." Ike, the aforementioned son, eavesdrops on the conversation and then comes in, just after Inga says, "Maybe this mail-order-bride business wasn't such a good idea. Maybe I should have stayed home in Norway and married the preacher's son."

The script read that at Ike's entrance, Inga was supposed to run out of the kitchen in embarrassment, but Fenny unintentionally dropped the silverware she was holding and then, bending under the table to retrieve it, bonked her head.

The director said, "Cut!" but, surprising everyone, did not order Fenny off the set to ponder the audaciousness that made her think she could act. Instead he said, "Print it," and then asked Fenny if she'd do the same thing in the next take.

"What was your motivation for that?" whispered Boyd Burch.

"Huh?" asked Fenny.

"Was Inga mad about something or did she want to prove something to Ike?"

"Gee, Boyd," said Fenny. "I just bumped my head. By accident."

"Dang," said Boyd. He had taken several classes on character analysis and his script was nearly indecipherable, marked up as it was by notes on motivation and sense memories.

The second take went even better. Fenny dropped the silverware, picked it up, hitting her head again on the table, and then, misjudging the placement of her chair, sat down on the floor.

The crew applauded after the scene ended, and Malcolm even managed a thin smile as he announced, "That's a keeper," and told the actors to take a break while the next shot was being set up.

"I'll bet that's how Tracy and Hepburn felt after they did a scene," said Boyd as they walked off the set.

"I don't know about that," said Fenny.

"I wish I knew how to make things up like that."

"Well, it's not that hard," offered Fenny. "I mean, all you do is let your character say what you'd think she—or he—would say."

They had walked out onto the back porch.

"I'd be afraid I'd say something really stupid."

As it was, Boyd did something really stupid by grabbing Fenny and kissing her full on the mouth.

"Boyd!" she cried, pushing him away. "What did you do that for?"

The actor looked back at her, a look of bewilderment spread across his movie star features. "You didn't like it?"

"No, I didn't like it," said Fenny.

Boyd Burch punched the wall.

"Yeoww!" he said as his fist made contact, but his apparent pain did not stop him from punching the wall again and then again.

Not quite believing anything that was happening, Fenny stood there for a few moments, until she realized that if she didn't step in, the actor was going to seriously injure himself.

"Boyd," she said, pulling on his arm. "Boyd, stop it."

He looked at her wildly, and for a moment Fenny feared she might join the wall as a recipient of Boyd's rage.

"Come on, let's take a walk," she said. Her instinct told her he wouldn't turn on her, but if he did, her quick reflexes would save her. She tugged at his sleeve. "Come on, you'll feel better."

He let Fenny lead him down the steps to the gravel road. They walked without talking, Boyd rubbing his hand, which was now starting to *really* hurt. They walked past the barn and along the row of white cedars planted as a windbreak.

"I am so sorry," said Boyd finally. "I feel like such a fool—it's not like I'm a molester, you know."

So stunned was Fenny by Boyd's self-punishment that she had nearly forgotten what had spurred it.

"I know you're not a molester, Boyd," said Fenny. "Still—why'd you kiss me?"

As they walked, he had been massaging his sore hand; now he stopped to look at it. "What did I do to my hand?" He held it out for Fenny to see. "You think makeup can fix it up?"

"Probably. Really, Boyd, I'm surprised you didn't break anything. You were really going to town."

" 'Going to town,' " said Boyd, grinning. "My grandma used to say that. And she also used to say, 'You're a pistol, Boyd.' And so are *you*, Fenny."

They walked on, looking out at the sumac that sprung up in bloodred streaks down along the county road. Fenny was just about to press Boyd for more of an explanation as to his behavior when he spoke.

"Don't ask me to analyze every little thing, okay, Fenny? Because I can't. You know me—I'm just a dumb cowboy."

"You are not," began Fenny.

"Tell my agent that . . . or my dad. Honest, I don't know why I kissed you. I mean, dang, you're pretty and all, but I like littler girls. Did you ever see how tiny Jean Arthur was standing next to Gary Cooper?"

Fenny shook her head.

Boyd laughed. "Can you tell I'm a big movie fan? My grandma and I used to stay up late and watch old movies. I could be *worn out* from working the ranch all day—my dad didn't think his kids were kids as much as field hands—and on my way to bed when Gran would say in this little sneaky voice, 'The Maltese Falcon is on, Boyd,' or 'Ever seen *Mogambo*?' " He smiled at the memory. "And I always stayed up. We'd eat popcorn, which she couldn't make for beans— it was always full of old maids—and drink root beer out of bottles."

"You sound like you really love her."

He nodded. "I did. She died three months after I took off for Hollywood. Gran was the only one who never laughed at me when I said I wanted to be in the movies. She always said, 'Why not? Beats stepping in cow pies and pitching hay.' "

The actor sighed. "About that kissing, Fenny. I guess I just thought that maybe if we got together, you could teach me stuff."

Fenny could see David the p.a. out on the porch, looking around, obviously for them.

"I think they need us back on the set," said Fenny. Putting her fingers to her mouth, she whistled and waved to David when he looked in her direction. "We'll be right there," she yelled through cupped hands.

"Okay," yelled David.

"It's just that you're so good," said Boyd.

"I am?"

Boyd nodded glumly. "A natural. You can do comedy like Carole Lombard and drama like Bette Davis."

"Carole who?" asked Fenny, her grasp of movie history hardly as broad as her co-star's.

"Malcolm needs you now," yelled David.

Fenny took Boyd's arm. "We're coming!"

"So do you think you could help me sometimes?" asked Boyd as they neared the farmhouse.

"Help you? How?"

"I don't know," said Boyd, rubbing his sore hand. "Do what Malcolm can't do. Help me be Ike."

"I'll try," said Fenny, even though she had no idea how she was supposed to do something like that.

"I used to think rich people were strange," said Lee that evening. "But they're nothing like movie people."

"Aren't most movie people rich?" asked Bill.

"Grace says Malcolm is," said Fenny, "and she says Boyd is, too— or at least on his way. But I don't know about anyone else."

"And what about you?" Lee's voice was teasing. "You never did tell us how much you're making on this movie."

Fenny's face colored; Sig and Wally had always taught her it was rude to talk about one's income. "More than I make running Sig's Place and the Bait & Camp."

Lee laughed. "Oh, come on, Fenny, tell us."

"I'll tell you if you tell me how much you make a year from all your O'Leary Exports stocks."

"All right," said Lee, conceding defeat. "Case closed."

Sitting on a bench swing that hung from a sturdy branch of an elm tree in the garden Lee had cultivated in Arvid Nelson's backyard, they were taking a break from hunting down any late-season raspberries.

Mr. Nelson, in his prime, had been quite a gardener himself, but now, in his nineties, was bedridden. He rented Lee the huge garden plot in his backyard for the sum of five dollars per year plus all the fresh produce she cared to give him. Lee often had to work on the garden in the late afternoon or early evening, after the cafe was closed, and he would direct his nurse to push his hospital bed up to the window so he could watch and garden vicariously through Lee. Occasionally Lee would make late-night visits to the garden, and this was fine with Mr. Nelson; his sleep was deep and sound, and Lee could have used a backhoe and still not disturbed him. On this evening, she had enlisted Fenny and Bill to help her in her berry mission.

It was dark, and the flashlight Lee had used to look through the dried-up bushes was turned off. Crickets were hiccuping their tuneful chant and wood smoke from a neighbor's barbecue pit lolled around the air, tangy and sweet.

"Any more?" asked Fenny, who had been given three berries.

"Sorry," said Lee. "You get a pretty meager harvest this time of year."

The swing creaked as they moved back and forth.

"I've got some candy," offered Bill.

"You've always got candy," said Fenny.

"I know." Bill reached into his jacket pocket. "And I hope I always will."

He handed Lee and Fenny each a Hershey's Kiss.

"Those raspberries were good, Lee—the few I had—but if you ask me, there's nothing like a piece of candy." He pulled the little paper flag, loosening the foil. "Every piece is like a little present."

"Because they're so sweet?" Lee enjoyed hearing a grown man expound on the glories of candy.

"Well," said Bill, "that's part of it. But mostly it's because you get to unwrap it."

"You get to unwrap fruit," said Fenny. "Well, some. Like bananas or oranges."

"Yeah, but peels and skins aren't *wrapping*. They're not gold or silver or sparkly." He dug into his pocket—a veritable holding bin of candy—and took out a handful of assorted candies. "My favorite wrapping was for Bonomo's Turkish Taffy. Remember that? It was a rectangle of hard taffy you'd hold in the palm of your hand and then

slap it on a tabletop or a sidewalk—*whap!*—remember?" Both
Fenny and Lee smiled at the enthusiasm in his voice. "Then you
opened up the wrapping and it was silver on the inside, shiny as a
mirror, and holding all those broken bits of taffy." He sighed at the
memory and dropped a miniature box of Milk Duds in Lee's hand,
and a piece of hard butterscotch into Fenny's.

"Mine's just a box," said Lee. "It's not wrapped."

"The box is the wrapping," said Fenny. "It's like when you get a
sweater for Christmas and it's just wrapped in the department store
box—it's still something you get to open, right, Bill?"

"You catch on quick."

Smiling, Fenny pulled at the twisted ends of the yellow cello-
phane containing her butterscotch disk. "So, Bill, you think that if
candy wasn't all wrapped up, people wouldn't like it as much?"

"Well, let me ask you this: If there were a bowl of these"—he
held up a Hershey's Kiss—"and a bowl of circus peanuts, which
ones would you pick?"

"Circus peanuts," said Lee. "You mean those orange marsh-
mallow things?" At Bill's nod, she added, "Oh, I hate those things."

Fenny laughed.

"If you didn't, though," said Bill, serious about his research even
though his subjects were not, "if you liked them equally, which
would you pick?"

"Actually, I do like circus peanuts," said Fenny, leaning forward
to talk to Lee. "But you can only eat a few of them before they make
you sick. So I'd have to say I'd go for the Kisses."

"Okay, then," said Bill. "I've proved my point."

He hadn't, but neither Fenny nor Lee minded. They were just
happy to sit in a swing in a backyard garden on a balmy autumn
night, pressed against Big Bill. They swung back and forth,
watching the moon and smelling the last valiant fall flowers—the
asters and mums and marigolds—that hadn't yet retreated back into
the earth.

"Fenny," said Lee, getting back to their earlier conversation, "if
you need any financial guidance, I can help, or Heine. Or maybe
you should ask Frau Katte; she knows a lot about the stock market."
Lee shifted her position as if she were uncomfortable, but what she

146 • Lorna Landvik

really wanted was to press herself closer to Bill. "You could talk to her, too, Bill."

"Me?" said Bill with a laugh. "What for?"

"Don't tell me you're the kind of guy who keeps all his money in the bank."

"Lee, you're making the assumption that I have money to *put* in a bank."

"And you don't?"

Bill laughed again. "Don't sound so shocked. It's not that uncommon a thing." He pushed the ground with his legs, giving the swing more momentum.

"Well, I know that, I just meant—"

"Don't you bank any of your checks from the Bait & Camp?" asked Fenny.

Bill shook his head. "I just cash them."

"What do you spend them on, then?" asked Fenny, knowing it really wasn't any of her business but sensing that Bill didn't mind talking about it.

"Well, I keep my candy stash current . . . I pay a little to Mae for letting me squat on her land . . . and I send a little home to my mother."

"But don't you worry?" asked Lee. "Don't you worry about not having any money for a rainy day?"

"Umbrellas don't cost that much."

"Oh, Bill." Lee had always had a cushion of money (in her case, it was more like the whole couch) to support any present or future fall she might take; it worried her that Bill did not and, too, that he didn't seem to care that he did not. "What if something happened to you and you needed to be taken care of?"

"Then I'd hope those who loved me would line up for the job."

Fenny pressed her thigh against his, a signal that she'd be willing to line up for *something*.

She herself had been putting money into a savings account for years; first as a girl who importantly carried red-and-white bank deposit envelopes to school on "bank day," then as an employee of her parents' shops, and then as a benefactee of her parents' estate and an insurance settlement. She didn't save with an eye to the future as much as she saved because she wasn't a big spender. She would rather do most anything than shop.

"Well, Bill," Lee said, "don't you think that's a pretty juvenile attitude to have? Don't you think it would be wise to plan ahead a little?"

The dry leaves of the elm whispered as a breeze ruffled through them.

"I don't know," said Bill, his voice quiet, reasoned. "To me, planning seems to get in the way of living."

The swing jerked as Lee scrambled off it.

"Oh, Bill!" She stood facing him, her hands on her hips. "That sounds like the philosophy of a teenage boy with a six-pack and a borrowed car!"

Bill chuckled. "Get back in the swing, Lee, we're unbalanced."

"I'll say," said Lee, but she sat back down and they resumed their swinging, looking beyond the garden to the moon floating just above the weather vane perched on Arvid Nelson's garage roof.

"I don't know," said Lee, trying for neutral ground. "I know I would worry if I didn't make *some* plans."

"I do make *some* plans," said Bill. "I plan to be awake in the day and asleep in the night."

"Come on—that's leaving everything to chance; that's taking no responsibility for anything at all!"

"Okay, I oversimplify. But what, really, is the point of making plans when the ones we make are so often undone?"

Lee opened her mouth to speak, but Bill forged on.

"Take you, for example, Lee. You planned to live happily ever after with that husband Mitch of yours—"

"Marsh."

"And look what happened. You planned to live a certain life and here you are, flipping pancakes up in the North Woods."

Lee thought about this for a moment. "Yes, but once my plans changed, I had the financial wherewithal to make those changes. And that's all I'm saying, Bill; you need to be prepared for when your plans do change."

"Lee, if you don't make plans, how can you tell if they change? You just take what comes down your path, and if you don't like it, you cross to the other side. Like my Aunt Mae says, 'The Great Spirit will provide.' I guess it's up to the person to decide if what's provided is enough."

Lee sighed. A part of what Bill said made sense to her, but in large part she found his philosophy naive and . . . unsettling. While she knew money was no magic elixir, it certainly did make a lot of things easier.

But that's okay, she thought, suddenly struck by a revelation. That's why we'd be so good together. He'll provide the ride on the trapeze and I'll provide the safety net. It was the perfect balance. She was almost gleeful, and wanted to share this insight with Fenny, but instead she leaned forward and remarked upon her friend's quietness.

Fenny smiled. She had been paying some attention to their debate, but not as much as she had been paying to Mr. Nelson's compost heap.

"Look," she whispered, pointing to the racoon who was methodically picking its way through the garbage, tossing aside an apple core for a half-eaten cob of corn.

The animal suddenly sensed its audience and, turning toward them, his eyes shiny gold pieces, he stood straight up, then jumped over the railed fence and onto a garbage can, knocking its lid off.

A light switched on in the house and then, through an upstairs window, Arvid Nelson's nurse leaned out and told the yard's occupants that gardening hours were over and why didn't they go home before they woke up the whole block.

They tumbled out of the swing and, following the swath of light Lee's flashlight cut through the darkness, they raced out of Mr. Nelson's backyard, giggling and pushing one another like kids running from the neighborhood witch.

Malcolm Edgely awoke in his suite at the Northlands Inn before his wake-up call. Getting out of bed was not his favorite part of the day, and when he was working, he ordered his production assistants to supplement his wake-up calls by knocking at his door every five minutes until he personally answered the door to snarl, "I'm up already, I'm up!"

He stretched and wiggled his toes and realized he was smiling, inciting an even bigger smile, because smiling was seldom on Malcolm Edgely's morning agenda.

Belting his silk robe around him, he smiled again, this time over what good shape he was in; there were no extra inches of flab gathering at his waist, no potbelly, no love handles. He pulled the heavy drapes open and saw the last of night fading out of the sky. Dawn was beginning to rise like a pink fog.

He ordered a big breakfast from room service, and when it was brought up, he gave the waiter a twenty percent tip. This was momentous; it was hard to squeeze ten percent out of the director. But Malcolm was feeling good—better than he had felt in years.

All night long he had dreamed vividly of his mother and father and their small house in Winnipeg; he dreamed of his sister Jean, the French director Anatole Baccarult, the actor Don Tolle—people who'd been important to him, all people who were now dead. He wasn't the type to put much stock in his dreams, but these were so real, so full of life, and each person he dreamed of seemed to impart the message that they loved him, loved the essential Malcolm, the person underneath years of pain and bitterness.

The prospect of another day of work heartened him, too. *Ike and Inga* didn't fit any particular genre, and Malcolm was a man who liked strictly defined genres. He had decided it was an action/romantic comedy/period piece. *Whatever* it was he was directing, the daily rushes (which he let only himself, his first a.d., and the projectionist see) were *good*. Finally he was seeing in Fenny Ness what Harry Freed had called "star quality, Malcolm, good old-fashioned star quality." There was something honest in her face, a directness. She could say one of Christian's occasionally over-the-top lines and yet you believed her, couldn't turn away from her and the truth of her performance. The cowpoke was benefiting from her company, too; day by day he could see Boyd's hammy gestures quieting, his fight for the camera's attention fading.

Malcolm hadn't known what had happened yesterday, but when Boyd and Fenny returned to the set, Boyd did a wonderful scene in which he let his vulnerability, so often encased in the protective crust of leading-man machismo, finally show.

Lingering over his pot of tea, Malcolm answered his wake-up call with a cheery "Good morning," and when a p.a. knocked on his door, he opened it and smiled, causing David, for one brief moment, to think he'd knocked on the wrong door.

His driver, too, did a double take in the rearview mirror when Malcolm got into the backseat and said, "Good morning, Ed, how are you?"

Malcolm had never inquired as to Ed's health; the question surprised Ed so much that he didn't respond by rote but gave it thoughtful measure and then answered that, all in all, he was fine, but he had this pain in his lower back that was bothering him.

"I'll send my masseur 'round to see you," said Malcolm. "He can take kinks out better than a hot iron."

Ed gripped the steering wheel and told himself to keep his eyes on the road and concentrate. He was used to chauffeuring the old Mr. Edgely; this Mr. Edgely made him nervous.

Sitting back in his seat, Malcolm looked out at the evergreens poking up into a big blue sky, rolled down his window a couple inches, and inhaled, smelling the lake and river and the early tang of approaching autumn. He was surprised that the depth of his happiness hadn't lessened; it felt as if he had been driving endlessly through a tunnel and at last had exploded into the light of day.

Twenty-five years ago, Malcolm had been nominated for a Directors Guild award for his direction of *Summit's Pass*. He was thirty years old and thought that he had as much to do with the earth moving as the moon or the sun. He had shot the movie in Wales with a British and American cast and had fallen in love with Donald Tolle, the son of a Blackpool pub owner and the picture's second lead. It was a reciprocated love and it was the happiest summer of Malcolm's life. Don was not jealous of the time and demands made on the director; rather, he was stimulated by them, and the two men would stay up late at night, talking over shots and rewriting dialogue and debating whether to use a classical or contemporary score. When they realized their wake-up call was only a few hours away, they would go to bed, and more than once Malcolm wept from the joy of it.

Summit's Pass was the story of James Summit, a British spy and superhero who saved the free world from a terrorist plot to assassinate all NATO leaders.

The movie still held up and was a popular video rental, but Malcolm couldn't watch it. *Summit's Pass* was his best movie, honored around the world, but Don Tolle was in nineteen scenes and Malcolm couldn't bear to see him.

After *Summit's Pass* wrapped, the two men vacationed in southern Italy. Malcolm, on the way to town to buy groceries, would often slip into the tiny church and sit among the old women dressed in black, who always smiled and nodded at him, as if they were happy he was among them. Kneeling, Malcolm would squeeze his eyes shut and thank God for Don. Frightened and repelled by his sexuality, he had spent years denying it; and when he had finally faced up to who he was, it seemed to him he had been given Donald as a reward. He was awed and humbled by his good fortune.

And then one evening, after he had been to Rome for the day to talk to an Italian producer about a joint venture, he came back to find the rented villa empty.

There was a note, scrawled on the back of an airmail envelope, and it read, "Sorry, Malcolm, I had to go back to her."

Turning the envelope over, Malcolm read the return address of a Mrs Donald Tolle of Clapham Common, London. He held the envelope to his nose as if it were a tissue and inhaled. It may have been the last thing Don had touched, and Malcolm struggled to breathe in his scent.

The director threw himself into affairs and one-night stands, but no one made him forget Don, which turned his anger and rejection into something even bigger, turned it into a poison. He hated Don for his cowardice (how many times had he sworn he was leaving his wife?), for going back to a life that, while easier, was still a lie.

But today, in this rare *fine* mood, Malcolm could even think of Don fondly, with gratitude. Life seemed at once so big and full and beautiful that Malcolm wondered, half seriously, if there was something in the water. He bounded up the steps of the old school where the day's shooting was scheduled and called to Bonnie Price, the script supervisor, and told her how pleased he was with her work and had she just cut her hair?—it was very stylish, very stylish indeed.

When Malcolm entered the schoolroom, all talk and laughter ceased. The director walked down the center aisle, his hand trailing over the desktops that sported inkwells and sat on iron-scrolled legs.

He noticed the bucket filled with coal near the old black stove and the teacher's podium in front of the dusty blackboard.

He flipped through the pages of the old *McGuffey Reader* that sat on the teacher's podium and then looked at his crew the way a minister looks out at his congregation.

"Excellent job," he said when his eyes found the set decorator. "Really excellent."

Tears jumped into the set decorator's eyes—she had been expecting a tirade and not a compliment. She blinked hard and smiled. "Thanks, Malcolm," she said, and because she didn't know what else to say, she turned to the coat hook and began rehanging jackets.

David the p.a. ventured forth with a cup of coffee, and Malcolm regarded him with a smile. He was a tall and earnest-looking young man whose thinning, curly hair would soon be swirling down shower drains. The director wondered if the p.a. was gay; it was so hard telling these days—straight men seemed gayer and gay men seemed straighter.

"Good morning, sir," said David, handing Malcolm the coffee. "You seem to be in a good mood today, if you don't mind me saying so."

"Don't mind at all," said Malcolm, lifting up the plastic lid and blowing on the coffee. "I'm feeling awfully good today."

"Great," said the p.a. He smiled broadly and turned to attend to his many tasks.

"By the way," said Malcolm, "I've really been impressed by your work on this picture. When it wraps, I'd be happy to provide you with any kind of reference."

"Thanks," said David. "Thanks a lot." He looked at his watch. "Well, I guess I'd better get the Talent."

"By all means."

Like a politician, Malcolm moved around the room, joking with the same men and women he'd treated like serfs a day ago.

"Be prepared," said David to Fenny as she came out of the makeup trailer.

"For what?" She opened her mouth and wiggled her jaw, hating the heavy feel of the pancake makeup on her face.

"For a new Malcolm."

"Oh, no," groaned Fenny.

"No, I mean new and improved. The guy's a new man—polite, friendly."

She stopped by the catering truck and ordered coffee. "Polite and friendly?"

"See for yourself—it might not last long."

When Fenny climbed the schoolhouse steps, Malcolm was standing in the door's threshold and he extended his arms toward her. She had no choice (there was no room to sidestep him) than to accept his hug.

"Fenny, I've been remiss in not telling you what a wonderful job you've been doing. I couldn't imagine a better Inga."

"Thank you," said Fenny, pushing herself away so that she could breathe. "That's awfully nice of you to say."

"Yes, well, I think I'll focus on the nice for a while," he said, "seeing as how I could be accused of overworking the awful."

"You could," agreed Fenny.

In the first scene to be shot, Ike and Inga, before anyone else had arrived for the town meeting, were trying to convince Miss Owens, the schoolmarm, to help them organize a dance to bring together the town's warring factions.

It was going well; the actress who had been hired as Miss Owens played the role with a good mixture of flintiness and dedication. They got the shot in three takes, all of which Malcolm claimed were "excellent."

Lunch was long and served outside. Malcolm circulated among the long tables, chatting with the best boy, asking the gaffer where he got his jacket, inquiring as to the least toxic lawn care products with the greensman. In one lunch break, Malcolm talked to more people than he had during the whole shoot. If someone had taken him aside and asked him why, he would have been hard-pressed to answer. For some reason a light had been switched on and he was interested, interested and curious in all these people who were helping him to make his best movie in years.

"Mr. Edgely, where do you want the extras?"

Malcolm looked up at the extras coordinator, surprised.

"They're here already?"

The coordinator nodded, pointing. Malcolm followed the direction of her finger and saw two buses disgorging dozens of pioneers, lumberjacks, and fur traders. He looked at the Rolex watch a producer had given him.

"Lord, time flies. Well, I suppose it's back to the grindstone."

The extras had spent the morning in the gymnasium of the high school, the men separated from the women by a partition as they changed into wool britches with suspenders, wide-sleeved collarless shirts, calico dresses, and shawls.

"Oh, Miss, you're just a prairie flower," said Frau Katte.

Miss Penk, her condominium of hair brushed down and into a gingham bonnet, was not so sure.

"Why don't they let me show my hair, Katte? You know how I feel about my hair."

"They covered mine up, too," complained Lee, tugging at her skirt waistband, which was about an inch shy of the comfort zone. "I look like an Amish reject."

Mary Gore, facing one of the mirrors that leaned against the wall, sighed at her reflection. "Calico," she said. "Who looks good in calico?"

In the men's area, Heine was delighted over his transformation. He looked just like an old tintype of his grandfather, standing in front of the family farmstead.

The mayor, too, was pleased with his costume, especially the wide-brimmed felt hat, which he felt gave him a certain élan.

Big Bill had supplemented his generic turn-of-the-century-man costume with a vest Mae Little Feather had made ("If they don't let you go as an Indian in the movie, at least give me a little free advertising"), a vest the costumer wanted to buy from him then and there.

"A hundred bucks," she offered.

"I'll tell you what," said Bill. "You go down to a place called Sig's Place on Main Street and you can get yourself one for half the price."

Giggles rippled through the groups as the extras coordinator and a few p.a.'s herded the extras and under-fives (actors hired out of Minneapolis who had a few lines). This was it; they were going to be in a movie.

Malcolm sat near the blackboard; the scene would be filmed in three shots. In the first, the cameras would face the crowd as they debated whether or not to allow a community dance.

He rose when everyone was in the room, smiley as an emcee.

"I zought he was supposed to be an old crab," whispered Frau Katte.

"He was," said a p.a., overhearing. "Until today."

"Welcome, people," said Malcolm. "It's a pleasure to have you on the set today."

"Why, he's as cordial as all get-out," said Miss Penk.

"Reminds me of my cousin Selmer, the undertaker," whispered Heine.

"This is what's going to happen," said Malcolm. "You are a group of townspeople who have been brought to a meeting to debate the merits of a dance. Some of you"—he gestured to a trio of women to his left—"like the idea, and some of you"—he pointed at the mayor and Heine—"do not. In the first take, I want you to react freely to what Ike"—he nodded at Boyd, and then toward Fenny—"or Inga says."

There was a smattering of applause from Fenny's friends. She shook her head at them, furiously.

"I couldn't agree with you more," said Malcolm, and he turned toward Fenny. "In fact, I think all of us deserve a big round of applause."

There was a moment's silence and then everyone clapped, first tentatively, then with great vigor.

Malcolm laughed, holding up his hands.

"People, people, let's reserve our energy for the shoot. Now, if the first take doesn't go well, don't worry about it, we'll do it again with more definite assignments. And remember—I want animation and conviction, and wait until you hear the word 'action.'"

The clapper marked the scene.

Sound and cameras began rolling, and Malcolm called out the word that had begun to thrill him again.

"Action!"

Boyd as Ike stepped to the podium.

"Friends, neighbors, I'm not here to cause problems."

"The heck you're not," called back one of the under-five actors.

"Yeah," shouted a few extras, and Malcolm nodded at the quick studies.

The scene progressed well; there was a good balance of dissent and favor, and Boyd's monologue had a nice crescendo to it.

Fenny stood to the side; she was trying to look properly supportive and, except for sneaking the occasional surreptitious look at Bill, who stood against the back wall, she did.

The cries of the crowd rose as Boyd finished his speech and Malcolm thought they just might have gotten it on the first take and he felt a rush of adrenaline fill him—how he loved this!—but as he stood to call *Cut!* the rush of adrenaline became something else, became a pain like an elephant jumping on his chest, the pain of a madman holding his heart and squeezing it with all his might, the pain of the thing that felled his father and his father's father: a myocardial infarction.

He gasped for air that wasn't there, and as he fell toward the floor, he looked toward the crowd in astonishment, looked at a few dozen pioneers and fur traders and in the back behind them all, he smiled at the old Italian women dressed in black, who nodded and smiled back at him.

Chapter 13

"Who *but* me?" asked Christian Freed, his voice rising to an octave more familiar to a Vienna Boys Choir soloist. "Who knows this story the way I do? I'm its *creator*, for chrissakes."

He didn't pace the floor of the hotel room so much as he spun across it like a whirling dervish.

Rather than risk getting a headache watching him, Harry, who had flown in as soon as he was given the news of Malcolm's demise, chose to fill a piece of hotel stationery with doodles of international flags. He could draw the flags of fifty-eight nations, but countries changed their borders so fast now, for the life of him, he couldn't remember if Hungary was still Hungary or part of a republic. If it was still Hungary, he couldn't remember its flag, so he made up his own—a silhouette of the Gabor sisters.

"Well?" said Christian, his voice shrill. "Well?"

Harry finished the tip of Zsa Zsa's nose. "Well, what?"

"*Uncle Harry.*"

Harry sighed and put down his pen. Looking up at the pinched white face that was his nephew's, he filled his lungs and released a sigh.

"So . . . ," he said, pulling at the skin below his eye. "So you think you could direct this picture?"

Christian nodded so fast, his teeth rattled.

"You *know* I could, Uncle Harry—all I need is a chance, all I've ever needed is—"

Harry held up his hand like a traffic cop. He did not need to hear his nephew grovel on top of everything else.

"Let me think for a minute," he said quietly. He rested his head in his open palm and closed his eyes.

Christian *did* know the story better than anyone; that was in his favor. What wasn't was his lack of any directorial experience, his lack of people skills, his lack of leadership . . . there were so many lacks, Harry didn't see how he could give Christian the go-ahead. It would be like handing the reins of a bucking bronco over to someone who had never even ridden a pony.

"There are plenty of directors I could call on," he began.

"I know that, Uncle Harry, but—"

"Don't interrupt me, Christian," said Harry, causing his nephew to press his lips together and sit down on the bed.

"I could pick up the phone right now and call Marc Chess or Keith Watkins or Lucy Donavan—"

"Lucy Donavan? She couldn't direct her way out of—"

"*I'm* talking, Christian."

Christian made a zipping gesture across his mouth.

"I just don't know if you're up to inspiring the troops, Christian—"

"Well, Malcolm sure wasn't! He was a bear to work with until his last day, when suddenly he shows up wearing this happy face—"

"This is a test, Christian. If you lack the self-control to let me finish a sentence, then it's pretty obvious you lack the self-control to take charge of a motion picture."

Christian zipped his mouth again, and mimed turning a lock and throwing away the key.

"Now, I realize you're my nephew, Christian, and blood is thicker than water, but sometimes blood isn't *better* than water."

Christian's eyes bulged with the desire to say something.

"Now, obviously I believe nepotism has its place—after all, it's gotten you this far—but is its place at the helm of a Hollywood motion picture?"

Christian squirmed, his eyes bulging even more. He waved his hand like a child seeking permission to go to the bathroom.

Harry went on as if he didn't notice. "Admittedly, Malcolm wasn't the easiest guy to work with, but at least he had *worked*; he had the experience, he knew what goes into making a picture, and that sort of confidence goes a long way in—"

Christian was now waving his arm like a beauty queen trying to acknowledge everyone on the parade route.

"All *right*," Harry said, annoyed. "So what do you have to say for yourself?"

The rational case Christian was ready to make for himself was forgotten. Instead, he begged.

"Oh, please, Uncle Harry," he said, clenching his hands. "Oh, please, please, please, give me a chance."

Harry looked down at his flags of all nations, pleased at his interpretation of Hungary's. On one hand, directing a picture was a big deal; on the other hand, it wasn't brain surgery. Wasn't even knee surgery, Harry thought; not even cyst removal. It wasn't as if Christian wouldn't have a lot of help. The assistant directors certainly knew what they were doing; the crew was able, the cast was good . . . and thank God, there was always the editor to solve a multitude of problems. He doodled some more, enjoying for a few more moments letting his nephew squirm, and then he put down his pencil and in a weary voice said, "Okay, Chris, let's see what you can do."

Christian jumped at his uncle, practically knocking him down in a hug.

"Can I tell everybody? They're all down in the bar."

"Why not?" said Harry. "And tell them not to get too snockered. We've got a lot of work to do."

Malcolm's agent, who had made the trip to Tall Pine with Harry, insisting that it was "no prob," would accompany Malcolm's body back to Canada, where he was to be buried in the family plot.

When Harry offered to join him, the agent had brushed the lapels of his Armani suit and asked, "Why? I mean, why bother? Everyone knows what a prick Malcolm was—I'm only here because he made a lot of money for us, and besides, I get a bonus—sort of a 'service beyond the call of duty' thing."

Harry had felt a deep swell of pity for the friendless, bitter man who had been Malcolm, whose own agent was accompanying his body to its final resting place only because a cash bonus was involved.

"Well, I'll see you at the memorial service, then," said Harry.

"Ha!" barked the agent. "If the Guild even decides to have one!"

Harry felt even sadder when he heard of Malcolm's drastic personality switch; it seemed unfair that the one day Malcolm chose to be kind and supportive and interested in his fellow human beings was the day he kicked the bucket. Did he have some sense, Harry wondered, some holy voice whispering in his ear, advising him to rack up some brownie points while he still could? Harry was at the age where death was more a close-up than a long shot; he thought about it more, worried more about things like his fat intake, his prostate, and the consistency of his arteries.

After Christian left his room, Harry sat staring at his flag doodles, thinking of Malcolm.

"I hope you're happier in heaven than you were on earth," he said quietly, and then he added a P.S.: "I hope you made it there."

The cast and crew dealt with Malcolm's loss by drinking at the Wild Wolf Lounge at the Northlands Inn. They weren't a bereft crowd as much as they were a confused one; what was going to happen to *Ike and Inga*? When they heard the news that Christian would be taking over as director, their partying continued; again, not so much in celebration, but as a way to further numb themselves in the face of unbelievable events.

Fenny knew wakes could be raucous occasions (Lutherans had hushed and solemn "visitations"), and the improvised gathering held for Malcolm (she was unsure if it qualified for a wake if his body wasn't present) was certainly that. The large majority of the group was plastered and, while Fenny was willing to drink to Malcolm's memory, she felt it was disrespectful to drink to inebriation.

"I'll bet Sheriff Gibbs'll be called in pretty soon," said Fenny, who had fled the bacchanalia at the Wild Wolf for the calm of the Cup O'Delight. "When I left, Grace Aisles was trying to get up a topless conga line."

"As mayor, I should go down there and check that out," said the mayor.

Heine nodded. "I'll be happy to assist you."

"I bet you would," said Lee, laughing.

"It doesn't sound like they're exactly mourning that Malcolm guy," said Slim.

"I think everyone feels bad that he died," said Fenny, "but they're not exactly going to miss him."

"I'll never forget the feeling of blowing air into a dead man," said Mary Gore, for the fifth or sixth time. (She and Big Bill had been the ones who performed CPR on Malcolm after he collapsed, and she would go home that night and pen a three-page poem, "Blowing Air into a Dead Man.") "At the beginning, I felt maybe we had a chance to revive him, but after a few minutes, I could tell it was for naught. I could actually feel a change in temperature."

Bill nodded. "It was weird. With every compression, I could feel his life slipping away under my hands. It was like trying to hold on to vapor."

"Poor guy," said the mayor. "I heard he was only fifty-five."

"So young," agreed Miss Penk.

"You just never know," said Frau Katte.

"Got to live for today is what you've got to do," said the mayor.

With a sigh, Big Bill rose and walked slowly to the piano. Lee and Fenny watched him closely.

Frau Katte nudged Miss Penk.

"Zere both like dogs," she whispered, "following zere master's every step."

Bill played a glissando and then launched into "O, Canada."

Most everyone in the Cup O'Delight knew the lyrics, having heard the anthem played before countless hockey games, and they joined in. It was as perfect and fitting and solemn as a hymn. Tears slid down Fenny's cheeks, and she was not the only one crying. Of course, she thought briefly, maybe it was easier to cry for a man like Malcolm if you *didn't* know him. Either way, she was grateful to Bill for the emotion his music inspired; everybody, even Malcolm, should have tears falling on the day of their death.

At the Wild Wolf Lounge, Christian's announcement of his appointment as director hadn't gone over as well as he would have liked; of course, everyone was either drunk or unconscious, so what did he expect?

Once he found out where Fenny had gone, he went to the Cup O'Delight, hoping to get a better reaction from his leading lady. He wasn't happy to see the usual suspects there, but at least they were sober and not doing the limbo with a mop purloined from the housekeeping closet.

As the big Indian played the piano, the barking busboy and the fat waitress sang. Christian had to admit that, for such an odd-looking crew, they sounded pretty good. The two old dykes were dancing with the two old guys, and the certifiable "poetress" was swaying by herself like an unpopular Deadhead.

Fenny was busy writing something at the counter and didn't notice Christian until he sat next to her.

"Writing yourself more lines?" he asked.

"Christian!" she said, surprised. "What are you doing here?"

"I just had a meeting with Harry," he said. "I'm *Ike and Inga's* new director."

Fenny flinched, as if she'd just received a small electrical shock.

"You're *Ike and Inga's* new director?"

Christian nodded. "It's what I've always wanted to do. Like Uncle Harry says, the director is king. Well, actually he says the producer is king, but I think he's wrong about that. Tomorrow I'm going to powwow—oops," he said, looking in Big Bill's direction, "I'm going to *brainstorm* with Harry and we'll pick up shooting on Monday . . . right where we left off."

Fenny nodded, taking in the news. She supposed it wasn't so surprising that Harry Freed had entrusted his nephew with the direction of a motion picture—he had, after all, entrusted her with a starring role.

"So what are you writing?" asked Christian after Fenny failed to speak.

"What?" She looked down at the unfolded napkin. "Oh. I was . . . I was trying to write about Malcolm. You know, like a eulogy. I wanted to somehow pay tribute to him. It didn't seem like he got . . . much tribute."

"Can I read it?" asked Christian, picking up the napkin.

"Malcolm was a director," read Christian. "His last picture was *Ike and Inga.*"

He and Fenny sat for a moment, both of them staring at the metallic red disks on the wall.

"Beautiful," said Christian finally. "Who could ask for a more touching tribute?"

Fenny laughed. It wasn't the best joke, but it was the first time she could remember Christian making one.

"I didn't have the easiest subject," she said, and then both she and Christian swiveled around on their stools to listen to Bill wail on the piano as Slim and Lee sang "Tutti Frutti."

"What a day," said Fenny as she helped Lee bus the dishes left over from the Polka Night.

"You must be exhausted." Lee covered up half a rhubarb pie with plastic wrap. "Why don't you go home, Fenny, get some rest? I've got plenty of helpers here."

Fenny and Big Bill exchanged a meaningful look. They had an understanding that this night was as good as any to tell Lee about their relationship, or at least the start of their relationship.

"You're going to need a lot of rest," said Slim, placing cups in the bus tub. "Working with that Christian guy."

"He wasn't so bad tonight," said Fenny.

"He's scared out of his mind," said Bill.

When the wall phone rang, Fenny wondered, What next? Had all the revelers at the Wild Wolf Lounge been thrown in the pokey and were now soliciting bail?

Lee answered the phone, and it took only seconds before the color drained from her face. Fenny knew immediately who it was.

"Just stop it!" Lee yelled into the phone. "Stop it right now!"

Slim pushed aside the bus tub. He grabbed the receiver from Lee and in a voice unsettling in its cold calm, he said, "Listen, you bastard, you're the one who'll be a dead man if you call here again." Then he hung up the phone and put his arms around Lee.

"What?" said Bill, standing, the broom in his hands. "What's going on? Who was that?"

Lee disentangled herself from Slim's arms and adjusted a bobby pin that had loosened from her coronet braids.

"That," she said, "was my ex-husband."

"The bastard," added Slim.

"What did he say?" asked Bill. "Why is he a bastard?"

Lee straightened menus in their holder. "Wouldn't you call a person who threatens to kill you a bastard?"

Fenny felt her heart race. "Is that what he just did?"

"That's what he always does," Lee said. "That is, when he's not asking me to remarry him."

"Then you've got to do something, Lee," Bill said. "Get a restraining order out, notify the police, find a—"

"Bill," said Lee—and Fenny couldn't help but hear the tenderness in her friend's voice—"I'm all right. Marsh is in Chicago. He does this all the time—it never amounts to anything. It's just . . . bothersome."

"Bothersome?" said Bill. "Threatening your life is more than bothersome."

Slim lifted his fists and, imitating the *Wizard of Oz*'s Cowardly Lion, said, "Then I'll threaten him right back. Roar! Roar, I say, roar! Let him come here—I'll pulverize him!"

His impersonation was so good and his audience so wiped out from the events of the day that they couldn't help but surrender to laughter, which only egged on Slim more, impersonating everyone from Dorothy to the Wicked Witch, and as they watched Slim "melt" to the floor, it seemed to Fenny that the opportunity to make a confession about her burgeoning love life had passed.

Fenny expected there to be excitement on the set because of the personnel change, but she was surprised at its degree.

"What's up?" she asked David the p.a. as everyone bustled around, saying things like "How do I look?" and "Ten million viewers!"

" 'Today's Day' is here."

"Why?" said Fenny. "Because of Malcolm?"

David nodded. "They're doing a story on dead directors."

"Today's Day" was America's most watched and most prestigious morning show, and while the program prided itself on its hard-hitting journalism, it offered as much "soft" news as its competitors, but always cloaked (however loosely) around an important theme.

"Drew Hellinger died last week," he explained. "A spotlight fell on him."

"I worked with him once," said Doug Woo. "He had a big coke habit in the eighties."

"They're going to go for some superstition thing," said the p.a. "Watch—the segment will be called something like 'What's Haunting Hollywood?' "

"Or 'The Final Cut,' " offered Doug Woo. " 'Why Are Our Directors Dying?' Film at eleven."

The production secretary sidled up to Fenny and told her she was due in makeup.

"They're going to go with you right after Boyd."

"Go with me where?"

"Oh, Fenny, Marcy Mincus is interviewing you! You and Boyd!"

"But not me," pouted Christian.

"They got some tape of you standing by Malcolm's old director's chair," said Harry, who was planning to stick around for a day or two to make sure Christian could handle things.

"Some *tape*," huffed Christian. "Big deal. I'm the main character in this frickin' drama—I'm the one who's saved the day, the guy stepping in for the dead guy."

"That may well be," said Harry, humoring his nephew. "But you're just the writer/director, and that's not as sexy as the good-looking leads. Sex sells, Christian—even in the morning."

Fenny had the unnerving sensation of being the latest model to come off the assembly line. She was brushed, sprayed, powdered, and buffed before shoved onto the kitchen set, where, surrounded by lights, cameras, and a half circle of people, Boyd Burch was wrapping up his interview with the morning star of television, Marcy Mincus.

"Thanks for that revealing moment," she said as Boyd brushed aside a tear with a curled forefinger.

"Jeepers," whispered Fenny to Harry, "what happened to him?"

"Marcy Mincus is what happened," said Harry. "You be careful in there—she's a barracuda."

The former psychotherapist and current newswoman smiled at the camera. "After these messages, we'll be back with a young woman whose story blends chance, risk, and the opportunity for redemption—Hollywood style."

"Is she talking about me?" asked Fenny.

Harry nodded grimly. "Like I said, she's a barracuda. You watch out."

Marcy Mincus would never take *all* the credit for the incredible ratings jump of "Today's Day"; but she would take her share, which she figured was about eighty-five percent. She interviewed celebrities the way a psychotherapist would, bound and determined to find deep secrets and hidden angst. But now, as a newswoman, she had no obligation to try and help these people work through their pain and suffering; she merely exposed it for all to see. Nothing was as it seemed for Marcy Mincus; *everyone,* from the easygoing president's wife to a well-loved character actor, had some trauma she or he wanted to reveal. She was famous for making her guests cry or confess to a variety of sins, ranging from adultery to grand theft to a sex change (this offered up by a romance novelist dressed in ruffles and curls). Some savvy critics thought she ambushed her guests in tabloid-style reporting at its worst; everyone else was convinced of her legitimacy by her credentials, her use of clinical terms, and her near-genius-level IQ (which she managed to mention at least twice a week). To the viewing public, Marcy Mincus was Dr. Sigmund Freud, Barbara Walters, and Attila the Hun rolled into one. Her features were hard but her frosted blond hair luxurious, and her on-air wardrobe consisted of miniskirts and suit jackets worn without a blouse underneath so that she could expose a little décolletage and still appear businesslike.

Fenny was led over to the interviewer's circle and outfitted with a microphone, and as she sat down, Marcy Mincus patted her hand and said, "We're on a live satellite feed, the latest ratings tell us we've got over ten million viewers, but don't be nervous. Whatever's meant to come out will come out."

Fenny felt as if she were getting a warning disguised as reassurance, and she didn't like it one bit. In fact, Marcy Mincus reminded her of the kind of doctor who promised nothing would hurt before jabbing the patient with a foot-long needle.

The television show's floor manager counted down and then pointed to Marcy, whose smile switched on like Christmas lights.

"America, we're here with Fenny Ness, a young actress who until a few short weeks ago was digging worms for a bait shop—"

"Actually, I don't dig—" said Fenny, but Marcy hadn't stopped for any input and her words completely overrode Fenny's.

"What I'm sure America would like to know, Fenny, is what are the psychological ramifications of having your life so abruptly changed, first from going from small-town hick to Hollywood player, and secondly, of having the man who's been your tiller, your guide, to up and die on you?" Tilting her head, Marcy squinted her eyes, their color a contact-lens lime green.

"I don't think Malcolm up and died on *me*," said Fenny. "I mean, that's sort of a selfish way of looking at his tragic death, wouldn't you think?"

The look of concern on Marcy's face hardened.

"And as far as being a Hollywood player," said Fenny, "I don't think I am—since I don't really know what that is. And the same goes for 'small-town hick.' "

Marcy blinked several times. "You've never heard of a small-town hick?"

"I didn't say that," said Fenny. "I just don't know exactly what one is."

Marcy revealed her large white teeth; a smile, Fenny guessed.

"I would say a hick is someone . . . someone who's not in the action, not a part of the real world."

"That's right," said Fenny in a robotic voice. "I am not a part of the real world."

"I didn't—" sputtered Marcy, who would have stopped the tape if this hadn't been live. She did not appreciate being teased, if that's what was happening. "I understand," she said tersely, looking at the notes on her lap, trying to get back on track, "that your parents died in a terrible accident several years ago, leaving you with some major abandonment issues?"

Fenny felt as if the woman had punched her in the stomach, but instinctively she knew not to show it. Marcy Mincus was the type of woman Sig would have felt no compunction in booting out of her store, and Fenny was not about to dishonor the memory of her parents by succumbing to the woman's tactics.

"I'm sure you'll understand that some things are too deep to discuss in a three-minute interview," said Fenny quietly.

"Tell us how you felt when you heard the news that you were orphaned."

Fenny stared at the reporter as if she were daft and continued to stare until the seconds ticked uncomfortably by, silent seconds that were taboo on television.

The look of concern Marcy had arranged on her features was replaced by her joyless smile. "All right, then," she said brightly. "I guess you're not the sharing type. Can you at least tell America how a young girl, virtually untrained in the art of acting, landed a starring role in a major motion picture—well, I guess a Harry Freed production isn't exactly major. Anyway, I've been told that you were supposedly 'discovered' while working in your *deceased* father's bait shop, but was there something else that got you this part—something the public is unaware of?"

Anger consumed Fenny—here Marcy had managed to slur Harry and work in her father's death, again—but she was not going to step in any trap the newswoman so obviously laid. She would give away nothing, or at least nothing that Marcy Mincus wanted, so she looked at her hands and with an offhanded shrug said, "Well, I did poop in my pants."

There was more silence, more dead air—the one thing Marcy Mincus the broadcaster tried to avoid at all costs—and in those moments, Fenny realized that in trying to swat away the pest that Marcy Mincus was, she had stung herself; she had admitted on national TV that she had pooped in her pants. If a second more had passed, the tears that Marcy Mincus hunted would have come, but the interviewer thwarted her own mission by saying, "I don't really see the humor in that."

"Well, believe me, I didn't, either," said Fenny, who like a ventriloquist's dummy moved her mouth but had no idea where the words came from. "But it got me the job."

Over the laughter of some crew members, Marcy said, "So you decided the thing to do to win the leading female role in a major motion picture was to . . . as you say . . . poop in your pants?"

"I really didn't 'decide,' " said Fenny. "Those things just sort of happen. But I'm told whatever can distinguish you from the crowd . . ."

Beyond the bright lights and cameras, the crew cracked up.

"All right," said Marcy, and her jaw muscles clenched like little fists. She decided to move on to a topic that might throw the little smart-ass. "So what does your boyfriend think of this movie business?"

"I don't know," said Fenny cheerfully. "I don't have one to ask." She knew better than to reveal *anything* about herself.

"Oh," said Marcy, finally smelling blood. "You don't have anyone special to share this very special time with?"

"I have a lot of special people to share this very special time with," said Fenny, who by simply repeating Marcy's words made them sound completely silly. "Just not a boyfriend."

Twin spots of red emerged through Marcy's pancake makeup onto her cheeks. How had this interview gone so wrong? She'd had Boyd Burch blubbering about his emotionally distant father and his popcorn-popping granny in sixty seconds!

"Penny—uh, Fenny! I'm sure America's enjoyed your refreshing simplicity, but surely you've fought some battles to get where you are today: Anorexia? Bulimia? Drugs? Sexual abuse?"

After each suggestion, Fenny shook her head until Marcy Mincus, defeated, looked into the camera and said, "We all should be so lucky," and then, surprising everyone, the woman who had made dozens of people cry on live television began to cry on live television herself.

Not knowing what else to do, Fenny reached over to touch the newswoman's hand.

"Oh, no, no," said Marcy, flinging off Fenny's touch, "don't feel obliged to comfort me. Make a joke! Go ahead—you're young, you're beautiful, you have a major Hollywood career to look forward to—don't put yourself out for *me*."

"Go back to New York for the weather," hissed the director into his headset.

Someone hollered, "We're clear!" and then there was a swarm of people around Fenny and Marcy Mincus, most of whom hoisted up the bawling television interviewer (while smiling at Fenny or giving her the thumbs-up sign) and led her off the set.

It seemed to Fenny that she could not move; disbelief had frozen her.

The smell of Harry's spicy cologne provided enough neural

stimulation to enable her to turn her head. Harry was squatting next to her chair, glee smeared all over his face.

"You got her!" he whispered triumphantly. "You speared the barracuda!"

Only Boyd couldn't celebrate Fenny's triumph over Marcy Mincus; the leading man was too angry at "that she-dog making me come off like such a little baby," but that evening his agent called and told him she'd been fielding calls all day from producers and directors who said they'd seen a new depth and sensitivity in him and maybe a lunch date should be arranged to talk about some projects. She didn't tell him that eighty percent of the time they added things like, "And what about that Ness kid? Wow! She really socked it to old Marcy. You don't know who's representing her, do you?"

No, no sense spooning more onto Boyd's full plate of insecurities . . . but it wouldn't hurt her own interests to find out ASAP just who Fenny's agent was.

When Fenny reported to makeup the next day, a cup of coffee was delivered to her as well as a pile of newspapers.

"Harry wanted you to look at these," said David the p.a.

"Does he think I'm getting behind on current events?" she asked as she unfolded a front page.

Her picture loomed up at her from *USA Today*. Her picture also loomed up at her from the *Los Angeles Times*, the *New York Times*, and countless papers in between, with the exception of the *Tall Pine Register*, which only published weekly.

"So how do you like yourself splashed all over the newspapers?" asked Harry, hopping into the trailer as David stepped out.

Fenny, dumbfounded, had no response.

"I love what that guy in the *Times* says about Marcy Mincus finally getting the tables turned on her," said Harry, sitting in the makeup chair next to Fenny's, "and how about *USA Today*? 'The real "poop" is that Marcy Mincus finally got called on her guerrilla tactics.' " Harry laughed, shaking his head. "Beautiful. You couldn't buy better publicity."

"But Harry," whispered Fenny, "I told everyone I pooped in my pants!"

The producer slapped his knee. "I know, I know, I couldn't believe it. But you pulled it off! You told the truth and no one's ever going to believe it!" He cackled and Fenny wouldn't have been surprised if he got up and did a little jig.

Sharen, the makeup artist, came into the trailer and looked at the papers spread out on the counter in front of them.

"I did that bitch's makeup once for a *TV Guide* cover," she said. "She had me crying before I got to her eyebrows." Sharen put a towel around Fenny's neck. "That answer you gave her about how you got the movie . . . ," she said, shaking her head. She dipped a sponge into pancake foundation and dabbed color onto her cheek. "Priceless. You're my new hero."

"Oh, please," said Fenny, who was beginning to get a headache.

Harry cackled again. "And *Variety!* Did you see *Variety?*" He pulled the Hollywood trade paper out of the pile and began to read from it:

"For months this reporter has been uncomfortable with the way Marcy Mincus interrogates her interviewees, grilling them until they admit something that's nobody's business but their own. Well, yesterday morning Fenny Ness, a young, newly discovered actress, gave Ms. Mincus her confessional; a riotous, hilarious riff, patched together with wit and charm and wild tall tales, and puncturing, with the simple answer '*I pooped in my pants,*' all that is self-important and manipulative and grandiose about Ms. Mincus and the entertainment world itself."

Harry smacked the newspaper with the back of his hand. "You know what this is going to do, Fenny? This is going to sell tickets."

He said it the way a cheerleader predicts victory, and she smiled weakly, feeling both bemused and disloyal, just as she had in high school when she couldn't summon up paroxysms of enthusiasm over the big game.

Chapter 14

The circus came to Tall Pine, only instead of clowns and acrobats and lion tamers, there were television, radio, and newspaper reporters, photojournalists, camera crews, and magazine columnists. Everyone wanted to interview Fenny or anyone who knew her.

Wishing to avoid the camera crew parked out in front of her house, Fenny had spent the night at Lee's, and what her host lacked in tidiness, she made up for in hospitality. There was a thermos of O'Delight waiting for Fenny when she woke up.

The cafe was open on Sundays only in the summer, but there were so many people that Lee said she couldn't in good conscience turn them down. LaDonna Stewart from the talk show "LaDonna!" had eaten blueberry pancakes there this morning, sharing counter space with a reporter from *Folks* magazine. The turnover was so rapid that Bill had been pressed into service, taking orders for Lee and collecting dirty dishes for Slim.

Fenny browsed through the Sunday edition of the *Chicago Tribune* Lee still subscribed to. It was stuffed with more ads than the *Tall Pine Register* could print in a decade.

Finishing a cup of coffee, she leaned back in the pillowy softness of Lee's couch and looked idly at a column titled "People in the News." She cringed when she saw Marcy Mincus's picture. The accompanying blurb said that Ms. Mincus had checked herself into a treatment center, location undisclosed, after realizing she needed to give herself the kind of "personal attention" she had been giving to everyone else.

"Then I feel sorry for you," muttered Fenny.

The telephone rang and she answered it without thinking, even though she realized before she said hello that it was probably a reporter.

"Did you see the paper?" asked the caller.

"I was—"

"It's all your fault, bitch! None of this would have happened if it wasn't for you, you fat cow—"

"I beg your pardon—"

"Who is this? Lee?"

"No it's not, this is—"

"I don't care who *you* are, you just tell that pig Lee thanks a lot for everything."

Before Fenny could respond, the caller hung up and dead air filled her ears.

It didn't take much to figure out it was Marshall Stouffer calling, but why was he so upset about what was in the paper? Was there more about Tall Pine or the movie than she'd seen, or was the despicable Mr. Stouffer a devoted fan who didn't like any negative publicity about his idol, Marcy Mincus? But, Fenny wondered, what did Lee have to do with Marcy Mincus?

Curious, Fenny methodically paged through each section of the paper and struck gold in the business section.

"Clements and Hoffman Broker Accused of Fraud," read a small headline near the bottom of the page. The article claimed Marshall Stouffer, son of the late James Stouffer, former ambassador to Bolivia, was being investigated by the Securities and Exchange Commission on charges of customer fraud. The accompanying photograph showed a man oozing confidence, or arrogance. Fenny creased the newspaper and circled the article in ink, putting it on the coffee table where even amid the clutter Lee would be sure to see it.

She spent the weekend giving interviews. Whenever the "poop" issue came up, Fenny calmly admitted that, yes, she did indeed do the dirty deed, no pun intended. All the interviews were favorable; everyone thought she was a real card to keep up a joke like that and, too, all of them shared a special glee in seeing Marcy Mincus fall.

Within hours, Fenny's words and images would be broadcast over airwaves, printed in more magazines and newspapers, and the American public, who a week ago had no idea who or what a Fenny Ness was, began to feel they knew her and, more important, were glad they did.

By Monday, the media that had swooped in like hawks had swooped out, sated, and Fenny returned to what had become an entirely different workplace. Tension had been swept off the set as if by a brisk housekeeper. There was a giddiness that came from all the attention (usually the only kind of movie that got publicity while still in production was the big-stars, big-budget sort that no one working on *Ike and Inga* had ever been associated with), but mostly it was that "Malcolm the Terrible" had been replaced, even though by what could possibly turn out as "Christian the Even Worse."

"He's too small to be intimidating," Grace told Fenny in makeup. "He's like a chihuahua you can't take seriously because no way is his bite gonna hurt."

Christian was embarrassed to near tears on his first day as director; the shot had been set up, the actors posed, sound and camera rolled. Christian thought the cast was playing a trick on him—why were the actors just standing there? He felt himself edging closer to what his mother called one of his "hissy fits" until Doug Woo leaned toward him and whispered, "Maybe you'd like to say, 'Action.' "

"I knew that," he snapped. "I was just testing you. Action!" He felt his ears grow hot and he knew they were a bright red beacon, signaling his embarrassment to one and all. After he yelled, "Cut!" and rushed off the set mumbling something about getting something to drink, Doug Woo scolded the snickering cast and crew, reminding them, "This is the guy's first time up. Give him a break, huh?"

Harry, who had sat observing everything from a far corner of the set, nodded to himself, thinking this whole thing might be pulled off after all.

The others took Doug's plea as a call to armistice; why not try to get along and have some fun?

Fear improved Christian's personality (at least on the set), tapping a heretofore unknown reservoir of humility in him. As a writer, he thought he knew all the answers; as a director, he knew he didn't. He needed help, and he sought it. He listened, too—to Doug Woo, to Bonnie Price, to other crew members, even to his actors—and so, despite his occasional flare-ups, the making of *Ike and Inga* went from an ulcer-inducing experience to one of good cheer and an esprit de corps.

Harry was able to return to L.A. with the knowledge that Christian might not be the greatest captain in the world, but at least his crew wasn't planning a mutiny.

"It's like going from detention to the cafeteria," Fenny told Big Bill. They were driving to Miss Penk's and Frau Katte's house, where they had been invited to a dinner party. "It's actually fun."

"As all work should be," said Bill. He looked out the window and after watching a geese formation, turned to Fenny. "You know how Heine has all his pet issues—nuclear disarmament, clean air—"

"And gun control," said Fenny. "Never forget gun control and world peace."

"Right. Well, if I had a pet issue, do you know what it would be?"

"Me?"

"You're not an issue."

"Okay, then. What? What would be your pet issue?"

"Fun."

"Fun?"

Fenny took one hand off the steering wheel and held an imaginary microphone and in her best Marcy Mincus voice asked, "Don't you think that's kind of a trivial issue?"

"Oh, I beg to differ," said Bill into the invisible mike. "Fun is profound . . . and if you vote for me, I'll work my hardest to see that there's fun in the home, on the job—"

"Fun on the job?" said Fenny in her shrill Marcy voice. "Why, I've never had an ounce of fun in all my years in front of the camera."

"Then maybe it's time for a new job. A job where they let you take more breaks and . . . and hold group sing-alongs, dances during lunch, prizes, games—you know, make the workday more like a party. Now what do you say? Do I have your vote for fun?"

"Yes, you have my vote for fun," said Fenny, grinning. "You have my vote for anything."

The first thing Big Bill saw when they entered the small house on River Street was a French Impressionist painting in the entryway.

"Oh, my God," he said, startled. "That's a Renoir. A real Renoir."

"Pretty, ya?" said Frau Katte, hanging up their coats.

She led them into the living room. The rooms weren't big, but by design had a sense of roominess.

"It's a Prairie Style house," explained Miss Penk. "Those Prairie Style architects really knew how to wring every single inch of space out of a room."

Complementing the architecture was the house's decor. It was apparent that neither woman suffered from timidity—the walls of the living room were a deep scarlet, the walls of the dining room were the color of a ripe peach, and the walls and cupboards of the kitchen were gold. But the walls' placement and color were nothing, *nothing* compared to what hung on them. They were filled with paintings, paintings that, to Big Bill's educated eye (he hadn't worked as a guard in the L.A. County Art Museum for nothing), were original. Paintings by artists of this century and past. Bill stared, his mouth open.

"We're so glad it's getting chilly," said Miss Penk as her guests sat down. "It gives us the perfect excuse to light the fireplace."

"Enough of za chitchat," said Frau Katte. "Red wine, white wine, beer, or somezing harder?"

"I'm having the wine," said Lee.

"Well, then I'll have the same," said Bill, sitting by Lee. "*You* look great."

Lee giggled—Big Bill had that effect on her. She was wearing a navy blue silk tunic and matching trousers that she had gotten at a Chicago boutique realistic enough to acknowledge there were women in the world over a size ten. The color set off Lee's blue eyes and her red hair, but Fenny knew that the certain glow Lee had was not due to clothes or cosmetics, but to Bill. Guilt dampened her party mood, and she resolved that Lee would know the truth about her and Bill . . . soon.

"Where's Slim?" she asked, sitting on a slippery antique sofa.

"Miniature golfing with Heine and the mayor," said Lee.

"Miniature golfing?" said Bill. "It's freezing outside."

"Not quite," said Miss Penk, pouring wine. "Although it is supposed to get down to thirty-five degrees. Besides, they keep the golf course open until after the first snowfall."

"Crazy northerners," said Bill. He accepted a glass of zinfandel from Miss Penk and looked at the wall opposite him. "Although I will say, some of you sure have amazing art collections."

"Zanks. We've spent many hours on zis couch, just looking."

"And this is your newest prize, isn't it?" said Lee, gesturing not to a painting but to a Tiffany lamp perched on a skirted table.

"Ya," said Frau Katte. "We won zat in za Belton Furniture Store contest."

"First prize was a massaging recliner," said Miss Penk. "Comfortable, but ugly as sin."

"We definitely zought we got za best deal."

"Wait a minute," said Big Bill. He couldn't say he was familiar with what was up for grabs in the sweepstakes world, but he was fairly certain a contestant couldn't win fine art by mailing in box tops. "The . . . uh . . . art can't be from contests?"

The women got a big charge out of this.

"Oh, zat's a good one, Bill," said Frau Katte, adjusting the fez that threatened to become unmoored as she laughed. "Now, *zat* would be a contest."

"Why don't we show him what we have won," suggested Miss Penk, and she stood up, gesturing for everyone to follow along on the house tour.

"Well, we can't show you za trips we've won," said Frau Katte, "but we do have slides."

"Lucky for you our slide projector broke," said Miss Penk. "We won that piece of junk in a contest, too; otherwise we would have returned it a long time ago."

They went into the kitchen, fragrant with their sauerbraten dinner cooking in the oven, to view the three kitchen appliances they had been awarded—a food processor, an air popcorn popper, and a coffeemaker.

"Of course we never use zat," said Frau Katte loyally. "Za only coffee we'll drink is O'Delight."

"Thank you," said Lee, bowing.

In their forest-green bathroom, Miss Penk pointed to towels, a filigreed plant stand, and a doctor's scale. "All from contests," she said.

A portrait of a boy decorated the walls of the aqua-blue bedroom. "Zat's Alphonse," said Frau Katte as Big Bill studied the photograph. "Miss Penk's son."

"I didn't know you had a son," said Bill.

Miss Penk nodded, a veil of sadness falling over her face. "He was fourteen years old in that picture. He's thirty-two now."

"Zese are all contest winnings," said Frau Katte, opening a closet door to reveal shelves filled with contest loot: cases of face cream, creme rinse, assorted brushes, hot rollers, hair dryers, and electric toothbrushes.

"It looks like a drugstore," said Lee.

"Don't even ask to see za basement," said Frau Katte. "Zat's where we keep all za automotive supplies."

Big Bill was tickled that his hostesses were getting such a kick out of showing off their contest booty (their tour was completed by a quick jaunt through the backyard to look at the speedboat moored on a trailer in the driveway) when the real prizes worth looking at were hanging on their walls.

"I hope you don't mind me asking," he said as they sat at the dining room table after their dinner, "but I know you can't completely live on contest winnings. And your art collection alone must have cost a . . ." Bill waved his hand in a gesture of erasure. "Sorry. It's none of my business."

"Oh, nonsense," said Miss Penk. "I've never understood why everyone's so shy about talking about money. People will confess to everything but their annual income." She rose to get an apple tart off the buffet counter. "We live on my army pension and investments. My Katte knows how to play the stock market."

The Swiss woman nodded, the tassel of her green fez jumping. "It doesn't take as much skill as playing za contests, but I enjoy it."

"I guess so," said Bill. "And obviously, you know how to pick 'em. My God, to be able to afford a Renoir, Monet, Léger, Picasso, Hopper—"

"Aren't they fabulous?" said Miss Penk. "And to think before I met Frau Katte, the only Dutch Masters I knew about were the cigars."

"She always finds a way to squeeze in zat joke."

"Well, it's true," said Miss Penk, blushing.

"Tell him how you started," prompted Lee.

"Okay," said Frau Katte, happy to oblige. She put a dollop of whipped cream on the tart and passed it to Fenny. "My fazzer was a farmer—a *well-off* farmer, who worked land zat had been in our family for centuries. Zere was only my sister Marni and I to inherit all zis land—we both would have been set for life—but when he died he left his entire estate to my sister, and do you know why? Because I had told him I liked women better zen men—I vas never za type to hide zings—"

"Isn't she brave?" asked Miss Penk, serving Big Bill his dessert. "I hid things until I was forty-four years old."

"I mean, I really zought I wasn't telling him anyzing he didn't already know, but in his will he said he wouldn't sacrifice family land and za family name to someone who obviously had no use for eizer one. But I was za farmer in za family—I loved being out in zose fields, working za land. Marni couldn't have cared less. She wanted to go off and live in Lucerne." Frau Katte emptied her wineglass and stared at it for a moment.

"He did leave me twenty zousand Swiss francs, sort of a consolation prize, I guess. I left Switzerland right after his lawyer gave me za check and made it up to a little town outside Munich. Zat's where I met Miss Penk—"

"My husband and I were both stationed in Garmisch, this beautiful little Bavarian town, and Katte and I met sitting on the patio of a ski lodge."

"Ya, she spilled hot chocolate all over me; she was pretty hard to ignore. But right away I knew, she was za one for me."

"I, of course, would admit no such thing, but I kept going up to that ski lodge hoping to see her—"

"And I kept showing up!"

The two women laughed, winking at each other from across the table.

"But we were talking about money," Frau Katte reminded Miss Penk. "I started investing zose francs while I was in Deutschland. I wanted to show my fazzer zat I could make somezing he gave me grow. I guess it was my way of not giving up on him, even zo he had given up on me."

"His terrible loss," said Miss Penk, shaking her towered head.

"I made a killing in a Swiss pharmaceutical company, and in keeping with za Swiss theme, I bought my first painting—a Klee. Every time I hit big in a stock or a fund or a future, I buy a painting. It's my reward for being so smart." She took a bite of the tart she hadn't had a chance to sample. "Umm, zat's good, if I do say so myself." She took another bite before turning toward Fenny. "So," she said, "how's za big romance going?"

A wave of silence rolled across the table. Then Fenny found herself stammering and Big Bill cleared his throat as if trying to dislodge a hairball. Lee, confused to be out of the loop—Fenny usually told her everything—leaned across the table and said brightly, "So what's this news, Fenny? Who's the guy? Do I know him?"

"Well, of course you do, Lee. He's sitting right across from you."

The sound Fenny made was that of a baby chick in distress; a tiny little peep. Lee's mouth dropped open and could not seem to close to form words.

"Katte," scolded Miss Penk. "Talk about letting the cat out of the bag."

"What?" asked Frau Katte innocently. She looked at Lee. "You mean you didn't know? Oops." She wagged her finger at Fenny and Bill. "I would have zought you'd told her by now."

The power of speech returned to Lee. "You and Bill?" She pushed her chair back and rose from the table. "*You and Bill?* Fenny, how could you?"

"Lee, I—" began Fenny as Lee ran out of the room.

"Lee!" said Bill, giving chase.

Fenny had risen out of her seat, but she couldn't seem to muster any further movement and so she half crouched, half stood until she heard the front door slam. That noise propelled her backward into her chair with a thud.

"Katte," said Miss Penk in a low voice. "That was a dirty trick."

"What?" asked Frau Katte, but then, realizing her feigned innocence wasn't going to play, she shrugged her shoulders. "I zought she should know. I didn't zink it was fair zat she didn't."

"Well, how did *you* know?" asked Fenny.

This question elicited a laugh from the two older women.

"Oh, Fenny," said Miss Penk. "Katte can sniff out a love affair a mile away."

"Zat's right," said Frau Katte, sniffing the air in demonstration. "I'm za bloodhound of love."

Bill had walked Lee home ("Well, most of the time I chased her," he explained later to Fenny. "She only let me walk with her for the last half block"), but she rejected his offer for further discussion over a cup O'Delight.

"I'd just as soon be alone right now, Bill," she said as she fumbled with the key of the door leading to her upstairs apartment.

"Lee, we didn't plan this, it—"

"Goodnight," said Lee, and without looking at him, she pushed the door open and went inside, slamming it behind her.

Fenny had left the dinner party shortly after Bill and Lee, and now at home, she passed the time waiting for Bill by working on a table runner. She was a good crocheter (having learned as a child from one of Sig's clients) but an infrequent one, drawn to it only when she was out of sorts or anxious about something. Counting stitches lulled her, and she liked something productive coming out of her worry.

She waited for Bill with increasing anxiety—what was taking him so long?—and when counting stitches no longer offered her solace, she flung down her crochet hook and raced out the door, into the rain and her old Comet.

Fenny had just driven down the long gravel road that served as the driveway and was about to turn onto the county road when through the windshield she saw Bill.

"Where're we going?" he asked brightly as he got in the passenger side, droplets of water flying off his black poncho.

"Bill, what took you so long?"

"Took me so long? I walked as fast as I could."

"So how's Lee?" asked Fenny, putting the car in reverse and backing up toward the house.

"Not so hot." He turned on the radio, asking, "You mind?"

Fenny put the car in park. "Are we staying out here?"

"Why not?" asked Bill. "I like being in a parked car in the rain. It's cozy."

The station selection was limited by location and weather, and Bill could tune in only some inane instrumental disco. He turned the radio off.

"I knew we should have told her a long time ago, Bill."

He sat back in the car seat, sighing. "Fenny, there wasn't anything to tell a long time ago. There isn't even that much to tell *now*."

"What do you mean by that?"

"We've had a few—what?—kissing sessions? I don't think 'kissing sessions' exactly qualifies as a *torrid affair*."

"Well, I thought we were at least heading in that direction," Fenny said in a small voice.

"Did you?" Big Bill sat up and took one of Fenny's hands in his own. "That's news to me. *Good* news." He pulled her to him and kissed her.

"Oh, Bill," said Fenny, leaning back to catch her breath. "Where did you think we were heading?"

"Someplace, I guess. But we were going so slow I didn't know if we'd ever get there."

Fenny blinked back the tears that welled up in her eyes. "I wanted to see you more, but you know how late they've had me working on this movie." She swallowed hard. "But even if I wasn't working so much, I just . . . I just needed to go slow. I needed to know you were the one."

"The one what?"

"The one . . . the one I was finally ready for."

"Finally ready for?" A line of water dripped off the hood of the poncho and onto Bill's cheek. "Good God, Fenny, are you telling me you're a virgin?"

"Why?" she asked sharply. "Is there something the matter with that?"

"No, no." Bill tried to take her hand, but she had folded her arms and turned toward the driver's-side window. Light from her house shone as if through a gauze, and she wished desperately she was inside, doing nothing more demanding than counting crochet stitches.

"I'm only twenty-two, you know," she said. "I know that's *old age* as far as virginity goes, but for me it's just . . . twenty-two."

Rain drummed against the top of the car like impatient fingers. Fenny sat wedged against the door, arms crossed, trying to contain the shiver that vibrated her body. "Well, why don't you say anything?" she said finally, and in answer, Big Bill reached across the car seat and took her in his arms.

"What do you want me to say?" he asked, kissing the top of her head. "Why didn't you tell me you were a virgin? I thought you kept putting me off because you didn't really like me."

"Didn't really like you?" As she pressed against Bill, Fenny's shivering increased.

"Here, let me get this off," he said, pulling off the wet poncho and throwing it in the back seat.

"Didn't really like you?" repeated Fenny. "Oh, Bill, I . . . I *really* like you."

His mouth found hers and they kissed, and the rainy world outside their car dissolved into a blur.

"What's this?" asked Bill, his fingers pushing a hard little pellet inside Fenny's bra.

"Nothing," said Fenny, plucking out the courage bead and putting it in her jeans pocket.

They pulled and tore at their shirts and pants as if they were being burned by them, and there on the blue and white vinyl seat of the Comet, as the windows fogged up, Fenny surrendered that which heretofore had not been captured.

She cried a little afterward, for a stew of reasons. She knew she had made the right decision, but she felt the small measure of regret anyone would feel in giving away something they'd had all their lives.

"And why," she complained to Bill, "why did I have to lose it in a *car?*"

"Don't you think 'lose' is the wrong word?" asked Bill. "I've always thought the word should be 'gained.' And besides, I don't think it's the place that matters, but the person," said Bill. "I lost my virginity on a beach in Waikiki—paradise, right?"

Fenny waited for him to go on, and when he didn't, she asked softly, "And it was awful, huh?"

"No, no, it was great. Not because of the place, but because I was with the right person."

"I don't know that I'm consoled," said Fenny dryly.

She had cried, too, from the joy and wonder of the experience, from the feel of Bill, the man she loved, filling her up, and finally, from sheer relief at finally having gotten through it.

It was too cold to lounge around in a car in late September during a rainstorm, and they dressed quickly. Big Bill turned on the heater long enough to warm up the car, and he held her, stroking her hair, her shoulders, and her back.

Fenny felt drowsy and content, thinking how nice it would be to drift off, when suddenly Bill's whole body tensed.

"What is it?" she asked, startled.

"How could I be so stupid?" he said. "I was just carried away in the rush of everything, I—"

In the dark car interior, Fenny smiled, pleased at her worldliness. "Don't worry, I'm on the pill. I have been for over a year."

"In anticipation of a night like this?"

"That, too," said Fenny, laughing. "But mostly to regulate my periods."

Big Bill shifted his long legs, hoping to find any overlooked spare room. "So why didn't you ever tell me about being a virgin?"

Fenny looked into Bill's deep brown eyes, their eyelashes thick and straight as a doll's.

"I don't know," she said after a moment. "You don't talk much about your past—especially your *sexual* past. Why should I talk about mine?"

"Because you don't have one?" Bill suggested.

"True." She waited for a long time before she began to talk again. "I went out with guys in high school, but I never had a serious *boyfriend*. I guess I've always had sort of a romantic idea about the 'first time'—I mean, I wanted it to be with someone I really cared about. And then after Sig and Wally died, I guess I sort of shut down. I didn't have the time, or the desire, for anyone." She looked up at Bill. "Until you."

"I'm honored," said Bill, and he kissed her. "Lars Larson told me a lot about your parents on that camping trip we took together. He said they were the best-matched couple he'd ever met."

"They were," said Fenny, feeling her eyes water. "The only thing I ever heard them argue about was breakfast. Wally always had a big, elaborate breakfast—eggs and bacon, waffles and strawberries—and Sig couldn't see how anybody could have more than a piece of rye toast and coffee in the morning. They agreed on all the big things, though, loved the same things, loved being with each other."

"I like hearing you talk about them," said Bill.

"It's . . . hard to talk about them. I always fall apart."

"My mother never said much about my dad—I guess she was afraid of falling apart, too."

"Did she ever tell you anything?"

"That he was tall. And that he loved macadamia nuts."

"That's all?" said Fenny.

Bill nodded. "Pretty much. And I've only seen one picture of him. Of my mother and him. He had his hands on her big pregnant belly. On me."

"Oh, Bill," said Fenny. She opened the car door. "Come on inside."

"But it's still raining."

It didn't matter to Fenny, who raced inside the house, leaving Bill with little choice but to race in after her.

After getting a photo album off a shelf, she sat down on the couch and opened it to the last page.

"Look," she said, pointing. "I've got the same picture."

Bill looked at the photograph of a man with his hand on a woman's pregnant belly.

"Proud parents-to-be," he said, reading the little paper flag underneath the picture. He put his arm around Fenny and they sat for a moment, looking at the happy smiling couple preserved on Kodachrome.

"Sig loved writing these captions," said Fenny. "She said, 'Every picture tells a story, but you want to make sure it tells the right one.' "

They looked through the whole book, Bill pausing on the page at the beginning that displayed some of Wally's school pictures.

Bill read some of the handwritten captions. "Headed for Juvenile Hall," read the one under the picture of a scowling sixth-grade boy, and "Member, Narcoleptic Society" accompanied a photograph that caught a freshman Wally with his eyes closed.

Bill laughed, carefully examining each picture.

"Mae told me what she remembers about my dad as a boy," he said finally. "She said if there was trouble to be found, he'd find it. But every time he visited her, he'd bring her a little present. A penny, a bouquet of dandelions, you know, stuff a little boy thinks is a good present." Bill sighed. "It's funny how bad you can miss someone you've never known, but I've always felt this connection with him, like we'd have been the greatest of friends."

"You probably would have been, Bill." Fenny looked at a picture of a teenage Sig mugging for the camera. ("Pretty Is as Pretty Does," read the caption.) "My mother could do birdcalls. She could whistle in a way that sounded like two people whistling. And my dad . . . my dad used to sing me this one lullaby in Norwegian. He sang it to me every night . . . even when I wasn't a kid anymore."

It dawned on Fenny, as she said those words, how sad it was that Bill didn't have more memories, but how nice it was to share hers with Bill, to show him her parents' pictures and laugh at Sig's captions.

"Hey," she said, "here we are talking about parents and I'm not falling apart!"

"No, you're not," said Bill.

"So far losing my virginity's been very good for me."

Bill leaned forward to kiss her again, thoroughly in agreement.

Chapter 15

The national media had left Tall Pine, but that wasn't to say the town had been deserted. There was still the occasional television crew from Fargo or Duluth roaming Main Street, and knots of people wearing cameras around their necks showed up at the movie sets and wandered the town, hoping for star sightings or, if unsuccessful in that venture, a good souvenir.

"They're not like tourists," complained Heine. "It's like they want something from us—no, it's like they *expect* something from us."

"It's only going to be for a little while," said the mayor, who happily posed for any picture anyone might want to take of him. "We'll probably miss them when they're gone. And you can't deny that business is up."

"I'll say," Lee said, refilling cups. "I must have made at least two hundred pancakes yesterday."

"A lot of movie people have been coming in," complained Pete. "And believe me, they can be real heels."

Instead of gratefully filling orders, Pete was annoyed by all the extra business he was getting. Not only did showbiz folk have expensive shoes, they were meticulous about their upkeep, and he had to take repairs home just to keep up. This infringed on his beloved shoemaking, an infringement that made Pete anxious. There was no goal in his life as compelling as the one to finish Lee's twelfth pair of shoes, for then he would present them all to her, along with his declaration of love.

And now that his love for Lee wasn't quite a secret anymore, he had to move all the faster, before his feelings became common knowledge and conversation fodder at the Cup O'Delight counter.

Big Bill promised him that he wouldn't say a word—not even to Fenny—but Pete didn't know Bill well enough to be one hundred percent reassured.

Bill had been walking home from the Bait & Camp when he came across the shoemaker fishing off a dock on Tall Pine Lake. He had jimmied his fishing pole into a cutout in the wood so his hands were free, it looked to Bill, to scale whatever it was he had caught.

"Hey," he said, "what'd you catch there?"

Pete jumped, and the thing that Bill had assumed was a bass or a sunny flew out of his hands.

"This isn't a fish," said Bill, bending down to pick it up, "it's a shoe."

"My . . . my sister Phyllis has a craving for a fish supper tonight," said Pete, "so I brought some of my work out here with me."

"Why, this is . . ." said Bill, ignoring the man's outstretched hand as he inspected a dangling strap with a needle and thread attached to it, "this is a shoe-in-progress. Pete, did you *make* this?"

The shoemaker nodded.

"I've seen enough of Mae's stuff to know good craftsmanship, Pete, and my God, that is *good* craftsmanship. You could have a whole other business—I'd bet people would—"

"Please, Bill," he said, still holding out his hand.

Bill handed him the shoe, which Pete stuffed in his jacket pocket.

"Now if you'll excuse me," he said, going to his fishing pole, "something's biting."

He pulled in a skimpy perch that wouldn't even make a meal for a fashion model and threw it back in the water. With one foot up on the dock railing, he recast his line and looked out on the lake.

"Bill," he said presently, "I hope you don't mention this entire incident to anyone."

"Incident?" said Bill, confused. "What incident?"

"Not to anyone," said Pete, a forcefulness to his tone Bill had never heard before. He stood in profile to Bill, his eyes squinted even though the afternoon sun was mild.

Bill was still not sure he understood the man. "You mean about the shoe? Why wouldn't you want me to mention the shoe? It's a piece of work, Pete—why, I bet you could get a couple hundred bucks for a pair like—"

"The shoe is not for sale. The shoe—shoes—are for Lee."

Bill didn't quite understand what Pete was saying, but he knew it was important. He folded his arms and leaned against the dock, his belt buckle clicking against the top railing.

"The shoes are for Lee," Bill repeated, hoping Pete would elaborate on the statement.

The shoemaker's squint got tight until it looked as if his eyes were completely shut. He reached up once, to palm his oiled hair, and then he flicked his chin, as if dislodging a bug.

"Bill, I've been making some shoes for Lee," he said finally. "They're presents. Presents I'm going to give her . . . because I love her."

Bill drew in a gust of air, but he disguised his surprise by pretending he had to cough. "Must be coming down with something," he said, coughing again, and then he asked, "Does Lee know about them?"

Pete shook his head. "She doesn't know about the shoes, she doesn't know my feelings." He looked at Bill, relaxing his squint just a bit. "And I hope you'll let me be the one to tell her."

"I won't say a word," said Bill.

"To anyone?"

"If that's the way you want it."

"That's the way I want it."

For several minutes, Pete reeled in his line and cast, reeled in and cast, reeled in and cast, and the two men concentrated on this activity as if it were a job they were highly paid to do.

"I'm sort of a late bloomer when it comes to women," said Pete finally. "I guess I was just waiting for someone like Lee to come along."

"Lee's worth waiting for, all right," said Bill, and he was surprised at the lump growing in his throat, surprised at the sadness that settled in his chest, knowing the likelihood of Lee reciprocating Pete's feelings was virtually zip.

Hearing Bill's assessment, but not the emotion in the big man's voice, Pete was encouraged to continue. It felt good to share feelings, felt good to give wing to the secret he had held close to his heart for so long.

"She always gives my bill a little slap when she sets it next to my plate," said Pete, awe in his voice, as if describing the most romantic of gestures. "And when she pours my coffee, she kind of tilts her head so I can see the sparkle of those little diamond earrings she wears."

Bill bowed his head and looked down at the water, feeling like a priest listening to a confession that was beyond his scope of counsel.

Pete didn't notice. "She hums when she's at the grill, Bill—did you notice? And sometimes she sings morning songs to me—I'm usually her first customer—you know, 'Zippedy Doo Dah' or that 'Oh, What a Beautiful Morning' one."

Bill snuck a look at Pete, and even as he couldn't quite believe what the man was saying, he couldn't deny that Pete *beamed* as he said it.

Pete turned, catching Bill looking at him. "I know I sound a little foolish," he said, and a faint blush mottled his face, "but I feel like the luckiest guy alive."

There was a tug at his fishing pole, and this time Pete reeled in a nice-sized sunfish. "Surprise, surprise," he said. "Phyllis is going to get that craving satisfied after all." He unhooked the writhing fish and threw it into a bucket. "I'm not blind, Bill, I know Lee has a crush on you—"

"Pete, I don't—"

"Thank goodness you've got a crush on Fenny!" He wiped his hands on his pants leg. "After Phyllis hurt her back, I was so busy trying to take care of her and earn a living that I didn't have much time for women. But as they say, 'All good things come to those who wait.' "

"Yes, they say that," agreed Bill.

Pete stuck out his hand. "So all this is hush-hush, right?"

"Right." The men shook hands and Bill added, "Good luck," wishing that that was all it would take for Pete to get what he wanted.

The door opened and Lee braced herself for the onslaught of tourists armed with cameras and questions and a certain aggression; like Heine said, they acted as if they were owed something.

But it wasn't an autograph hound from Hibbing or an aspiring actor from Alexandria.

"Fenny!" said Frau Katte.

"Fenny," said Heine, with not as much enthusiasm.

Lee said nothing at all, but excused herself and went into the back room. Slim came out shortly after.

"What'll you have?" he asked so curtly that Fenny drew in her breath and blinked hard against the battalion of tears that were ready to fall into position. Slim's friendship was one she thought she could always count on.

"Uh . . . coffee?"

Slim poured her a cup, placing it in front of her so that some sloshed on the counter. He then joined Lee in the back room.

The Swiss woman leaned toward Fenny. "You tell Bill I'm glad you two came out of za closet. No one should have to keep zeir love a secret."

"Thanks," said Fenny, feeling herself tearing up again.

When it became obvious that Slim was not going to refill her coffee cup, Fenny left the cafe, leaving a dollar tip as a statement. What exactly that statement made, she wasn't sure; she just knew it felt good in a perverse way to leave it.

"You say hi to Bill for us," said Miss Penk, and Fenny nodded, as grateful as if she'd been given a blessing.

Lee's hurt was a weight Fenny hated carrying but didn't know how to put down.

"Do you think," said Bill that night, interrupting Fenny's monologue about how bad she felt about Lee, "that we can change the subject?"

There was a slippery rustle as he shifted his position inside the sleeping bag. They were in his tent, which of late had become their favorite place of rendezvous. Fenny would park her car far enough away so that Mae Little Feather wouldn't hear its approach and, with a flashlight for illumination, walk along the river to Bill's tent.

"You weren't in the Cup O'Delight. She hates me, Bill! She wouldn't come out of the back room the whole time I was there!"

"But that, Fenny, is not your problem."

"Easy for you to say."

"It is. It's very easy for me to say, because it's true." Bill rolled to his side, propping his head up under his hand. "Look, Fenny, if you're going to feel guilty about Lee, at least take some comfort that it's a clean guilt."

"Clean guilt," said Fenny. "What's that?"

With his palm, Bill brushed Fenny's hair back. He loved the feel of her hair and the contour of her head underneath his hand.

"Well, Fenny, you didn't set out to hurt Lee—it's that your feelings and hers intersected at the same point. And that point was me."

Fenny leaned forward and kissed Bill lightly on the lips. "That point *was* you," she agreed. "So I should feel 'clean' guilt about that? As opposed to 'dirty'?"

"Exactly." Bill adjusted the backpack he used as a pillow. "When you set out to hurt a person, you *should* feel dirty guilt. Clean guilt is for when you hurt someone, but it's not intentional."

"You seem to have experience with guilt."

Bill shrugged, and when he didn't say anything further, Fenny said, "If you and Lee *had* been together, I might have done something intentional to . . . to get you to be with me."

"Give me some credit, Fenny; I have free will, you know. You couldn't have done *anything* to be with me if I didn't want to be with you." He cupped her face in his palm. "Let's just forget about feeling guilty altogether. Let's just *feel*."

He kissed her, and she took his advice; in that tent shadowed by fading firelight, she *felt*.

Afterward, they lay on their backs, looking up at the night sky through the mesh skylight of the tent.

"This is getting to be one of my favorite views," said Big Bill, and then, shifting his arm under his head, he said, "Ow," and fished out the thing that had poked into his skin.

"Here's one of those things again," he said, holding the small bead up to better see it in the moonlight.

"Oh, that's mine," said Fenny, but when she reached for it, Bill pulled his hand away.

"What is it?" he asked, rolling it between his fingers.

"Please, Bill, give it to me."

Hearing the urgent tone in her voice, Bill gave it to her.

"What is it?" he asked gently.

Fenny reached down and dug up her jeans crumpled at the bottom of the sleeping bag. She put the bead in their front pocket and then stared up through the skylight.

Bill rolled to his side and, softly brushing aside a lone tear that meandered down her face, he asked again, "What is it?"

"Promise you won't laugh?"

"I won't laugh."

"It's a courage bead . . . from a necklace that broke. From a necklace my mom and dad sent me right before they died."

"Oh, Fenny." He tucked one arm under her head and with the other pulled her close to him. They lay quietly for a few moments until he asked, "Why do you call it a courage bead?"

"Sig called them that. She said local legend had it that whoever wore them would be brave and adventurous . . . but I think she made that up."

"So does it?" asked Bill.

"Does it what?"

"Give you courage."

Fenny's laugh was one sad, quick note. "I doubt it. I mean, I don't carry it with me for courage . . . I just carry it to keep Sig and Wally close—if that makes any sense."

Bill kissed her. "That makes a lot of sense. So where's the rest of it?"

"The rest of the necklace? In an envelope in my dresser."

"Do you ever think of restringing it and wearing the whole thing? Wouldn't that be easier than carrying a little bead around?"

"Probably," said Fenny, and her voice sounded as if it were clouding up. "But—and this sounds stupid—I don't want to wear the whole thing . . . until I've earned it. Until I am really, truly brave."

Bill kissed her again and then he held her, hoping his strong arms around her would comfort her in a way words could not, and together they watched the northern sky until they fell asleep.

Autumn was in full swing, bringing to Tall Pine its bright colors and cooler temperatures. Fenny rode her bike to the set every morning, usually at dawn. She rode along a path forged through the woods and around the lake, through an explosion of color wet with dew, past the deep jewel red of sumac and turkey oak trees; past yellow birches and aspens, and past basswoods, silver maples, and choke-cherries whose leaves sported every color in between.

In the morning, before the sun had cranked up its full power, it was cool on the path, almost cold, and the seasonal decay from the lake and from the dying leaves left a slight tang in the air.

It was a long ride to the farmhouse where they had been shoot-ing, especially from Big Bill's tent, where she had been spending most of her nights. But she needed the long ride, if for nothing else than to provide her with a little peace. Not that things weren't going well on the set—they had never been better. Christian was far easier to work for as a challenged director than as a frustrated writer, and Boyd had relaxed on the set, deciding he didn't need to analyze his every line and entrance. He had taken on Fenny as a confidante, and confide he did, about everything from his goals ("I'd like to be as respected as Henry Fonda—he's in the Six-four Club, you know—as mysterious as James Dean, and have Elvis's Elvisness") to his troubled relationship with his father.

"You know what he told me the last time we talked?" he said one day during a lighting change. "After he told me he'd like to whup my ass for crying on national TV, *then* he said, 'You're lucky you're in Hollywood, because Hollywood's the only place that hires people as dumb as you.'"

"Oh, Boyd," said Fenny, "you're not dumb."

"Then why does everyone say I am?"

"'Everyone' doesn't. And those who do are wrong."

"Really?"

Fenny looked into Boyd's perfect-for-the-screen blue eyes.

"You know what you want and you've gone after it *and* succeeded at it—that's smart."

"It is?"

"Of course it is. It's just that you're so handsome people don't want to think that you can be smart, too."

"They don't?"

"No, they don't."

Boyd took Fenny's hand and kissed it. "Much obliged for the pep talk, Miss Fenny." He kissed her hand again, this time with a little more feeling. "You know, maybe I'm wrong about you not being my type."

"You're not wrong, Boyd," said Fenny with a laugh. "Now let go of my hand."

Fenny shifted to a higher gear, making her legs pedal harder as she rode the inclining path that was studded with rocks and wandering tree roots. Breathing deeply, she got to the Heneghan farmhouse feeling invigorated and ready for the day's work.

The day's work, however, was delayed due to technical problems. Shooting was scheduled to begin at ten, but by the time one problem was fixed, another arose.

Lunch had long been served and costumed extras sat in the open tent, eating second or third desserts, reading the paper, or playing cards.

"No, I don't want to sign a petition," said Marv Kozlak, finishing another cup of coffee. Marv was a keyboardist who, along with his Merry Men, had been hired out of Minneapolis to play for the Harvest Ball scene.

"Are you saying you don't support a wind-power study?" asked Heine, who had collected almost a hundred signatures during lunch.

"No, I'm not," said Marv. "I just don't believe in mixing music with politics."

"Ah," said Heine, raising a finger. "In today's world, you've got to mix politics with everything."

"Let's go tune up," said Marv, who was already a little put out by having to play with Heine and his friend Corby Deele, musicians who didn't come *close* to his band's level; he certainly didn't want to waste his time arguing politics with the accordionist.

Marv wanted to enjoy every minute of the day—after all, he and his Merry Men had been in plenty of movies (most often shot at wedding receptions by a tipsy relative of the bride), but never in a *Hollywood* movie.

They went into the barn and climbed onto the hay bales that served as their makeshift stage. The professional square dance caller was already there, having cut short his lunch for extra rehearsal with the Sunshine Dancers, a square dance troupe out of Superior, Wisconsin. The dancers didn't need the extra rehearsal as much as the caller did; for the life of him, he couldn't remember calls he had been making for over forty years.

Outside, Mary Gore found Lee and Slim watching the crew set up the finally-fixed crane that would be used to shoot into the roofless barn. "Have you seen Fenny?"

"No, I haven't," said Lee coldly. "And if I did, I'd look the other way."

"I see we're still upset about Bill," said Mary. "So many have, that never touch'd his hand, Sweetly suppos'd them mistress of his heart." She smiled. "Shakespeare. From 'A Lover's Complaint.' "

The words that escaped Lee didn't escape Slim.

"So many have, that never shut her mouth, secretly wished to have that honor," he said, in a high British accent. "Knutson. From 'A General Complaint About You.' "

As Lee laughed, Mary's smile curdled and she tightened her bonnet bow under her chin. "Well, you're sounding awfully normal today."

Slim growled at Mary.

"I guess I jumped the gun," she said to Lee. "In calling him *normal.*"

Slim growled again, this time baring teeth, and Mary Gore scampered off like a poodle confronted by a mastiff.

"All right, people," said the first a.d., his voice amplified by the megaphone he held to his mouth. "Thanks for your patience. Our problems seem to be solved, so we're ready to start the outdoor dance scene. If everybody could take your places, please."

Dozens of pioneer women joined dozens of frontiersmen. They had all been assigned "partners" earlier by the extras coordinator. At least a third of the extras were from Tall Pine, the others culled from a casting session Emma Tuttle had held in Minneapolis.

Fenny and Bill emerged from her trailer. She wouldn't admit to hiding out, but she thought the less opportunity she had for running into Lee, the better.

"Hey, there's Fenny Ness," said a young actress for whom this job constituted her big break into showbiz (previously it had been her stint as an usher at the Guthrie Theatre).

"Oh, yeah," said Will Bick, the teenage son of the hardware store owner. "I know her." He raised his voice. "Hi, Fenny—how's it going?"

"Hi, Fenny!"

"Great stuff in the newspapers, Fenny!"

"Way to get that Mincus, Fenny!"

" 'I pooped in my pants'—that's telling 'em, Fenny!"

People she knew and people she didn't know called out their greetings, comments, and advice like a boxing audience welcoming their contender to the ring.

In the crowd, Fenny felt a flush of fear: who were all these people calling out to her, reaching for her?

Fortunately, the panic was short-lived, replaced by an abrupt laugh when Frau Katte and Miss Penk, in costumes, sidled up to her.

"You look like the grandma in *Little Red Riding Hood*," said Fenny to Miss Penk.

"And don't tell me . . . ," said Frau Katte, grinning, "I look like za big bad wolf."

"She's trying to get into character," explained Miss Penk. "Even though we're just extras, she did what you said that Boyd Burch does. She wrote up a whole history of our characters."

"Ya," said Frau Katte. "Miss Penk is a poor rich widow, and I'm za gold digger who's come to take atvantage of her."

The weather certainly was cooperating for the day's filming. The skies were the color blue that shows up only in autumn: a gaudy turquoise. The pine trees that loomed above them were such a deep green, they appeared black. The temperature hovered in the low sixties, which for the movie crew was verging on the nippy side but was balmy to the natives.

The a.d. again made instructions through his megaphone. "Could we have the professional dancers on the road leading to the barn, and the number one couples on the left side and the number twos on the right?"

This was the sequence that had Fenny nervous. It involved choreography, and although Fenny claimed her ineptitude on the dance floor came from a lack of training, in truth she was just a lousy dancer. All she needed to do was waltz up the center of the road and into the barn, but if she had been told to juggle the drumsticks *and* the bass fiddle belonging to Marv Kozlak's Merry Men it wouldn't have daunted her more.

Plus her character was supposed to be mad at Ike for flirting with the judge's daughter visiting from Baltimore. Fenny couldn't just concentrate on counting her steps; no, she had to act, too. When Christian and the actors and the dancers and the band and the crane operator and the crew were all in their places, the first a.d. called for quiet and Fenny whispered to her co-star, "You've got to help me out on this one, Boyd."

"You got it," said the actor, as confident of his dancing as Fenny was not.

Boyd Burch had taken not only dozens of acting classes, but countless others that might help and broaden his career—fencing, Rollerblading, tap, jazz, and ballroom dancing; tax preparation (he had a business manager now, of course, but still took pride in his ability to decipher a W-2), self-hypnosis (he never could put himself under, but he got a lot of napping in), speed reading, and a one-day seminar on "The Psychology of the Talent Agent." In one miniseries he got to sword-fight, but rarely were his other learned skills called into play. When they were, as was the case today, he was thrilled.

Sound and film were rolling, and Christian called, "Action."

Marv Kozlak and His Merry Men, aided by the equally merry Heine and Corby, began to play "Turkey in the Straw." The professional dancers began to dance in the middle of the road, the women's dresses twirls of color. One camera dollied beside them on a track, another shot the action from a perch inside the barn, and the crane camera captured the aerial view. Fenny and Boyd stood out of frame, waiting for their music cue, and when they heard it, Boyd took Fenny's hand and led her out to the middle of the dancers.

"Ike Forrest," she said with Inga's Norwegian accent, "I told you, I don't want to dance. Why not ask that little *flicka*, the mayor's daughter?"

"I don't want to dance with that *flicka*," said Boyd/Ike, pulling her to him. "I want to dance with you."

"I don't share the same wish, Mr. Forrest," began Fenny as Boyd grabbed her around the waist and began to dance. She had another line but could not seem to get it out, seized as she was by giggles.

"Cut!" called Christian. "Fenny, Inga's mad at Ike, remember?"

Pressing her lips together, Fenny nodded. She hated to screw up such a big scene.

Places were called again, the music started up, and Ike led Inga out to the middle of the dance floor.

"I don't share the same wish, Mr.—" said Fenny again, and as Boyd grabbed her and started dancing with her, she burst out giggling again.

"Cut! Fenny, what is your frickin' problem?"

"I'm sorry, Christian," she said, raising her voice to the director, who was at least twenty-five feet away from her. "It's just that I'm . . . ticklish."

"Well, why didn't you say something? Boyd, hold her somewhere else. Avoid the ribs."

"Will do," said Boyd.

During take three, when Boyd grabbed Fenny, he moved his hand so his fingers wouldn't rest on the back of her rib cage, but it didn't matter.

"I don't share the same— Huh, huh, huh, hoo, ha ha, chh chh, oooh, hee chh hoo!"

"Cut!"

"Christian, I held her different!" shouted Boyd. "I didn't touch her ribs!"

"Fenny, I'm thinking of coming down there and inflicting some bodily harm."

Marv Kozlak, watching the whole thing from his perch on the hay bales, shook his head, not only as a reaction to the young actress's unprofessionalism, but also in an attempt to deny to himself that all of a sudden, he was feeling sort of punk.

"Sorry, Christian, it's just that there's something about Boyd's fingers, I don't know, they're like little claws jabbing right into my sides."

"Oh, and thank you very much," muttered the actor.

"He says he's barely touching you now."

"I know, but 'barely' is almost even worse. It's just imagining those little claws ready to jab me."

"You're going to have more than claws jabbing you if you don't get it together, okay?"

"Okay."

She blew take four.

"I don't share— Huh, huh, huh, hoo, ha ha, chh, chh, oooh, hee chh, hoo!"

The dancers were getting especially agitated—they were the ones who had to put out all the physical exertion over and over again. The women stood with their hands to their hips, their feet arranged in various ballet positions. The men checked their watches, and then remembered the costumer had made them take them off.

"I expected her to be a lot more professional," said the woman who was going to parlay her role as an extra into a modeling and commercial career back in Minneapolis.

"I've never seen her like this," said the young Bick boy, who really hadn't seen her much at all. Even though Bick's Hardware was right next door to the Cup O'Delight, the boy never went in, as his father, Fred Bick, had a thirty percent share in the Dog Haus and when he and his family dined out, they took their meals there.

There were other murmurings from extras and Merry Men and even the core of Fenny's friends, who hadn't gotten to dance yet, their turn interrupted every time by Fenny's giggle fits.

"I zink she's cracking up," suggested Frau Katte. "From all za pressure with her love life. And from ruining zat Marcy Mincus's career."

"Oh, honestly," said Miss Penk. "Fenny didn't ruin Marcy Mincus's career. But if she keeps this up, she'll ruin her own."

"Maybe one of us should talk to her," said Frau Katte.

"Or him. Someone should talk with Christian," said Mary Gore. "Artist to artist." She brightened. "I'll volunteer."

Any sympathy the crowd had for Fenny quickly evaporated as Fenny began laughing again in the next take. The young woman from Minneapolis who was hoping for her big break scowled, in judgment of Fenny's behavior and also in reaction to the sudden wave of nausea she felt.

"Cut!" ordered Christian. "Let's take a break, everybody!"

Christian took Fenny outside and began walking her around the barn. If he didn't move, he was going to blow his cool. They had just about circled the barn when Christian could no longer hold in his words.

"Fenny, excuse my French, but what the fu—"

"Excuse me, Christian—"

Fenny and Christian turned around to see Mary Gore, holding up her skirts, rushing toward them.

"We're trying to have a discussion out here," said Christian, his voice condescending.

"I'm sure you are, that's why I'm here."

Christian pinched the bridge of his nose.

"I do not need this," he said.

Mary took in a deep breath. "I just thought that since you're having so much trouble with the scene, why don't you just incorporate Fenny's ticklishness into it?"

Christian opened his mouth, but it was as if her effrontery took away his ability to speak for a moment. "What sense," he finally managed to say, "would it make for Inga to be laughing in this scene?"

"Well, I'll tell you," said Mary, her face shining underneath her bonnet. "For the same reason Fenny's giggling right now. Because she's ticklish. Couple that with Inga's anger over what she thinks is Ike's interest in another woman and, presto!—you've got yourself one endearing little scene!"

Christian was just about to tell Mary what to do with her endearing little scene when David the p.a. raced over to them.

"Christian," he said, panting. "We've got a crisis."

"I'm working on it, okay?" snapped the director.

"No, I mean on the set."

"Another one?" said Christian. "What?"

"Well," he said, leading everyone back into the barn, "it appears some people have gotten sick."

Marv Kozlak and one of his Merry Men, both of whom had an odd green tinge to their faces, rushed past them, covering their mouths with their hands.

"I hope they make it," said David, but seconds later the sounds of retching told them they had not. "We might have to move the Porta Potties closer."

The same odd green colored the faces of over a dozen people inside the barn.

"What is going on?" asked Christian as a woman in a calico dress vomited into a bucket.

"We think it's food poisoning," said David the p.a. "The same thing happened when I was working on the 'Katy Jo Pruitt Christmas Special' last year. Then it was deviled eggs. The chicken tetrazzini seems to be the culprit now. We're taking everyone who ate it to the hospital."

Christian felt a rush of relief—he'd had the meat loaf—and dismay.

"How many people ate it?"

His question was answered when the first a.d. got on the megaphone.

"Would everyone who ate the chicken tetrazzini report to the vans at the end of the driveway?"

Christian counted fourteen people, some of them in the throes of illness, others seemingly fine, leaving the barn.

"Fenny, tell me you didn't have the tetrazzini," said Christian, thinking the day would be completely shot if his leading lady got sick.

Fenny shook her head. "I didn't even come out of my trailer for lunch. David brought me a bowl of soup."

Christian exhaled a blast of air. "Good. David, go get Boyd for me, will you?"

The leading man looked hale and hearty.

"I didn't eat lunch," Boyd said. "I worked out instead."

Christian took the actor's head in his hands and kissed him on the forehead. "Bless you and your buff body." He turned to David. "So who are we missing that we really need?"

"No principals," said David, "just extras—except for Marv Kozlak."

"Who?"

"The musician," the p.a. reminded him.

Christian scanned the barn. Everyone looked at him expectantly, hoping their Hollywood experience wasn't about to be waylaid by something so unglamorous as a case of salmonella.

"Fenny," said Christian, jamming his hands in his tight pockets, "where's Big Bill?"

"Bill? He's . . ." She scanned the barn and, when she found him, pointed. Immediately, Christian was headed across the barn.

Standing by an old plow and in conversation with Miss Penk and Frau Katte, Big Bill suddenly found himself confronted by the diminutive director.

"This is your big chance, Bill," said Christian, holding his arms out as if measuring the whopper of a fish he caught.

Bill crossed his arms and looked at Fenny, who stood behind the director, but Fenny could only answer him with a shrug.

"Here's the thing," continued Christian, looking straight into Bill's chest. He'd have to tip his head back too far to make eye contact, and one thing he'd learned as a short man was to never make adjustments for someone else's height—let the tall person bend down or duck his head. "Our keyboardist got ahold of that bad chicken, and we need a new one."

"You need a new bad chicken?"

Christian's smile was sour. "We need a new keyboardist. So how about it?"

Bill squinted his eyes and looked at the musicians on the hay bales. "Well," he said slowly, "I was sort of counting on dancing with Miss Penk here."

"I'll pay you three hundred dollars," said Christian.

"And Frau Katte and I were hoping to cut the rug, too."

"Five hundred."

Bill shrugged and turned to his friends. "Ladies, I guess we'll have to take a rain check."

He followed Christian over to the band, where Heine enthusiastically introduced him to the remaining Merry Men.

"How's the light holding up?" Christian asked Doug Woo.

"I'd say we've got about an hour left," said the cinematographer.

Christian's mind was whirling with information, ideas, and worries. Would that be enough time to shoot the scene? Would Fenny ever stop laughing? Would anybody sue the production company for food poisoning? Were they liable? At times like this he wanted nothing more than to be sitting at his "Perky the Puppy" desk, flying airplanes made out of his rejected script pages.

"Should I call places?" asked the first a.d.

"In a minute," said Christian. "First I've got to talk to Fenny and Boyd."

"*What?*" asked Boyd when Christian, much to his own surprise, told him they were going to do what Mary Gore suggested.

"Fenny'll just keep giggling," he explained. "Boyd, act just like you're put out by that, just like you've been doing."

"You would be, too, if Fenny kept—"

"Listen, we've already wasted enough time. I want to get right to this. Fenny, ad-lib some lines about why you're giggling; you know, because you're ticklish, et cetera, et cetera, and Boyd, if anything comes to you, say it, too."

"What if I can't think of anything to say?"

"Then tell a knock-knock joke!" Christian pinched the sides of his nose. "Look, Boyd, I'm not asking you to invent a soliloquy—just frickin' react to Fenny!"

He tugged at the hem of his sweater and turned to face the extras. Suddenly, he felt very much in control.

When action was called, Big Bill started playing a jazzy "Turkey in the Straw" that made Marv Kozlak's pale in comparison. The dancers were inspired by the new vigor in their music and matched it in their steps. The energy on the set was different, hepped-up and bordering on wild, but not quite there. Through the camera lens, it looked perfect and was just what Christian wanted.

As Fenny said, "I don't share the same wish, Mr. Forrest," Boyd grabbed her in his arms and, true to form, she started giggling. There were a few couples who almost stopped dancing, certain they were about to hear *Cut!* but they had been briefed well by the extras coordinator, as well as various crew members ("Whatever you do, don't stop until you're told to!"), and continued on, professionals that they were.

"What is so funny, Inga Anderson?" asked Boyd, who was so delighted with this bit of improvisation that he couldn't help laughing himself.

"I guess I'm ticklish," said Fenny, giggling a little, and then responding to Boyd's laugh, she added, "And maybe you are, too?"

"I don't think I'm ticklish. Maybe just tickled."

Christian almost fell off his perch at camera one. He couldn't believe it. Boyd Burch, who wouldn't have been allowed to *bus* the Algonquin Round Table, let alone sit at it, had just improvised the perfect Ike response.

"Oh, Mr. Forrest," said Fenny, blushing. "I don't know why you're toying with me."

"I'm not toying with you." He moved his hand, which made Fenny giggle again. "Here," he said, moving his hand again. "Is that better?"

Fenny stopped laughing and nodded. "You're sure you're not having second thoughts about me as your bride? You're not smitten with the mayor's daughter?"

"I'm smitten," said Boyd, "but not with her."

They both laughed then, and danced into the center of the crowd, and then, as rehearsed, the extras joined in. Miss Penk and Frau Katte, paired with extras from the Twin Cities, danced, Slim and Lee danced, and Mary Gore, who was beside herself with the success of a scene she felt she co-directed, danced with a middle-aged man who had bragged that he'd had the lead in *Man of La Mancha* in high school.

The camera operator on the crane followed the turning, hopping, gliding figures as they danced into the roofless barn, filmed them as the music shifted and the square dance caller began calling out moves. He filmed the wider, overhead shot as camera two, on a dolly, followed Ike as he took Inga's hand and led her through the dancing crowd and out a side door.

When Christian called, "Cut! Print it!" everyone applauded and, just because he liked to accompany a good mood, Bill led the band in a quick refrain of "Happy Days Are Here Again."

Chapter 16

Although Hollywood operated more out of a sense of debt ("I owe you a favor") than gratitude, Christian Freed, when thinking of Malcolm Edgely, was truly grateful. The director's heart attack had been the falling domino that set off his appointment as director as well as a wonderful chain of events: Marcy Mincus's nervous breakdown on TV, leading to the media descending on Tall Pine, leading to publicity usually reserved for events like air disasters, or senators caught with call girls, or fashion models opening their signature restaurants. Everyone seemed to know about *Ike and Inga*, and how often were people aware of one of Harry Freed's movies while it was still being filmed?

"I just gotta find a way to keep the publicity going," Christian told Clark VanDrake. He had called the Yale graduate and fellow "Perky the Puppy" writer on the "Perky the Puppy" WATS line; this, after all, was a business call of sorts. Clark VanDrake had a crafty, devious mind, which was totally suited to dreaming up wild and warped scenarios, as well as to writing children's cartoons.

"You are a greedy little bastard," said Clark. "That's what I like about you."

"Thanks," said Christian. "I return the compliment. So how do I keep this tidal wave flowing in my direction?"

"Anyone else sick on the set?"

"Everyone's the picture of health," said Christian gloomily, "although I could see Grace Aisles getting a sexually transmitted disease."

"Not newsworthy enough. You need something with drama, human tragedy, high stakes. Any depressed types ready to off themselves?"

"No," said Christian, as if disgusted by the group's good cheer.

"How about a big fire? Burn the whole set up on the last day of shooting?"

"Clark, I'm an *artist*, not an arsonist."

"Yeah, right. Well, maybe you'll get lucky and get a natural disaster. A cyclone or something."

"A cyclone? Is that the same as a tornado?"

"Am I a fucking meteorologist? All I'm saying is death and destruction, that's what guarantees publicity. I gotta go now, I'm right in the middle of a 'Perky' episode."

"How is the little bitch?" Christian asked.

"I've got a horny bulldog after her," said Clark, "but it'll never get past the censors."

"Oh, well," said Christian, "you can only try."

Ron Feldman was organizing his stuntmen when Christian got to the set that morning. Today was the day of the logjam, and the cast and crew had assembled on the narrowest part of the Tall Pine River, barely two hundred feet across. There were no sightseers, owing in part to the early hour and to the fact that most of the tourists did have lives they eventually had to return to.

The sightseers' absence, however, further convinced Christian that the movie needed more publicity, and he allowed himself to daydream, thinking how nice it would be if maybe there was an accident or two.

"Okay, men," Ron was telling his crew, "remember, the trick is to stay in the middle of the log. Don't try to outrun it; just feel its pace and keep up with it."

The half dozen stuntmen nodded. They had flown in the day before for rehearsal (all outfitted with wet suits underneath their flannel shirts and overalls) and had pretty much mastered the art of logrolling. It was okay work, but not on the adrenaline-pumping level they preferred; it was no jumping off moving vehicles or cliff diving or running through fire.

"Looking good, guys," said Christian, and because he never knew what to say around men so much bigger and beefier than himself, he added, "Just remember, you're stuntmen. Don't try to act."

The crowd scenes had been shot the day before on the banks of the much wider Rainy River (Christian directing the Cup O'Delight regulars and other extras at different intervals to "look amazed!" "look scared!" "look surprised!"); today's shoot involved only a few cast members and the stuntmen.

Fenny was on the riverbank, trying to keep warm on the brisk fall morning by playing Frisbee with Boyd.

"Ready for the big scene?" Christian asked.

"I guess," said Fenny.

"Remember, this is where Inga realizes she really loves Ike and isn't scared to commit to him."

Holding her skirt against her thigh, Fenny lifted her leg and caught the Frisbee underneath it.

"Show-off!" yelled Boyd, laughing.

"Did you hear me, Fenny?"

"Yes, Christian," said Fenny in a singsong voice. "Inga realizes she really loves Ike and isn't scared to commit to him."

"I just don't want you to miss the subtext."

Boyd Burch didn't miss any subtext, grazing but not hitting Christian's head with a perfectly aimed Frisbee.

"Sorry, Christian!" he shouted.

"Actors," muttered Christian, patting his head to see if his hair was all messed up. "You try to make it easy for them and they just turn on you."

Miss Penk came down to see Ron Feldman and his men in action. She had met the stunt coordinator while working as an extra on the set, and the two had clicked. They shared a love of sports and keeping fit, but most of all, she told Frau Katte, "he reminds me of my son. A big, white muscley version of my son, but he and Alphonse have the same gestures, especially in the way they touch their throat when they're thinking."

It pained Frau Katte deeply that she couldn't give Miss Penk the thing she most wanted: a reconciliation with her son. Alphonse's father had won custody of the boy and had intercepted all letters and phone calls. After a while the letters would come back unopened, "no such address" marked on them. It was only the occasional briefings from Miss Penk's former, semi-sympathetic sister-in-law that kept them posted, and when she sent a graduation announcement ("I just wanted you to know that Alphonse is doing fine, even though you did desert him"), Miss Penk had decided nothing was going to stop her from seeing her son. Sitting high in the bleachers, her heart nearly bursting with pride and hurt, she had watched him accept his magna cum laude diploma from the University of Virginia.

She was able to plow through the crowds after the ceremony to find him, throwing herself into his arms. Her ex-husband flung her off him as if she were a bloodsucker.

"Alphonse and I have nothing to say to you," he had said in his cold, cold voice.

Miss Penk looked at her handsome, grown-up son, imploring him to say otherwise, but he didn't. She saw pain in his eyes, but he was his father's son, and in seconds the pain had been replaced by a cold anger and he turned on his heels and walked away. It was the last time Miss Penk had seen him.

Lately, in secret, Frau Katte had written to Alphonse, imploring him not to judge his mother, but to love her as she loved him.

"We have a lot of pictures hanging in our house," she wrote, "but yours is the one she looks at the most. Sometimes she will just sit there in front of it and I see the tears she wipes away."

Frau Katte didn't expect a return letter, but she desperately hoped for one, meeting Monte Barsch at their mailbox almost daily, taking the letters from him the way a child grabs for a present.

"Okay, people," called the first a.d., "places."

The first scene to be shot involved the birling, or logrolling, contest between a group of lumberjacks. It wasn't an official contest per se; in the story the men are trying to break up a logjam but, manly men that they are, turn this venture into a competition. A truckload of logs had been brought down from Canada. The current of the river they were shooting on wasn't too fast, but was fast enough for men balancing themselves on logs. They had earlier shot at the wider Rainy River, using different angles, and this footage would be used in cutaways.

The logjam looked puny, but through the magic of the camera, stock footage, and the editing room, Christian knew it would look massive and threatening. Three cameras would be used to get as many angles as possible. Once the men fell in, they'd have to be dried off and recostumed, so Christian, ever aware of Harry's admonitions to watch the budget, hoped to do it all in one take.

There were two "log wranglers." Their jobs were to get the logs to the stuntmen from where they stood on the "logjam," which was built out of a dozen tethered logs and looked something like a raft. The log wranglers were also in wet suits and stood in chest-high water while pushing the logs to the stuntmen; once shooting started, they would swim underwater until they were out of frame.

Once the marker board clapped and Christian called, "Action," motion filled the water. On the logs, the stuntmen moved as if they were on tightropes, arms extended, moving as gracefully as dancers.

"Over here, Jed!"

"Move it out, Ulysses!"

"Out of my way, Ike!"

The stuntmen shouted to one another as the logs rolled on the slate-blue river. All of the stuntmen performed serviceably, combining grace and athleticism as they treaded the rolling logs.

"Watch out!" yelled one stuntman on cue and, running in place, fell backward, spectacularly, into the water.

One particularly acrobatic stuntman ran forward, backward, then, in a real show of manly manliness, stood on his hands on the log before tumbling into the water, too. Christian had okayed the stunt, even though it seemed hokey. One by one, the stuntmen took their falls on cue and took them well, especially Boyd Burch's stunt double, who managed a clean back flip. It was a perfect take, and when Christian called, "Cut! Print it!" he gave everyone the thumbs-up.

Miss Penk applauded as the young men got out some distance downriver and into the trailer awaiting them.

"Way to go, Ron," she yelled through cupped hands, and the stuntman, his teeth chattering, acknowledged her with a jaunty wave before climbing into the trailer. He was a little disappointed there wouldn't be another take; he himself was the sort of person who liked extra insurance, and besides, it had all been so anticlimactic. It was such a tame stunt—who couldn't jog on a log? At least there was a fight scene he'd have to block, although that wasn't anything like falling off an office tower. Oh, well, he figured, it still beat digging ditches. He could say this with some authority, as he had in fact, one hot dusty summer, dug irrigation ditches.

Only Boyd and Fenny were in the next scene, and when they were called to their places they held hands, helping each other over the group of logs that had been tethered together.

"Man, these things are slippery," said Fenny, trying to get her balance. They only had to walk across the width of six logs to get to the place they were supposed to sit down.

"Just hold on to me, Fenny," offered Boyd chivalrously, although he was holding her hand a lot harder than she was holding his. Logs were not his favorite walking surface, especially logs floating on water.

"Okay, you guys, sit right there," instructed the first a.d. "We're going to be shooting with the three cameras"—he pointed to them—"so, any questions?"

Both actors shook their heads.

"Okay, kids," said Christian from the riverbank. He had an annoying habit of calling the actors kids, even those like Grace who were older than him. "The town's timber supply is safe, the world is good, and you two are in love. Let's get this thing done so we can get some lunch, okay?"

"Ike, I wanted to apologize," began Fenny as the cameras rolled.

"Don't," said Boyd, putting two fingers to her mouth. "I should be the one who apologizes. I've been the skunk here and I'm sorry for it."

Fenny felt tears come to her eyes. She was Inga, accepting his apology.

"Oh, Ike," she said.

"Oh, Inga."

Boyd slowly pulled the strings of Fenny's bonnet and leaned forward to kiss her.

"Cut! Print it! Let's just do it one more time," said Christian. "Just a little slower."

They did it one more time, slower, and it was a keeper.

"All right," announced the first a.d. over the megaphone, "lunch!"

Because they were hungry, because it was chilly sitting on those logs, Fenny and Boyd both leapt up, forgetting the precarious flooring they were on. The logs were tethered at the end, and to a tree on shore, but only loosely, and they began to shift in the water. Boyd accidentally stepped between two logs, into the water, and, righting himself, he stood back to give himself a wider base for balance, but he misjudged the distance and fell into the water.

"Help!" He bobbed to the surface to admit his secret shame. "I can't swim!"

"Grab on to a log!" said Fenny. "He can't swim!" she yelled to those on shore.

The dozen logs, still tethered together at one end, came apart at the other and fanned out, leaving wide spaces of water in between. It was in one of those channels that a frantic Boyd grabbed her hand, but the logs shifted again, one knocking Boyd across the shoulder. He slipped underwater, and Fenny followed him in.

The first a.d. and Doug Woo plunged into the water. The logs were close to the shore and they were beside Fenny shortly, ducking in and out of the water, looking for Boyd.

On shore, Christian stood frozen, watching. Here was what he had been hoping for, praying for; more calamity, which would in turn result in more publicity. As that awful little phrase *Be careful what you wish for* screamed in his head, he screamed back, *But not this! I didn't want anyone to get hurt . . . well, not hurt bad—especially the leading man!*

Christian watched as Doug and Fenny dove underwater, watched as the first a.d., holding a log for support, went into deeper water, calling for Boyd. Another body whizzed by him and into the water; it was Miss Penk, who had shed her sweater and her trousers. With neat, quick strokes, she swam past the jumble of logs.

Bile rose in Christian's throat; he thought of all the times he had dismissed Boyd Burch as "that dumb cowboy, a guy who's lucky he's got good looks because his head isn't much good for anything else."

He put out a prayer to any God that still might have the patience to listen to him: *Please let them all be okay, let them be okay.* He added an earnest *Especially the leads!*

When he heard Fenny shout, "We've got him!" relief flooded through him in a sensation so vivid that he thought for a moment he wet his pants. Fenny and Miss Penk, swimming against the current, held Boyd between them. They hoisted him over a log, where he coughed and sputtered. Then, with their arms resting on the log, the makeshift rescue squad kicked and kicked, bringing the log to shore.

"Should we get him to the hospital?" asked Christian as everyone waded out of the water.

"No, I'm all right," said Boyd, his relief at being saved replaced by embarrassment. He collapsed on the sand. "Ain't no need for a hospital."

"Don't even sit down," said Christian. "Everyone needs to get their wet clothes off." He did not like the color of their faces, which had odd dusky casts.

"Your shoulder's okay?" asked Fenny, her teeth chattering.

Boyd moved it, tentatively. "Yeah. A little sore."

"Come on," said Miss Penk. "Christian's right. We all had better get out of these wet clothes."

"That won't take long for you," said Christian, unable to help noticing that in her underwear, Miss Penk had a pretty good body.

There was a flurry of motion, a stomping of feet as Ron Feldman and his stuntmen brigade, now in dry clothes, ran to them.

"What the hell?" cried Ron. "Why didn't someone come and get us? Boyd, are you all right? Is everyone okay? Jesus, Boyd, you should have never been out on those logs if you can't swim. Why didn't you tell me you couldn't swim?"

Weakly, Boyd shrugged his sore shoulder. "You didn't ask."

"All right, men, move them out," ordered Ron, and before anyone could protest, Boyd, Doug Woo, Fenny, Miss Penk, and the first a.d. were each lifted up by a stuntman and carried to Boyd's trailer, which was the most obvious choice, seeing as it was the biggest.

Christian jogged along helplessly, and when the trailer door was shut before he could enter, he stood outside, feeling ashamed and alone. These feelings were deep and real, but Christian's psyche wasn't built to sustain deep and real feelings for long. Knowing he wasn't going to be of any help just standing there, he decided to check out the lunch tent, and as he walked past assistants scurrying by with towels and dry clothes, he began to chuckle, thinking of Miss Penk's tower of blond hair and how, soaking, it still kept its shape, its only change being in its direction. Wet, it swooped over one side of her head, looking like an odd and porous stocking hat. The Leaning Tower of Miss Penk. Thinking about her hair made him think about the state of his own, and as he approached the catering truck, he wondered if he dared risk getting a haircut in Tall Pine, at a place called Corby's Clip Joint.

It was a celebratory group that met for the Tall Pine Polka that evening. Miss Penk had invited the movie people to attend, and many of them accepted, seeing as disaster averted is an excellent excuse for a party. Boyd came, happy to be alive and wanting to spend time with those most responsible for that state, i.e., Fenny and Miss Penk. Christian came because Boyd was alive and the movie wouldn't have to be reshot *and* because he wanted to show off what he thought was the best haircut he'd ever gotten in his life. (He was still marveling over the fact that it had cost him only seven dollars, *including* a tip, at Corby's Clip Joint, whereas at the Très Beau Salon in Tarzana, haircuts cost ten times that much.) Ron Feldman came because he was happy Boyd was alive *and* because he hoped Bonnie Price, the script supervisor on whom he had a crush, would be there.

The regulars were of course happy that Boyd was alive, but some of them also had good news independent of the leading man throwing off the arms of the Grim Reaper.

Frau Katte took a letter out of her pocket, snapping it in the air.

"Look what Miss Penk and I got in za mail today." She cleared her throat and, making sure she had everyone's attention, read from the letter. " 'Dear M. Penk'—only one of our names can be on za entry blank—'Congratulations! Zesty Spice Foods is happy to inform you zat you are za winner of our Why I Like Zesty Spice Foods Contest. You and a guest'—zat'll be me—'will be flown out to San Diego, home of za Zesty Spice Foods Company, for one fun-packed weekend. Details to come, but in za meantime—congratulations!' Signed, 'Vera Brady, Contest Coordinator, Zesty Spice Foods.' "

Applause filled the cafe.

"San Diego has a great zoo," offered Ron Feldman, "if you're into zoos. Still, you'd think Zesty Spice Foods could send you to someplace a little more exotic."

"Oh, San Diego will be fun," said Miss Penk, whose hair had completely recovered from the morning's swim and sat high on her head, blond and swirled. "I've always wanted to go on that *Queen Mary.*"

"Well, you gals aren't the only ones who got a letter today," said Heine. "Gladys Triggs, one of our state senators, no less, wrote to me today saying that thanks to the concern of citizens such as myself, she's rethinking her position on the Boundary Waters."

"Heine's against the use of motorboats and Jet Skis in this particular wilderness area of ours," Miss Penk explained to the Californians who'd never heard of the Boundary Waters.

Bonnie Price nodded. "It's the people who are going to make the difference; we've just got to unite our voices."

"Right on," said Christian derisively. He had seen enough about power in Hollywood to know how much the "people" counted. The looks of his fellow revelers, however, told him they weren't going to tolerate any nonsense from him, and he amended his remark. "But you have a point there, Bonnie."

Mary Gore suddenly ran to the middle of the cafe, like an actor who was late picking up a cue. She was wearing her fringed *Angel Motors* jacket and a long patchwork skirt.

All talk, clinking of spoons against cups, scraping of chairs stopped. Mary stood still, posed like the Statue of Liberty. Under normal circumstances, the heckling would have already begun, but because of all the new guests, the regulars decided to hold back.

"Give me your tired, your weak, your poor," she began in a loud, taunting voice. "Give me your disenfranchised, your disabled, your disliked. Give me your geeks, your nerds, your social misfits. Yes, I will offer them life, liberty, and the pursuit of happiness, but an offer is not a promise. In the end, I will simply *grind them up!*" She shouted this and Boyd, mildly alarmed, looked at Lee to see how the owner of the place was handling Mary's public raving, but she seemed unaware of anything but the coffee she was pouring.

"Whew," said Mary, fanning her face as she sat down. "I don't know where that one came from."

"Probably za devil," whispered Frau Katte, ignoring Miss Penk's elbow nudge. "Someone should call an exorcist."

Grace Aisles, Doug Woo, and David the p.a., who were sitting at the counter, all laughed. Each had been thinking the exact same thing.

"Thanks," said Boyd as Lee filled his cup. "Any idea when Fenny might be showing up?"

The natural hostess smile that had been on Lee's face disintegrated.

"No, I don't," she said, moving down the counter with her coffeepot.

"Good one," mouthed Grace, who got regular updates on Fenny's personal life while the two were in makeup.

"What?" protested Boyd, and after Lee finished refilling coffee cups and went into the back room, Grace filled Boyd in on the romantic plot—and its actors—that had been happening in real life, off the set.

"Too many people," complained Slim, turning on the dishwasher. "When I get done with this load, I'm going out there as a mad dog and chase them all out."

Lee chuckled, in spite of her bad mood. "Good idea. And bite that Boyd Burch for me, will you?"

Slim started taking dirty cups out of the bus tubs and placing them in a gridded rack. "Why?"

Folding her arms, Lee leaned against the door of the walk-in refrigerator.

"He asked me where Fenny is. People should know not to ask me about Fenny."

"That's why I don't like all these strangers here," said Slim. "They don't know the rules. They don't know Fenny used to be your best friend but now you hate her."

She stared for a moment at Slim, who continued to casually stack cups. "You know I don't hate Fenny," she said finally. "I just think friends should respect friends' feelings."

Slim lifted the rack and set it next to the dishwasher. He still felt bad for giving Fenny the cold shoulder the last time she'd been in the cafe. "Are you respecting hers?"

Lee opened her mouth to say something but then shut it again.

"People fall in love with who they fall in love with," said Slim. "It's hard to fault someone for that."

"Yes," said Lee, and her blue eyes seemed brighter beneath a sheen of tears. "But I fell in love with Bill first."

A buzzer went off and Slim lifted the hood of the dishwasher. A cloud of steam rose like a genie toward the ceiling.

"I fell in love with Bill first," he said in a perfect impersonation of a pouting three-year-old, and before Lee could answer him he hoisted up the rack of newly washed dishes and pushed open the swinging door.

He was behind the counter when Mayor Lambordeaux came through the front door.

"Gettin' cold out there," said the mayor, hanging up his plaid wool jacket. "We might just get some frost tonight."

After this weather report, the mayor didn't join the others in the booths or take a seat at the counter, but instead went to the center of the cafe, took a deck of cards out of his pocket, and asked Bonnie Price to think of a card, any card.

When she said she had, and after elaborate shuffling and a few magic words, the mayor pulled out the jack of clubs from under Frau Katte's fez.

"That's it!" said Bonnie. "That's the card I picked!"

"Why are za cards always under my hat?" asked Frau Katte.

"Because no one else wears one," said Miss Penk.

"What exactly is going on?" Grace asked Lee, who emerged from the back room once she got bored listening to the dishwasher motor.

Reflexively, Lee grabbed a pot O'Delight. "How do you mean?"

"Well, that poem Mary recited, for one. Who was she supposed to be? The Statue of Liberty with a bad case of PMS?"

"Yeah, and now your mayor comes in and does card tricks," said Doug Woo, holding up his cup for a refill. "What gives?"

Lee held up her finger, acknowledging Mary, who was sitting in a booth, pointing to her cup.

"Well," she said, leaning toward the trio. "It's what we call doing the Tall Pine Polka."

"So what is that?" asked Grace. "Sort of a talent show? Is there dancing involved?"

"Yes," said Lee, "and in answer to your second question— probably. We do like to entertain ourselves, and somebody usually dances before the night's over. But the Tall Pine Polka is more a state of mind."

"What kind of state of mind?" asked Doug Woo. "Is it a Zen kind of thing?"

Lee laughed. "No, I wouldn't say that. Frau Katte," she said, summoning over the Swiss woman, "tell these people exactly what the Tall Pine Polka is."

"Hmm," said Frau Katte. She tilted her head and the cord of her fez hung at an angle. "I guess you could call it a state of mind."

"She already said that," said Grace. "That wasn't any help."

"Yeah," said Doug. "We still don't get it."

Just then Miss Penk and Ron Feldman stood facing one another, each striking a karate pose. Miss Penk yelled something unintelligible and Ron Feldman yelled something unintelligible back.

"Well," said Frau Katte after they watched the martial arts exhibit for a while, "I guess it's drinking za best coffee in za world, eating delicious desserts . . . and spending time with people you feel at home with. And when a person feels zat comfortable, zat free . . . well, zen souls are bared, songs are sung, and dances danced."

"Sounds like a cult thing," said Grace. "Souls bared—singing and dancing."

"Speaking of dancing," said Doug, "why don't we?"

To accompany Miss Penk and Ron Feldman's posing, some wise guy had selected "Kung Fu Fighting" on the jukebox and now two stuntmen were doing the Hustle, and doing it well. Christian and Sharen the makeup girl danced next to Heine and Bonnie Price. Laughing, Grace and Doug boogied across the checkered linoleum.

"Have I ever told you how pretty you photograph, Grace?"

The actress smiled at the cinematographer, realizing that he just might be amenable to an invitation to her room. "Tell me later," she said. "For now, let's just dance."

The last song of the evening was a request made to Heine by one of the dancing stuntmen.

"It's our anniversary," he explained, "and our song," and as Heine played "Love Is a Many-Splendored Thing" on his accordion, the two men danced cheek-to-cheek.

"Just like Fred Astaire and Fred Astaire," marveled Heine as he and the mayor walked home. "Not that I have anything against gay people—"

"Nope, me neither," said the mayor.

"But still, I thought people might think by playing 'their' song I might be endorsing what they do—not that it's up to me to give my stamp of approval, or anything." Heine stopped on the sidewalk to button up his coat. "Although I do think they'd be happier if they gave up that kind of lifestyle."

"A *lot* happier," agreed the mayor. "If you ask me, you've gotta be pretty miserable to live a gay lifestyle."

"Yeah, but then you look at Miss Penk and Frau Katte. They seem pretty happy."

"Well, that's sort of different," said the mayor. "They don't have a *gay lifestyle*. They just love each other."

Heine nodded. "Right." He held the collar of his coat tighter and turned onto the sidewalk leading to his house. "I think you called it on that frost, Mayor."

"Frost? I'm betting on snow now." He looked at his watch, bug-eyed. "Look at the time. I hope Dolly's not awake or I'm going to catch h-e-double-toothpicks."

" 'Night, Mayor."

"Goodnight, Heine."

Chapter 17

The mayor's weather prediction was on target; late the next afternoon, it started to snow.

"Snow in October?" said Grace Aisles, looking out the window of the Wild Wolf Lounge. "Is this part of that greenhouse effect?"

"Nah," said the bartender. "This is part of living in northern Minnesota."

Grace and Doug *had* spent the night together and were now spending their day off together.

"Let's go outside," suggested Doug. "We can build a snowman or something."

"Okay!" said Grace, but as she pushed herself away from the bar, she paused. "Wait a sec." She looked at the bartender. "I suppose you need mittens and stuff to build a snowman, huh?"

The bartender nodded. "Makes it a little more comfortable."

Grace turned to Doug. "Did you bring mittens?"

The cinematographer shook his head. "Why would I? I mean, who'd think it was going to snow in October?"

"Exactly." Grace pulled her stool to the bar again. "I'll have another."

"Me, too," said Doug. "But this time, make it a double."

Fenny, a native, was prepared to meet the snow, early or not.

"Come on, Bill," she said, pulling winter wear out of the closet. "You can wear my dad's stuff."

"Where are we going?" said Bill, who had been content playing a game of Scrabble—for money—by the fire.

"It's the first snowfall!" said Fenny impatiently, zipping up her parka.

Rising, Bill sighed. "And I suppose there's some Scandinavian ritual we have to complete?"

Fenny held her father's down jacket in her arms for a moment before holding it out to Bill. "Well, I wouldn't say it's a Scandinavian ritual," she said, "but it's a fun one."

"It better be," he said. "I was just about to score a triple word." Bill put his arms in the sleeves and shrugged the jacket up over his shoulders. It was extra-large but still a little snug on Bill.

"Wally used to say that was the warmest jacket he'd ever had," said Fenny with a little catch in her voice. "He said the only thing that kept him warmer was the love of his two girls."

"Maybe I shouldn't wear it."

"Oh, no, he'd like you to."

She handed Bill a pair of gloves with long cuffs and, dressed for the snowy world, they went out to meet it.

"Now our fun begins," said Fenny as she drove the Comet into a small parking lot lit by Chinese lanterns.

Snow was flying fast and furious and the windshield wipers were a steady metronome during the half-hour drive. Bill thought they were plowing their way through a blizzard, but when he voiced that opinion to Fenny, she laughed.

"Bill, blizzards are *wicked*. This is just a little snowfall."

They both got out of the car, Big Bill pulling tight the strings of his hood until only a small circle encompassing his eyes, his nose, and his mouth was exposed.

"What is this place?" he asked, nodding toward what looked like a little white shack.

"The Great Ball of China," said Fenny.

"The Great *Ball* of China," repeated Bill, as if saying the words aloud would help him understand just exactly what they meant.

"That miniature golf course I told you about. They close down the day after the first snowfall."

Bill nodded as if everything made perfect sense to him.

Fenny tucked a mittened hand in the crook of Bill's arm.

"It's sort of a tradition here to play a game on the first snowfall," she explained. "Kind of like counting down the New Year, or shooting off fireworks for the Fourth of July."

"It doesn't look like it's a very popular tradition," noted Big Bill, looking around the nearly empty parking lot.

"A tradition doesn't have to be popular to be meaningful," said Fenny.

As they walked under a wooden arch and into the shack that served as a ticket booth, two cars pulled into the lot.

"Welcome to the Great Ball of China," said the woman who sat playing solitaire at an old nicked desk. The heating coils of the space heater next to her glowed orange.

"So," said Fenny, her eyes sparkling. "The first snowfall."

"Yup," said the woman, who obviously didn't share Fenny's excitement over the event. "If you ask me, they should close down on Labor Day, but I just married into this crazy family, so what do I know?" She looked at what she could see of Big Bill's face framed by his hood. "How's it going, Nanook?"

Bill's smile was tight. "How much?"

"Four dollars," she said, and made change for Bill's ten. "The balls and clubs are over there."

"Follow me," said Fenny, and after she selected their clubs from a rickety rack, Bill did.

They walked downhill on a path, also lit by plastic lanterns. It was only when they were down the hill that the Great Ball of China could be seen.

"Ye gads," said Bill.

Made in the early 1960s by three brothers who had been raised in the Hunan Province by missionary parents, the Great Ball of China was a painted plywood construction of pagodas (Holes 1, 4, and 5), dragons (Holes 2 and 9), a wok (Hole 3), a bamboo forest (Hole 6), rice paddies (Holes 7 and 8), and ending with Hole 10, which was a Buddha. All of these landmarks were bordered by the Great Wall itself, a three-foot-high plywood fence painted a tired gray.

"And I thought an active volcano was something to see," said Bill. The falling snow was glittery, lit by a sun that had managed to shine through a break in clouds as it began its descent, and Fenny and Bill were content to stand at the beginning of the Great Ball, taking in all its kitschy magnitude.

"It's somezing, isn't it?"

Bill and Fenny turned around to see Frau Katte and the Cup O'Delight gang—with Pete, who had been cajoled to stand in for the mayor, who was at a waterworks meeting—making their way down the slight incline.

Fenny was delighted to see her friends, but her enthusiasm was tamped down when Bill whispered, "There's Lee. And she's armed with a golf club."

"Come on, let's choose sides," said Miss Penk, on whose tower of hair was perched a jaunty tasseled stocking cap. She ordered everyone to line up, and after they had counted off, she told the "ones" to form a line to the left and the "twos" to go to the right. Everyone was as obedient as schoolchildren under the direction of a bossy gym teacher, even Fenny and Lee, who wound up on the same team.

"Okay," said Miss Penk, who gathered the twos—Fenny's group—into a huddle. "Let's play smart and keep our eyes on the ball."

A coin was flipped, and the ones—Heine, Bill, Frau Katte, and Slim—were up first.

Frau Katte wiggled her hips a little and then putted the ball over the thin layer of snow that covered the AstroTurf path leading to a small pink and gold pagoda. She shot wide, the ball missing the cup, which was just inside the pagoda's door.

"Sheiss," she said. "Zis snow is giving me a hook shot."

Slim went next. He eyed his target, eyed the ball, and then, keeping his eye on the target, he hit the ball. Snow parted as the ball rocketed across the AstroTurf and directly into the door of the pagoda like an expected guest.

Slim jiggled his head slightly in an abbreviated swagger.

"Nice shot," affirmed his team.

Heine nodded, acknowledging what he thought was Slim's *lucky* shot, and then readied himself. He, too, studied his target and his ball, and when he thought he understood the trajectory needed, he hit the ball. Like Slim's, it was a clean shot that zipped through the snow, but unlike Slim's it was slightly off, and hit the pagoda to the left of the door, sending the ball back a good six feet.

There was plenty of encouragement from the ones and plenty of jeers from the twos, or at least part of the twos. Lee and Fenny, who kept as far away from each other as they could, stood sullen and silent.

By Hole 6, the teams were tied, with no thanks to Bill, who felt as displaced on this snowy putt-putt course as his teammates would have felt hanging ten on a surfboard.

"Now I'm getting serious," he said, assuming an exaggerated golfer's stance. This hole consisted of a crooked path with sprouts of wooden bamboo placed at odd angles, the objective being to get around the bamboo and to the panda, whose open mouth held the cup.

Bill's ball hit the wood-planked border of the path, hit a bamboo "forest," ricocheted off that and against the other side of the path, and then, in an amazing exhibition of luck over skill, shot right into the panda's mouth.

"Yes!" said Big Bill, pumping his club in the air.

Beyond the Great Ball of China, the sky was darkening, the sun already having slipped below the horizon. The snow was swirling, its motion matching the churning anger building inside Fenny. While Lee was pointedly ignoring her, her very presence was making her mad—Fenny was tired of being thought of as the bad guy—and when it was her turn, she smacked the ball so hard that it was launched over the panda's head and into Mongolia.

"Nice shot, Fenny," said Heine. "But this is *miniature* golf, remember?"

"Sorry," said Fenny tightly, and after setting down another ball, she did exactly the same thing.

"Hey, Fenny, relax," advised Miss Penk, who took any athletic competition seriously. "We don't want to just *give* them the game."

Fenny nodded; as irked as she was, her competitive spirit hadn't completely dissolved. She hit the next ball vigorously, but not wildly, and she was rewarded with a hole in one.

The temperature seemed to have dropped as the golfers finished the ninth hole (the dragon) and walked under the archway that led to the tenth.

"Wow," said Big Bill, "will you look at that."

At the end of a winding path sat a big gold-painted Buddha whose smile was almost a leer. Snow sat on the top of his head, giving him a white toupee, and covered his shoulders like a shawl.

The golfer had to get his/her ball past a fork in the path labeled "Temptation," over a bridge called "Enlightenment," through a tunnel called "Nirvana," and into the Buddha's outstretched hands.

"A lot of people zink it's a little sacrilegious," said Frau Katte.

"They had a big write-up in the paper last year," said Miss Penk. "For its thirtieth anniversary. The brothers that opened it—if I remember correctly, their names are Matthew, Mark, and John— anyway, they said this was their way of paying homage to a great country and great spiritual beliefs."

"Yeah," said Heine, "but look at the smile on that guy. Imagine the hubbub if it was Jesus sitting there smiling like that, ready to receive a golf ball in his hands."

Big Bill strode purposefully to the built-in tee. He was all business now; any wandering thought had been lassoed and brought into the tight corral of his concentration. He stared at the little white ball and then let his eyes follow the wandering path it must take, past life's obstacles and stages and into the hands of the Buddha himself.

He held his breath and putted. It was a sweet hit; the ball smartly avoided Temptation, zipped over Enlightenment, and just when it seemed he was going to have the unbelievable good luck of getting a hole in one, the ball found Nirvana too tough an obstacle to go through and bounced back. It took Bill another shot to get into the hands of Buddha.

"You're cookin' now, Bill," said Slim, the first civil thing he'd said to the man.

The ones beat the twos by three strokes, but everyone agreed it had been close and stared happily back to parking lot, their breaths frosty plumes in the snowy air.

There was so much good-natured congratulations that no one, except Fenny, heard the word that Lee said softly, but distinctly, as she passed her.

"Whore."

The two women had been keeping their distance; Lee was always the first to shoot on the twos team and Fenny last, and when they were watching the other team they made sure there was plenty of space between them.

Fenny's mouth hung open; she was the type of person who hadn't inspired a lot of name-calling—up until now, "prude" was probably the most inflammatory (and uttered by a college boy whom she refused to sleep with)—and to be the recipient of a word like "whore" stunned her.

"Collecting snowflakes?" asked Frau Katte, passing her, and it took Fenny a moment to realize what she meant. She shut her mouth and caught up to Lee and said, "Bitch."

Lee stood still, smiling expansively at Fenny until everyone had passed and they stood under the archway near the ninth-hole dragon.

"What did you say?" asked Lee, her tone as pleasant as a lady dispensing supermarket samples.

"Oh, believe me"—Fenny smiled—"it'd be a pleasure to repeat it: *Bitch.*"

"Then permit me the same pleasure: *Whore.*"

"Is everything okay?" asked Pete, who throughout the game had quietly taken his turn and then tried to unobtrusively position himself as close to Lee as possible.

"Everything's fine," said Fenny. "I'm just talking to this bitch, is all."

"And I'm conversing with this whore," said Lee.

"Oh, my," said Pete. He wasn't sure who pushed whom first, but suddenly Fenny and Lee were under the dragon, a tangle of flailing arms and legs, of auburn braids unleashed from their moorings, and then the two women were locked in an unfriendly bear hug, staggering back and forth like marathon dancers ready to be disqualified by the judge.

Pete finally succeeded in separating them by worming his body in between theirs.

Shocked, he held them apart like a referee in a cage match.

"What's gotten into you two?"

"She called me a whore!" cried Fenny.

"Well, she called me a bitch!" said Lee.

Pete knew how to break up a fight but not how to moderate the following peace negotiations. "Uh, I guess I'll leave you two to work this one out yourselves," he said, adjusting his Russian-style fur hat over his pompadour. "But remember: Friends don't hurt each other."

The women's labored breaths were their only response, but as they didn't fling themselves at one another, Pete felt he could leave Lee in good conscience. He felt nauseated by what he'd seen, and if he got sick, he didn't want Lee to see it, so he hightailed it to the parking lot, where, he was fairly certain, the people weren't calling each other names or grappling one another to the snowy ground.

Watching him scamper down the path, there was something about his brave, scrawny body that filled Fenny with shame.

"The first time Pete joins one of our little outings and we start a fistfight." She shook her head and then said softly, but loudly enough to be heard, "I'm sorry."

Lee's tongue pushed out from the side of her cheek and Fenny saw tears glistening in her eyes.

"I'm really sorry," said Fenny again. "It's just that . . . well, I'm not a whore."

Lee blinked, but it was too late; a twin line of tears ran down her cheeks. "And I'm not a bitch."

Next to the dragon's claw, she sat down, almost swooning, as if the events of the past few minutes were too much for her.

"I know," said Fenny, picking up Lee's beret, which had been knocked off in the melee. "But still," she said, batting the snow off, "to call a person a *whore*."

"I hate that word—it just popped out of my mouth."

"And I hate my word," said Fenny. "But it was the only thing I could think of to call you back."

Lee's mittened hands swabbed at her wet face. "Can tears freeze?"

Sitting down, Fenny shrugged. "I guess. Once I ran out with wet hair to get something out of my car, and on the way back to the house, my hair was clinking together."

"Are you kidding?"

Fenny shook her head. "It was really cold, though. Much colder than it is now."

Both women sat quietly, watching the snow twirl and dance in the pale light cast by the plastic Chinese lanterns.

"Looks like we were the only ones to take advantage of the last day of the miniature golf season," said Lee presently.

"Some tradition, huh? And I built it up to Bill to be this big thing."

In the following silence, Fenny wanted to kick herself for bringing *the* hot topic into their newly forged neutral zone.

"I'm sorry," she said again.

Lee nodded. "I feel so stupid. I know I didn't have any claims on Bill . . . I just didn't want anyone else to." Her voice quavered like that of a singer trying to find her note. "I want to be your friend again."

"Oh, Lee," said Fenny, and their down jackets made a slippery sound when they hugged one another.

Chapter 18

It was late afternoon (Christian wanted to get the sunset in; not necessarily because the scene called for it, but because he always liked a good sunset on film) and the cast and crew were set up in front of the old white clapboard church a few miles outside Tall Pine. They were shooting what would be the last scene of the movie, but the fifth-from-the-last scene to be shot. (Fenny still found the out-of-sequence shooting jarring, but had tried to adopt Grace's movie-making credo as her own: "If it made sense, it wouldn't make sense.")

"Looks good, Doug," said Christian. "Although I'm wondering if maybe you'd like the church a little more to the left. Then you'd get that lonesome-looking tree in; it might give us some good contrast."

After looking through the viewfinder, Doug nodded. It was always a pleasant surprise when Christian made a good artistic decision; and it gave Doug hope for all of mankind.

In an earlier scene, Ike and Inga had argued about what kind of wedding to have. Ike, a man who couldn't be bothered by public opinion, had surprised Inga by his desire to have "a big wedding with the whole town turned out." Inga, in turn, surprised Ike (who asked, "Don't all women like a big to-do?") by requesting a wedding with just the two of them and a preacher ("I don't want to share the day with anyone but you and the Lord, Ike").

Inga prevailed, which had made sense to Christian when he wrote the scene and now made even more sense to him as a director, as it would save the production another expensive crowd scene. The only shot of the bride and groom would be as they came out of the church, Ike carrying Inga down the wooden steps and to their carriage, as the preacher wished them a happy life from the doorway.

The snow Mayor Lambordeaux had foretold a few days earlier didn't stay, and the temperature had climbed up and stabilized in the mid-forties.

The first take went well, except that when they got into the wagon, the horse took his time before finally moving.

"Let's do it again," said Christian. "But this time, try to get a little more life out of that second-rate National Velvet."

"My agent called again," said Boyd as they walked back to the church. "Now she wants to fly out here to meet you."

"She sure doesn't take no for an answer, does she?" asked Fenny.

"She ain't supposed to," said Boyd. "She's an agent."

Many agents, who drooled over the prospects of her brilliant career and their ten percent of it, had tried to telephone Fenny, but she had no answering machine (unfathomable in Hollywood) and so their recruitment was left to fax machines and second-party phone messages. Dozens of messages and faxes piled up for Fenny in the production offices, but after reading a few of them, she advised the production secretary to recycle them into scratch paper; she wasn't interested in agency representation.

Boyd, in the production office to pick up his per-diem check, heard this, and was impressed.

"So, you're gonna go the lawyer route, huh?"

"The lawyer route?"

"Yeah, that's when you hire a lawyer to look over your contracts to make sure you're not giving up your firstborn or nothing. You save the agent commission and you get the peace of mind that everything's on the up-and-up."

"Actually, Boyd," Fenny had said, "I'm not going the lawyer route *or* the agent route."

"Fenny hasn't decided if she wants an acting career," said the production secretary, with whom Fenny had briefly discussed the matter.

"Not want an acting career?" asked Boyd, bug-eyed. "What's the matter with you?"

Fenny shrugged. "There are other things to do in life, you know."

"Yeah, but who wants to do them?" said Boyd, shaking his head.

Now, as the leading man and the leading lady climbed the

wooden church stairs, Boyd said, "I got you all figured out, Miss Fenny Ness. You're just playing hard to get."

"Boyd, I've told you, I like you, but as a friend."

Boyd laughed. "I'm talking about your *career*. You're holding off all these agents so they'll want you even more."

Fenny knew there were some concepts Boyd just couldn't grasp, her disinterest in a Hollywood career being one of them.

"Okay, you're right," she said. "You saw right through me."

"I knew it," said Boyd. "So what should I tell Mimi?"

"Tell her when I start thinking about getting an agent, she'll be the one I'll be thinking of."

"Okay, kids, let's do it again," said Christian.

The sun had just slipped under the edges of its colorful western blanket as the just-married couple triumphantly descended the stairs, the beaming preacher (a veteran of dinner theaters in suburban Minneapolis) waving goodbye.

Bonnie Price, the script supervisor, thought it might work better if the couple were to skip down the steps together, signifying the equal partnership, thinking that Ike carrying Inga smacked of paternalism, and just as she was jotting down the note to give to Christian, Boyd Burch tripped.

He would claim it was on Fenny's trailing dress, but footage would show that he had simply misjudged the width of the step.

Fortunately, it was the last step, so the pair didn't tumble down the entire flight of stairs. Unfortunately, Boyd was holding Fenny, and when he fell, he fell on her.

What probably would have been a fall injurious only to Boyd's ego became more when Fenny, whose arms had been wrapped around Boyd, instinctively let go to try to break her fall. The combined weight of her and Boyd landed on her outstretched arm and both of them heard the snap of bone, which would have been horrifying enough without the terrible *thunk* that followed, when Fenny's face met with one of the rocks that lined the walkway to the church. In less than a second, blood spurted from her mouth and she felt unnaturally jagged points where her two front teeth used to be.

"Cut!" screamed Christian.

"My teeth!" screamed Fenny.

"Your arm!" screamed Boyd, scrambling off her and seeing her forearm bent at an angle at which a forearm should never be bent.

Boyd's words alerted her to the extreme pain in her arm, but still, Fenny's concern was over her teeth, the pieces of which she could see on the bloody rock.

"My tee!" she screamed again, through an increasingly fat lip.

In the hospital waiting room Boyd punched one fist into the other.

"Oh, why couldn't it have been me?" he moaned, for at least the tenth time. He felt awful, clumsy and unprofessional and terribly guilty.

"It's all right, Boyd," said Christian, pacing behind the couch. "It was an accident."

A *stupid accident*, Christian wanted to add, but didn't. What accidents *weren't* stupid, weren't caused by a moment of distraction, a second of not looking? Still, couldn't Boyd have fallen on his own time, without Fenny in his arms? Christian sighed, feeling bloated from holding in the fit he wanted to throw.

When a doctor appeared, everyone in the lounge stood up.

"Her arm's broken," said the doctor, addressing the whole group rather than just one person. "Compound fracture. The radius came right through the skin."

Boyd groaned; he hated that he'd caused something so serious.

"As for her lip—well, she definitely won't be playing the trumpet for a while." The doctor laughed a little, trying to be entertaining for the movie people. When they didn't change their sober expressions, he cleared his throat. "Actually, more than her lip is split. The cut extends about a quarter inch past the lip." He demonstrated the area of injury on his own mouth, with his pinkie. "She's got five stitches. Our dental surgeon's on his way and we think he might be able to reattach one of the teeth, but the other one's too broken up."

"I'll pay for everything," said the contrite Boyd, " 'less, of course, she's got insurance."

By late evening, Harry and his secretary had flown in and met in Christian's hotel room for a conference with the beleaguered director.

"We should make a rule," said Harry grimly. "Further bodily injury to any cast or crew member will no longer be tolerated."

"I'm starting to think the whole thing is jinxed," said Christian. "Maybe we're filming on some sacred burial ground or something."

Harry's secretary passed out copies of the five scenes that remained to be shot.

"And speaking of filming," she said, riffling through the papers, "what are we going to do about it?"

"Well, let's see," said Harry. "How many more scenes do we have to shoot?"

"Five," said Christian, folding a stick of gum and adding it to the wad already in his mouth. "And Fenny's in four of them."

"Hmmm," said Harry, tapping his two pointer fingers on the table. "And how long did they say her cast would be on?"

"Six weeks."

"Right," said Harry. "And her mouth? How long before that heals?"

"The doctor said it would be healed enough for makeup in about a week and a half."

"Hmmm. And when were we hoping to wrap?"

"By Halloween," said Christian. "The end of next week."

"Hmmm." He tapped the table furiously, adding two more fingers. "I guess now would be a good time to take suggestions."

No words were spoken, but the room was filled with the noise of nerves: Christian's gum cracking, Harry's tapping, and his secretary's pen clicking.

"Well," said Harry finally, "I guess we could just shoot around her, like they did in that movie Boris Karloff made. He died before they were done, and they used the back of some extra's head and pretended it was Boris's."

This suggestion was not met with much enthusiasm. The tapping and cracking and clicking started up again.

"Maybe we could just shoot her good side," said Harry, "the side she didn't fall on."

"The trouble is," said Christian, "her lip split right here." He pointed to the vertical groove between his nose and mouth. "Right in the middle where this funny thing is."

"Philtrum," said Harry's secretary, who didn't do crossword puzzles for nothing. "That's called your philtrum."

"What I haven't learned from this lady," Harry said, smiling at his secretary. "But be that as it may," he said, forcing himself to continue, "being that it's right in the middle, it'll show from either side. Plus her lip's swollen up about twice its normal size." He had been able to see Fenny briefly, and she wasn't a pretty sight. "And there's also her cast to consider. I mean, we can throw a shawl over that arm, but what do we do in the scene where she's racing Ike on horseback?"

Christian ran his hands through his newly cut hair. "It's hopeless," he said. "We'll just have to wait until she's recuperated."

"That," said Harry, whose keen eye was always focused on the production finances, "is impossible."

"Well, we're frickin' insured, aren't we?" said Christian.

"Yes, Christian," said Harry, straining to keep his temper, "we're *frickin'* insured. But the big question is: So what? We wait six weeks and we have entirely different weather to contend with; shots that don't match, conflicting schedules—why, Boyd Burch is already in negotiations for a movie that starts in the middle of November, and Doug Woo leaves for North Africa the tenth—"

"All right, all right," said Christian. He was still running his hands through his hair, and his eyes were closed. "So we can't wait. What can we do?"

Harry's secretary's pen-clicking stopped. "I have an idea, boys."

Two anxious and questioning faces looked at her, begging her for answers.

"Remember when Fenny couldn't stop giggling and that . . ." She snapped her fingers, trying to remember the name. "That Mary Gore suggested that you incorporate that into the scene?"

Christian and Harry both nodded, but suddenly Christian stopped.

"Wait a second," he said, "how do you know about that?"

Harry looked at his nephew with a mixture of pity and exasperation. "Well, Chris, Doug Woo told me."

"Doug Woo told you? What is he—your paid spy?"

"He's my paid cinematographer," said Harry calmly. "He spies for free."

The bubble Christian had been blowing popped, and he dragged the remnants of gum off his lip.

"That does it," he said, pushing himself away from the table. "I will not have my work undermined and questioned at every turn by my own crew! An artist cannot be expected to comply to—"

"Christian, sit down," said Harry, not in the mood for any of his nephew's histrionics.

Christian sat.

"Doug Woo doesn't undermine or question your work in the slightest. All he does—at my request—is occasionally fill me in on what happened on the set. He gives me a different perspective from yours, that's all. What he might think important, you might not . . . and vice versa. The whole 'giggling dance' scene, for instance. You didn't think it was important to tell me it was Mary Gore's idea, whereas—"

"I wasn't trying to keep anything from you, Harry, I just—"

Harry raised his hand like a traffic cop. "Let's not waste time, Christian." He turned to his secretary. "I believe you were telling us your idea?"

Harry's secretary took a sip of the tepid coffee that room service had sent up. She pushed her glasses up on her nose, ready to do business.

"Well, why not do the same in this case? Incorporate what we've got? Use the wedding footage—show Boyd falling with Fenny in his arms, and then shoot the rest of the movie with Fenny's visible injuries."

Christian swatted the air as if a fly were buzzing around. "You don't understand; it's all out of sequence. The wedding scene is the last scene in the movie. How can she have a fat lip in earlier scenes if she doesn't get it until the end?"

"Maybe you'll just have to change the ending."

"And how do you propose I do that?" Christian's voice was at its most patronizing and Harry was about to scold him, but his secretary didn't give him a chance.

"Write more scenes."

Christian was delighted with her answer; he leaned back in his chair and laughed. Not only did he laugh, but he slapped his knees and held his stomach until Harry told him to cut it out, couldn't he see she was only trying to help? And then he said, wait a minute, maybe her suggestion wasn't so bad after all; what were the alternatives? And then Christian shook his head and asked if they were aware it took him three years to write *Ike and Inga* and he was not the kind of writer who could do quickie patchwork, and then Harry said that maybe they should bring in a writer to help him, and Christian wondered whom they could bring in at the eleventh hour, and then Harry's secretary suggested Mary Gore.

"She's the one who thought to leave in the giggling," she reminded them. "She knows the movie and she is a writer."

"Writer," scoffed Christian. "She's a frickin' *poetress*, and a lousy one at that."

"Bad writing never stopped a script from being made," said Harry. God knows he had made plenty of movies from poorly written scripts. He dragged the phone across the table. "Let's call her. Time's a-wasting."

And so Mary Gore, who was sitting at her kitchen table, eating sardine sandwiches and tomato soup with her father, got the call she had been waiting for all her life.

"Daddy-o," she said, hanging up the phone, "that was Hollywood calling—and it was for me!"

Fenny studied her mouth in the hand mirror Lee had brought her. Now that the Novocain had worn off, her upper lip was a throbbing, swollen mess, accentuated by what looked like a black bug crawling up the middle of her lip. Her arm hurt, too, but she had been given industrial-strength Tylenol and her mouth consumed so much of her attention the pain was easy to ignore.

She parted her lips slightly (it was amazing how this slight movement made her want to yelp in pain) to better survey her teeth. Her beautiful white teeth. Even the most modest person has one or two private vanities, and Fenny's teeth were hers. She loved them, and apparently wasn't alone in her regard. During her one year at college, the boy sitting next to her in her government class had compared her teeth to the perfect democracy.

"There's a place for each one of them," he had said breathlessly, "with no bullying incisor or molar squeezing them out."

Fenny thanked him for his comment and privately asked the professor for a seat change.

Now she struggled to lift her throbbing lip high enough to see a democracy in shambles. The left front tooth, cut cleanly in half by the fall, had been reaffixed, and the dentistry was so well done that she couldn't tell if the faint line of demarcation was real or imagined. The left tooth, however, or what remained of it, looked as out of place in Fenny's mouth as a hobo at a debutante's ball. Only a jagged vee of white peeked out from her gum line; it looked like a puppy's tooth, small and sharp and pointed. A rush order had been placed on the prosthetic crown, but the dental lab could only move so quickly and, too, her doctor wanted her lip to heal more before subjecting her to the dental procedure.

At the hospital, Harry had told Fenny he'd get her a room at the Northlands Inn so she wouldn't have to be alone in her house, but Fenny accepted Lee's invitation to stay at her place. Bill wouldn't be able to nurse her; didn't even know that she was in need of nursing, as he had left for Canada with Mae Little Feather the day before, to pick up deer hides from her supplier.

Fenny had actually been happy he was going; she wanted time alone with Lee to further cement their fractured friendship. Happily, any awkwardness between them evaporated after her accident; Lee rallied to her side as the old friend she was, and their estrangement seemed far away.

"How're you doing, Fenny?" Lee asked, tucking an O'Leary Exports cashmere afghan around her patient.

"Good," said Fenny softly.

"Slim made you this downstairs." Lee set a vanilla malt on the coffee table.

"Extra malt powder," said Slim. "That's my secret."

Fenny tried to purse her lips around the straw. Even this tiny effort hurt.

Slim sat on the floor by Fenny and, putting his head in her lap, whined.

"Hello, old dog," she said, her words sounding thick. "I've missed you."

"Likewise," said Slim. "So don't get in any more fights with Lee."

"Harry called while you were sleeping," said Lee. "They're having a big meeting to decide what's going to happen."

"I feel so bad," said Fenny.

"I'll bet you do, honey. Do you think it's time for more Tylenol?"

Fenny laughed, but the position laughter put her mouth into was too painful. "No, I don't mean bad that way, although I do feel bad." She took a sip of the thick malt. "I mean, I feel bad that I've screwed up the movie."

"Fenny, it's Boyd who fell, not you."

"I know. But just let me feel guilty, okay? It helps me forget the pain."

The phone rang.

"And I'll bet this is Boyd again," said Lee, guessing at the caller's identity. The poor actor had been calling with apologies every half hour.

Lee picked up the receiver and a moment later shouted, "I have nothing to say to you!" She slammed the phone down. Her face was as white as the moon shining through the uncurtained window.

Slim was immediately to his feet. He picked up the phone and yelled into it, "*What is your problem?*" and slammed the receiver down, harder than Lee.

"He stays on the line," Slim explained to Fenny. "The bastard stays on the line just to provoke Lee even more."

Fenny's battered teeth began to chatter. "He's been calling a lot lately, hasn't he?"

Lee nodded. "About every other night now, since he got caught cheating all those clients. He goes to trial next month—my brother says there's a good chance he'll go to jail." She sighed deeply. "I keep my fingers crossed."

"I've told her to get her number changed," said Slim, looking crossly at Lee.

"What's the point?" said Lee. "He'd just find another way to reach me."

Christian now had no doubt that hell existed—he was experiencing it firsthand.

Mary Gore arrived at his hotel room the next morning, bright and early, wearing, of all things, her caftan with the tiny mirrors embroidered into it.

"Aw, geez, did you have to wear that?" asked Christian, herding her quickly inside. He didn't want anyone to get the idea that he might be *entertaining* this lunatic.

"Your uncle warned me that you might not exactly be thrilled to be working with me," said Mary Gore, throwing her *Angel Motors* fringed jacket on the bed. "And to that I say, *Je comprends.* In a perfect world an artist shouldn't have to deal with another artist coming in and putting her thumbprints all over his work. "But this isn't a perfect world, is it?"

Christian swallowed hard, thinking the possibility of throwing up was a real one. What had he ever done to deserve punishment like this?

"Well, don't just stand there," said Mary Gore, going to the round table near the window. "We've got words to smith."

They worked until the afternoon without a break. Twice Christian got up, grabbed a pillow off the bed, and screamed into it. Once Mary Gore called him a spoiled little baby, frightened to spread his creative wings. Christian suggested long-term therapy as a way of ridding her of her crackpot artistic delusions once and for all. Mary wondered aloud where Christian would be if he didn't have an uncle in the movie business. Christian remarked that he had heard townspeople had found the perfect use for *Angel Motors*—as toilet paper.

Still, in between insults and stomps around the room and screams into pillows, they worked, and by the time Harry and the room service waiter came knocking on the door, they had mapped out an outline of the new ending.

"I thought you might be hungry," said Harry as the waiter wheeled in the cart. "So I took the liberty of ordering you lunch.

"I ordered fish," he continued as the waiter lifted the silver lids off the plates. "Brain food. And here we've got lots of vegetables . . . and lots of rolls here—you'll need carbohydrates for stamina." He signed for the bill and tipped the waiter, who left smiling, twenty dollars richer than when he came in.

Harry helped himself to a pumpernickel roll and, buttering it, he asked, "So how's it going?"

He sat on the edge of the bed, listening to Christian and Mary alternately tell the revised story of Ike and Inga in between bites of brain food and carbohydrates.

"See, Uncle Harry," said Christian, "the reason Ike fell on the steps in the first place is that he was dodging a wild bullet fired by Ulysses Coltraine."

"He's the lumberjack Ron Feldman played in that logrolling scene," said Mary Gore. "We're building up their rivalry in another scene."

"Which'll save me from hiring another actor," said Harry.

"Don't say I never saved you money," said Christian.

"So Ike," continued Mary, "by falling on Inga, actually saves her life—"

"Not a bad wedding gift for a groom to give to his bride, huh?" said Christian. "And we've got a great bedside scene—Inga lying there, her face all beat up, her arm broken, thanking Ike for marrying her and saving her life, all on the same day."

"It'll be a scene of pure poetry," said Mary, "a scene exploring the depths of romantic love, the limitless—"

"Okay," said Harry, having heard enough. "I better let you geniuses get back to work. Our goal is to stay on schedule—and Monday morning's only"—here Harry checked his watch—"thirty-some hours away."

It was after midnight when Mary finally picked up her *Angel Motors* jacket, lying in a heap on the bed where she had thrown it.

Christian leaned back in his chair, exhausted but exhilarated. With a sense of wonder, he watched the wide-hipped, forty-something woman in the ridiculous mirrored caftan put on her equally ridiculous fringed jacket; when had she turned into the perfect writing partner? When had she stopped sounding like a nut and started making sense? In less time than it sometimes took Christian to write a line of dialogue, she and Christian had written five new scenes and a whole new ending.

"We'll do the polish tomorrow morning," said Christian, his hand rooting in a nearly empty bag of potato chips.

"I suppose even diamonds need to be shined," said Mary, convinced that not just good scenes, but true art, had been created in that hotel room. "Same time tomorrow morning, then?"

"I'll have breakfast sent up."

"Oh, goody," said Mary, for room service was a perk of the movie business of which she was especially fond.

Chapter 19

That Sunday evening, Harry brought his leading lady the revised script, explaining that Christian and Mary Gore had spent the weekend in a frenzy of rewriting.

"We may have created a monster," he told Lee and Fenny. "Now they're actually talking about collaborating on another project."

"*Mary and Christian?*" said Fenny. "Somehow I just don't see it."

"I know," said Harry. "Hollywood will never be the same."

Fenny riffled awkwardly through the revised pages with her good hand.

"They're keeping in Boyd's fall?" she said, briefly reading a section.

"Oh, it's an integral part of the story line now," said Harry. "Read on. You have three scenes in which you get to show the world your stitched and swollen face."

"I do?" asked Fenny, but when she finished reading, she nodded her head. "It works for me."

"You're willing to go before the cameras looking . . . like that?"

"Sure," said Fenny. "I just want to get this thing *done*."

"You're a trouper, Fenny Ness." Harry had worked with a lot of leading ladies, and his instinct was always to protect them from anything that might show them in a bad light. The idea of Fenny's unfortunate accident being incorporated into the script offended him; he felt she was being taken advantage of.

"Fenny, you do realize that you don't have to agree to this?" For a brief moment, the producer part of Harry wondered if he was going crazy, trying to talk an actor into delaying a movie and consequently costing the production money. "You can ask for more time off to recuperate. It's perfectly understandable that you don't want your face to be seen twenty feet high on the movie screen in the condition it is now."

"Oh, Harry," said Fenny, "everyone will think it's makeup anyway. And it does make the ending a lot better."

"I, for one, appreciate your chivalry," said Lee.

"And I appreciate your appreciation," said Harry.

The black stitches holding her lip and skin together moved slightly as Fenny, as much as she could, smiled. "I don't know how much of a kissing honeymoon this will be," she read from the script, "but I can make up for it in hugging."

Harry's smile was unreadable.

"Oh, my darling Inga, how will I ever forgive myself for hurting you?"

"You saved my life, Ike. Thanks to you, my broken skin and bones will mend."

"You know the funny thing, Inga? You have never looked more beautiful to me than at this moment."

"Perhaps my husband has an affection for jack-o'-lanterns I was not aware of. Or maybe it is that in the fall you suffered injury to your head?"

"The only injury I thought I might suffer is a broken heart, Inga. That would be my fate if anything happened to you."

"Oh, Ike."

"Oh, Inga."

Silence filled the room as they kissed, and when Christian called, "Cut!" the crew burst into applause.

"God," said Doug Woo, thumping his chest, "that gets you right here."

"Great job, Mary," said Harry. He had decided to stay in Tall Pine until the movie wrapped ("Maybe I can ward off some of these accidents," he told his secretary, who had flown back to L.A.), and watched the new scenes being filmed.

"And you, too," he said to Christian.

"Thanks," said Christian. He was in such a good mood that he didn't even mind Mary taking a little of the glory. The scene *was* good, packing an emotional wallop that he knew would have audiences crying into their popcorn.

"Don't take this the wrong way," he said to Fenny after she got out of the four-poster bed. "But I think your accident is the best thing that happened to this movie."

"Glad to be of service," said Fenny, holding up the voluminous skirt of her nightgown so it wouldn't drag on the floor. "If there's any other way I can be of service—oh, maybe by breaking a leg, or how about if I sustain a nice skull fracture?—well, you just let me know."

"Fenny, I didn't mean—"

"I know you didn't," said Fenny. She sighed. "A person just doesn't like to hear how *pleased* someone else is over her injury."

The next day Fenny wasn't needed on the set until midmorning and so she decided to see how Gloria Murch was handling things in Bill's absence.

"My goodness," said the pastor's wife when she saw Fenny, "you look absolutely awful!"

"You should see the other guy," said Fenny. Using her good arm, she lifted an erratically woven pot holder off the hand of the display mannequin.

"Let me guess—Roberta Paulsen."

"Oh, Fenny, don't make fun of Roberta. You know her cataract surgery didn't go well and—"

"I'm not making fun of her," said Fenny, "I'm just wondering why you have to hang her pot holders all over the place. I think people'd be more likely to buy them if they didn't see them up close."

"Fine," said Gloria. She began yanking pot holders off the mannequin's hands, off the metal sculpture deer antlers (it had been her mother's last acquisition for the store and the one Fenny had chosen, out of sentimental value, never to sell), off the hat rack by the door.

"And does she have to be wearing these?" asked Fenny, gesturing toward the mannequin, who displayed a sweatshirt appliquéd with puffy gingham flowers and an apron that was embroidered in uneven calligraphy, "Kiss the Cook—It Adds Spice to the Meal."

"Alida Loberg made those!" said Gloria Murch, as if knowing who the craftswoman was might change Fenny's mind about the craft. "And I think they're darling!"

Fenny was about to say, *My point exactly*, when the bell above the door jingled.

"Mae!" said Fenny, pleased not only that she had been interrupted, but over the interrupter and what her presence meant: Bill was back! "When did you get home?"

The old woman, carrying a shopping bag, looked at Fenny as if she were crazy.

"I didn't go anywhere," she said, walking to the display counter and setting her bag on top of it. "You know you got a bug on your lip?"

"It's not a bug, it's stitches." She went behind the counter. "And I thought you and Bill went up north to get some deer hides."

The old woman began taking beaded wallets out of her bag. "This one I'm charging thirty dollars for," she said. "It give me a damn blood blister on my thumb."

Gloria Murch *tsk*ed; she never understood how people could use profanity around a clergyman's wife.

"Mae," said Fenny, trying to keep the urgency out of her voice, "didn't you and Bill go up north?"

The woman cocked her head, surveying Fenny through eyes nearly buried under the wrinkled drapery of her eyelids. "No, I ain't been up north. Can't say as Bill has or not. Ain't his keeper and neither are you." She looked at Fenny's arm. "You want me to sign that cast?"

"No, thanks." Feeling short of breath, Fenny took the invoice the old woman gave her and walked to the cash register. She opened it, and after looking at the figure on the invoice, she carefully counted out Mae's money, willing her hands to stop trembling.

"You know," said the old woman, folding her money and zipping it into a pouch she wore around her neck, "I don't mind doing business with you—no, I *like* doing business with you. You're as fair as your ma was. But I will tell you this." Mae leaned over the counter, curling up her forefinger in an invitation for Fenny to come closer. "I don't want Bill to have nothing to do with you. So if he's somewhere he shouldn't be according to you, then I'm glad. I got a friend's granddaughter up in Manitoba who's interested in him, and I'm hoping he takes the bait."

She turned sharply, startling Gloria Murch, who had moved into a better eavesdropping position.

"My, them's big ears you have," she said, walking past the pastor's wife. Raising her voice to a singsong, she added, "The better to hear you with."

The bell jingled, and Mae Little Feather didn't bother to shut the door as she left. Fenny and Gloria Murch stood absolutely still, listening to the old woman's cackling, until it was erased by wind and distance.

Fenny was sullen in the makeup trailer, sitting silently in her chair with her arms folded over her chest.

"And then they dragged her," Grace was saying, "kicking and screaming into rehab, with about five hundred photographers taking her picture."

"I worked with Mara on *Lucky Linda*," said Sharen, standing behind Grace, appraising her finished makeup. "She was zonked on downers then."

The two women were discussing the latest tribulations of one of Hollywood's highest-paid actresses.

"See, that goes along with my theory," said Grace. "You can have a huge talent—and admit it, Mara Reynolds does—but she's gone through, what—three husbands? At the end of the day she goes home to an empty house."

"You don't think you can have both?" asked Sharen.

"Sure," said Grace. "If you can ever find the man who's not afraid of your talent—who doesn't think it's like some big attack dog—ready to go after him just because he wants to pet its master."

Sharen laughed. "You make a lot of sense, Grace. Although I never heard of talent referred to as an 'attack dog.' "

"Not just talent—brains, beauty, skill of any kind—it all threatens men."

As Sharen began work on Fenny, Grace regarded her fellow actress.

"So what's up with you?"

"What do you mean?" asked Fenny as Sharen sponged foundation on her face.

"What do I mean?" asked Grace derisively. "I mean, we have a certain level of gossip that we aspire to here in the makeup trailer, and if you can't contribute to it, you should at least have the good manners to act interested in it."

Fenny, who wasn't planning on sharing any information, surprised herself. "Oh, Grace, Bill lied to me!"

She told Grace and Sharen of her run-in with Mae Little Feather that morning.

"Oh," said Grace, waving her hand, "that's nothing. I thought you were going to tell me something good—like he's got a wife and family back in Hawaii or that he's a transsexual or something."

"That would be something *good*?"

"You know what I mean." Grace regarded her friend in the mirror. "But to tell you the truth, I think you're jumping the gun as far as calling Bill guilty. Maybe his aunt lied—maybe they did go to Canada to get whatever you said they were getting—"

"Deer hides," interjected Sharen.

"Whatever. But doesn't it make sense? His aunt doesn't like you, so why shouldn't she want to stir up trouble?"

"And lie to me?"

Grace laughed. "You sound so wounded, Fenny. Wouldn't you rather have her lying to you than Bill?"

Fenny nodded.

"So forget about it. Don't worry about anything until you talk to Bill." She stood up, holding out her hand. "Now come on, let's go watch Ron and Boyd play cowboys."

Ron Feldman found his role as the logrolling lumberjack, Ulysses Coltraine, expanded, and he couldn't have been more pleased.

"This is the first time I've had more than five lines," he said. "This is a real acting job."

He had gone over and over his lines with Bonnie Price, who was not only a responsible and diligent script supervisor but an astute director, coaching Ron as they went over the script.

"Remember, Ron," she said, "Ulysses is a tough guy, but he also loves Inga. Maybe if you could show some of his hurt at her rejection, we'd feel more for him."

The scene to be shot would appear in the movie before Boyd's fall, and establish some of the rivalry that led up to the firing of the gun. As Mary Gore explained to Fenny, "The testosterone level will be volcanic."

They were shooting in a corral (really a pen, but movie people seemed to have a need to give things fancier names) on the Heneghan farm. Both men were looking over a horse they wanted to buy.

"I don't think you could handle a horse like that," Ulysses said to Ike. "She needs someone who lets her know who's boss."

"Why is it, Ulysses, that you're always so worried about who's boss over who?"

The two men baited each other for a while before Ike got on the horse and started riding it around the corral. Ulysses chased him on foot until he got the brilliant idea to jump on another horse and chase Ike around the pen. The two men continued arguing and then the scene ended with Ron the stuntman stepping in for Ron the actor, jumping from his trotting horse to Boyd's. He missed, landing in the dirt. When Ike offered his hand, Ulysses said, "I'm not going to take the hand that's trying to take away the hand that's meant for me."

The crew applauded when Christian ordered a print.

Boyd offered Ron his hand after the last take, and clapped him on the back.

"Dang—I felt like I was acting with Laurence Olivier on a horse!"

"Thanks, Boyd," said Ron, rubbing his shoulder. In the last fall he had landed funny, but the resulting muscle spasm took little away from his euphoria. He had acted!

For the next scene, Mary Gore sat next to Harry, watching Ron Feldman/Ulysses get off his horse in front of Ike's barn and tearfully apologize to the newlywed couple about "firing that pistol just out of pure orneriness."

"I's just shooting up at the sky," said Ulysses. "Just sorta like a shout or scream. Sorta like my protest against what you were doing . . . gettin' married and all."

"He is *good*," whispered Mary to Harry.

Harry nodded. Like Fenny, Ron was a natural, but adding to the ease he brought to the role was the role itself, which seemed tailor-made for the stuntman: big tough guy who only wants to be loved.

Ike swung himself up on his new horse.

"Well, we did get married, Ulysses. And if you want to show you're really sorry, you'd help me get my bride up on this brand-new horse. I want to take both of them for a ride."

Ulysses obliged the request, lacing his fingers together to make a stirrup for Inga. She stepped onto his hands and he gave her a boost up into Ike's arm. She then settled herself in front of Ike, drawing her broken arm close to her body and holding the saddle horn with her other hand.

"You take good care of Miss Inga, now," said Ulysses, and hearing the catch in his voice, Mary felt tears come to her eyes.

"That, Ulysses, is my intention," said Ike, and pressing himself to his bride, he kissed her. Inga leaned back and turned her head, returning Ike's kiss.

"Hee-yah!" said Ike, and with a toss of her head, the horse trotted off down the road and out of frame.

"Cut!" said Christian. "And help me write my Oscar speech!"

To say that Fenny was shocked to see Bill at that evening's Polka Night would be to say the universe is vast.

He was at the piano with Lee, and both were so deeply engrossed in an improvised blues duet that neither turned around at Fenny's entrance.

Fenny tried to walk casually to the counter, even though she felt she had been hit with a stun gun.

" 'Allo," said Mary Gore, who at the counter was writing in a black leather notebook. "*Ça va?*"

"Just fine," said Fenny in a tone that spoke otherwise.

"Mary's writing a screenplay that'll take place in Paris," explained Miss Penk.

"I think I've found my métier," said Mary. "Although I won't give up my poetry. I couldn't do that to the world."

"Oh, please try," said Frau Katte.

"You're looking much better," said Slim, pouring Fenny a cup O'Delight.

"I feel better," Fenny fibbed. Actually, she was near tears; first Bill lied to her, and now he was completely ignoring her.

Slim leaned over the counter and, inches away from her face, studied her lip.

"You know, when you have those stitches out, you might have a little scar."

Fenny nodded glumly.

"But from what I can see, it's going to make you better-looking than you already are."

"Puh," said Fenny, blowing air out of her mouth.

Slim squinted his eyes. "No, really, it'll sort of outline your upper lip and give it—"

"Fenny!"

Fenny felt Big Bill's arms around her waist, felt his smooth face next to hers, smelled his outdoorsy smell laced with peppermint candy and coffee, and the smell almost made her melt in his arms. Almost.

She sat up stiffly. Without being asked, Frau Katte moved down a seat, giving Bill the stool next to Fenny's.

He still kept one hand on her back while he sat down, swiveling to face her.

"How's your arm, Fenny?" he asked, a line of concern cutting into his brow. "And your mouth—my God. Go like this." Bill bared his teeth and looked at Fenny's as she mimicked him. "Hey, the one looks good. When will they fix the other one? Oh, Fenny, Lee told me all about it. I'm so sorry."

It looked as if Fenny was still displaying her teeth, but in truth, her mouth had frozen into a grimace. She was torn by warring impulses: she wanted to throw her arms around Bill and she wanted to slug him; she wanted to tell him how much she missed him and she wanted to scream at him for lying to her. Instead, she sat on the counter stool, looking at him as if he were a host who'd just served her something that tasted vaguely rancid.

"Fenny," said Bill, "what is the matter with you?"

But Fenny was saved from having to formulate an answer by Lee, who asked Fenny if she had heard the music she and Bill had been playing and did she think Lee should turn the Cup O'Delight into a blues bar?

"Where's my ax?" said Heine, picking up his accordion, and when he launched into a blues chord progression, the group laughed and kept time by slapping the counter with the palms of their hands.

The night was shaping up in typical Polka style, but Fenny, who had missed the gatherings desperately while she and Lee were feuding, was in no mood to enjoy it.

"So where were you?" she asked Bill.

With a big smile, Bill pushed aside the look of guilt that jumped onto his face, but not before Fenny saw it.

"Where was I *when?*" he asked, his voice as sugarcoated as a kid's breakfast cereal.

"When you said you were with Mae Little Feather!"

Fenny wasn't aware she had used some unnecessary volume but figured it out when all other conversation in the Cup O'Delight abruptly ended. Fenny didn't care—if she and Bill were going to have an argument, everyone would hear about it sooner or later; why not give it to them firsthand?

"What *are* you talking about, Fenny?" asked Bill the way an understanding counselor talks to a patient about to be committed.

"Oh, Bill!" said Fenny. She swiveled away from him in disgust, but then, having more to say, swiveled back. "Mae came into the shop! She said you didn't go up north with her!"

Bill's face didn't so much turn red as it darkened—his version of a blush—and his jaw muscles pulsed under his skin.

A silence filled the cafe and people who didn't itch felt a need to scratch; people who didn't care what time it was checked their watches; and people who didn't have colds sniffed and cleared their throats.

Finally Frau Katte, who thought Bill was rude not to answer Fenny, spoke.

"Zo," she said, fiddling with the sugar dispenser. "Where were you?"

"I was up north," said Bill evenly, not taking his eyes off Fenny.

"Up north with your *aunt?*" said Frau Katte.

"Katte," scolded Miss Penk. Even though she was dying to know the answer herself, she thought Frau Katte's imitation of a court-room prosecutor was a little pushy.

"No, Frau Katte," said Bill, still looking at Fenny. "I wasn't with my aunt."

The mayor couldn't resist jumping into the fray. "Then why'd you tell Fenny you were?"

"I had my reasons," said Bill.

"Listen," said Lee, uncomfortable for her friends. "This is really none of our business. This is between Fenny and Bill."

"Still," said Mary Gore, "if they choose a public place to air their *problèmes d'amour*, then I think by rights we can be interactive participants."

"Mary," said Fenny, leaning against the counter to better look at her, "I think I speak for the entire group when I ask you to please *shut up.*"

Making fun of Mary was a sport the entire group enthusiastically participated in, but this was different. There was not an inch of teasing in Fenny's voice; her tone was so mean and cold that Slim, hardly a defender of Mary's, felt obliged to say, "Hey, now, Fenny, come on."

Slim's censure, on top of everything else, was the spring that cata-pulted Fenny off her stool and out the door.

Bill looked at his friends, shrugged, and followed after her.

"Darn it," said Heine. "That's one pickle I would have liked to hear Bill get out of."

The mayor chuckled. "He's going to have to do a lot of fancy foot-work, that's for sure."

"I can understand her being upset," said Mary, patting the tubes of her flipped hair. "But to take Bill's betrayal out on us—"

"Mary," said Lee, wiping the counter harder than she needed to for mere stain removal, "we don't know what the story is, we don't know if there's been a 'betrayal,' we don't really know anything."

"I know I could go for some pie," said Miss Penk. She was a

careful eater who knew when her calorie intake left her enough leeway for a treat, and when it did, she didn't like to deny herself.

Slim turned on a switch and as the glass case began to rotate, everyone sat for a moment, thinking their own thoughts as they watched the slow carousel of lemon meringue, pecan, and strawberry-rhubarb pies.

Chapter 20

The atmosphere on the last day of shooting was as festive as a carnival. Hugs and kisses accompanied every greeting and gifts were exchanged.

"You are some picture-taker," said Boyd, impressed over the candid photograph Doug Woo had given him. "I should use this for my eight-by-ten."

Grace Aisles gave little green leather pine trees imprinted with the words "Ike and Inga."

"They're to put on your key chain," she explained shyly.

Ron Feldman gave jump ropes with attached cards (made up at Gore Printing for a discount) that read, "For your heart. Make sure you give it a daily workout. Love, Ron."

Fenny had stayed up late the previous night, making brownies with Lee. These she gave to her movie friends, wrapped in wax paper bags and tied with ribbons.

Her card read, "It's been sweet," and she was somewhat embarrassed by the simple sentimentality, but it had been two A.M. by the time the last batch of brownies was done and she didn't have a lot of time to spare on poetry.

However, Mary Gore did. She had made up a commemorative "movie issue" of *Angel Motors* for public distribution but, now that she was officially part of the movie, decided to give copies to the cast and crew. The magazine featured such poems as "Christian/His Bark *Is* His Bite" and "Honoria, Child/Woman/Vixen/Angel."

"Who's Honoria?" asked Grace, flipping through the pages.

"Me," said Fenny, wishing Mary would stick to screenwriting, where her obnoxiousness factor wasn't so overpowering. "Anyone else around here look like the child/woman/vixen/angel?"

Harry gave watches and Boyd gave engraved pens ("Yours, Ike").
"What a haul," said Fenny, putting her presents in her bag.

"An unusually good haul," agreed Grace. "I think relief has a lot
to do with it."

Christian, who loved presents, accepted his gifts happily, although he didn't particularly care for the style of the watch his uncle
gave him and he knew the green leather key chain attachment
would wind up in the bottom of his hotel room wastebasket. It didn't
occur to him that he could have been a giver instead of just a receiver until Grace asked him where her present from him was.

Christian aimed a fixed smile at her. "My first gift to everyone,"
he said, "was my script. My second gift to everyone was my direction."

"My gift to you was my performance," said Grace, the insincerity
of her smile matching Christian's. "But I still give you an end-of-the-
shoot present, oh, just because it's sort of traditional."

"I'm not a traditional kind of guy," said Christian, and immediately sensing the power of the words, he filed the sentence away in
his writer's memory. Later he would pull it out and it would become
the catchphrase of *Deke York, Bounty Hunter.*

The last scene shot would actually appear in the middle of the
movie. Because Inga wouldn't have taken the tumble with Ike yet,
Fenny's face would be partially obscured by a big bonnet. A shawl
covered her arm cast. The long camera angles and blocking would
work to hide Fenny's infirmities, and the only close-ups were to be
of Boyd.

The scenario, as the new writing team of Freed & Gore wrote it,
went like this: Inga, wanting to be more than a mail-order bride,
wanting her groom-to-be to love her freely, with no sense of obligation, decides to take the train back East and then a freighter all the
way to Norway. Ike, who finds it hard to say the words Inga so desperately wants to hear, tries to stop her from getting on the train. Ultimately he jumps on the train as it slowly begins to leave the station.
This causes Inga to jump off. Ike follows. We get a comic effect here
of the two of them jumping on and off until finally the train's speed
prevents their little game.

Fenny, of course, wouldn't be able to do any of the jumping on
and off ("I thought you were trying to write stuff to accommodate
my broken arm and smashed-up face," she told Christian, who

replied, "We did. But this scene just sort of took over. It's not all about *you*, Fenny"), and Harry was about to spring for the expense of flying out a stuntwoman, but then Ron Feldman convinced Christian to use Miss Penk.

"She's about the same size as Fenny, she's in great shape, and you'd save yourself some money."

"Gee, I appreciate the thought, Ron," said Christian, "but in case you haven't noticed, Miss Penk is black. Fenny is white."

"Christian, it's going to be a long shot. Nobody will be able to see her features anyway. And she can wear makeup."

Christian started to protest that a woman Miss Penk's age could never pass for a woman of Fenny's age, but then he remembered how she had looked in her underwear after helping rescue Boyd. Hers was *not* the typical over-sixty body. And Ron was right; the cameras were shooting at a distance and makeup could change her color. . . .

"Okay," said Christian, throwing his hands up. "Why not? I mean, this has been kind of an unconventional movie. Why *not* bring in an old black dyke in white greasepaint and let her jump on and off a train?"

"She'll do great. Just don't call her names, okay?"

After they had shot her sequence, Fenny stood with Frau Katte under the awning of the old train station. A few extras acting as train passengers had been brought up from Minneapolis, and some townspeople and a lone news reporter from nearby Roseau watched the proceedings with the rest of the cast.

"So how does it feel to be all done?" asked the reporter, sidling up to Fenny.

"Done?" said Fenny, surprised at the emotion she felt. "I am done, aren't I? I don't feel done. I mean, the movie doesn't feel done." She paused, shrugging her shoulders. "I don't know how I feel."

"How's your mouth feeling?" asked the reporter. "Now, I personally think your lip looks pretty sexy."

"Listen, bub, either write your story or go bozzer someone else. We're trying to watch za movie."

"Excuse me for breathing," said the reporter, whose news features were as unoriginal as his lines. He sauntered off to bother someone else.

"It does seem strange zat it's over," agreed Frau Katte. "And even stranger—I'm going to miss a lot of zese people."

"Me, too," said Fenny. More than sadness, however, she felt relief and excitement. She wouldn't have to put on a corset and a wig every day! She wouldn't have to speak in a Norwegian accent. She wouldn't have to deal with any more Marcy Mincuses or reporters from Roseau who wanted to ask her out. Most important, she could get back to her old routine, albeit her old routine factoring in Bill.

They had had a long discussion the night she ran out of the Cup O'Delight.

"Mae and I *were* going to go get her deer hides," he said as they sat on one of the lakeside benches. "Then she heard from her sup-plier—sounds covert, doesn't it?—her *supplier*—that he didn't have enough hides for her because he'd wasted a week's worth of hunting by being sick—said he had some kind of wicked flu, I guess, and—" Hearing Fenny's sigh, Big Bill stopped. "What's the matter?"

Fenny looked out at the dark lake. "You seem to be explaining a lot without really telling me anything."

"I'm getting there, I'm getting there," said Bill. Knowing Fenny was right made him all the more defensive. He reached in the pocket of his jeans jacket. "Candy?" he asked, tapping Red Hots out of a box.

Fenny stuck out her hand and Bill poured a little red heap into her palm. She was beginning to feel sorry for Bill; it was painful lis-tening to him try to worm his way out of his deception.

"I think these were hotter years ago," he said, shaking the box. "But I think they had to make an adjustment for blander tastes."

Again Bill heard Fenny sigh.

"Okay," he said, like a child finally convinced there's no more wool to be pulled over his parents' eyes. "Mae canceled her plans, but I thought, Why should I? Why shouldn't I go on a little vacation—I mean, all this stuff with you and me and Lee . . . who wouldn't want to get away from it for a while?"

The October night air was chilly, and Fenny hunched up her

shoulders and burrowed her chin into her upturned collar. "Bill," she said softly. "Lee and I had made up by the time you left."

"I know that. But all the stuff leading up to that . . . I don't know; I was tired. I wanted to get away."

"From me?"

This time it was Bill's turn to sigh. "From a lot of things, but yeah, from you, too. I just wanted some time to think."

"You could have told me that, Bill. You didn't have to lie about it."

"I didn't really *lie*," said Bill. "It's not like I was shacking up at my secret girlfriend's house."

"Well, where did you go?"

"Up north—I camped out, okay? So, see, I didn't really lie—I just didn't tell you that Mae had changed her plans. Sorry. I guess I didn't want to have to explain myself."

"Like you do now."

"Yeah, like I do now."

"So any more lies I should know about?" Fenny was half teasing and so was surprised when after a moment Bill said, "Well, I didn't leave school because I wrecked my knee playing football."

"You didn't?" asked Fenny, amused that he chose to confess such a benign lie.

"No, I left school because I was thrown in jail."

"What?" She could no longer admit to being amused.

Bill laced his fingers together and stared at them awhile before he spoke.

"I didn't just get a football scholarship, Fenny, I got a music scholarship, too. Nobody in my family had ever gone to college, so this wasn't just a big thing; it was huge.

"Newspapers were interviewing me—'The Piano-Playing Wide End,' stuff like that—and so there I was, this cocky kid, acting like the King of the World, when actually . . . I was scared stiff."

"What were you scared of?"

"Oh, lots of things. Mostly being in a world I didn't think I deserved . . . and having everyone find out I was a fraud."

"Who would find out you were a fraud?"

Bill laughed without humor. "Everyone. Everyone in the whole school. You know what they used to call me out on the football field? 'Don Ho/Geronimo.' It was sort of a cheer. Every time I caught a pass, everyone in the stands would be yelling, 'Don Ho/Geronimo.'

"I didn't think it bothered me—I just thought it was a good-natured nickname. But after our last game of the season there was this big party and everyone was breaking training because football season was over; I mean, we were all *smashed*. Then this guy, Dwight Ellis the Third or Fourth, some rich guy, starts asking me if I get my love of alcohol from my Don Ho or my Geronimo side and then he starts doing this little dance, half war dance—complete with war whoops—and half hula. And I just lost it."

"How?" asked Fenny, her voice a whisper.

"I beat him up," said Bill simply. "I beat him up and broke three of his bones with my bare hands—my hands that I was always so worried about hurting out there on the football field."

"Oh, Bill," breathed Fenny.

"I heard each one snap—it was just a little louder than when you pull apart a wishbone."

A breeze rippled through the grass and then Fenny saw it move across the milky white reflection the moon had cast on the lake.

"Was . . . was he okay?"

"He was back at school—in two casts—a couple of days later."

"And you?"

"I was arrested for assault and battery. Spent a little time in jail, and . . . well . . . after that, well, I just couldn't go back as the *felon freshman*. I was too ashamed." He looked at Fenny, squinting his eyes in the dark. "My poor mother—first my dad broke her heart, then I did." He cleared his throat. "So, any more lies you want cleared up?"

"Are there many more?"

Bill shook his head. "Not really. I just never like to publicize that one. Makes me feel like a bigger loser than I am."

Fenny made an involuntary *tsk*. "Oh, Bill. You're not a loser."

"Fenny, you don't understand—I wrecked whatever chance I had in football and whatever chance I had in music."

"Bill, you're a wonderful musician."

Bill shook his head. "I played cover tunes in a hotel band, Fenny. Now I play the piano in a *diner*. I think that puts me right up there in the top ranks of loserhood."

"I don't believe that, Bill," said Fenny. She took her empty sleeve, the one her arm in its cast wasn't using, and pulled it across herself, in an effort to warm up. "And I don't believe you do, either."

"I do right now. I think of all the things I was going to be and what I am: a guy who drifted into town and works in a bait shop."

"Bill, you're so much more than that! You just have a different philosophy, remember? Make no plans but enjoy whatever the day brings?"

"That, Fenny, is the philosophy I've been fooling myself with for a long time—the philosophy of a loser who doesn't want to admit he's a loser."

"*You are not a loser!*" She sniffed from the cold. "Do you love me, Bill?"

Big Bill looked startled at the change of topic, and then alarmed. "I—I don't know," he stammered. "Do you love me?"

They stared at each other like trapped animals looking into a mirror until they both had to laugh.

"Well, do you?" asked Fenny after they had enjoyed their little joke.

"Do you?" repeated Bill.

"Hey, that's not fair," said Fenny, exasperated. "I asked you first."

"I know, but women know the answer to these things better than men."

" 'Better than men,' " mimicked Fenny. "You're just trying to weasel out of answering."

"I don't see you making any bold declarations."

"Well, I'm just . . . I had . . ." Fenny stopped, not knowing what to say. "It's hard for me," she said finally. "It's just that I . . . I loved Sig and Wally so much and then they . . . died. I don't know, now love seems so . . . *risky*."

"Because of how much it hurts if you lose someone you love?"

"I guess."

"Then we just have to figure out a way to be brave enough to love one another."

"Oh, Bill," said Fenny. "You make me want to be that brave!"

"Likewise, Fenny." Bill kissed her cheek then, not wanting to hurt her patched mouth, and Fenny could smell the cinnamon candy on his breath. They sat on the park bench for a long time, Bill's lips on Fenny's cheek, warming her cheek with each breath.

"Okay," said the first a.d. after Ron Feldman and Christian had conferred with Miss Penk and Boyd. "All quiet on the set!"

"I get goose pimples every time I hear zat," whispered Frau Katte.

Fenny nodded her head, surprised to admit, "Me, too."

The scene was marked, sound and film rolled, and Christian called, "Action!" The train cars, pulled by an old steam engine that had been brought up from a train museum in Duluth, started slowly moving.

"I hate Miss Penk's face zat color," whispered Frau Katte. "She looks spooky."

On cue, Miss Penk grabbed the vertical railing and easily jumped on board. Boyd followed. Startled to see him next to her, Miss Penk jumped off. Boyd followed. The train was now picking up speed.

"Zis is starting to scare me," said Frau Katte.

"Me, too," said Fenny. Considering past history, it seemed an accident was just waiting to happen.

Miss Penk, whose gait was now a trot, jumped onto the train. Boyd followed. Miss Penk jumped off. Boyd followed, skidding a little.

"I don't like zis at all," whispered Frau Katte. This time Fenny's mouth was too dry to answer.

Now Miss Penk had to run to catch the train. She jumped and, grabbing the rail, stumbled.

Frau Katte gasped, but Miss Penk, who was not a brown belt in karate for nothing, was able to compensate for her loss of momentum and hoist herself onto the moving train.

"*Mein Gott im Himmel,*" whispered Frau Katte.

Boyd easily jumped aboard and then, for the last shot of the movie, Miss Penk jumped off. Boyd followed. Their momentum thrust them forward and they ran a few steps. It was the perfect exit, except Boyd's foot caught the end of Miss Penk's dress and with a great ripping sound, the long skirt, let out that morning in the bodice to accommodate Miss Penk's slightly wider waist, tore off. Miss Penk stumbled forward, but she had barely hit the platform before she was up on her feet. In her pantaloons, she marched three steps to Boyd and, in an inspired bit of improvisation, walloped him across the face.

"Cut!" yelled Christian. "Print it!"

Cast and crew applauded.

"Sorry, Boyd," said Miss Penk, brushing the dust off her gloved hands. "I just thought that's how Inga would have reacted."

Holding his face with one hand, Boyd rotated his jaw.

"Everyone's an actor," he muttered.

Chapter 21

The wrap party at the Northlands Inn was loud and raucous, and several times the front desk clerk had to call the night manager, who in turn would sheepishly tell the revelers that some complaints had been filed and could they keep it down, please?

"Keep it down?" slurred Christian, putting his arm around the night manager's shoulder. "Why would we want to do a silly thing like that?" He rarely drank to excess because he knew he couldn't handle his liquor well, but tonight he didn't care—they had made it through the shoot!—and his trips to the bartender were regular, if not steady.

"You just tell those muds-in-the-stick that this is a frickin' movie company that's having a little party and if they don't like it, they can shove it up their—"

"Christian!" said Harry, putting his arm around his nephew and pulling him off the night manager. "Why don't you go sit down and let me talk to this nice man."

"I love you, Uncle Harry," said Christian.

"I'm sure you do, Christian. Now go away and let me try to straighten this thing out."

In a quiet conversation with the night manager, Harry learned that all the complaints had come from the same people—two English professors who made yearly visits to the Northlands Inn.

"So you see, sir, we really can't afford to offend them," apologized the night manager, who, if it were up to him, would order a rum collins and join the party himself.

"Tell you what," said Harry. "Extend an invitation to them. Here, give them my card." Harry dug for something in his wallet. "Tell them we'd be honored if they'd come down and join us."

Ten minutes later Mr. and Mrs. Rance Storr from Omaha, Nebraska, were lecturing Harry on the state of literature in North America, and Harry made a mental note to never try to appease people complaining about noise, because, inevitably, they were bores.

Fenny, Big Bill, Lee, and Slim had escaped to the domed poolroom, where the women reclined on white plastic chaise longues and the men sat on the side of the Jacuzzi, their legs in the water, plates of food on their laps.

"These movie people sure know how to throw a party," said Bill, wiping his fingers on a napkin imprinted with the words "Ike and Inga." "Did you get any of those little cheese puff things? Man, they're good."

Slim swabbed a shrimp in cocktail sauce. "I like the shrimp myself. Seafood tastes pretty exotic when you're thousands of miles away from any ocean."

The two men sat companionably, eating their fancy foods and drinking their fancy drinks.

"Oh, darling," yelled Fenny from across the room. "Run and get me another plate of food, will you?"

"You're not a movie star anymore," Bill yelled back. "Get it yourself."

Slim chuckled, his cheek bulging with another shrimp.

"I'm glad you two are together," he said, wiping a blob of cocktail sauce off his chin. "Take it from me, Bill, it doesn't pay to lie to your woman."

"Thanks for the advice," said Bill tersely. He set his plate to the side and leaned forward, arms crossed.

"I only offer advice I feel qualified giving," said Slim quietly. "I lied to my wives all the time. And I've got two divorce certificates to prove it."

"So what'd you lie to them about, Slim?" asked Bill, regarding the white-haired man who looked older than his years. He had known Slim was married twice only because Lee had told him; the man rarely confided anything of his personal life to Bill.

"Because it was easier than telling the truth," said Slim, and he stared at the water bubbling and surging around his legs for so long that Bill assumed that was all he had to say on the matter. "I suppose it's because you're scared first," he finally said. "Scared of getting caught doing something you know your wife doesn't want you doing."

"Like what?" asked Bill, having some ideas of his own but wanting to hear Slim's.

"Like going a little crazy, for one." Slim looked at Bill, and his eyes were so sorrowful that Bill was sure the man was going to cry, but then, to Bill's surprise, a grin broke across the gloom of Slim's face. "See, I kept lying about how I felt after I got home from Vietnam — had to be strong, you know — 'I'm fine, I'm fine — nothing's the matter with me,' I'd say, even when I'd wake up from nightmares dripping wet with sweat or when I'd flinch at loud noises. Once my mother-in-law, the first one, dropped a cake pan and I practically hit the deck. I couldn't stand the thought of them thinking that I wasn't man enough to handle war, so I lied and lied . . . and then I started barking."

"I've heard that bark," said Bill, nodding.

Slim laughed. "I only did it a couple times in my first marriage, but it was enough to send Marilyn to the lawyer's. Well, that and a general breakdown in communication. She wasn't the type that believed in counseling, either; once she wanted out, she wanted *out*. And guess what?"

"What?"

"She married her divorce lawyer."

"No shit," said Bill, feeling free to laugh because Slim did.

"Then I met Ginny," said Slim, taking a sip of his strawberry daiquiri. "She was a real easygoing Earth Mother type, but even those kind can only take so much barking."

"Which you were still doing?"

"Oh, yeah. Even more so. It just kept building and building. I was a Normal Joe on the job — which, believe me, took a whole lot of concentration — but once I got home, I needed some kind of release."

"It's kind of an *odd* release," conceded Bill. "I mean, most guys would turn to booze, or pot, or other women."

"Well, see, this is the thing, Bill. I felt like I was going crazy, but when I barked or howled or mooed—whatever—I didn't. It was like my little secret, my little joke; doing the thing that made people really think I was crazy was the thing that was making me feel sane."

"Hmmm," said Big Bill, thinking. "So you sort of designed your own therapy?"

"Exactly," said Slim, pleased to be understood. "But you know, I'm no doctor. So sometimes I get carried away. Sometimes I over-prescribe. Sometimes I just have fun with the shock factor."

"You're starting to make more and more sense. And that worries me."

The two men laughed.

"So what ever happened to Ginny?"

"Ah, Ginny," said Slim, and a trace of the sorrow came back into his eyes. "I heard she married a chiropractor. Did you know she could read the funnies backwards?"

"No, I didn't," said Bill, getting in his head a picture of a woman reading a comic book while sitting the wrong way in a chair.

"Every morning she'd sit down at the breakfast table, open up the paper to the funnies section, and start reading. 'Yram Throw'—that was 'Mary Worth,' and 'Ogop'—that was 'Pogo,' and 'Tnemtrapa G3.' " Slim smiled, remembering. " 'Apartment 3G.' "

"It got so I even started understanding her." He raised his glass. "Ot Ynnig."

It took Bill a moment before he caught on. "Oh," he said, raising his glass to Slim's. "To Ginny."

"So don't lie," said Slim. "Even if you think you're doing it to protect them—they still don't want you to lie."

Suddenly Christian stumbled into the domed poolroom. He was followed by the rest of the cast and crew, and the acoustics of the room gave each drunken reveler's shout a muffled echo.

"Par-*tay!*" Christian was a general ordering his troops, waving his glass like a flag.

Harry was happy over the change of venue—it gave him a chance to ditch the English professors—but just when he thought he was going to be able to relax and enjoy the party, the night manager buttonholed him, complaining that the hotel didn't have a lifeguard on duty and couldn't be held responsible for any accidents.

But Ron Feldman, overhearing, told the manager to relax; he was sober and a former Santa Monica Beach lifeguard.

"And her," he said, pointing over to Fenny, "she saved a non-swimmer just the other day."

"Is that right," said the night manager, impressed; and, fairly certain that there would be no casualties, he relaxed enough to okay the request that a portable bar be brought in.

"You should go into acting full-time," said Boyd Burch when Ron joined him at the glass-topped table he, Bonnie Price, Miss Penk, and Frau Katte had sat down at. "You're *good*."

"Thanks," said Ron, touched because he knew actors usually didn't encourage any potential competition.

"Are you thinking about it?" asked Miss Penk. "Would you give up your stunt work to concentrate on acting?"

Ron shrugged his big stuntman shoulders. "I don't know. I'm flattered that you think I could . . . but, I don't know, it seems kind of risky thinking of giving up the known for the unknown—especially in Hollywood."

"It's risky to give up the known for the unknown anywhere," said Miss Penk. "The question is: What would make you happier?"

Ron laughed. "Maybe neither."

"What do you mean?" asked Frau Katte.

Everyone looked up as Christian skipped by, a life preserver around his waist. He tripped, but caught himself before falling, and then struck a pose like a ballerina.

"Everybody—get up and boogie!" he ordered, and then, executing a clumsy grand jeté, aimed himself toward another group of people.

"So you were telling us zat you might not want to do stunt work or acting in Hollywood?" reminded Frau Katte.

"Oh, yeah," said Ron. He looked at Bonnie Price and smiled. "Well, you see, Bonnie and I have sort of been talking about getting married and getting into farming."

"Married!" said Miss Penk.

"Farming!" said Boyd.

"We're just talking," said Bonnie, brushing back her bangs. "We don't want to jump into anything—we want to make sure this isn't just a movie romance—but if it isn't, eventually we'd like to get out of Hollywood and buy some property. Maybe raise horses . . . or grow apples."

"We'd appreciate any advice you might have for us, Boyd," said the stuntman.

"Here's some—don't do it!"

Ron chose to ignore Boyd's exhortation and said to the others, "We haven't really sorted out the details. See, Bonnie's got a teaching degree and she could do that anywhere, and I . . . well, I've always wanted to make a living off the land."

"I zink it's a wonderful idea," said Frau Katte. "Like Boyd, I was raised on a farm."

"Ranch," corrected Boyd, snobby about the distinction in the way westerners are.

"Well, when we get ours, you and Miss Penk can come to visit," said Ron.

"It's a deal," said Frau Katte.

"What is with you people?" asked Boyd. "First Fenny's ready to blow off a big career, and then you want to go live on a *farm*. What's so bad about Hollywood, anyway?"

Walking by at this precise moment, carrying a tequila sunrise for his wife and a Campari on ice for himself, was the professor Rance Storr, whose students privately referred to him as "Rancid Bore."

"Oh, my dear boy," he said, stopping in front of Boyd. "Don't get me started." He took a sip of his Campari. "But let me just say, when Western civilization is tottering, it will be Hollywood who gives it its final push into the abyss."

With that declaration, the professor bowed and made his way back to his table.

"That's Hollywood booze you're drinking," called Boyd. "This is a Hollywood party you're crashing!" He shook his head. "Fuckin' hypocrite." He looked up at Miss Penk and Frau Katte. "Excuse my French."

"We say za same zing in German," said Frau Katte. She cupped her hands and called after the professor. "Fucking hypocrite."

"Hello, folks," said Christian, lurching up to a small group of people sitting in lounge chairs. Still wearing the life preserver around his waist, he staggered, lost his balance, and fell next to the chair Fenny sat on. "Oh, goody," he said, putting his arm around her. "You're the one I wanted to sit next to anyway."

"Christian," said Doug Woo, "I'm going to have the bartender cut you off."

"No, no, no," said Christian, waving his hands. "Let's not cut off anything. God, I love you, Dougie!"

"Now I know he's plastered," said Doug to Fenny.

"But like I said," said Christian, batting Fenny's knee, "you're the one I wanted to sit next to. You're the one I wanted to tell—oh, don't smile at me, I can't stand to see that poor little snaggletooth of yours—anyway, I wanted to tell you how proud I was of you. Yes, you. There was no way I thought you could ever pull it off, but you did. And in no way did you embarrass yourself . . . well, hardly any way."

"Gee, thanks, Christian," said Fenny.

"Even drunk, he can't give a decent compliment."

"Oh, hello, Gracie. I didn't see you hiding there."

"I'm not hiding, Christian. Although if I'd have seen you coming, I would have."

"Wiseass," said Christian, shaking his head. "Always a wiseass." He turned to Lee. "Did I say hello to you yet?"

"I don't think so," said Lee.

"Well, then: Hello." He squinted, studying her. "You know, you have really pretty eyes. I mean, really, really, really pretty. They're not just blue . . . they're navy blue."

"Christian, I think Harry's looking for you."

"He is not, Fenny, you just don't like me flirting with your friend." He looked Lee up and down with his unfocused eyes. "Your big, big, *big* friend."

"All right, that's enough," said Fenny. She stood and, with her good arm, lifted Christian up by the crook of his, and like a Girl Scout on a mission, escorted him across the tiled floor. When they reached the edge of the pool, Fenny pushed him in and then brushed her hand against her chest as if she had just put down something dirty.

Christian bobbed up in the water, the life preserver still around his waist. He misunderstood the cheers, thinking they were somehow in praise of him, rather than what had been done to him. He waved to the crowd, twirling around in his preserver so as not to miss anyone.

This elicited even more cheers, and then Grace Aisles, who understood when a party was ready to shift gears, jumped into the water. She was followed without hesitation by a stream of revelers, and the wrap party for *Ike and Inga* ended as it should: with swimmers in various stages of dress and undress in the pool and Jacuzzi, with the soundman adjusting the hotel's sound system so the elevator music blasted into the poolroom, with the professor from Omaha soliciting advice from Ron Feldman as to how to build up his upper body, with a visit from Sheriff Gibbs, who warned everyone to keep it quiet and then asked Boyd Burch for his autograph ("You're my niece's biggest fan"), and with Christian standing in the corner, his arms resting limply on the life preserver, throwing up into the pot of a plastic dieffenbachia.

Driving Slim and Lee home, Fenny lost Bill as a passenger when he asked her to pull over.

"Are you okay?" asked Fenny, the wheels of her car crunching on the road's gravel shoulder.

"I don't think so," said Bill. He opened the passenger door and lurched out. Immediately, those in the car heard the sound of retching.

After a moment, Bill walked around the car and tapped Fenny's window. She rolled it down.

"Cheese puffs and banana daiquiris," he said with a sheepish smile. "Lethal, man."

"What can I do?" asked Fenny.

"Nothing, but thanks. I think I'll just walk home, though. I could use the night air." He bent down to kiss her but thought better of it. "I'll see you tomorrow."

Fenny didn't resist Lee's invitation to spend the night; she was too tired to drive back home.

After saying their goodnights, Fenny settled into Lee's couch. Lee kept a cluttered house, but at least she had high-quality clutter. One of the things Fenny loved about staying at Lee's was the bed linen. That sheets could be an item of function *and* luxury was news to Fenny; these were remarkably soft and, when topped with a cashmere afghan, gave Fenny the sense of being wrapped up in a fine, soft cocoon. She drifted off easily, happy that the movie had wrapped, happy about the fun she'd had at the party, happy about Bill (not that he had puked, but just all-around happy about his existence).

Just before dawn, she sat bolt upright on the couch, awakened by screams.

"It's Slim," explained Lee, tying her bathrobe as she ran past. Fenny kicked off her cocoon and followed Lee out her door, across the hall, and into Slim's efficiency apartment.

"No! No! We're going down! Help! *Help!*" This last plea was screamed with such anguish that Fenny felt breathless, as if she had been punched in the stomach.

Lee raced to Slim's bed and, sitting next to him, shook him gently.

"Slim, Slim, wake up. It's okay, Slim."

"Help us! Oh, God, help us!"

Fenny stood helpless, shivering in her T-shirt and underpants.

"Slim, it's all right. It's all right, Slim, wake up."

One final scream for help gave way to groans, and finally whimpers.

"Fenny, put some water on for tea, okay? Make the chamomile that's on the counter."

"Okay," said Fenny.

With shaking hands, Fenny made the tea in Lee's kitchen, sloshing it all over the tray as she carried it to Slim's apartment.

Slim was awake now, but looked dazed, as if he hadn't quite accepted the transition into consciousness. Lee still sat next to him, her arm around him, talking to him softly.

"See, Slim, there's Fenny," she said. "She's brought some tea. Remember, we always have tea after you have one of your nightmares?"

Slim nodded shakily.

"It's our little ritual, remember? And tonight Fenny's going to join us."

Slim nodded again.

Lee moved over, making room for Fenny, and the three sat on the bed quietly drinking their tea.

When they were done, Lee asked Slim if he was okay, and when he nodded, she took his teacup and kissed him on the cheek.

"Then get some sleep," she said, "and no more bad dreams, okay?"

Back in Lee's apartment, Fenny washed out the cups.

"Oh, don't do that," said Lee. "Leave them till morning."

"It is morning," said Fenny, nodding toward the window that looked out at a beginning sunrise.

Lee groaned, looking at the wall clock. "I open up in a half hour."

"I'll help you," said Fenny.

Downstairs in the cafe, Lee brewed the first pot O'Delight and they talked about Slim.

"It's been so long since he's had a nightmare," she said, "I forgot how scary they are."

"Boy, I'll say," said Fenny, who was standing at the stainless-steel prep table by the sink, awkwardly mixing up pancake batter under Lee's careful supervision. "Can you think of anything that might have set it off?"

Lee shook her head. "A little less oil, Fenny." Impatiently, she pulled the pot away from the machine and held a cup under the filter to collect the dripping O'Delight. "He drank a little last night, but that doesn't usually affect him. Not like Bill."

"I know—I've seen Bill drink twice, and twice I've seen him get sick."

Lee looked in the mixing bowl to check the progress of the pancake mix. "Now, don't overbeat it," she said.

The bread man and the dairy man made their deliveries and then customers began to trickle in: Heine and the mayor, Grace Aisles and Doug Woo.

"I can't believe it," said Grace as Fenny, with her good arm, loaded a tray with dirty dishes. "Yesterday you were a movie star, today you're a busboy."

"That's showbiz," said Fenny. "So how come you're up so early? You were still in the pool when we left."

"Doug and I are leaving today."

"You are?" said Fenny, a rush of emotion blowing through her. "I thought you were flying out tomorrow."

"We decided to drive," said Doug. "We're going to rent a convertible and drive through the Rockies."

"You'll probably get snowed on," said Mayor Lambordeaux.

"Then we'll put the top up," said Grace. "Doug wants to photograph each state we drive through from the perspective of a convertible."

"What a good idea," said Lee. "Will you send me some copies?"

"Sure," said Doug, focusing his camera on Lee and taking her picture.

"That I won't miss," said Lee with a thin smile. She hated having her picture taken.

"Sorry," said Doug. "I just can't resist taking pictures of beautiful women."

"And that's why Mr. Doug Woo has won, over many contenders, the prize of Miss Grace Aisles," said Grace. She leaned toward him and kissed him. "He always knows the right thing to say."

Eggs fried, bacon sizzled, and pancakes bubbled as the Cup O'Delight began to fill with people. Miss Penk and Frau Katte came in, followed by David the p.a., Ron Feldman, and Bonnie Price. Other crew members drifted in. Two movie fans from Cloquet sat at a booth and giggled, hoping Boyd Burch would show up. Sheriff Gibbs stopped in to fill up his coffee thermos.

"That was quite a party you movie folks threw," he said, standing by the cash register, digging in his pocket for change.

"Ya, but it wasn't quite up to zat New Year's Eve party Sig and Wally had zat one year," said Frau Katte slyly. "Remember, Sheriff?"

The law officer rubbed his nose with a crooked finger, trying to hide his embarrassed smile. He had taken full advantage of his off-duty status that night, taking regular trips to Sig's spiked punch bowl.

"Put a little cream in there, will you, Lee?" said the sheriff, eager to change the subject.

Lee added a dollop of cream to the coffee and screwed on the thermos top. "Have you seen Pete, Sheriff? He's usually never this late."

Sheriff Gibbs shook his head. "Nope. But if I see him, I'll tell him you're looking for him."

Pete would have loved hearing this news; he was in desperate need of courage, and to know Lee was asking after him would have given him some. He sat in his small shoe store, the "Closed" sign still turned out toward the street, wiping the sweat that beaded up on his forehead as soon as he wiped it away.

His heart beat the way it did when he'd had too much O'Delight, and he breathed slowly, in and out, in and out, trying to calm it.

The source of his discomfort was a black plastic garbage bag that sat in the middle of his scuffed wood floor. Chuckling a nervous *Ho ho ho*, he had planned on toting it over his shoulder like Santa Claus into the Cup O'Delight, but somewhere between his car and the bank, his resolve evaporated, and he raced back to his store, hoping no one had seen him.

"What are you," he now scolded himself out loud, "a man or a mouse? They're just shoes, for crying out loud, just shoes."

But he wasn't fooled; they weren't just shoes, they were part of Pete's declaration of love, the declaration he was going to make that day . . . if he could only move.

He had finished Lee's twelfth pair of shoes the previous night. They were beautiful; sling-back navy-blue leather pumps on a stacked heel, decorated with an onyx button. He could imagine the way Lee's pretty legs would look in them, the way the back strap would set off her nicely tapered ankles.

"And they match your eyes, Lee," he whispered to himself. "You'll be navy blue from head to foot." He shook his head, not liking the image of a bruise the words evoked. He amended himself. "You'll look nice.

"Come on, Pete," he told himself. "Up, up. Get up. You can do it. Whatever she does, it won't be the end of the world." "Whatever" in this case meant outright rejection, and to Pete, it would be the end of the world, but he was trying to buttress himself. He hadn't been listening to his Dale Carnegie tapes for nothing.

It was his growling stomach that finally convinced him to get up.

He was a man used to an early breakfast, and his body protested at change in routine.

"All right," he said, palming both sides of his Brylcreemed hair. "On with the shoe."

He took the cheesecloth bag containing the navy blue pumps off the top of the pile in the bag, deciding not to overwhelm her with the whole kit and caboodle.

He tried to whistle as he walked to the Cup O'Delight, but the cold wind pulled the tune out of the air and ran away with it.

"Pete!" said Lee as the man entered the cafe. "We were wondering what had happened to you!"

Pete couldn't stop a wide smile of pleasure. "Just got a little tied up."

Everyone laughed, assuming he had made a shoe pun when in fact he hadn't, at least intentionally.

He sat down at his usual place, the stool on the end, next to Miss Penk.

"You look like the cat who swallowed the canary," she noted.

"I do?" said Pete, feeling warmth radiate from under his plaid collar on up to his cheeks. "Well, I feel pretty good." And he did. He felt as good as he could remember feeling, proud of himself for doing what he promised himself he'd do, excited about the prospects; happy to see the usual crowd eating breakfast . . . and seeing Lee.

"What's that?" she asked, gesturing toward the bag in his lap.

Courage scampered out of Pete like a hamster out of an opened cage.

"Uh . . . it's . . . just some work I've got to take home."

"Oh," said Lee. "Coffee?"

He didn't know why he didn't present her with the shoes then and there; but he was waiting for the timing to be right. Waiting for a few more of the movie people to leave, waiting for the cafe to be filled with only his friends, who would applaud his declaration. Or wouldn't they? Pete looked surreptitiously at the mayor, at Miss Penk and Frau Katte. Would they think he was worthy enough for Lee, or just some heel?

Cut it out, he reprimanded himself. Get ahold of yourself!

He welcomed the coffee Lee poured him, wrapping both hands around the cup.

"The movie's over," she told him. "Did you hear?"

"Endings are also beginnings," said Mary Gore, breezing up to the counter, the folds of her long skirt sweeping the floor like a velveteen broom.

"So what's that mean exactly, Mary?" asked Heine.

"It means, Heine, that I'm going to Malibu, California, to launch my career as a screenwriter."

"No kidding," said Frau Katte. "When?"

"Oh," said Mary, holding her skirt and swaying back and forth like a coquette, "I'm looking at Monday."

"Are you going for good?" asked the mayor hopefully.

"I'm not going for *bad*," said Mary. "But will I stay there forever? Methinks not, for Tall Pine is my muse's home."

"Well, for goodness' sakes," said Miss Penk.

"So Lee, I need two coffees to go," said Mary. "I'm going to break the news to Dad, and I figure I'll soften the blow with some O'Delight."

"It might be the best news he's heard in a long time," muttered Heine.

Mary accepted the paper cups of coffee. "I'm off!"

"I'm glad," whispered Frau Katte.

Mary's departure seemed to inspire others: Ron Feldman, Bonnie Price, and David the p.a.

"Well, as long as people are saying goodbye, we might as well hit the road, too," said Grace Aisles.

"That's right," said Doug Woo. "There's a lot of great light out there right now."

"Is *everybody* going?" said Fenny, suddenly feeling she was standing on what was becoming an abandoned ship.

"I'm not leaving until tomorrow," said David the p.a. "But I've got an appointment at the barber's. Christian recommended him."

Grace stood up and hugged Fenny.

"It's been swell," she said. "See you in Hollywood."

Fenny leaned away from the hug. "What makes you think so?"

Grace laughed. "Because I'm smart. And because I know the pull of Hollywood is stronger than you think."

"I'm not feeling it now," said Fenny, standing stationary to prove it. "See?"

"Wait a little while," said Grace.

After a flurry of hugs and promises to write and call, everyone was gone.

Fenny leaned against the counter, watching them outside the window. She saw her friends get into the Northlands Inn van that would take most of them to the airport and two of them to the car rental agency. She saw David the p.a. across the street, going into the Clip Joint. She saw Christian pull up in his Alfa Romeo and wave to Mary, who ran over to talk to him. Fenny sighed. She was more than ready to get back to real life, but still . . . it was sad seeing her friends go.

Pete's comfort level rose, now that the only movie people in the Cup O'Delight were Fenny and the one-day stuntwoman, Miss Penk, but they didn't really count as movie people. He wanted witnesses to his declaration of love, but witnesses he was friends with.

"I wonder when Slim'll think about coming down," said Lee, looking up at the ceiling.

"And Bill," said Fenny. "I hope he got home all right."

Now, Pete said to himself, tell her now! Do it now! Before she goes and checks on Slim.

Pete cleared his throat. "Lee, I—"

"You want some more coffee, Pete?" Lee held up the pot.

"No, I . . . I just wanted to tell you—"

He faltered; he had prepared himself for the possibility of Lee's rejection, but not this look of outright horror on her face. Her expression was then mirrored on his own face; the last thing he wanted to do was cause her pain, but then he saw that she was looking past him, over him toward the door.

He swiveled a half turn on his stool.

Pete's recollection of the events to come would stop at a certain point, but there were those at the counter who insisted time stilled and everything moved in slow motion, and others who argued everything happened in a blur of speed.

What Pete did see were two men. One, a stranger wearing an unbuttoned coat that looked a little thin for the weather, came through the door, and the other, not yet in, waving to someone, was that little Hollywood screenwriter/director guy.

He heard the stranger say, with a terrible smile on his face,

"Anyone know where I can get a good cup of coffee?" and then as Pete saw the man reach inside his coat and pull out a gun, he heard Lee cry, "No, Marshall!"

Instinct propelled Pete, an instinct to help Lee. He jumped up, leapt into the air in front of Lee just as the first shot was fired.

He felt it the way he'd feel a firecracker—no, a stick of dynamite going off inside his body. There was an internal explosion and then he fell backward on the counter, a stain spreading out from under him like a crimson shadow.

Noises—screams and the sound of bodies hurling themselves to the floor and glass breaking and silverware clattering—filled the cafe.

"This one's for you, bitch!" screamed Lee's ex-husband, and fired again, but his aim was too high, and the bullet hit one of the ornamental red disks that floated against the back ceiling. It crashed onto the stainless-steel prep table.

"And this!" Marshall fired again, and Miss Penk, desperate, jumped up to push Frau Katte out of the range of fire.

All this happened so fast that Christian, who had been waving to Mary as he walked into the Cup O'Delight, scarcely had time to comprehend what was going on and certainly didn't have time to stop the momentum of his body from slamming into the assassin.

Christian bumped into him hard enough that Marshall Stouffer stumbled forward and fell to the floor, and then Slim, who had just gotten into the back room and was tying on his apron when he heard the commotion, burst through the swinging door.

The screams magnified—Frau Katte was keening—as Marshall scrambled up, looking for Lee, but Slim was bearing down on him so fast that he couldn't do anything but fire at him as the white-haired man knocked him to the floor.

Both men yelped, Slim because he realized the heat in his boot was from a bullet, the gunman because the weapon was knocked out of his hands. Fenny was surprised to hear how lightly it skittered across the floor; she expected a full, weighty sound, a sound relative to the gun's power.

"All right, freeze!" said Christian, grabbing the gun, which had stopped its slide directly in front of him. But there was no way Marshall Stouffer was about to obey his order. Slim tried to hold him to the ground, but Marshall bit his hand and when Slim reflexively drew it back, he jumped up. Christian, paralyzed, held out the gun, certain that was what the killer wanted, but Marshall didn't see it, didn't seem to see anything as he burst out the door.

Limping like the maimed man he was, Slim ran after Marshall Stouffer, who ran fast but recklessly, ignoring one basic rule. He did not look both ways when he crossed the street, and because he didn't, he ran straight into Professor Rance Storr's Chrysler Le Baron.

There was a squeal of brakes and the thump Stouffer's body made as the car hit him. He flew in a full arc—"like an underhanded pitch," Slim would recall later—and fell, crumpled and broken, next to a rake display at Bick's Hardware.

"He ran right out in front of me!" wailed the professor, walking in tight circles in front of his car, his arms held wide enough to catch a medicine ball. "Right out in front of me!"

In the cafe, Heine yelled, "Somebody give me a hand!" and he and the mayor lifted Pete's bandy legs and pivoted him so that he lay on the length of the counter.

Lee rose from her crouched position behind the counter, her hand cupped over her mouth. She felt as if she were in a dream, she prayed she was in a dream, but the smell of gunpowder and blood and bacon burning on the grill was too real to be a dream.

"Oh, Pete," she said, taking the man's hands in hers. "Oh, no."

Pete managed a smile; he knew he was dying, but the fact that he was dying in the arms of his beloved was a great comfort, a gift, really, beyond the scope of his most hopeful imaginings.

Slim hobbled back into the cafe. "Call for help," he shouted, and Fenny, nodding dumbly, staggered into the back room.

Slim had seen enough men dying on the battlefield to know that Pete was going to join them, but he leaned close to Pete's face, smoothing his greased hair with his hand and whispering, "Hang on, buddy, everything'll be all right."

Pete smiled wanly; he was enjoying all the attention and was only sorry that it would be short-lived—just like himself, he thought, and smiled again.

But the hole in his chest was a vacuum and he could feel his energy, his consciousness being sucked out of it, and so he gathered his strength, squeezed Lee's hands, and said, "I love you, Lee," and then, using a shoe pun he had never had occasion to use, he added, "You're my sole's delight."

His freckled eyelids fluttered as he smiled the last smile of his life, and then he was gone.

Part Two

Chapter 22

News crews came from all across the country to cover the sensational story of the small town/Hollywood murder. Print journalists, their bags filled with pads of paper and tape recorders, chased after local citizens while photographers shot the town of Tall Pine and especially the Cup O'Delight (even though its windows were now boarded up) from every possible angle. Even Marcy Mincus, knowing a good story, was tempted to revisit Tall Pine, but her therapy group talked her out of it.

Christian, besieged with interview requests, held court in his hotel room. He was hailed as a hero, "the screenwriter [although he reminded them at every opportunity that he was a director, too] who couldn't have written a more bizarre scenario for himself," the man who had tackled the killer and then snatched away his gun.

"This diminutive man may not look like a hero," intoned one newswoman into the camera, "but strength comes from the size of the heart, not the fist."

Christian got a little tired of all the references to his size, but as long as the word "hero" was mentioned more times than "small" or "slight" or, God forbid, "tiny," he would grin and bear it. Or at least bear it; grinning wasn't a very seemly thing to do, considering the circumstances.

And Christian wanted to be seemly. He wanted to be rich and famous and interviewed and talked about, but he didn't want to appear to be taking advantage of a terrible situation. At least not obviously.

"What do you think, Harry?" he asked his uncle. "Do you think I should put a moratorium on all these interviews, or just keep the big network ones, or what?"

"I don't really give a damn," said Harry. For the first time in his life he was weary—weary of a world that got all jazzed up by guns and violence and moviemaking.

He had been talking to his secretary on the phone as he packed for his return to L.A. when the front desk came on the line and said he had an emergency phone call. It was from David, one of his p.a.'s.

"There's been a shooting at the Cup O'Delight, Harry. Some townspeople have been hurt, and—"

"Christian?"

"He's fine. Harry, I've got a car. I'll come and pick you up if you like."

"Thanks. I'll be outside."

"I'm really getting tired of this place," said Harry, as they drove up to the hospital where Malcolm had died and Fenny had been treated.

In the hallway, they saw Fenny standing outside the lounge area and rushed over to her.

"Oh, Harry—Lee's ex-husband went berserk and Slim got shot in the foot! The doctor said the X ray shows it was a clean shot; it didn't go through any bones, he says his prognosis is pretty good."

"What else?" said Harry, knowing from Fenny's breathless recitation that there was more.

"Miss Penk's in surgery. We haven't heard anything, but I saw her in the cafe, and— Oh, God." She fell into the producer's arms and Harry held her for a moment.

"Do you remember Pete?" she said, lifting her head. "He ran the shoe repair shop?" At their nods, she added, "Well, he's dead."

"No," said Harry.

"He died in Lee's arms," she said, "and I swear, he was smiling. Do you know what his last words to her were?"

Harry and David shook their heads dumbly.

"He said he loved her," said Fenny, "and that she was his sole's— you know, the shoe kind—delight." She gasped as if she couldn't catch her breath. "He was in love with Lee and she didn't even know it."

Harry's knees buckled when they went inside the waiting room.

Everyone looked shell-shocked, staring off at some unknown point, not talking. Most of them had blood splattered on their clothing, except for Frau Katte, who was drenched in it. The Swiss woman sat silently on the vinyl couch, holding her arms to her chest, rocking back and forth.

"Harry," said the mayor, "did they tell you about your nephew?"

"David said he was all right!" said Harry, his voice high with panic.

"Oh, he's fine," said the mayor. "In fact, if it wasn't for him, the whole thing probably would have been a lot worse. Not that it already isn't."

"Where is he now?" asked Harry.

"Last I saw, he was on his way to the men's room," said the mayor. "He was looking a little green around the gills."

"What about Lee?" Harry didn't see her in the waiting room.

The mayor shook his head. "Now, *that's* who I'm worried about."

Sheriff Gibbs was worried, too. He had taken Lee into the tiny chapel that smelled of carpet shampoo and at his first question— "You say the perpetrator was your ex-husband?"—she leaned against the pew in front of them and, cradling her head in her arms, began to sob. It didn't seem as if she was thinking of stopping anytime soon.

Sheriff Gibbs patted her back until his arm got tired. He counted the ceiling tiles and then started in on counting the dots in the ceiling tiles, but then he finally got the bright idea to question Lee later.

"Don't worry, it's not like there aren't other witnesses," he said softly. "We'll talk later, when you're more up to it."

Sheriff Gibbs went off to find Heine and the mayor and then thought out loud, "Say, I wonder if anyone's contacted Pete's sister," and figuring that probably no one had, he went to the pay phone by the pop machine to do his duty.

"Oh, most merciful God," whispered Lee when she heard the door quietly shut behind the sheriff. With her head buried in her crossed arms, her voice sounded amplified. "Please help me, God. Please, please help me." Her tears ran down her face and onto her arms, and she could taste their salt. She could also smell and taste

Pete's blood on her. Frantically, she started licking a long red stain on her forearm that less than an hour ago was inside Pete, *Pete's lifeblood*, and that's how Fenny found her, licking herself like a wounded animal.

Fenny sat down in the pew, frightened.

"Lee," she said.

She jerked her head up, and Fenny drew her breath in as if she'd been hit in the stomach. Her eyes were puffed to slits, her face wet with snot and tears and, near her chin, blood.

"*Lee*," she said again.

"I was just tasting him, Fenny," she said, her voice panicked. "I thought, that's all I have left of Pete now. The taste of him."

"Oh, Lee," said Fenny, feeling there was no oxygen in her, feeling like she was going to pass out.

Lee sat up, a mark on her forehead from where it had pressed against the edge of the pew.

"Oh, Fenny, it's all my fault. How can I live with myself? I don't want to live with myself!"

"Lee, it's not your fault," said Fenny, but her words sounded lame and comfortless and so she just sat silently with her friend, listening to the sound of her own heartbeat fill the room.

Big Bill walked to Tall Pine, invigorated somewhat by the cool, sunny day and the exercise he took in it, but he knew nothing could revive a system impaired by the god-awful combination of cheese puffs and banana daiquiris better than a cup O'Delight.

When a state trooper told him he couldn't turn on Main Street, he thought there was some filming going on. When he saw Gloria Murch standing with a small crowd of people, he was about to ask her who was minding the store, but before he could, she asked him if he'd heard about the shooting.

"No," said Bill, "but that's what I assumed was going on."

"You *thought* a shooting was going on?"

Big Bill looked at the pastor's wife, puzzled.

"No," he said, "I thought *shooting* was going on. You know—" here he looked through the viewfinder his curled fingers made and cranked his other hand in the air—"movie shooting."

Gloria shook her head, her agate earrings jangling. "No, Bill," she said, "I'm talking about a real shooting. Some nut—they say it was Lee's ex-husband—opened fire on the Cup O'Delight."

"What?" But Bill was off running toward Main Street before Gloria could answer.

"You won't be able to get in!" she shouted after him.

He couldn't; yellow police tape surrounded the building the Cup O'Delight was housed in.

"It *must* be movie shooting," whispered Bill to himself, even as he knew the movie had wrapped the day before. He was unable to grasp the reality of the situation, unable to think that the chalk out-line on the sidewalk in front of Bick's Hardware might have really held a body inside; unable to think that his Fenny might have been at the cafe and . . . his mind refused to consider more.

"Bruce," called Bill, seeing one of the sheriff's deputies, "what's going on?"

"A bloody rampage," said the young deputy, who as a boy had an entire bedroom wall devoted to posters of Serpico. "Lee O'Leary's ex-husband came in with a .22 and an agenda."

"Was anyone hurt?" Bill said, swaying back and forth, trying to get a look inside the cafe.

"I'm not at liberty to say," said the deputy.

"Bruce!" pleaded Bill. "Was Fenny inside? Was Fenny hurt?"

The deputy, who was only three grades ahead of Fenny in school, considered this question for a moment and, then realizing he probably wouldn't be giving away any classified information, said, "No, sir, I saw her get in Sheriff Gibbs's car with Miss O'Leary."

"Where did he take them?" shouted Bill, wanting to smack the officious little twerp.

"I believe they all went to the hospital," said Deputy Bruce.

Bill began running, past the clots of people who stood on the sidewalk, past a news crew that had already arrived from Interna-tional Falls, and past the little red building whose sign read, "Pete's Shoe Shack." He didn't stop running until he was inside the hos-pital lobby.

"Fenny!" he shouted. Seeing her come out of the chapel, he practically tackled her. "Oh, Fenny, I am so sorry!"

"Bill!" She clamped her good arm around him and they stood in the middle of the hallway until a patient pushing an IV stand asked them quietly if they'd mind moving.

"Let's go sit in there," said Bill, nodding toward the waiting room.

"No, let's go outside."

They pushed open the hospital doors and sat on the steps, never letting go of one another.

They both cried as Fenny told Bill the whole story, told him the strange and stupid thoughts—would they take down the rest of those ugly metallic disks now that one had been shattered by gunfire? would everyone run out without paying their bill? who sang "Afternoon Delight," the song that was playing on the jukebox? was her arm in the cast throbbing because she had rebroken it or just because she had been lying on it?—that had run through her head as she lay on the tile floor at the Cup O'Delight, listening to the pop of gunfire.

Slim was able to walk, on crutches, up the church steps to Pete's funeral. Flanked by Fenny, Big Bill, Lee, and Harry, he began a low growl as they passed the phalanx of whirring cameras, passed the news reporters, their microphones thrust out and wagging, taunting them. Fenny wasn't exactly sure, but she thought it was on the third step that Bill began to growl, too, and then the others took up the call. The newspeople looked at one another, baffled, as the group climbed the church steps, growling and snarling like a pack of wild dogs.

Lars Larson and his sons carried Pete's sister Phyllis up in her wheelchair. There had been occasional discussions of putting in a wheelchair ramp at the church, but the discussions had never moved past the talking stage. Pastor Murch didn't see a need; anyone disabled by age or illness used the back door, which opened onto the parking lot. But funerals, like weddings, demanded spectacle, and everyone used the front entrance for them.

The wheelchair was made heavier by the silent thoughts of the four who carried it: What if we drop it? The mental strain made them physically strain, so that their muscles were tensed and their grips white-knuckled.

Neither Pete nor Phyllis was a member of Benevolent Father's, but when Pastor Murch offered to host the funeral in his church, Phyllis agreed. Pastor Murch felt somewhat close to the man; after all, Pete had resoled his shoes for over fifteen years, and besides, the press attention couldn't hurt the church, which was now involved in its annual pledge drive.

The barking crew grew silent as they entered the church. All of them were wearing black, except for Lee, who wore navy blue, wanting her dress to match the sling-back pumps the sheriff had given her the evening of the shooting.

"We found this on the floor," he had said as she loosened the bag's drawstring with trembling hands. A card sat atop a layer of tissue paper and when Lee read it, she groaned, which brought Fenny into the room from where she'd been washing the dishes that had amassed in Lee's kitchen.

Fenny read aloud the card Lee gave her: "Lee, you shoe are special to me. Pete."

Gingerly, Lee spread apart the tissue paper, not knowing what to expect.

"Shoes of Love by Pete," said Fenny, taking a shoe out and reading the stamp on the leather inner sock. She looked at Lee. "Pete made these?"

Lee took out the other shoe and held it in her hands, running her fingers along the soft leather. "I . . . I guess so," she said. "Oh, Fenny, aren't they beautiful?"

"Try them on."

Lee bowed her head. "I . . . don't know if I can."

"Sure you can, Lee. Pete would want you to."

Tears splashed Lee's hands as she bent down to put on the shoes. She stood up and walked across the room and back to the couch, a sobbing model.

The sheriff coughed; it seemed as if they had forgotten his presence.

"You know, there's more at Pete's store," he said. "I was going to bring them by tomorrow, but with all those press people—well, maybe it'd be easier for us to go now when they're not out in the streets. That is, if you're up to it."

Fenny would rather wait for Big Bill, but she saw in Lee's face how much her friend needed her.

Main Street was dark and blessedly free of any camera crews or tourists. Sheriff Gibbs brought them inside the tiny store, pulling the shade before he turned the light on.

"Those are for you," he said, gesturing toward the garbage bag in the middle of the floor.

Lee and Fenny pulled over the short wooden stools that stood against the window and opened the bag. When Lee saw what was inside, she wondered why God was so thoroughly punishing her; did He really think she could take any more heartbreak?

"Listen to this one, Lee," said Fenny, reading from a card: "I'm always on an 'upper' when you are around."

"Here's hoping you never give me the 'boot,' " read Lee. The card was inside a bag holding a pair of ankle-length boots. Lee put one hand inside one of the buff-colored boots and rubbed the outside with the other. She had never seen or felt such finely crafted shoes, and there had been a time in her life when her taste in shoes was an expensive one.

"I had no idea Pete could do this," said Lee softly as they looked through the bag.

"Phyllis told me he had a thriving mail-order business," said the sheriff. "She said he worked on them in a little workshop in the spare bedroom. He would pick up his orders from a P.O. box in International Falls, and when the shoes were done, he'd mail them off from there. He didn't want anybody to know about his shoe business."

"Why?" said Lee, stroking a pair of pebble-grained loafers. "Why wouldn't he want anyone to know he could do this?"

The sheriff shrugged. "If I knew one one-hundredth of why people did things, Lee, I wouldn't be a sheriff. I'd be head of the FBI."

The next morning, Lee had driven out to Pete's house and asked Phyllis if she could see his workshop, the place where he had made all her shoes.

"I 'spose," said Phyllis, "though I can't think why you'd want to." Pete's sister wheeled her chair over a plastic runner in the hallway and to a small room.

"This is it," she said, gesturing with her arm.

Pete's tools were arranged in neat rows. Labeled glass jars held "thimbles" and "seat rivets," "eyelets" and "heel nails," rolled-up "welts" and "shoelaces." Labeled drawers held "bottom fillers" and "counter stiffeners," "shanks," "seat lifts," "inner socks," and "back linings." Neat piles of cut leather were in cubbyholes, as were wooden molds. In the center of his worktable was a handwritten note.

Lee picked it up and read it.

> Dear Pete,
>
> I live a fast-paced life as an investment counselor. I fly around the world, checking out burgeoning markets for my clients. However, I'm also an aspiring novelist and I'd like a brisk, yet sensitive shoe that reflects this! Is this enough or do you need more information?
>
> Yours sincerely, J. M. Stiveson.

"What's this?" she had asked Phyllis.

The woman rolled closer to Lee and looked at the note. "Pete had all his clients write a little something about themselves. He called them 'personality profiles'—he said they helped figure out the right kind of shoe to make."

Lee had shaken her head, thinking she knew nothing about the man who had sat quietly at her counter every morning, leaving the same tip, telling the same jokes.

Now, sitting in church, listening to Alma Forslund sing a quavery "Shall We Gather at the River," Lee shut her eyes. She was as tired as she had ever been; tired in the way that made her think maybe it would be best to go to sleep and never wake up.

She had fought with Fenny on the way to the church. She'd been reciting a litany of guilt Fenny had heard at least a dozen times—how everything was her fault, how if she had never married Marshall Stouffer none of this would have ever happened, etc., etc.—and Fenny finally lost her cool.

"Lee, would you shut up, please? Marshall Stouffer was crazy. Are you responsible for the acts of a crazy man? Are you responsible for Pete loving you so much that he'd take a bullet for you?"

"Oh, Fenny!"

"Do you think Pete would want you to feel guilty over his taking a bullet for you? Hardly! I'd think he'd think you were, well . . . *devaluing* what he had done. He'd have wanted you to celebrate being alive. He wanted you to be alive, Lee."

Lee leaned her head against the car window and, looking at the sky, said softly, "Sorry, Pete. I can't celebrate yet. I can't even *think* of that now."

In the church, the organist played "Now the Day Is Over" as the mayor, Heine, and four of Pete's cousins carried Pete's coffin out, and as Lee watched it, sadness rose up like floodwaters and there she sat, in the middle of it.

The worst part was that she knew the sadness was only going to rise, only going to get deeper; she would be in sadness that threatened to drown her because immediately after Pete's service, she would be heading to Duluth, to hear whether or not Miss Penk had made it through another night.

The wounded Miss Penk had been taken to the harbor city after it was determined her injuries were too grievous to be treated in a small hospital, and the Cup O'Delight regulars made sure there was always someone to sit with Frau Katte. Lee would drive down with Slim after Pete's burial; she had asked Fenny to come along, but Fenny had declined.

"I'm getting my tooth fixed in the morning," Fenny reminded her. "I'll go down after that—after I take care of some things here." It was left unsaid that what Fenny had to take care of was Bill.

She was worried about him. She was worried about all of them; who could go through what they had just gone through without damage? But Bill was suffering not because he had been at the Cup O'Delight that awful morning, but because he had not.

"I should have been there, Fenny," he had cried, and like a child, he buried his head in her breast, his arms wrapped around her. "I should have been there to protect you."

"Oh, Bill," Fenny had said, smoothing his shiny black hair, "can anyone really protect anyone?"

Chapter 23

Lee sat in the hospital cafeteria, thinking that if she had been blind-folded, she would not be able to identify what she was eating, which was an egg salad sandwich dispensed from a vending machine. It tasted more of its plastic wrapping than it did of egg or mayonnaise, and this struck Lee as an occurrence so sad that tears sprang to her eyes. She wasn't surprised at her emotion over bland, plastic-flavored egg salad; even more innocuous events had her sobbing. She was forced, for instance, on the drive down from Tall Pine, to pull over on the side of the road because she had happened to read a bumper sticker on the fender of a passing car.

"Lee?" Slim had asked quizzically as she laid her head on the steering wheel and wept.

"That—that bumper sticker," she had blubbered. "The one that read, 'Commit random acts of kindness'!"

"Yes?" said Slim patiently, but Lee offered no more explanation, and cried for a good five minutes before Slim suggested that maybe he should drive the rest of the way.

She cried again when she saw a cat sitting on the porch of a boarded-up house in Hibbing and when she saw a group of girls playing hopscotch in Hermantown. Everything struck her as un-bearably sad; everything was capable of heartbreak and pain.

"Slim," she said during a brief reprieve from her crying, "I think I'm losing it."

"Take it from someone who's lost it," said Slim. "You're not losing it."

"But I can't stop crying."

"There's a lot to cry about."

Lee was limp now from crying; she could barely sit up in the hospital cafeteria, had barely the strength to lift the cup of weak coffee to her mouth. She blew her nose on a thin square dispenser napkin, wondering how long a person could cry before she parched herself, when Big Bill suddenly appeared at her table. She was so startled, she hiccuped.

"Bill!" she said as he pulled out a beige plastic chair. "What are you doing here?" She leaned, looking past him. "Is Fenny here, too?"

He sat his big frame in the inadequate chair, which squeaked a protest. "I wanted to see how Miss Penk was doing, so I hitched a ride down with the Murches. I heard the whole long story of their courtship and the even longer story of Pastor Murch's days in the seminary." He shook his head. "Remind me never to hear that story again."

Her eyes still brimming with ears, Lee smiled. "Is Fenny here, too?" she asked again.

Bill shook his head. "We sort of had a fight."

This information—or any information on Bill and Fenny's relationship—normally would have been of great interest to Lee, but her pain was so big that she couldn't summon up interest for something as everyday as a lovers' spat.

"The Murches went up to see Miss Penk, but I didn't want to see her with them," Bill continued. "Is she bad? Is that why you were crying?"

Lee blew her nose, realizing too late that the napkin didn't have the absorbency power to contain all that she blew. Embarrassed, she daubed at her nose with another napkin and then drew in a raggedy breath.

"Well," said Lee. "The good news is that she's not going to die. The bad news is that she's not going to walk."

"Oh, Jesus," whispered Bill.

Lee nodded in sad assent. "Imagine Miss Penk not walking . . . not running, not waterskiing or fencing or kickboxing or whatever that kung fu stuff was."

"What will she do?" asked Bill, and his rhetorical question was answered with, "We'll figure it out."

Hearing Frau Katte's voice, Bill stood, embracing the squat

woman in his arms. Slim sat down at the table with Lee and helped himself to her uneaten sandwich.

"Ick," he said after one bite, "it tastes like plastic."

"I had to get out of zere," said Frau Katte, sitting down. "Za Murches take up a lot of air in a room."

"You should be in a car with them," said Bill. He took the old Swiss woman's hand. "I am so sorry, Katte."

Tears filmed in Frau Katte's eyes, but she blinked them away. "Oh, pish," she said. "I was sure I vas going to lose her. Now I am not. Miss is alive!"

Her love and devotion hung on each simple sentence like flower buds, and Lee sniffed, feeling her relentless tears begin to gather.

"How's Miss Penk taking all of this?" asked Big Bill.

"Well, she's a little mad right now. You know," she said, her voice lowering, "she told me she was walking down zat tunnel of light you always hear about. She said it was za most peaceful feeling she ever had—she said she felt like a baby being held in one hundred arms of love." Frau Katte readjusted a bobby pin that kept her fez tethered to her head, composing herself as her chin trembled. "She said she wanted to be in zat tunnel, in zose arms forever, zen—boom—it got all black and it felt like she had been dropped and zen she opened her eyes and she was in za hospital room."

"Oh, Katte," said Lee, taking the older woman's hand.

"She said za only reason she didn't scream was because she saw my face."

Two candy stripers sat at a nearby table and their giggly conversation concerning a "babe" named Trevor was all the more jarring having come directly after Frau Katte's tale of her companion's near-death experience.

"Let's go see Miss Penk," suggested Lee. "I'm sure she's had enough of the Murches."

Even though Miss Penk ignominiously fell asleep during Gloria Murch's recitation of food served at Pete's funeral, the couple considered their pastoral visit a success and left, assuring Frau Katte that everything was "in God's hands."

"I don't zink so."

"What?" asked the pastor's wife, unsure she had heard Frau Katte correctly.

Pastor Murch smiled wanly. "What do you mean, Katte?"

The Swiss woman looked at her partner snoring softly on the bed. Her dyed and processed hair had been taken down from its high perch and hung over her shoulders in limp waves, the sight of which touched Frau Katte deeply.

"What I mean is, I zink it started out zat way—everyzing being in God's hand. But I zink God let go a long time ago."

"Katte," interrupted Gloria, who had better things to do than listen to blasphemy in a Duluth hospital room.

"Why would God *want* everyzing in his hands?" continued Frau Katte. "Zat's like a big bully who won't let anyone else play with his ball." She shook her head. "No, God might have started za whole game, but I zink He . . . or She . . . wants to see how we play it."

"Well, that's just absurd," said Gloria, and she had plenty more to say, but Pastor Murch ushered her out of the room, reminding Frau Katte to call if she needed anything.

While Miss Penk slept, Slim and Frau Katte played gin at her bedside and Lee and Bill decided to take a walk along the rocky shoreline of Lake Superior.

"Well, it's almost like the ocean," said Bill, looking at the horizon where the dark gray lake met the pale gray sky. "Even has waves—sort of."

Those were the only words spoken for the duration of their hour walk, other than Lee commenting on how chilly the wind off the water was and Bill offering her his jacket. It was only when Lee slipped on the rocks and fell that their silence was broken . . . by her wailing.

"Lee," said Big Bill, sitting on a rock next to her. "Lee, are you all right?"

Unable to speak, Lee shook her head and held up her scraped palm.

"Here," said Bill, taking out a wad of paper napkins and pressing them to her wound. "I took these from the hospital cafeteria, in case we ran out of Kleenex."

There was no reduction in the volume of her wailing.

"It's not really your hand that's hurting, is it?"

Lee shook her head. "It's . . . everything . . . else," she said in between sobs.

Bill nodded. "I figured." He readjusted his position on the hard rock and put his arm around Lee. "Do you want to stay here and cry or would you rather walk and cry?"

"Stay . . . here . . . and . . . cry."

"Fine with me," said Bill. "Although this wind is awfully cold. Still, I like bad weather when I'm feeling lousy—it makes me think the whole world is joining in on the grief."

Lee shivered, hugging her knees to her chest.

"I . . . like . . . feeling . . . bad . . . when . . . I'm . . . feeling . . . so . . . bad."

Bill nodded as if this made perfect sense to him.

"Fenny told me how you feel that it's somehow your fault."

Lee's wail mimicked that of an ambulance siren.

Bill tightened his grip and drew Lee closer. "Lee, Lee," he said, unable to suppress a small laugh over her vocal magnitude. "Lee, you know it's not your fault."

Lee drew her palms across her face. "I . . . was . . . the . . . target," she began, "I . . . was . . . the . . . one . . . who . . . was . . . supposed . . . to . . . get . . . shot."

"No one was supposed to get shot." Bill's voice was stern. "Your ex-husband was crazy—that's why he was your *ex*-husband."

"Still . . . ," said Lee, "my . . . ex-husband . . . my restaurant . . . Pete . . . Miss Penk . . . I'm . . . so . . . sad . . . Bill. So . . . sad . . . and . . . sorry."

"Me, too, Lee," said Bill, feeling his own tears well. "I keep thinking that if I were there . . . . well, I *am* big. I could have stopped something."

A young couple, just off work and on their daily power walk, passed on the nearby walkway, their arms pumping. If they noticed the distressed duo sitting on the rocks, they gave no evidence of it, pausing not an iota in their rhythmic breathing and conversation concerning IRA vs. Keogh contributions.

Bill and Lee sat huddled together until the blue-gray curtain of dusk fell and the sky and the waters of Lake Superior were the same color.

When a shiver spasmed through Lee, Big Bill decided it was time they headed back to the hospital and see if Miss Penk was awake yet.

And so, unwilling to let go of each other, they held hands, stepping over the rocks and sticks and occasional flattened pop can that littered the shoreline.

After Pete's funeral, Fenny and Bill had skipped the church luncheon in favor of sitting in front of the Shoe Shack. She hated those luncheons; at the one held after her parents' memorial service she wanted to yell at everyone for having appetites, for being able to help themselves to hot dish and make jokes about the doughiness of Gloria Murch's hot-cross buns.

A measure of respect needed to be paid, and that is what led her to tie a black ribbon around the outer doorknob of Pete's Shoe Shack and to sit quietly on the bench outside, the one Pete sat on in mild weather while resoling shoes or nailing cleats onto heels.

Bill was quietly following along with Fenny's ritual—that is, until he spoke.

"Shhh," shushed Fenny. "I don't want to talk right now."

Not only had she been shaken by the violence that had occurred inside the Cup O'Delight, but the violence that had taken place outside. She had seen the car strike Marshall Stouffer, had seen him flying through the air, had seen his broken and bleeding body on the sidewalk, and as much as she tried to resist it, she couldn't help but picture her own parents being flung through the air, couldn't help but hear that horrible smack and squeal of brakes. She had imagined their deaths before, but now she had a frame of reference, and it terrified her.

Bill pressed his lips together and folded his hands like a boy chastened for his chattiness in Sunday school.

They sat there for a long time, and Bill tried to chart how long by the travel of the sun. Trouble was, it was overcast, but even if the sun had been shining, Bill didn't know if he'd be able to tell time by it. His lack of knowledge of the natural world shamed his Chippewa side; his Aunt Mae knew the outdoors—knew not only the time by the sun but the time by the moon, and also what weather it foretold.

"You got all that knowledge inside you," Mae told him, "you just got to trust it enough to come out."

Apparently Bill wasn't trusting enough; the only way he was going to be able to tell the time was if he had a watch.

He then tried to count the paper turkeys in the display window of Sunstrom Sundries across the street, but it was a game that didn't occupy him for long, seeing as there were only five. (It was Mrs. Sunstrom who decorated the windows for upcoming holidays, and Thanksgiving always seemed to get the short shrift, because, as she explained to her husband, "There's only so much a person can do with pilgrims and turkeys.")

Bill then tested his vision by reading the signs placed in Denton's Grocery, first with his right eye closed and then with his left eye shut. He wasn't sure, but he thought the lettering was sharper when read with his right eye. With his left eye shut, he was trying to read a license plate of a car parked far down on Main Street when Fenny spoke.

"Bill, I think we ought to see other people."

"*What?*" said Bill, and Fenny was almost as jarred as he was by her words. She had, after all, intended to comfort Bill, knowing how much in need of comfort he was. She felt like an actor who'd been given a script completely different from the one she had memorized and yet, now that she had said one line, felt a need to commit to it.

"I just think we should take some time off from seeing each other exclusively, and—"

"Fenny," interrupted Bill, "you're just upset about all that's happened. You don't really want to see other people."

Fenny's laugh was as dry as a rasp. "I don't? What makes you think that?"

"Because *I* don't. And we think about each other the same. I mean, we both . . . we both . . ."

"Love one another? The thing that we've both been hoping to be brave enough to do, let alone brave enough to say?"

"Fenny, please. This has been hard on all of us. Don't make it harder."

Fenny's laugh now could hardly qualify as one. "Come on, Bill, say it. It's not so hard. Just curl your tongue up a little and say 'l-l-l-love.' "

"Love," said Bill, staring at his big folded hands. "Love."

Fenny's laugh was cruel. "Well, at least you can say the word."

Bill heard the wind snap the courthouse flag, still at half-staff, heard the metal ching of its pulley against the pole, heard the cry of a blackbird up on a telephone wire; his ears seemed sharp as a wolf's, seemed to fill with dozens of faraway noises and sounds, and yet they could not absorb the words that came out of a mouth just inches from them.

They both sat staring at the doorknob of Pete's shop. The black ribbon tied around it spiraled in the wind.

"Why are you saying these things?" Bill said finally. "I don't understand."

Fenny did not exactly understand, either, but she felt a strange power in saying them, and anything that made her feel powerful now had to be a good thing.

"It's because I wasn't there to help, isn't it?" said Bill. "Just like I wasn't there to help when you and Lee got in that fight with those tourists at the Midsommer's Eve party." Bill took Fenny's hand, which lay in his own like a cold, limp fish. "Well, that's the last time," he said. "The last time I'll ever let you down. From now on I want you to always count on me."

"Oh, Bill," said Fenny with a sigh. "Don't make promises you can't keep. No one can count on anyone, really."

With that she stood up, hugging her cast to her side, and began to walk to her car, still parked at the church. Fenny's words had been like blows to Bill and, KO'd by them, he just sat on the bench, watching her go.

At home, Fenny tried to crochet, but the angle in which she had to hold her broken arm made it too awkward an undertaking. She tried reading, but the words were meaningless hieroglyphics. Finally, feeling both guilty and confused over what she had said to Bill, it seemed clear to Fenny that the only thing for her to do was to leave town. She needed time to think by herself, with no distractions but

Mother Nature. She packed her camping gear and decided to go to Canada, to a place she had often gone with her parents, but she hadn't driven more than a quarter mile before she decided she couldn't leave Bill completely in the lurch. She drove to Mae Little Feather's to tell him of her plans.

That he wasn't in his tent didn't exactly surprise Fenny as much as it disappointed her, but seeing an empty paper bag (probably empty of candy), she flattened it and wrote Bill a quick note:

> I'm not sure I meant those things I said, Bill. I'm not sure of anything except that I've gone on a little trip to think things out. We'll talk when I get back—and I hope the words will make more sense. Sorry about everything, Love (I'm pretty sure), Fenny.

She laid it on top of his sleeping bag, but not before sealing the words with a kiss.

Zipping the tent door shut from the other side, she noticed the Norwegian sweater that she wore as a robe in the tent now that it was getting cold.

"Wait'll you see my line of tent lingerie for spring," she had told him, to which Bill had answered lasciviously, "I can't."

Now she reached over to take the sweater, which would serve her well camping.

Back on the road, she felt, not exactly a lightness, but a sense that the weight of all that had happened, the weight that was bearing down on her, had shifted slightly and might not crush her after all.

From her kitchen window, Mae Little Feather watched the car drive off, and when she was sure it was long gone, she scurried down to Big Bill's tent to see what was what, and when she saw the note written on a brown paper sack, she took it, because that white girl had no right leaving something like that on her nephew's sleeping bag.

Chapter 24

Two days and two nights in the semi-wilds of Canada were a tonic for Fenny. She was a hard-core camper, never bothered by weather that would have sent those less hardy to the nearest Motel 6. And the temperatures had been dropping steadily, a reminder that winter had begun its heavy-footed march forward; the next snow that fell would not be a seasonal aberration like the Great Ball of China snowfall, but the one that would be the first in an ongoing five-month stream.

Fenny was not one to complain about the cold; in fact, she welcomed it. She wondered why so many people carped about the cold, when all a person had to do was dress for it: good hat, good boots with two pairs of wool socks, good mittens, and lots of layers.

"You wouldn't go deep-sea diving without the proper equipment," she once told Lee, who hated cold weather.

"I wouldn't go deep-sea diving *with* the proper equipment," Lee answered.

Cold, even *cold* cold, did not faze Fenny at all, and she embraced the beauty that was literally frozen by the weather: the ice-coated tree branches, the vast slopes of snow, icicles hanging from roof gutters like swords belonging to a brigade of snow warriors. Fenny loved walking in the silence of a deep winter's day, her frosty breath reminding her with every exhale of her very aliveness, her nostrils pinching together as the mucus inside froze. She loved the *squinch* sound her boots made in the snow, the quiet of the natural world, hunkered down and in hibernation.

Of course, it was nowhere near that cold and, although frozen dew whitened the grass in the morning, no actual snow had fallen.

Sitting in front of a roaring campfire as the night pulled its shade around her, it was easy to believe that nothing much had changed; that if she were to be transported back across the border and into Tall Pine, all would be well; Lee would be at the Cup O'Delight pouring coffee, Pete would be making shoe puns, and Miss Penk and Frau Katte would be swiveling on the counter stools, debating which kind of pie to split. And she and Bill would be together.

"I guess I've made up my mind, Bill," she said out loud, staring at the fire, "and I guess I've decided on you." She crawled into her sleeping bag (she couldn't pitch a tent with one good hand and she had always liked to sleep under the stars anyway), feeling as happy as she was able to feel under the circumstances.

She slept deeply on that cold Canadian night, the way a person does when she's made what she's sure is the right decision.

Bill, on the other hand, spent an uncomfortable and wakeful night on the floor at the foot of the double beds occupied by Lee and Slim.

"Why is it," he asked the next morning, trying to stretch out the kinks in his back, "that the floor of a motel room is harder than the ground I usually sleep on?"

"Pine needles," said Slim. "Pine needles are a softer cushion than carpet."

After square sausage sandwiches at a fast-food restaurant, they drove to the hospital, but Frau Katte assured them that she was fine by herself, and besides, she had appointments with several people regarding how to manage Miss Penk's at-home care.

Lee and Slim and Bill drove back to Tall Pine, discussing their own plans.

"I'm going to sell the Cup O'Delight," said Lee. "I'm going to sell the cafe and go somewhere."

Slim, stretched across the back seat, let out a small groan.

"Go where?" asked Bill, on the passenger's side.

"I don't know," she said. "I've just got to get away from here for a while."

Slim began whining like a dog who wanted to be let inside.

"Slim, cut that out. I can't handle any of that right now."

"And I," said Slim in a perfect Alfred Hitchcock impersonation, "can't handle any of what you're telling us right now. Therefore, I bark." He barked, so loudly that Lee flinched. She tightened her grip on the steering wheel.

"I don't know where I'm going, Slim," said Lee, "but wherever it is, and if you want to, you can come with."

"Can I come, too?"

Lee let out a dismissive "Tuh," and then asked, "What about Fenny?"

Bill had a funny feeling, not in the pit of his stomach, but at the top of his chest. He rubbed his collarbone, trying to believe it was just the achy beginnings of a flu but sensing it was the foreboding of something he did not want to be foreboded about.

"I don't know what's going on with me and Fenny," he said, looking out the window at the passing gray landscape. "We didn't just have a fight, Lee; we broke up."

"What *happened?*" she asked, and while her eyes were focused on the road, her ears gave Bill their full attention.

"Well, I'm hoping the things she said were said under duress and don't count," said Bill, "but I just can't help thinking that when I get back to Tall Pine, she'll be gone."

"Oh, Bill, Fenny doesn't go anywhere."

"She might go to Hollywood," offered Slim from the back seat. "You know how everyone's been bothering her to go to Hollywood."

"She says she hates Hollywood," said Bill, turning in his seat to face Slim, "or at least the idea of it."

Slim shrugged his bony shoulders. "When we were shot down in Quang Tri, there was only one thing I wanted to do, and that was *get out of Quang Tri.* I didn't care where—anyplace had to be better than *Quang fuckin' Tri.*"

"Even Holly-fuckin'-wood?" asked Lee. She was not one to use foul language, and so on the rare occasions when she did, it still had the power to shock.

"Lee O'Leary!" said Bill.

"You just let me out of the car if you're going to talk like that!" said Slim, in Gloria Murch's voice, and then they laughed, and for the rest of the ride home, with little jokes and impersonations, they tended to that laughter carefully, the way they would a fire, making sure that it never went completely out, fanning a spark until a new blaze burned, because keeping that laughter alive was, for the moment, the sanest thing they could do.

Bill got out of the car at the boarded-up Cup O'Delight but didn't follow Lee and Slim up the stairs to their apartments, instead choosing to walk to Fenny's house.

"Good luck," called Lee after him.

That funny feeling in his upper chest flared up again as he rounded the slight curve of road before the Ness house and saw that her car was not in the driveway.

"Doesn't mean anything," he said, and without stopping, he turned around to walk back to his tent.

Mae Little Feather was peeling apples at her kitchen table, her feet propped up on the vinyl chair across from her, occasionally looking up at the little portable TV perched on her counter to see what idiot had bid two hundred and fifty dollars for an automatic breadmaker.

"Too high, too high," she heckled, along with the studio audience. She was merciless, and would have gotten into name-calling had she not seen, through the kitchen window, her nephew.

She almost cackled with glee, thinking of the note that lay shredded at the bottom of her wastebasket.

She watched him enter his tent and was thrilled when, not a minute later, he emerged and began walking toward the house.

"That you, Bill?" she said innocently as he knocked on the door before opening it.

"None other," said Bill, settling himself into one of Mae's yellow vinyl kitchen chairs. He folded his arms and looked at the TV and then back at Mae, whose face gave no indication of her near-overwhelming desire to giggle.

"Hey, Mae," said Bill, fingering the clay saltshaker that a potter relative had made. "You didn't happen to see Fenny around, did you?"

"Fenny?" she said lightly. "Well, yes, I did, Bill. I happened to be doing the ironing yesterday afternoon when I seen her come by."

"Really?" asked Bill. "How did she look?"

"She looked like Fenny, I reckon. Although, as I recall," said Mae, squinting her hooded eyes, "she did go into your tent empty-handed and come out carrying something. Sweater, I think."

"A sweater?" asked Bill, and then the implication of what that meant made him slump in his chair. She took her sweater, her *tent robe*, the one she brought for extra warmth now that it was getting so cold at night. Taking it meant that she wasn't planning on spending any time soon in his tent.

"What?" said Mae, noticing Bill's change in demeanor. "Should I of told her not to take it? Did she steal it?"

"No, no, Mae. Nothing like that. Well," he said, standing up, "I guess I'll walk to town. Do you need anything?"

"Could use something sweet. Unless you got something?"

Bill riffled through his jacket pockets, which further validated his sense that life as he knew it was falling apart, because for the first time in recent memory, he was without a single piece of candy.

In town, Bill walked slowly past Sig's Place, hoping to see Fenny inside, but saw only Gloria Murch, who was dressing a mannequin in another of the appliquéd sweatshirts she thought belonged in every American woman's wardrobe.

He felt as aimless and lonely as a dropout whose friends have all stayed in school. With the Cup O'Delight closed, there was no central place to go and hang out, have coffee, and ask the one question he most wanted an answer to: "Have you seen Fenny?"

He was idly examining a roll of Cyclone fencing in front of Bick's Hardware when Lee, agitated and out of sorts after hanging up on her brother Gerald (who didn't seem as concerned about her well-being as he was in her future plans with the cafe), saw Bill through her apartment window. She was downstairs and outside in a minute.

"Bill, don't stand here," she said, taking his arm. "That's where Marshall . . . landed."

"Uhh," said Bill, as if he'd stepped in something he didn't want to step in.

Lee pulled him across the street.

"So Fenny wasn't home, huh?" she asked, shivering in the cold.

Bill shook his head. "Mae said she saw her in my tent. She took her sweater." His voice broke.

"Oh, Bill, come on, I'll get you a cup—" She stopped, her own voice breaking, as she looked at the boarded-up windows of her cafe.

That evening, Lee and Big Bill were in Hinckley, Minnesota, gambling in a casino that smelled of the barbecued beef from the buffet dinner being served in the dining room and the cigarette smoke that was supposed to be contained in the small smoking area but managed to drift out. They were a little high, but only from adventure.

The idea to get away had seemed to ride in on the cold wind that flapped the awning of Bick's Hardware.

"Let's get out of here," said Bill.

Lee's deep blue eyes flashed. "I was thinking exactly the same thing."

Slim had brushed aside Lee's concerns about leaving him alone.

"I'm not a baby," he said gruffly. "I can manage to feed myself— just tell me where you keep the pablum."

"But your foot—you can't get around so well and—"

"I can get along fine, Lee."

"Well, I don't know when we'll be back," said Lee, not really knowing what their plans entailed.

"Have fun. And don't worry—I promise not to play soccer or run any marathons."

Bill and Lee drove in a smug, excited silence, as if they couldn't believe they were breaking through the heavy curtain of shock and grief that had been drawn around them and into some sort of light.

It was a series of road signs advertising the fun to be found in Hinckley ("The Fun's Just 100 Miles Away!" "The Fun's Just 50 Miles Away!") that gave them a destination.

"Let's gamble," said Bill. "Let's sit in a dark casino and drink cheap drinks and watch showgirls in feathers walk by."

"I don't think Hinckley has showgirls," said Lee. "But I'm game for the rest of it."

They played blackjack first, along with a farmer from Yankton, South Dakota, and a woman who kept sucking in her loose dentures. The dealer had the impassive, bored look of someone who desperately needed a new job, or at the very least a coffee break.

"Here, let me get this," said Bill, paying for their chips with two twenty-dollar bills he took out of his pocket.

"Thanks," said Lee with the surprised gratitude of someone who assumed she'd be paying for everything.

The farmer from Yankton, who'd taken a reprieve from his wife's family reunion to try his luck, quit after he'd won back his initial investment; if he was any more late for the family get-together, his wife would start telling her snoopy sisters all about the little problem he'd been having in bed lately.

Lee and Bill were each riding a seesaw of wins and losses, but the denture-sucker was cleaning up.

"You seem to know your way around a blackjack table," noted Bill.

The woman drew in her choppers. "I took a class at the senior citizen center. Only class I ever took there that's paid off." She sucked her teeth in again and directed the dealer to "hit me." Winning the round, she cackled as she collected her chips. "I took ceramics once—what a joke that was—everything I ever made looked like spoilt fruit. Then I took some kinda massage class, and let me tell you, when I practiced what I'd learned on a fellow classmate, he was hollering for 'uncle.' Said it felt like I had ruptured his kidneys or whatever organs you got there in your lower-back area." She talked easily in between choosing cards and righting her dentures and was heading deep into a discourse about a class that taught how to cut vegetables to look like flowers—"only I cut myself right there in my thumb and needed four stitches before I ever made a radish look like a rose"—when Bill and Lee decided to cut their losses and look for other entertainment.

After Bill cashed in another forty dollars for quarters (refusing Lee's offer to chip in), they sat down at two video poker machines.

"Don't be so chintzy," said Bill, after Lee put a quarter in and proceeded to play the hand. "You've got to bet big to win big."

"All right," said Lee, putting in five quarters, and without having to discard anything, her cards came up a straight flush. Lights lit up and quarters rained down from the machine like silver hailstones.

"Lee!" said Bill. "Lee, you're rich!"

"We're rich," said Lee. "Those were your quarters."

Lee's take was five hundred dollars, which was winnowed down to three hundred by the time they decided a second big win was probably not in their cards, or on the video screen.

"Let's go hear Lorenz Ferré," said Lee, who had noticed his picture on a "Now Appearing!" sign as they had entered the casino.

"Lorenz Ferré," said Big Bill. "You've got to be kidding."

"Oh, come on," said Lee, pulling on his arm. "I'm getting carpal tunnel working this video machine."

The lounge was only a third full.

"Big fan club," whispered Bill as they were led to a table.

"Shhh," whispered Lee.

Their waitress served them their drinks (they each had one rum and Coke before switching to plain Coke) as Lorenz Ferré launched into a smarmy version of "Downtown."

"And that's why I hate the guy," said Big Bill. "He doesn't sing a song so much as mangle it."

"I feel sorry for him," said Lee. "It used to be you couldn't turn on your radio without hearing his hit songs and now he's singing in a half-empty casino lounge."

"Hit *song*," corrected Bill. "He had one hit song: 'Purr Little Kitty.' And that song *stunk*."

"Still," said Lee, "you couldn't turn on the radio in the early seventies without hearing it."

Lorenz Ferré's four-piece band kicked into the instrumental section of the song, leaving Lorenz to twirl the cord of his microphone above his head as if it were a lasso.

"He is really pathetic," said Big Bill.

Mr. Ferré turned his attention to Bill and Lee, knowing that they were talking about him. He winked and smiled, his ego seemingly too big, even in the midst of such a small audience, to conceive that anyone talking about him might not be talking favorably.

"Oh, my God," whispered Big Bill, trying not to move his lips as he talked. "If he isn't the sorriest—"

"Shut up, Bill," said Lee with a fixed smile. She was too polite to laugh at a performer who wasn't trying to be funny, but it was a politeness she was having a hard time with.

"Why does he keep winking at us?" she whispered, feeling slightly panicky from the laughter that wanted release.

"He thinks we like him," said Bill.

"Downtown" ended and the first few bars of the song on whose coattails Lorenz Ferré had been riding for years began.

"Oh, no," groaned Bill.

Many professions have incorporated a certain cheesy earnestness into their personas (any salespeople pushing used cars or door-to-door beauty products), but none can match the lounge performer trying to sell a song. Lorenz Ferré's lip twitched, his shoulders and hips twitched; he was a shivering, shuddering piece of animal magnetism—at least in his eyes.

> *"More than catnip I'm every feline's dream,*
> *Yes, I'm the tomcat who can make them scream.*
> *Every Persian, every Calico, every Siamese*
> *First they say 'meow,' then they beg, 'please.' "*

Lorenz Ferré had made it to the lip of the stage, and there he got down on both knees and with one curled finger beckoned Lee to him.

Lee's shoulders rocked from the force of laughter no longer containable.

Bill, laughing himself, nudged her and nudged her again. "Lee, he wants you to go up there."

"So purr little kitty," sang Ferré to Lee, "purr right now / Purr little kitty—umm, that's right—meow, *meow*."

Bill had no idea what compelled him to obey Lorenz Ferré's command, but he pulled Lee out of the booth and was dragging the laughing woman toward the stage. He marched her up the side steps and they stood on either side of the faded star, dwarfing him.

The singer took Lee's hand.

"Purr little kitty—umm, that's right, purr little kitty, *meow*."

Lee's laughter was like blows pummeling her; she held her sides, wondering how she'd have the strength to stand.

"We've got one frisky little kitty here," said Ferré to the audience.

"Why don't you take a hike, mate?" he whispered to Bill, his mouth still wearing its cheesy smile.

A small part of Bill thought how much he'd enjoy wiping that smile off the singer's face and sending him on his own little hike, *mate*, but a larger part was enjoying the absurdity of the evening too much, and so he backed away.

"Don't leave me, Bill!" spluttered Lee, still laughing.

"Oh, don't be afraid of this old tomcat," said Ferré, who hadn't let go of her hand.

The audience, though small, had been enthusiastic all along, and as the band launched into the final chorus, they stood up and applauded for Lorenz Ferré and their collective memories of him in his elephant bell-bottoms and leather vest singing one of the great make-out songs of all time.

"So purr little kitty, purr," sang Ferré. He held Lee's hand up and was dancing around her, his own personal maypole.

Tears pulsed down Lee's cheeks; her face was red from the intensity of her laughter.

"Purr, little kitty, purr—that's right—*meow*."

The lights blacked out and the audience went wild, but a voice in the blackness announced, "Thank you, ladies and gentlemen, for joining Mr. Lorenz Ferré—have a nice evening."

Lee stumbled around in the blackness, being pulled by the singer, who never did encores, mainly because of the limited size of his repertoire.

"Where are you taking me?" she asked, colliding slightly with a cymbal.

"I just want to talk to you—person to person," said Ferré. He pushed aside a curtain and they were backstage.

"Great show, Mr. Ferré," said the stage manager.

"Thanks. It was a nice crowd."

Lee had finally stopped laughing and she followed the singer, who still held her hand, down a hallway and to a door marked with a star.

She thought of her cabin mates at Camp Waganotoshi and how they had done an outrageous dance to "Purr Little Kitty" one night and how their thin-lipped counselor had come in and snapped off the radio, asking them what did they think they were, a bunch of sex-crazed deviates?—and then, regaining her cool, cleared her throat and told them they'd better hit the hay, they had a big day of canoeing ahead.

And now Lee was being asked to sit down in Lorenz Ferré's dressing room.

"Like a cup of tea, luv? Or something stronger?"

Lee looked at her hands, suddenly feeling shy and foolish.

"I . . . I really can't stay," she said.

"Nonsense," said Ferré. "You can stay. You just don't want to."

Ferré's voice was wistful, as if he were used to people who didn't want to stay. Lee, always an easy mark, shrugged her shoulders and sat down.

"I guess I just don't understand why you want me to stay."

"It's fairly obvious, luv. You're absolutely smashing!" With this declaration, the singer took a leap across the room, landing on Lee's lap.

"Ooof!" said Lee.

"God, how I love ginger-haired women!" said Ferré before plastering a big wet kiss on the side of Lee's face.

"Get off!" she said, and in case he wasn't thinking of listening to her, she gave him a good push.

Landing on the floor, he giggled as he got up, his jet-black toupee slightly askew.

"I love a feisty woman," he said, and he would have leapt into her lap again had she not stood up. "So come here and let's make mad love, luv."

Bill had found his way backstage and now rapped on the singer's door.

"Lee? Lee, are you in there?"

Lee hesitated one second too long, and Bill, putting the full weight of his shoulder against the door, pushed it open. Because the door was unlocked, this was an unnecessary gesture that caused him to tumble into the room and nearly fall down himself.

"Why, Bill," said Lee, impressed by his entrance.

"I didn't do anything," said Ferré, who was carefully walking backward toward the bathroom, which he planned to escape into if need be.

"Well, you did kiss me," said Lee mildly.

"He kissed you?" said Big Bill, playing the spurned lover. He moved slowly toward Ferré, his fingers curled, his big hands looking like bear claws.

Lorenz Ferré took a gulp of air and then dashed into the bathroom, punching in the little button lock on the doorknob.

"No lock can keep me out," said Bill in his deep, intimidating voice, and Lee, who had begun to laugh again, shook her head and waved her hand in a gesture of, *Enough! enough!*

Bill let the singer wonder about his fate for a few minutes and then rapped on the door.

"Come on out, Mr. Ferré. I was only kidding."

"You're not going to hurt me?" Ferré's voice was surprised.

"No, I'm not going to hurt you. I promise."

Slowly the doorknob turned, releasing the button lock. The door opened and from behind it emerged a sheepish, and bald, Lorenz Ferré.

"I took off my toupee," he said, as if neither Lee nor Bill could have figured that out for themselves. "I'm less likely to get hit without it." He went over to his makeup table and sat down. "I guess boyfriends don't feel as threatened by a bald sex symbol as by a sex symbol with hair, eh?"

Big Bill didn't bother to admit he didn't feel threatened at all; like Lee, he felt pity for the man.

Ferré seemed to read his thoughts and looked at Bill in the mirror.

"You just think I'm a washed-up little twit, don't you?"

Bill shrugged his shoulders.

"Come on, admit it."

"Okay," said Bill. "I admit it."

"Bill," scolded Lee as the singer began dabbing more foundation on his face.

"Oh, that's all right," said Ferré. "I think the same thing most of the time. Except when I'm onstage. It would be deadly to think that while I'm onstage."

"I loved 'Purr Little Kitty' when I was a teenager," offered Lee.

"Who didn't?" said Ferré. "It was a great song." He patted his makeup with a Kleenex and looked at Bill. "I gather you're not of the same opinion?"

"Well," said Bill slowly, not wanting to hurt the guy's feelings, but not wanting to lie, either, "I wasn't a particular fan. But I suppose for its time it was an okay song."

" 'For its time,' " scoffed Ferré. "Hey, mate, classics are classics."

Bill shrugged again. "Shall we go, Lee?" he asked, not feeling like getting in the ridiculous argument about whether or not "Purr Little Kitty" was a classic.

"Sure, go," said Ferré, waving his hand. "Leave. Everybody else does."

This is where the pity Big Bill was feeling for Lorenz Ferré took that extra step into loathing.

"Oh, please," he muttered.

"We can stay for a little while," said Lee.

"Lee, I thought we were driving back home tonight." Bill didn't really know what their plans were, but he hoped they didn't include sitting around with some self-pitying, washed-up—what was the word Ferré used?—"twit."

"Bill, we can get a hotel room. We don't have to go home tonight. Slim's not expecting me any particular time." She looked at the singer, who, bald and in his orangey stage makeup, seemed oddly touching. "Don't you have a manager . . . or an entourage to keep you company?"

Ferré laughed. "An entourage? The days of an entourage ended around the time the public figured out there was no follow-up to 'Purr Little Kitty.' "

"No 'Roar Big Tiger'?" asked Bill, rolling his eyes at Lee.

"What did you say?"

Bill mistook the man's tone for aggressiveness. "Hey, you *don't* want to get in a fight with me."

"No, no," said Ferré, standing up and going to the battered piano that was pushed against the wall. "Say what you said again."

"Hey, you don't want to get in a fight with me?"

Lee laughed. "No, Bill, he's talking about 'Roar Big Tiger.' "

"That's it!" said the singer. He played a C chord and sang, "Roar, big tiger." He shook his head. "No, that's not it." He played another major chord and sang the same three words. "Come on, come on, I know I've got something here."

"Are you serious?" Bill asked as he and Lee went over to the piano.

"You're bloody right I'm serious. I've been trying to think of a sequel to that song for years."

"You have?" asked Big Bill, astonished not only that the man hadn't been able to think of one, but that he wanted to at all.

"I'm not much of a songwriter," said Ferré, striking another chord. " 'Purr Little Kitty' came to me in a dream. The tune, lyrics, arrangement, everything."

"It did?" said Bill, again astonished. Once he had a dream in which he had wallpapered over the Sistine Chapel, but he had never written a song in his sleep.

Ferré struck another chord and sang the three words. It was apparent inspiration was being stingy.

"Bill, sit down," said Lee. "Play around with it."

"Me?"

"You?" said Ferré. "You play the piano?"

"No, *I* play the piano," said Lee. "*Bill* whales on it."

"Well, then," said Ferré, sliding over, making room for Bill on the piano bench. "Be my guest."

Giving Lee a smile that said, *I'll get you for this,* Bill sat down at the piano and his fingers quickly covered the keyboard. Ferré watched Bill's fingers as they played a blues riff, then a little of "Every Picture Tells a Story, Don't It," ending up with a dozen bars of a Bach concerto.

"I'm sitting next to Little Richard!" said Ferré.

Bill took off on the concerto then, adding minor keys and laying down a heavier bass and, in fits and starts, began singing.

> *"I used to be a tomcat, chasing tails all night,*
> *Thinkin' I had to have every pretty cat in sight."*

"Write that down! Write that down!" squealed Ferré, and Lee, finding a small tablet with the casino logo on its pages, began writing the words Bill sang.

> *"I thought 'cause I had nine lives, the party'd never end*
> *But I got older, baby, there were some things I had to mend."*

"That's beautiful! Perfect! Did you get that down, Lee?"

She looked at the tablet and read, ". . . there were some things I had to mend."

"Like broken promises," sang Bill, the words coming fast and furious, "and broken hearts, too, / But most of all, I had to admit that I was in love with you."

"Brilliant!" screamed Ferré. He squeezed his eyes and pressed his temples with his hands. "Play that again, so I can memorize the tune."

"I can write down the music," offered Lee.

"Oh, my God," said the singer, who himself had never learned how to read notes, "I'm surrounded by genius."

Within a half hour, Bill, with occasional lyric suggestions from Lee and Ferré, had crafted a song that told the story of an old tomcat who always fancied himself a tiger and who, after years of making all the felines purr, was now happily domesticated by one, and wanted to roar about it.

He played it several times, each with slight variations, but the main tune Lee was able to transcribe and she did, on page after page of the wallet-sized casino tablet.

"Write your names and addresses, too," said the flushed Lorenz Ferré. "I'll need to know where to send all the royalty checks."

"Yeah, right," said Big Bill, but as they celebrated with a bottle of champagne Ferré had the stage manager bring to the dressing room, he couldn't help humming the tune that the singer said would "blast its way to the top."

"I don't know about that." Bill laughed. "It's pretty hokey."

"Most pop songs are, mate." Ferré, obviously feeling better, had put his toupee back on. "But hokey doesn't matter as long as it's got a good beat and a tune you remember."

"Well, to hokey, then," said Lee, raising her glass. She looked at Bill. "Although I wouldn't call it that, Bill. I'd call it wonderful."

In that synergy that sometimes strikes, the three of them began singing "Roar Big Tiger" until the stage manager knocked on the door, telling the singer it was about time for the second show.

Bill and Lee played a few more games of video poker, and to their great surprise, Lee won seventy-five dollars, and they whooped and hollered louder than when she had won five hundred dollars, because they had beaten the odds a second time.

Watching them leave the casino, a security guard assumed they were drunk; they were arm-in-arm, laughing and knocking their hips together as if each were trying to upend the other. But one rum and Coke and one glass of champagne had inebriated neither one; they were intoxicated by the fun they'd had.

They walked in the general direction of their car, thinking they were headed to it and then Tall Pine, but another sign right across the parking lot determined their destination once again, a sign announcing a hotel with a swimming pool and Jacuzzi.

"A Jacuzzi," said Bill. "That would feel good about now."

"It is late," Lee agreed.

They were informed at the front desk that, sorry, the pool and Jacuzzi hours were eight to eleven. But once Bill and Lee were in their room, they decided that, sorry, those rules would have to be broken.

They scurried down the hallway and into the deserted pool area.

"All right," said Bill, "let's go!"

They stripped to their underwear and climbed in.

"Ahhh," said Lee as the hot churning water swirled around her.

"Ahh," said Bill, leaning his head back.

"Jacuzzi's closed!" said the security guard, suddenly appearing from behind a pinball machine.

Lee and Bill looked at one another, not willing to believe that their luck hadn't held out.

Bill looked at the skinny guard, whose collar was much too big for his neck. "It wasn't turned off," said Bill pleasantly.

"Doesn't matter," said the guard. "It's"—he looked at his wristwatch, which seemed too big for his wrist—"eleven fifty-two P.M. This area's been off-limits for . . . uh . . . fifty-two minutes."

"Oh, please," said Bill. "What'll it hurt if we stay just a few minutes? You can't kick out a couple who just got married, can you?"

The security guard's large Adam's apple bobbed once and then again. "You just got married?"

"Today," said Bill. "In Las Vegas. We were going to spend our honeymoon out there until we heard that the gambling was just as good in Dinckley."

"Hinckley," corrected the security guard. "We're pretty proud of our casino."

"And well you should be," said Lee. "It's beautiful. Better than the ones in Monaco."

"You've been to Monaco?" asked the security guard. "Oh, I'd

have given anything to go to Monaco. That Grace Kelly was something else."

"She certainly was," agreed Bill.

They sat in the water quietly, watching the guard's face.

"She's got my vote for all-time best-looker," he said dreamily. "Next to the wife, of course."

"Thank you," said Bill.

The security guard colored. "Um, I meant my wife. Not that yours isn't really pretty herself."

"Why, thank you," said Lee demurely.

"Okay, then," said the guard, looking around at the ghostly reflections the pool lights cast on the ceiling. "I guess I can bend the rules this once, seeing as you are on your honeymoon and all. Just keep the noise down and be out of here by twelve-thirty, okay?"

"Thanks," said Bill and Lee.

The security guard tipped his hat, and as he wandered away to make his rounds, Lee and Bill could hear his whispered exclamation: "Monaco."

Afterward, nearly limp with relaxation, they watched a movie on cable about a prostitution ring working out of the Pentagon.

"Hey," said Lee, "there's Grace Aisles!" She pointed to a woman heavily made-up and dressed in leather, standing next to an admiral at a fax machine. "I thought this was supposed to be a documentary."

"A docu-*drama*," said Bill, reading from the *TV Guide*. He watched the screen until Grace wasn't on it anymore and then dialed Fenny's home number. "She's not home," he told Lee after listening to the phone ring and ring. "I guess we did break up."

"Oh, Bill," began Lee, "she could be anywhere—"

"I know, Lee. That's the point."

They watched the movie for a while without speaking and then Lee looked over at Bill sprawled across his bed and saw he was asleep. She turned off the movie—it wasn't very good anyway, and it didn't seem as if Grace's character was going to make another appearance—and then switched off the light on the night table separating her bed from Bill's.

She woke up an hour later, to what she thought at first was Slim having another nightmare. Then, as she got her bearings, she thought she was hearing Bill's snoring, until she realized he was crying.

"Bill," she said, going to his bed. "Bill, are you all right?"

"I'm sorry, Lee. This is embarrassing—I . . . I . . . Lee, you don't have any clothes on."

Goose pimples jumped out on Lee's skin; her underwear had been wet from the Jacuzzi and she hadn't wanted to sleep in the only clothes she had brought with her. Completely forgetting her nudity in her desire to comfort Bill, she now got up quickly to get back to her bed, but Bill encircled her wrist with his hand.

"Or you could stay," he said, and although a thousand reasons why she shouldn't screamed in Lee's head, she answered softly, "Okay," and slid under the covers toward the musky heat of Bill's body.

Chapter 25

Shame was a posse, driving Bill out of that hotel room and warning him not to come back.

The sun had just started to show its pale face above the pink collar of the eastern sky when Bill slunk out into the parking lot. He had no idea where he was going, only that he had to go. Even though he knew he deserved it, facing Lee was punishment he was too cowardly to take; he needed to get out, to think, to forget.

If I felt any lower, he thought to himself, I'd be underground.

The emotion of their lovemaking had been so powerful that if Lee were younger, or vainer, she might flatter herself thinking she was its cause, but she knew that its strength was in its release; a coming-together of warm bodies, joined forces against all the grief and horror and sheer disbelief of the past days. She and Bill had held each other like drowning victims hugging life preservers, had screamed and cried as each wave lapped against them, had laughed when they were done, kissing each other's wet face, safe on shore.

They caught their breaths then, and laughed again, but it wasn't long before the enormity of what they had just done settled down on them like a blanket; a thick, heavy, stifling blanket, one they wanted to kick off.

"Lee, I—" began Bill, just as Lee said, "Bill, I—"

After a quick courtesy laugh, they shut their mouths, each waiting for the other to speak, and when an uncomfortable amount of time had gone by, they both spoke, again on top of each other's words.

"Bill, I have no idea—"

"Lee, you have to understand—"

Silence overtook them for good then because words seemed too small an expression, almost pointless, and they both lay quietly until Bill fell into a fitful sleep.

Lee watched his shoulder rise and fall with each breath.

I do love you, Bill, she had wanted to tell him, *but not in that madly-truly-deeply way I loved you when we first met. It took a while, but I got used to the idea of you and Fenny being together. I just adjusted my love for you to fit the circumstances. I had turned down the heat.*

She rolled over, her back facing his, thinking, I guess I didn't turn it down far enough.

After being on night watch so long with Slim, Lee couldn't sleep through any noise; but she pretended to when she heard Bill get out of bed, testing the springs every few moments. She wanted to speak to him, wanted to assure him that it was all right; she didn't expect anything from him now that they had slept together. She wanted to say all kinds of things, but couldn't, only breathed evenly, in and out, as if she were still sleeping.

Her eyes looked shut, but were open just a slit so she could watch as he dressed as quickly and efficiently as a fireman called to duty. Lee felt sad that he wanted to get out of the room that fast, but certainly understood his need to.

Out in the parking lot, Bill was startled by a quick, jarring honk and for a moment he felt almost nauseated, thinking it was Lee in her Bonneville, catching him trying to sneak away.

He never thought he'd be thrilled to see Lorenz Ferré, but that was the emotion he felt when he saw the singer, his head stuck out a bus window, waving to him.

"Hey, mate—where are you headed this early in the morning?"

Bill didn't answer right away, and from the look on Bill's face, Ferré was able to imagine all sorts of scenarios.

"You all right, Bill?" he asked as the last member of his band climbed on the bus. "Did you and Lee have a fight?"

"I guess we did . . . sort of."

"So now you're just wandering aimlessly around at dawn?"

Bill nodded. "I guess. I was sort of thinking of hitching a ride somewhere."

"Really? Where to?"

"Haven't figured that out yet."

"Well, if you're dumb enough to leave your lovely ginger-haired lady," said Ferré, "then you might as well hop in. We're going to Green Bay."

Bill couldn't have been more excited if he'd said Paris or Rome. Green Bay was what he needed right now: a simple answer. And so, with a hydraulic hiss, the door of the bus was opened and Big Bill climbed aboard.

Lee did not like the feeling of no underwear under her clothes, but there wasn't much she could do about it. Her bra and panties, which hours earlier had served as a swimsuit, were still wet. Lee pulled them from the towel rack and stuffed them in her purse. She looked around the hotel room slowly, as if she were checking to make sure nothing was left behind.

Snow had begun to fall as she ordered breakfast in a nearby restaurant, and she thought she was doing fine, she was surprising herself with her calm, but then a waitress served a customer at the counter a caramel roll and the two of them exchanged a joke, and Lee thought how just six days ago, that could have been her and Pete. That memory brought all the ones back she wanted to forget, in particular the most recent one: the one of her and Bill together.

Mae Little Feather always had the TV on when she worked, and somehow she was able to pay meticulous attention to her work while following the intricate plot lines of the soap operas.

She loved to watch white people acting like the fools they were, all dressed up in their fanciest clothes to have coffee—or an affair— with a neighbor.

Still, she thought, chuckling to herself, all the convoluted drama of the serial she now watched could not compare to the soap opera that was going on in—literally—her own backyard!

Fenny had driven up just after lunch. The ground was white from the snow that had been falling all morning. Out her window, Mae watched as Fenny parked her car behind a clump of trees—as if she thought she could sneak onto her property without Mae seeing her—and raced to Bill's tent. Bill's empty tent.

Mae hollered to Fenny from her doorstep.

"Bill ain't here!"

"What?" said Fenny.

Mae beckoned her closer. She wasn't about to scream her lungs out in the middle of a snowstorm.

When Fenny had climbed the woman's wooden steps, Mae opened the door for her.

"Come on inside," she said. "I don't want to get pneumonia talkin' on the back porch."

"Do you know where Bill is?" asked Fenny, getting right to the point.

"You want a Mountain Dew?" Mae had no intention of sharing any of her stash, but enjoyed playing around with the girl a little bit.

"No, thank you," said Fenny. "I'd just like to know where I can find Bill."

"I got some more vests you might want to take back to the shop," said Mae. "It'd save me the trip."

"Mrs. Little Feather, please! I just want to know where Bill is."

Mae pushed out her bottom lip and shook her head slowly, as if she had news but didn't want to share it.

"He left with that O'Leary woman," she said as if she couldn't believe it, either.

"Left? Left where? Where'd they go?"

Mae couldn't stop shaking her head. "Don't know. Bill didn't tell me. All's he told me was he was leaving. With her."

Mae was not only a talented artisan, she was also a good actor; she spoke her last line with resignation, as if its implications were clear.

Fenny was out of Mae Little Feather's kitchen before the old woman could say anything else—and she was prepared to say *a lot*—and as Mae watched her running through the snow to her car, she cackled, just like a witch getting a big charge out of the trouble she was brewing.

Fenny drove through the snow, her thumping heart providing a fast and steady bass to the rhythm of the windshield wipers. Whatever calm and perspective she had gained on her two-day camping trip was gone.

In town, she leaned on the doorbells of Lee's and Slim's apartments, until Slim opened his apartment window.

"It's faster to talk through the window than make it down the steps on these crutches," he explained.

"Is Lee back yet, Slim?" she asked, her head tilted back to look at him, and when he shook his head, she burst into tears.

"I'll come down," he said, and began to close the window.

"I can't stay," said Fenny. "I just want to know where they are."

Slim reopened the window. "I don't know, Fenny. Lee just told me they were leaving and they didn't know how long they'd be gone."

"She didn't say where?"

Slim shook his head. "I don't think she knew. They just wanted to get away."

"Fine," said Fenny, and before Slim could ask her where she was going, she was gone.

These were no teasing snow flurries that would melt before ever whitening the ground; this was steady, heavy snowfall, but Fenny found herself speeding as she drove back home.

"Slow down," she reprimanded herself as she nearly slid across the county road into Lars Larson's yard. "Going in the ditch is not going to help things."

She had decided what *was* going to help things, and that was a trip to California.

Heine and the mayor carried Miss Penk into the house she shared with Frau Katte.

"How's she doing?" asked Slim, standing on his crutches and watching as Frau Katte got a suitcase out of her car.

"Well," she said as she slammed the trunk door shut, "don't feel sorry for her. She'll have a fit if she zinks you're feeling sorry for her."

Slim nodded.

"Now, me, I zink I would love having people feel sorry for me. I zink I'd really milk za situation."

"You would not," said Slim, laughing. "You're tough as nails, Katte."

They began to walk down the walk that the mayor had shoveled earlier that day.

"It's easy to be tough as nails when you're not za one in za wheel-chair. Miss Penk's za hero in zis story, Slim. I'm just happy to do whatever she needs me to do."

Inside the art-adorned living room, the men and women ate a store-bought angel food cake that Heine had picked up.

"Sorry, guys," said Frau Katte, serving them instant coffee. "Zis is za best I could come up wiz."

"It's fine," said the mayor gamely.

"Sure," said Heine. "It almost tastes real."

Conversation was minimal, confined to remarks about the cake's fluffiness and assorted "Ummm" and "Ahh" sounds after sips of coffee, until Miss Penk put down her cup and told everyone to knock it off.

"The cake's stale, the instant's awful, and I can't walk. Let's admit what's true and get on with it."

An uneasy silence swelled in the room.

"Okay," said Miss Penk. "I'm going to give everyone three min-utes to tell me how sorry they are for me—three minutes to let it all out. Three minutes and then we'll be done." She looked at her watch. "Okay, on your mark . . . get set . . . go."

The silence didn't budge.

"Okay, that's two minutes and fifteen seconds," said Miss Penk. "You'd better let it all out now while you have the chance."

Slim leaned back on the couch and gave a mournful howl, and his expression of sorrow was all the rest needed to offer their own.

"Oh, Miss Penk . . . ," began the mayor.

"I'm just sick about this whole thing . . . ," said Heine.

"Miss, I don't know if ever I can forgive myself. . . ."

Slim howled, Frau Katte grabbed the Kleenex box and passed it to the mayor, and Heine apologized over and over.

Finally Miss Penk, who hadn't taken her eyes off her watch, held up a hand and said, "Stop."

"And then I wonder, if we had been able to overpower him right away—"

"Arrrroooooohhhhhh!"

"Heine, Slim," said Miss Penk. "That's enough."

"I think of you kickboxing on Polka Nights—"

"Mayor," said Miss Penk, her voice edged with anger. "I said, *that's enough.*"

A hush fell over the room.

"Thank you," said the woman whose tower of hair, at least, stood tall. "Now, this," she said, patting the arm of her wheelchair with her palm, "is not how I'd get around if I had the choice. But I don't. All pity would do is make me feel worse about something I have no choice about. Help, I'll take . . . but not pity." She looked at the three men sitting on the couch. "First thing I'll need is a wheelchair ramp built. You guys think you can do that for me?"

Three heads shook and Miss Penk exhaled deeply. "Good, because Katte told me *she* could build a ramp, and if any of you have ever seen my Katte with a hammer—"

"Hey, I'm good with a hammer!"

"Okay, then. It's the nails you have a hard time with."

The men laughed then, a little louder than necessary, and then Frau Katte, hearing the doorbell, got up to answer the door.

"It's probably anozzer hot dish," she said. "Gloria Murch and her church circle ladies have been sending over hot dishes up za ying yang."

It wasn't a contingent of blue-haired women carrying Tuna Noodle Surprises or South of the Border Hamburger Bakes; it was Mary Gore.

"I zought you were in Malibu," said Frau Katte.

"I was," said Mary. "I'm back now."

She stomped the snow off her boots and then stepped out of them, the little bells attached to the laces tinkling.

"Look who's here," said Frau Katte, and it was hard to tell if the tone of her voice suggested surprise or horror.

"Oh, Miss Penk," said Mary, "you're in a wheelchair!"

Miss Penk started, as if she had just been told the house was on fire. "You're right," she said, looking down, as if seeing the chair for the first time. "Katte! Katte, I'm in a wheelchair!"

Everyone, except for Mary Gore, laughed, and then Slim said, "Katte! Katte, I've got white hair!" followed by the mayor, who said, "Katte! Katte, I'm wearing socks!" and Heine, who exclaimed, "Katte! Katte! Today's Thursday!" and the exchange of obvious information went on until they all sat back, out of breath from laughing so hard.

"All right," said Mary. "I deserved that, I suppose."

"Actually," said Miss Penk, wiping a tear from her eye, "you didn't. There wasn't any way that you'd know I was in a wheelchair."

"There would have been if I had stayed around," said Mary, her big chin quivering. "But I was too scared. I had to run away."

The group was used to recitations of bad poetry or lectures or obscure quotations from Mary Gore, not confessions. No one had a comeback.

Mary sat down near the fireplace, pushing her embroidered denim skirt into the confines of the wing chair.

"I am so sorry, Miss Penk," she said, looking not at the woman in the wheelchair but at her own wringing hands. "I was so shocked by what had happened, I . . . I just had to leave. Like a soldier traumatized by what she saw in action, I had to desert." She sniffed, a phlegmy, gargly rattle. "Slim, now I have some idea what you went through."

Not really, thought Slim. *I* never deserted.

"So I fled," continued Mary, "away from the carnage and chaos of Tall Pine . . ."

The mayor and Heine exchanged looks; here was the Mary they knew so well.

". . . not able to attend the funeral of the cobbler Pete—"

"Za cobbler Pete?" said Frau Katte. "You make him sound like a pastry."

Mary was not about to be knocked off track. "Although I did hold a candlelight vigil for him on the beach, which unfortunately was interrupted by a police helicopter hovering right above me."

"Are candlelight vigils on the beach illegal?" asked Heine.

Mary *tsk*ed. "They weren't after me, Heine, they were looking for a robber. He had held up all these patrons in this ritzy seafood restaurant and was running away."

"Did they catch him?" asked the mayor.

"They did. He was trying to swim out to sea, if you can imagine that plan of escape. I mean, what was he going to do once he got tired?"

The group considered this for a moment before Mary plunged on.

"Anyway, Miss Penk, I'm sorry I didn't have the moral stamina to stay around and be a comfort to you and Frau Katte. I feel I let you down . . . I feel I let everyone down, and I'm sorry."

In truth, no one felt let down by Mary's absence, but they were sensitive enough to know that Mary wouldn't want to hear that.

"It's all right," assured Miss Penk.

"Don't worry about it," said Heine.

How does a person get so goofy? wondered Frau Katte.

"I came through town and saw that the Cup O'Delight's boarded up," said Mary. "What's going on?"

There was a moment's silence; the closing of their clubhouse was a painful subject.

"Well," said the mayor, finally, "Lee's gone."

"Gone?" asked Mary. "Gone where?"

And so they took turns telling Mary the story of how Big Bill and Lee took off on a little trip and only Lee returned, and then, finding out that Fenny had gone to Hollywood, left herself.

"For Hollywood?" asked Mary.

"She didn't say where," said Slim, who was the last person who talked to Lee. "She just said she had to get away."

"I'm confused," said Mary. "What about Bill? Why didn't he go with Fenny? Or did he?"

"No," said Frau Katte, who'd heard the whole story from Slim. "He left Lee in Hinckley. No one knows where he went."

Mary shook her head. "It's finally hit them."

"What?" asked Heine.

"The flee instinct. Remember when the big oak was struck by lightning and everyone scattered? Well, that's what's happening now—except that unlike mine, their flee instinct's been a little delayed. When in trouble, we run or we die."

"We didn't run," said the mayor.

"And we didn't die," said Heine.

"True," said Mary, and then, surprising everyone, she added, "Dad says I go around half-cocked most of the time. Sometimes I think he might have something there."

These were strange times in Tall Pine if Mary Gore was doubting herself.

The woman fingered the "Twyla Tharp for President!" button she had pinned to her long underwear top. "Then again," she said with a shrug, "criticism is vital to the artist's life. It's like a signpost, telling us we're going the right way."

Those in the room wanted to cheer; equilibrium was restored; Mary was still deluded.

"Is that coffee you're drinking?" she asked, nodding toward the cup and saucer on Heine's knee.

"Sort of," said Frau Katte. "But it's sure not what we're used to."

"*Nothing* like it," said the mayor.

Heine could only shake his head.

"Well," said Slim, lifting his still-healing foot off the ottoman and leaning forward, "what would you say if I told you there's a whole canister O'Delight just waiting to be put into a pot?"

Everyone started talking at once.

"What do you mean?"

"Are you sure?"

"How do you know it's O'Delight?"

Slim raised one black eyebrow; he was not a stranger to the theatrical gesture.

"I know because Lee always filled an extra canister every morning—just in case she ran out."

"And it's still there?" asked Frau Katte, awe in her voice.

"Yup."

"Well, why are we sitting around yakking about it?" asked Miss Penk. "Let's go."

Five minutes later they were making their way into the boarded-up Cup O'Delight via the back door.

"Whew," said the mayor, who was carrying Miss Penk, "you're heavier than you look."

"Oh, you're just saying that," drawled Miss Penk.

Slim turned on the lights in the back room and pushed open the swinging door, and in one quiet line they entered the cafe.

Underneath her heavy coat, Frau Katte felt goose pimples and she held on to her fez as if she were in a high wind. Tears filled both Mary Gore's and the mayor's eyes. Heine clenched his teeth.

"Thank God she had the place cleaned up," whispered Miss Penk.

Lee had hired a cleaning crew to scrub away the blood and sweep up all the broken glass, and everything was now in order, except for a red metallic disk that had been shot off its mooring and a bullet hole in the wall.

Mary Gore went over to the stool where Pete always sat and spun it. Somehow the gesture seemed exactly right, like a genuflection in Vatican City, and everyone took turns doing the exact same thing, the mayor holding Miss Penk in his arms as he did it.

"I've got to sit down," he said, panting.

"Well, set me down, then, you big baby."

"Where?" asked the mayor.

"How about a stool?" answered Miss Penk sarcastically, as if she were the brains of the group speaking to the brawn.

"Well, I . . . can you sit by yourself? I mean, can you . . . balance?"

"Yes, you nitwit, I can balance."

"Miss, how's he supposed to know zat?" Frau Katte patted her own leg at midthigh. "Zis is where za feeling stops for her. So, yes, she can sit by herself." She narrowed her eyes at her companion. "But she might find herself sitting alone if she keeps yelling at everyone."

"Sorry, Mayor," muttered Miss Penk as he set her on a counter seat. "Actually, nitwit's one of the nicer things I've called people lately."

"Are you okay *there?*" asked Frau Katte, wondering if Miss Penk was up to sitting where she had been during the shooting.

"It's where I always sit, isn't it?"

Everyone sat at their regular places then, leaving Pete's seat empty, and Slim went behind the counter to retrieve the canister sitting on a shelf.

"This is it," he said, holding it up with the same fanfare a magician holds up a hat he's ready to pluck a rabbit out of.

Applause ran down the counter, but as Slim poured water into a pot and measured the coffee into a filter, there was absolute quiet from his audience. It wasn't broken until he turned on the coffeemaker and it began to brew, and then there was another round of applause. They sat for a few moments, entranced as the first group of people gathered around a television set, watching the clear dark liquid stream into the pot and listening to the puffs and gurgles of the machine.

"Oh," said Frau Katte, "just za smell of zat makes me zink zat everyzing might be all right again."

"You know," said Slim, "I've been thinking." He looked into his friends' faces, one by one. "There's no reason why we couldn't open up this place."

"But Slim," said Mary, "Lee's not here."

"You know what, Mary?" said Slim. "I am aware of that. But one thing she's always told me is, '*Mi café es su café.*' "

"That means, 'My restaurant is your restaurant,' " translated Mary.

"Gee, no kidding," said Heine. "What does this mean?" It seemed Mary Gore's grace period was over; he had raised his hand and was about to hold up his middle finger, but then Slim announced that the coffee was done and goodwill once again reigned.

Slim went down the counter, filling everyone's cup to the halfway mark.

"We've got to savor it," he said as he poured his own half cup, and then, holding it up, he said, "To us. To us as we were, as we are now, and as we will be."

They clinked cups and then they all took a sip.

"Ahhhhh," was the common refrain, and then it was embellished.

"Oh, man," said Slim.

"*Mein Gott,*" said Frau Katte.

The mayor whistled.

Then Mary Gore, who couldn't really play despite years of childhood lessons, sat down at the piano and tried to bang out a version of "S'Wonderful" and Slim began singing, and for a time, as a cold wind stirred up the top layer of snow outside, something was revived that seemed dead: a Polka Night. It was a patched-together, off-key, ragtag version, but still, it *was* the Tall Pine Polka, and all present to witness it felt as if a tiny sprout of grace had shot up in what they had assumed was barren land.

Chapter 26

"I knew it," said Grace Aisles when Fenny called her from LAX. "I knew you'd be here sooner or later. I just thought it would be later."

"I'm just as surprised as you are," said Fenny. "Need a roommate for a couple days?"

"I'd love one," said Grace. "But I'm on the way to the airport myself. I've got three weeks of work in New Mexico—playing a school nurse, of all things."

"Oh," said Fenny, remembering that she was not a fan of impulse because chance played such a big part in its whole drama; chance had a leading role when she would have preferred it had a small walk-on.

"Hey, listen," said Grace, "meet me at the United ticket counter. I'll give you my key and you can house-sit for me."

"Really?"

"Sure, and if for some reason you're not there . . . well, there's a YMCA on Las Palmas."

"Here," said Harry, handing Fenny a pair of big black sunglasses. "You won't be so recognizable in these."

They were on their way to lunch and Harry had picked Fenny up at Grace's house in his classic Mercedes convertible (purchased thirty years ago after *Chorza, Star Maiden* became a surprise hit in Europe; the car ran so well that Harry had yet to replace it with a newer model) and, turning onto Hollywood Boulevard, a driver hollered out his window, "Fenny Ness! How ya doing?"

Being recognized outside of Tall Pine was an odd and unsettling experience for which Fenny had not been prepared.

In Grand Forks the flight reservationist had nearly squealed when Fenny stepped up to buy her ticket.

"Oh, my God, Fenny Ness—oh, I loved what you did to that Marcy Mincus and, oh, my God—that shooting—weren't you just terrified? You know, my husband and I thought we were doing a good thing when we moved up here, but it seems as if nowadays you're not safe anywhere—"

"I'd like a ticket to Los Angeles, please," said Fenny.

On the plane, two flight attendants and a half dozen passengers had recognized her, a phenomenon she found far more unnerving than exciting. Inevitably she was fooled for a brief moment whenever anyone approached her, asking, "Fenny Ness?" thinking that they were somehow related to her or perhaps an old classmate. Before she had time to be embarrassed about her forgetfulness, however, the person would ask her about Marcy Mincus or the shooting or when the movie was coming out and Fenny would be jolted into the world of fame, into a world where people she knew nothing about knew something about her.

"What am I doing here, Harry?" Fenny now asked.

"I don't know," said the producer. "I must admit I was rather surprised when you called. I honestly thought you weren't going to take the bait."

"The bait?"

"You really did strike me as a person who could be satisfied with a little sample of Hollywood. Most people couldn't, you know—but I thought you were different."

"Harry," said Fenny, glad she had put on the sunglasses so he couldn't see the tears that had welled up in her eyes. "It was too hard to stay in Tall Pine. I . . . I didn't know where else to go. Please don't be so disappointed in me."

"Oh, Fenny," he said, cursing himself for being so insensitive. He reached over to squeeze her hand. "It's not you—I'm just disappointed in everything lately. The world just seems to be such a . . . disappointing place."

Fenny agreed, but from the producer she had come to expect enthusiasm, vigor . . . not despair. "Harry, are you all right?"

"Sure. It's in my constitution to be all right—even when I'm fed up."

"So what are you going to do?"

"I thought we were trying to answer that question for you."

Harry, now on Sunset Boulevard, passed a stretch limo and then a Rolls-Royce. "Now tell me everything that's happened since I left Tall Pine."

And so Fenny did, and when she was done with her story, they had reached Venice Beach.

"For whatever ails you," Harry said, after advising Fenny to leave her shoes in the car. "A good walk in the sand is just about the ticket."

They walked holding hands, walked past a young woman who was indelicately trying to reroute her thong bathing suit, past a silver-haired man playing the bongos, past two children digging a moat for their sand castle.

"So you really think Bill and Lee ran off together?" asked Harry as they walked along the wet sand.

"That's what it seems," said Fenny.

"I just can't see it," said Harry. "Maybe it's just friends getting away."

"No," said Fenny, shaking her head. "I left a note for him, pretty much apologizing for the things I'd said; pretty much saying I was wrong and I wanted to make things right again. And he just left."

"Are you sure he got the note?"

"Harry, I put it in his tent. Right on his sleeping bag."

Suddenly a woman's screams pierced the air.

"My baby! My baby!"

A knot of people were gathered at the water's edge, watching a screaming bikinied woman run back and forth along the beach, and after the second or two it took her mind to process what was going on, Fenny took off.

Lunging forward, Harry stopped her progress by gripping her good arm.

"Harry, let go, maybe I can help."

"They don't need your help, Fenny."

"But I don't see a lifeguard and I'm a strong swimmer and—"

"Fenny, they don't need your help. In fact, your help would screw up their shot." He pointed to the cluster of people watching the distraught woman. "It's a movie."

Fenny looked closer at the group, which had now fanned out, revealing a man holding a camera and another with sound equipment strapped to him.

"Probably a student movie, from the size of the crew, but—"

"Oh, Harry, you should feel my heart." It still pounded from the adrenaline that had flooded through her body. She stood quietly with him, watching as three women, all in bikinis, ran toward the screaming woman, their inflated bustlines virtually bounceless.

"A movie?" Fenny said, her voice full of disbelief.

"A movie," repeated Harry, but in his voice was both apology and disgust.

Grace lived up in the Hollywood Hills, in a small guest house that had been the only part of an estate that hadn't burned down in a hillside fire that had flashed up one hot windy day, taking over a dozen homes with it.

Fenny planned for her date with Harry to be her only excursion for a while; she wanted nothing more than to headquarter herself on the chaise longue that was the centerpiece of the small backyard, to watch hummingbirds hover around the red splashes of bougainvillea that trailed down a trellis against the side of the house, and snooze, or read from several magazines she had mined from a great stack in the bathroom.

Idleness was something Fenny usually had to work hard at, but life had been so daunting lately—a day in which she cried less than the day before was progress—that boredom was a comfort. She agreed with Harry, who had counseled her to "just sit back and see which way the wind's blowing" and had gotten up to pour herself a glass of water from the cooler in Grace's kitchen when the phone rang.

She had been letting the answering machine pick up calls, but she was next to the phone now and automatically picked it up.

"Hello?"

"Fenny?"

"Yes . . . ," said Fenny, not recognizing the voice and not liking that she didn't.

"Fenny, Marv Gilman here. Grace called me from New Mexico

this morning and told me you were staying at her house—and let me tell you, when I heard that, I thought today is my lucky day, because Jon Hirsch—you're aware of Jon, aren't you, Fenny? He directed *Sunflower* and *The Day the Good Humor Truck Crashed*—which, by the way, won an award at the Venice Film Festival—anyway, Jon is all set to go on his new movie—*Winifred Jones*—only problem is, Kayla Bourne, who was signed to be his Winifred, just told him she's pregnant, five months along, so it's not like she's still in the undetectable zone—and anyway, Jon would love to take a meeting with you."

"Mark, thanks very much, but I—"

"Marv."

"Beg your pardon?"

"It's Marv. With a *v*, not a *k*."

"Oh, sorry, Marv. But what I was—"

"Grace told me not to take no for an answer," said the agent. "A driver's on his way to pick you up. Don't worry about what to wear, it's a totally casual thing, Jon just wants to get a sense of you as a person."

"Marv, really, I don't think I'm interested—"

Apparently Marv Gilman couldn't care less what Fenny was interested in, because he had hung up the phone.

Of all the nerve, thought Fenny, resolving that she just wouldn't answer the door, that was all, but when the doorbell rang and rang and rang, she felt sorry for the driver dispatched to pick her up and thought of the trouble he would get into if he didn't successfully complete his mission, and so she answered the door, and then found herself in the back seat of a limousine, steaming with anger over Marv Gilman's audacity and her own spinelessness. To the driver, however, she was the kind of person he rarely got to drive around in Hollywood: someone who chatted with him as if she might actually be interested in what he had to say.

As soon as she stepped into his sleek, steel-decorated office, Jon Hirsch knew Fenny was his Winifred Jones. He of course had been impressed by her sweetly subversive decimation of Marcy Mincus, but in person she was an even more powerful presence: a warrior, a Valkyrie in modern dress (well, fairly modern; what, he wondered, was with her ratty old Joan Crawford blazer?)—his Winifred Jones.

"Have a seat," he said coolly, not willing to give himself away.

Fenny sat in a black cushion that was surrounded by chrome hoops.

"Nice chair," she said, the way someone says, *Cute baby*, when looking into a stroller and finding a toddler with crossed eyes and a heat rash.

"A Von Muesen," said the director proudly. He had the biggest collection of Von Muesen furniture in Hollywood, a collection whose price was inestimable, now that the Belgian designer had died during a liposuction procedure.

Fenny and Jon Hirsch chatted aimlessly for a while and then the director asked her if she'd mind reading a few pages from the script and she agreed, giving what she thought was a hurried, I'm-bored-by-this reading, which, unbeknownst to her, was perfectly *Winifred Jonesian*, according to Hirsch, who wanted Fenny to sign on the dotted line *now*, but all he said was, "That was nice, Fenny; thanks for coming in. We'll talk soon."

He was speed-dialing Marv Gilman's number the moment Fenny left his office.

Big Bill dreamed of Fenny almost every night. They weren't bizarre or frightening dreams featuring melting clocks or faces, nor did Bill plummet to the ground, having been pushed off a phallic tower by Fenny; no, in these dreams Fenny did nothing but sit by Bill, usually facing a lake or a forest, and talk. Bill could never remember the conversations, but he always awoke feeling calm and happy, until he reached over and realized that Fenny wasn't in the sleeping bag next to his, that he wasn't in his tent at all, and then his calm happiness sputtered like an unknotted balloon losing all its air. He would remember where he was then, and whom he was with, and then he'd close his eyes, willing himself back to sleep.

For the past four months, Bill had been living with Lorenz Ferré. Some of that time had been spent in Ferré's home in Kansas City, Missouri ("It's my ex-wife's hometown and the first house that we bought when the 'Purr Little Kitty' money started coming in," he explained, "and the only one I managed to keep. The ex got the Lake Tahoe house"), but most of it was on tour, crossing the country in a bus and playing clubs and casinos and lounges with names like the

Firelight Room and the Cozy Corner. He had stayed in motels that smelled of insecticide and motels that smelled of sex, and he had eaten over three dozen chicken-fried steak specials in truck stops and at least fifty Cheeseburger Combos.

Bill had become the unofficial roadie, setting up and dismantling what little equipment the musicians used and running sound and lighting checks. He did everything he was asked, except to pilot the bus, which was a duty all the band members took turns at. No one razzed him about his fear of driving; many idiosyncrasies are forgiven and explained away as being part of an artistic temperament. For instance, Mike the bass player rarely wore socks and never underwear, believing that his musicality was affected by any lower-extremity constriction.

For these duties, Ferré paid him a small weekly stipend, plus room and board. It was a situation that kept Bill moving, and for that he was grateful.

Gratitude was too small a word to describe all that Ferré felt for Bill, the man who was going to help restore his career.

"I wish I could pay you more, mate," he said after a sound check at a dinner theater in Little Rock, "but believe me, your patience will be rewarded. Soon the money's going to be pouring in."

Bill laughed, not so much at the idea of money pouring in, but at the way Ferré said it. "Don't you know the love of money is the root of all evil?"

"So let's write about it in a song," said Ferré.

That was the refrain with which Ferré greeted any cliché, insight, or throwaway comment Bill might make.

"If you say that one more time," Bill said, "I'm going to have to hurt you."

"Can I help it if you're such a bloomin' songwriter?" asked Ferré. "Can I help it if we're the next Lennon and McCartney?"

"Tim," said Bill to the band's drummer, "isn't it about time for Lorenz's medication?"

The drummer finished polishing a cymbal with his shirt cuff and looked at his watch. "Nah, we like to medicate him as close to the show as possible. That way he forgets about half the songs and we all get to leave earlier."

The truth was, Bill and Ferré had written over twenty songs. None had come in an easy half hour the way "Roar Big Tiger" had (perhaps because these were more collaborative, Ferré putting in his two cents' worth as much as possible), but nevertheless they had been written, and as soon as they were finished with the final leg of their tour, the whole band would record them with hopes of putting out an album.

"Can you imagine?" asked Ferré. "The last time we put out an album was when they still *were* albums."

At first the songwriting was not done out of passion or because it fulfilled an artistic yearning, but simply because it was easy. Bill had only wanted ease; the complications of love had about done him in, and all he cared about were his basic needs. But lately he had been coming to the songwriting sessions excited, full of ideas and melodies, and it was always Lorenz who had to call it a night, claiming, "We need our bloody sleep, Bill!"

He had called his aunt the day he took off with Lorenz Ferré.

Mae gave no indication that she'd miss him; she only wondered whom she'd get to take his tent down.

"Well, Mae," said Bill, "just leave it up. I'll be back."

"When?"

"I don't know, exactly. But I'm sure I'll be back."

"Meantime, I've got to look at that thing through my kitchen window?"

"Mae, it's just a tent. How bad can looking at a tent be?"

"I like a clear view to the river," said the old woman.

From the phone booth outside a Wisconsin truck stop, Bill could see the band members boarding the bus.

"Mae, I gotta go. Did Fenny come by? Did she call?"

"I ain't seen hide nor hair of that girl. Oh—my kettle's whistlin'," said Mae, and then she hung up the phone, her hot water demanding more attention than her nephew.

The day Fenny's cast was taken off her arm was the day she shot her first *Winifred Jones* scenes, and for the next six weeks the set became her daytime fortress, a bunker where she could hide away from the people who approached her on the street, away from the phone calls and interview requests, away from her sorry and lonely personal life.

Fenny was a complete professional, on time, lines learned, and willing to implement any suggestions made. Once she got over the surprise of accepting the part (which only happened, she reasoned, because she couldn't figure out what else to do), she appreciated the opportunity her work gave her to at least *fake* emotion. Her work often brought tears to Jon Hirsch's eyes, but that wasn't necessarily a difficult feat; he was the sort who was moved easily, who in college had so frightened his date by the intensity of his emotion as they watched a revival of *Now, Voyager* that she returned his fraternity pin to him on the spot.

"No offense," said the young woman, a psychology major, "but I believe grown men who cry have latent homosexual tendencies."

Winifred Jones wasn't a period piece, although it did have dream sequences that took place in the eighteenth century, and it was those that Fenny enjoyed most: dressing up in a powdered wig and stays and brocade dresses whose sleeves were cornucopias of lace. Looking as if she were from another era comforted Fenny, made her forget, for a while, the depression and hopelessness that had settled in around her, and she never minded—even welcomed—when they fell behind schedule and had to shoot until it was late.

On those nights, she drove back to Grace's house in the car the studio had loaned her, uninterested in the Hollywood nightlife that spiraled out of dance club doors, out of restaurants, and onto the streets.

Grace was a true and solid friend, who seemed to know when Fenny could use company and when to retreat into her own room. Her boyfriend, Doug Woo, was on location in Thailand, and so she was somewhat displaced in the evenings, too.

"You know I must *love* the guy if I'm not out barhopping," she said one fragrant evening when, to Fenny's amusement, she jumped on the small round trampoline she kept in her backyard.

"Why are you doing that now?" asked Fenny.

"Because I didn't get a chance to this morning. Come on up."

"No, thanks."

"Come on," said Grace. "Have you ever seen the butts of trampoline jumpers? Like steel cantaloupes."

Fenny, reclining on the puffy-cushioned lawn chair, laughed. "I don't want a butt like steel cantaloupes. I just want to sit in the dark and drink my tea."

"You sound like a little old lady."

"Lee always used to tell me that."

"Still no word on her, huh?"

Fenny shook her head. "I'm sure Slim's talked to her, but he's not saying anything. Neither is Mae Little Feather." Fenny sighed. Gloria Murch, who was running Sig's Place in Fenny's absence, had told her over the phone that Mae Little Feather said she hadn't heard one word from Bill, that "he could be dead, for all I know."

Fenny sighed again and, hearing it, Grace once again urged her to join her on the trampoline.

"Come on, it'll cheer you up. Not only do you turn your butt into steel cantaloupes—it's a known fact that you can't jump and be depressed at the same time."

Muttering like the old woman she'd just been accused of being, Fenny pushed herself out of the chaise longue and joined Grace on the trampoline. Facing each other, they joined hands and began jumping.

"See, don't you feel better already?" asked Grace.

"No," said Fenny, but as their jumps became higher, her smile belied her answer.

"See, it has something to do with your hormones getting shaken up," said Grace, and as Fenny began to laugh, Grace did, too, until they were shrieking with laughter, holding one another's arms.

"Are we aiming," gasped Grace, "for the moon or beyond?"

"Beyond," answered Fenny.

Their jumps were getting high enough to become dangerous, and this element of possible injury was adding to what was becoming near-hysterical laughter. At least that's what Grace assumed, until she saw the tears on Fenny's face and heard the laughter had changed to sobs.

"Fenny," said Grace, locking her knees.

Her attempts to stop jumping, or at least slow down, upset their equilibrium, particularly Fenny's, who bounced off the trampoline and onto the grass. Grace stumbled after her.

"Are you all right?"

Fenny shook her head.

"What's the matter?" asked Grace, hunkered by her side.

"I hurt so much!"

Grace was alarmed now, thinking Fenny had maybe fallen funny and broken something—maybe her recently healed arm. "Where?"

"Here!" wailed Fenny, clutching her chest.

"Let me help you up," said Grace, putting her arm around Fenny. She was relieved that her friend wasn't hurt but knew that physical wounds were easier to repair than the ones Fenny was talking about.

Fenny let herself be led to a lawn chair.

"You stay right here," said Grace, even though there didn't seem much chance of Fenny wanting to escape. "I'll be right back."

She returned with two glasses of wine and the two women sat listening to distant traffic and Fenny's occasional sniffling.

"Did you know," said Grace, looking upward at the stars (if one could see the stars in L.A.), "that my next-door neighbor—you've seen him, the old screenwriter?" She lowered her voice to a whisper. "The one who eavesdrops on backyard conversations? Anyway, he says that in the thirties the smell of oranges here was so overpowering that he'd get dizzy."

She paused as if contemplating this.

"Can you imagine? The smells of the natural world being that overpowering?"

Fenny took a long sip of wine.

"I mean, to get dizzy from it!"

Fenny shrugged.

"I . . . I guess I was just struck by the idea of there being that much sweetness in the air—in L.A.!—although the fact that we can still smell the jasmine through all this pollution says something, I guess."

"I don't know how much more I can take," said Fenny, finally ready to talk. "First my mom and dad . . . and now my best friend . . . and Bill." Her voice went up about an octave when she said "Bill" and Grace thought she was going to lose it again, but Fenny took a deep breath and forged on. "I was finally starting to feel, I don't know—like the old me. I was finally starting to feel that life could be fun and wide open, exciting and . . . and full of possibility—I felt *loved*." She wiped at her eyes with the heel of her hand. "And then . . . then Pete was killed"—her voice softened to a whisper—"and everybody went away. The people I thought loved me went away."

Grace felt her own tears. She wished she could tell her that everything would be all right, that Fenny's life would be fun and wide open to all those things again, but while Grace had her flaws, lying wasn't one of them. Instead, she offered what she could.

She held out her hand. "Well, I love you, pal."

Both knew a consolation prize when they saw it, but still, it was *something*. For a long time, the two friends lay on the puffy-cushioned chaise longues, listening to the unique night music of crickets and sirens, their hands joined together, forming a bridge over the cool dark grass.

Boyd Burch's career was going pretty much according to plan; in fact, his agent, Mimi Schoals, had actually mapped out the trajectory his career was supposed to take and filled in pertinent notes and dates on little lines that she had drawn with a ruler. For instance, by *Blood of the Honeysuckle*, she had written, "exposure from this classy miniseries will push Boyd into the movies," and the notation by *Ike and Inga* read, "the part that shoves Boyd onto the A list." Her predictions had proven to be true; Boyd was now starring in his first big-budget picture, *Peanuts! Popcorn!* He was playing the part of Joachim Teague, a stadium vendor who, while lobbing snack items, is discovered to have a great pitching arm. The script combined action and romantic comedy and his co-star was none other than Paula Dunn, who had been a contender for the role of Inga. In this picture, she played the wealthy club owner, his mentor and ultimate romantic interest.

"If you don't get nominated for an Oscar for *Ike and Inga*," said his agent, who was spending a few days with her client on location, "then you sure will for this one. The dailies are *fabulous*, Boyd."

"Thanks, Mimi," said Boyd, looking at his reflection in his trailer mirror. Wearing a baseball uniform was new to him; ranch chores had always precluded his participation in organized sports. He mimed swinging a bat, watching his biceps flex.

"Speaking of *I and I*," said Mimi, who often referred to Boyd's movies by their initials, "I spoke with Harry Freed yesterday. They're premiering it at the end of the month."

"Dang, that soon?" asked Boyd. He'd had movies that didn't come out until a year after they'd been shot—and one that never came out at all.

"It's been almost five months," said Mimi. "I actually thought they'd speed it up even more—you know, to cash in on all the prerelease publicity."

"Where's the premiere?"

"Mann's Chinese."

"*Graumann's* Chinese," corrected Boyd, believing that the man who founded the famous theater was the man who should keep the title.

"It's kind of hard to believe that a Harry Freed production is premiering at the Chinese, but like I said, Boyd, this pre-publicity's helping out a lot. Harry's moving up, and you, cowboy, are moving *way* up." With that statement, Mimi held her arms out, because, after all, Boyd wasn't due on the set for another half hour.

Along with a group of *Peanuts! Popcorn!* people, Boyd and Mimi ate that evening at one of the many restaurants that advertised themselves as having "the best barbecue in K.C.!" They had just been served huge platters of ribs and fries and coleslaw when the movie's director stood up and said, "Tell me I'm not seeing things—Lorenz Ferré!"

The singer let out a shout of recognition, and after the two men threw their arms around each other, the director introduced his long-lost friend.

"Lorenz Ferré!" he said, slapping the man on the back. "This little Limey here gave me my first break—I was fresh out of NYU film school and he hired me to shoot his concert film!"

"I liked his ideas," said Ferré to the group that respectfully had put down their ribs and now discreetly wiped the sauce off their mouths and fingers, "and besides, he was dirt cheap."

"So what brings you here?" asked the director.

"Why, the barbecue," said Ferré. "It's the best in town. Plus I've got a house here."

"No kidding."

"Don't spend much time in it—I'm on the road eight months out of the year, but I'm working on an album now."

"That's great," said the director, and then to the group at the table he added, "Remember 'Purr Little Kitty'? It was the greatest make-out song of all time."

"I'm recording its sequel," said Ferré, "with the hopes that it'll put a whole new generation in the back seat. There's my mate who wrote it." He waved his arm. "Bill! Bill, come on over here!"

Across the room, Bill looked up from a discussion he was having with the band's drummer. "So we'll speed up the tempo on the bridge here," he said, drawing on a napkin, "and slow it down again for the chorus. Hold on," he said, seeing Ferré's furious gesture. He got up and as he walked in between the tables, this time it was Boyd Burch's turn to stand.

"Bill!" he said. "Mr. Big Bill!"

They, too, embraced; they weren't the old friends Ferré and the director were, but their unexpected meeting called for a physical re-action of some sort.

"I'll be a son of a bee, Bill, what are you doing here?" asked Boyd as extra chairs were pulled up to the table and stories exchanged.

Finally the drummer, who had waited patiently at the table in the back, approached the reunited friends. "I hate to be a party pooper," he said, "but we've got a session scheduled, remember?"

"Well, I for one can't wait to hear 'Roar Big Tiger,' " said the di-rector. "And all the other music you're recording. I'm at the Hilton—give me a call tomorrow. I'm going to need some good songs for this movie."

"Great," said Ferré, thinking, for the first time in years, possibility loomed.

Bill was quiet on the drive back to Ferré's house, thinking of his conversation with Boyd Burch. When the actor had mentioned Fenny, Bill had grabbed him by the collar and practically lifted him off the ground.

"Fenny—have you seen Fenny?"

"Sure, Bill, she's making a movie at Grandview Studios. Didn't you know that?"

Bill shook his head dumbly. In phone conversations, his Aunt Mae always claimed ignorance of Fenny's whereabouts (even though she had heard from Gloria Murch that the girl was in Hollywood).

"I saw her a couple days before I came here," continued Boyd. "Grace threw a little shindig—Fenny's staying with Grace, you know—and so, of course, she was there. Seemed to be in a bad mood, though."

"Bad mood," said Bill, "how?"

"Well," said Boyd thoughtfully, "just sort of quiet, I guess. Not so funny in that Fenny way of hers." He pushed aside his plate of bones. "So are you coming to the *Ike and Inga* premiere?"

"The *Ike and Inga* premiere?"

Boyd nodded. "It's in a couple weeks. You should come and surprise Fenny."

In Ferré's home studio, Bill played wrong notes and skipped entrances until Ferré called for a break.

"What's your problem, mate?" he asked as the other band members retreated to the porch for a cigarette break.

"Fenny," confessed Bill.

"Okay," said Ferré, "we'll work on 'Gone Girl,' then. You're in the perfect mood."

It was a savvy call on Ferré's part; "Gone Girl" was a plaintive ballad, and the sadness in Bill's heart found escape through his fingers and inspired Ferré's vocals, and after one take the musicians regarded one another with wide eyes, as if they couldn't believe what they had just heard, and the engineer in the sound booth said, "If that's not a number one song, I don't know what is."

Chapter 27

"And there's that handsome cowboy, Boyd Burch," said one of the breathless entertainment show anchors, whose movie premiere commentary reflected the same awe that past reporters had given to treaty signings or moon landings.

"Boyd! Boyd!" she shouted. "A few words for 'Entertainment Right Now'?"

Boyd ambled to the microphone.

"Ladies and gentlemen, Boyd Burch, star of *Ike and Inga*," said the reporter to the camera. "Boyd, can you tell us how you're feeling right at this moment?"

"Well, ma'am, I'd have to say I'm a little high." Immediately Boyd recognized his mistake. "I mean with excitement, not with . . . excitables."

The television reporter laughed. " 'Excitables.' *You're* the excitable, Boyd."

As he walked away, the reporter looked into the camera and with all seriousness said, "Ladies and gentlemen, I think it's safe to say we were in the presence of greatness."

In the limousine that was bringing the producer and female lead to the premiere, Harry confided to Fenny that "it doesn't matter if *Ike and Inga* is a hit or bombs; either way, I'm packing it in."

" 'Packing it in,' " said Fenny, "what do you mean?"

"I mean I'm leaving Hollywood."

"To where?"

Harry looked at his watch and then held his arm out. "Did I ever show you this?" he asked.

"Your watch?"

"No, no," said Harry, pushing up his sleeve. "The cuff lir ' s."

Fenny took Harry's arm and looked closely at the silver disk holding the cuff of his sleeve together.

Fenny squinted and read the fancy scrolled letters. "F.A.A." She looked at Harry, confused. "Were you a pilot or something?"

Harry shook his head. "No, I bought these cuff links when I was in the middle of making *Vice Squad Sergeant*. My lead actor just about shut down the production when he nearly overdosed on drugs; there was a fire on the set, our leading lady's soon-to-be-ex-husband was showing up on the set making threats, and we didn't know what the story was until the screenwriter handed us the pages he'd written the night before."

Fenny shook his head. "And after all that you still wanted to make movies."

Harry smiled broadly. "Exactly. Amidst all the turmoil, the clashes of great egos, the danger—I was having a ball. 'F.A.A.' became my motto, it was what moviemaking was to me—'fun above all.' "

"Bill talked about fun once," said Fenny wistfully. "We were talking about Heine's pet causes and Bill said he was going to make fun his."

"See, he's figured out what fun is—the natural by-product of doing something you love. When I was making movies, doing what I loved, anything could have happened—and often did—and it was all great fun to me. I think I was able to sustain that excitement longer than most, but lately it hasn't been 'F.A.A.'—it's become 'W.C.' "

"Water closet?"

The producer laughed. " 'Who cares?' Is everything that it takes to get those flickering images up there on the screen worth it anymore? See, when I answered, 'Who cares?' instead of, 'I do!' I knew that it was time to get out of the business."

"Harry, why is it I feel like you're telling me to do the same thing?"

"The only thing I'm telling you, Fenny, is to make sure whatever you do, you're having 'F.A.A.' "

The driver had turned off Hollywood Boulevard and made a

circle around the block so he would be on the right side as they approached the Chinese theater. Searchlights were streaking the sky, as if there were a giant game of flashlight tag going on. Fans on risers whistled and cheered.

"And the flashbulbs were popping like champagne corks at a homely girl's wedding."

"What?" asked Fenny.

Harry chuckled. "A bad joke a director once told me at another premiere."

The limousine pulled to the curb.

"So, are you ready?" asked Harry.

"As long as my dress stays up, I'm ready." She tugged at her strapless bodice, hoping her courage bead wouldn't be dislodged.

Grace and Ron Feldman were speaking to the phalanx of reporters, but Fenny sailed past them in the low-cut peach satin dress Harry's secretary had procured from the studio costume department. ("I'm not quite sure," she had told Fenny, "but I think Linda Darnell wore this in *Country Deb*.")

While waving and smiling, Fenny was unwilling to stop and chat to the reporters. She might have been more predisposed to talk to them if one clown hadn't called out, "How've you been since the slaughter in the diner?" reminding Fenny that their smiling, friendly faces belied their sharklike mentality to go for blood.

Harry, her escort for the evening, shrugged his shoulders at the reporters, all the while squeezing Fenny's hand and whispering, "Good for you. Don't play the bastards' silly little game."

In the theater lobby, Christian was holding court and, seeing his uncle and Fenny, he waved them over.

As Daria, the young actress who was Christian's date, asked Fenny where she got her hair done, Christian remarked to Harry, "I think the duke's been promoted, don't you?"

"Huh?" said Harry.

"You once said we writers were like the dukes in Hollywood royalty, remember?"

"Well, most writers are," said Harry regarding his nephew, who was dressed in a knee-length greatcoat. "But you, Christian, you're something entirely different."

"Thanks, Unc," said Christian.

"You're the palace jester."

Daria grabbed his arm before he could lob an insult back to his uncle.

"She did her own hair!" she said, as if announcing Fenny had discovered a cure for cancer. "And guess what? I've got to pee!"

Christian smiled thinly as she tottered off on her four-inch platforms toward the ladies' room.

"I wonder if the doctor who surgically enhanced her breasts could do something with her brain."

"Oh, real nice, Christian," said Fenny. "I wonder what you say about women who *aren't* your girlfriends."

"Fenny, dear," said Christian, taking her hands in his. "It's just that you've spoiled me. You made me think a woman *could* be smart and attractive at the same time."

"Oink, oink," said Fenny. "Who let you out of your sty?"

"Hollywood," answered Harry.

Christian laughed as if he knew they were joking, and then, recognizing another director, excused himself to go talk shop.

The lobby was filling with actors, movie and television executives, restaurant owners, and real estate tycoons and anyone else who might be remotely important and/or rich. Normally Harry would have been in his element here, mingling while subtly doing business; but his heart wasn't in it, and besides, he had more important things to attend to.

"Excuse me," he said to Fenny.

Boyd Burch approached with open arms. "Fenny, darlin'! You look just like Linda Darnell in *Country Deb!*"

Fenny hugged Boyd, a real hug, not the Hollywood kind where only the air is squeezed.

"Fenny," said a hard-faced woman, her hand extended. "Mimi Schoals. I'm Boyd's agent. I was hoping to be yours, too, but then I heard you went with Marv Gilman."

"I didn't go with any—"

"Trust me, you can do better. Marv Gilman does a fine job representing character actors, but you, Fenny, need an agent who knows how to represent a star."

"Well, I—"

The lights flicked on and off.

"Perfect timing," said Harry, reappearing by Fenny's side. "Let's go get our seats."

Harry escorted Fenny to two seats near the back of the ornate theater.

"I hope you don't mind aisle seats," he said, "but I've always got to get up and walk around during a premiere."

"These are fine," said Fenny.

They sat down, and as the music swelled and the credits began to roll, Fenny found herself holding her hands to her chest, her chilly, half-exposed chest.

Harry had seen the movie many times, of course, but he never thought he *really* saw a movie until he shared the experience with an audience.

"You see the *whole* movie with a crowd," he had explained to Fenny. "I spend so much time with the little bits and pieces of it, seeing it through editing, through scoring, through looping, but it's not until I'm sitting in the dark theater with Joe Blow in front of me chomping on popcorn and a couple behind me necking that I get the total movie experience."

Many of the cast and crew members had seen the finished product at a screening several days earlier, but Fenny had chosen not to attend; she wanted to experience the premiere as a virgin.

As most virgins are, she was glad she had waited. When the great curtains parted and the lush orchestral music swelled, Fenny was absolutely stunned. Chills cascaded through her body; when a shot of the old Heneghan farmhouse appeared and the credits scrolled over it, her hands, still at her chest, pressed against it, not so much for warmth but to contain her heart, for the likelihood of its jumping out seemed a strong one.

When Boyd Burch walked into the frame, an ax over his shoulder, she burst into applause, along with everyone else.

"Oh, Harry," she whispered, "it's really a movie!"

"What did you think we were making?" Harry whispered back. "Spaghetti?"

When Fenny saw herself on-screen, she gasped, and when the

audience applauded for her, she alternately wanted to stand up and take a bow, and bury her head in her arms.

It was an odd sensation, seeing herself twenty feet tall and in Technicolor, or whatever they called it nowadays. She felt detached, knowing that the gigantic, colorful image was Fenny, but she was also carried away enough to believe it was Inga Anderson, Norwegian mail bride.

She got so transfixed in what was happening on the screen that she stopped noticing Harry's comings and goings.

The audience, admittedly a biased one, seemed as entranced as Fenny.

When the harvest ball scene came on, and Inga was overcome with giggles, the people in the theater laughed and clapped like a French audience watching a Jerry Lewis movie.

Fenny laughed, too, as memories of that day came flooding back, of her desperation when she realized she couldn't stop laughing, of Mary Gore's smart idea of incorporating her giggles into the scene—and then there was a shot of the band and there was Bill, playing the piano in place of the food-poisoned Marv Kozlak.

Bill looked wonderful on the silver screen, his hair a shiny black rope down his back, his big shoulders bunched as his hands pounded the keys, his face wearing, as it often did when he played music, that look of possessing a wonderful secret.

"Oh, Harry," Fenny whispered, leaning in her seat. "I remember that day so well."

"Me, too," said Harry, only it wasn't Harry, it was Bill, or at least it was Bill's voice, and then Fenny turned her head to find out if it was really Bill or if she was going crazy.

She wasn't going crazy.

"Bill!" she said, loud enough so that people turned around to look at the jerk who was uncouth enough to talk above a whisper during a movie premiere.

All the feelings of anger and abandonment Fenny had been carrying around were dropped in that moment as she embraced pure, surprised joy.

"Bill! I—"

"Fenny! I—"

"Shhhh!"
"Shhhh!"
"Should we go out into the lobby?" Fenny whispered.
"Don't you want to watch the rest of this?"
"I guess." Fenny returned her gaze to the screen and she and Bill held hands as they watched the story unfold, knowing they could wait a few minutes for the unfolding of their own.

They were acceptably quiet until near the end of the picture, when Fenny let out a distressed "Oh," and Bill a gasp. These reactions were in response to Miss Penk, doubling as Inga, jumping on and off the train. Her athleticism and grace were startling, especially considering her age, and both Bill and Fenny shut their eyes for a moment because the picture of Miss Penk then was too painful when contrasted with the Miss Penk now.

The applause at the ending credits was tremendous, and afterward, in the lobby, people were so giddy they seemed intoxicated.
"The best movie I've seen all year!"
"I laughed, I cried—it had everything!"
"*The* romantic comedy of the decade!"

As Fenny was hugged by people she vaguely knew (Emma Tuttle, the movie's casting director, thanked her for "finally bringing me to the big time") and kissed by people she'd never met in her life, she was being told what a brilliant career she had ahead of her or what a fresh face she was or did she know she looked a little like Garbo except with not such a long nose?

Bill was on her left side and Harry on her right, but the press of people wouldn't let her talk to either one of them.

"Fenny, I think we got a hit on our hands!" said Boyd, and after giving Bill a high five, he said, "You don't know how hard it was keeping Bill a secret from you tonight, Fenny. Did he tell you that we met up in Kansas—"

"Boyd, hon, don't monopolize the conversation," said his agent Mimi. "Introduce me to this tall and *very cold* drink of water."

Mimi shook Bill's hand, not wanting to release it. "You played a very convincing piano," she purred. "Do you play anything else?"

"Bill!" said Grace, charging through the crowd with Doug Woo. She leapt into Bill's arms. "How'd you sneak into town, you devil?"

Mimi Schoals pulled Boyd away as if she were suddenly bored.
"Come on, cowboy, the press is waiting for you outside."

It was all a blur for Fenny, a blur of perfumes and colognes and
jewels winking in the light, a blur of evening gowns and tuxedos (a
number that would have cleaned out the entire stock of Sherry's
Wedding & Formal Rentals in International Falls), a blur of compliments and invitations to lunches and meetings and offers on the
spot of movie deals.

The celebratory dinner at a Japanese restaurant overlooking the
city was also a blur; Fenny remembered there was a lot of laughing
and toasts made, a lot of sushi jokes told, but it was only when the
limousine dropped Fenny and Bill off that she could finally do what
she had wanted to do ever since she realized Bill was sitting next to
her in the theater: take him in her arms and kiss him.

Grace had thoughtfully decided to spend the night at Doug
Woo's, and so with the high-octane hormonal surge of a prom
couple entering an unchaperoned house, they opened Grace's door
and it was barely shut before they were falling on top of one another.

It was all that the best of lovemaking is, the uniting of two people
for whom nothing and no one else exists. The whole outside world
closed down and there was only time and space for the two of them.

The intensity was such that of course Fenny had to cry afterward
and Bill cried, too, and then that release transformed into its cousin:
laughter.

"Oh, Bill," Fenny was finally able to say, "I missed you so much,
where were you?"

Bill began humming.

"Bill?"

"I'm giving you a clue." Bill hummed some more.

Fenny listened and then, finally recognizing the tune, sang the
few words she knew.

" 'Purr little kitty, hmmm, hmmm, hmmm, Purr little kitty.' That
song was in the jukebox at the Cup O'Delight."

"That's right," said Bill. He hummed more.

"So?" said Fenny, giving him a little nudge. "So what has that got
to do with anything?"

"Do you know who sang 'Purr Little Kitty'?"

Fenny sat up; in their frenzy, they hadn't been able to make it to Grace's guest room but had simply dropped to the rug on the living room floor. Now she leaned against the couch in a better thinking position.

"Um, I know he was famous a long time ago," said Fenny, "but no, I don't know his name."

"Lawrence," said Big Bill, "but spelled in a showbiz way, L-o-r-e-n-z. Lorenz Ferré."

Big Bill smiled and after a pause Fenny said, "And?"

"And what?"

"And why is it important that I know who Lorenz Ferré is?"

"Because, Fenny, he has been my friend and co-writer and employer for the last four months."

They could hardly put back on their formal clothes, so Fenny got her robe and a generic men's robe that hung on the back of Grace's bathroom, left over from the days when there were a lot of men who needed to wear it for one night.

("I never take it down," Grace told Fenny, "because it's a reminder of how lousy my life was before Doug."

"Why do you want to be reminded of something that's lousy?" Fenny had asked.

"I always like to be reminded of the bad so that the good seems even better.")

As Bill put on the too-small robe now, something shiny caught his eye.

"Hey," he said, picking a courage bead up off the floor, "I believe this belongs to you."

"Oh, thanks," said Fenny. "I was afraid someone was going to see it at the premiere—I've never had it in a strapless bra."

She took her purse off the coffee table and withdrew an envelope, and as she put the bead inside it, Bill heard the contents rattle.

"So all of your courage beads made the trip with you?"

Fenny nodded. "Wherever I go, they go."

Outside, sharing one of the puffy lounge chairs, Bill told Fenny everything, starting with his hurt over her decision to break up.

"And then when I got back to Tall Pine from seeing Miss Penk and you had just . . . just left," he said, "I couldn't believe it. I thought if you had left without telling me where you were going, then you really *were* serious. And then when I found out you took your favorite sweater—your tent robe—I knew you really did want to break up."

"But didn't you read my note?"

"You left me a note?"

"Bill! Of course I left you a note! I left it right on your sleeping bag."

They looked at one another, and it didn't take long before they reached the same conclusion.

"Mae," they said in unison.

"I can't believe she would be that low," Bill said, shaking his head. "Well, no; I guess I can. I guess what I can't believe is that I *believed* her. I knew she didn't want us to be together."

"I shouldn't have believed her, either," said Fenny. "After I came back—all I did was take a little camping trip—anyway, when I came back, I went to see you and that's when Mae told me you'd left with Lee. She made it sound like the two of you were off on a rendezvous."

Bill was glad his wasn't the kind of skin that showed his feelings easily. As it was, he felt a mighty internal blush, although he was far past embarrassment and deep into shame.

"Sure aren't any stars out, are there?" he asked, leaning back in the chaise longue. "Nothing at all like Tall Pine."

"I know," said Fenny. " 'Course, it's not just L.A. In most big cities you can't see the stars anymore. At least that's what Grace says." She squeezed Bill's hand. "So where did you and Lee go?"

Bill felt a physical pain in his heart; it was if his secret were a stone lodged in his chest and the stone had shifted and torn something. He wanted desperately to tell Fenny what had happened, and why, and that ultimately, as hackneyed as it sounded, it meant nothing, or at least nothing like it meant when it was between Fenny and himself—but he knew that any explanation he offered would be a flimsy seedling, unable to withstand the storm of betrayal Fenny had every right to feel.

"Actually," said Bill, "we went to Hinckley. To a casino."

"You went to a casino? Why?"

Bill fingered the worn terry collar of the robe he wore. "I don't know. It sounded good at the time, I guess—getting away from all the trouble—mindless gambling, you know. And then we saw Lorenz Ferré's show."

Bill skipped the part between attending the singer's show and meeting him outside in the parking lot and taking him up on his offer to go to Wisconsin.

"So you just up and went? What did Lee say?"

The stone in Bill's heart shifted again. "What could she say?"

"Well, to just leave her there . . ."

"Fenny, we were in *Hinckley*. A couple hours' drive from Tall Pine. It's not like I left her in an opium den in some country the United States doesn't recognize."

"Still," said Fenny, but lightly enough that Bill knew she didn't think it was that big a deal.

He breathed easier, knowing he had gotten past the hard part, and told Fenny of his own foray into show business.

"So we just recorded this album; Lorenz is going to sell it on TV—you know, like those cheesy 'greatest hits' compilation things, and we've sent the single, 'Roar Big Tiger,' out to a couple radio stations and the feedback's been pretty good."

"Oh, Bill, good for you. I'm so glad you're back to your music."

"What's the matter? A guy selling tackle wasn't good enough for you?"

"Bill; no, I . . . Bill, what makes you say something like that?"

"I don't know, Fen." In truth, he thought maybe he'd gotten out of his Lee story too easily and subconsciously wanted to get himself in a little trouble. "I'm sorry. I don't know why I'd say such a dumb thing. I didn't mean it."

Fenny closed her eyes and inhaled the sweet aroma of night-blooming flowers. "I'm just glad that you're doing something with your music—I mean, you're so talented and it brings you such pleasure."

"Well, we're just writing pop songs, Fenny," said Bill modestly. "But I tell you, it sure beats playing someone else's music. I wrote a song for you."

Fenny's voice was soft. "You did?"

"It's called 'Gone Girl.' I was so scared because I thought you were gone, for good."

Fenny laid her head on Bill's shoulder.

"And then I met Boyd Burch in Kansas City, of all places, and then he told Harry, who arranged this whole thing."

"Seeing you in that movie seat was the nicest surprise of my life," said Fenny.

"I was scared," confessed Bill. "I didn't know what you'd do. I thought you hated me."

"Hated you?"

"Well, maybe not hate. But I sure didn't know if you loved me anymore."

"You're talking about love pretty easily there, Bill."

"Well, I had a good English teacher. She always taught me to say what I meant."

"You mean . . . ?"

Bill got up off the chair and with his arms spread wide, he confessed. "Yes, Fenny, I mean I love you. I've loved you for a long time and I can finally say it. *I love you!*"

There was a slight pause and then Grace's neighbor, the old screenwriter whose open bedroom window had afforded him a ringside seat to any backyard conversation on which he cared to eavesdrop, called back, "So what are you waiting for? Tell him you love him back!"

Ike and Inga opened nationwide the next day, and to launch it, Fenny was booked on "The Gerry Dale Show."

They had Boyd Burch promoting the movie like P. T. Barnum: off to New York City to do all the talk shows taped there, appearing in magazine and newspaper interviews, and chatting on syndicated radio programs and on the Internet. Fenny, on the other hand, was only going to do America's number one late-night show.

"I know you hate to do publicity," said Christian during his sales pitch, "but we're only asking you to do 'Gerry Dale.' "

"Why 'Gerry Dale'?" asked Fenny, mimicking Christian's reverent tone.

"Because *everyone* watches 'Gerry Dale'—you go on there and it'll be like killing a whole flock of birds—no, a whole migration of birds—with one stone."

"What if I said no?" asked Fenny. She had already made up her mind to say yes—after all, it was her nature to be a team player—but she couldn't pass up a chance to tease Christian.

"Go ahead," Christian had said. "Go ahead, and sabotage my big dream, everything I've ever worked for, all my—"

"Okay, okay, Christian, I'll do it," said Fenny.

A person could wear a parka in the studio and not break a sweat.

"Why is it so cold in here?" Fenny asked the assistant who stood with her behind a set flat.

"Gerry likes it that way," whispered the assistant. "He thinks it keeps everyone on their toes."

Suddenly Fenny heard her name, and the assistant gave her a little shove and she was walking across a shiny floor and to a carpeted platform on which was positioned a couch, Gerry Dale's desk, and Gerry Dale himself.

"Miss Ness," said the former announcer in his deep, former announcer's voice. "Such a thrill to have you here."

He never let go of her hand until she was seated on the couch.

"So, Fenny," he said, taking a quick sip of water from his Gerry Dale mug, "how does a guy like me get to know a gal like you better?"

"Uh," said Fenny, thrown by the question, "what do you mean by 'better'?"

"Like 'man and woman' better."

"You're joking, right?"

Gerry stared at Fenny bug-eyed, and the audience erupted in laughter, thinking it was part of the act. Gerry was not King of the TV heap for nothing; he milked the laughter, biting his knuckles and looking wounded, which in truth he was.

Gerry Dale seldom booked actresses his own age (fifty-two), preferring to host young, attractive females under the age of thirty. He liked them as guests because they were good-looking, of course, but more important, because they were putty in his veteran hands.

"Okay," said the host, obviously staring at her chest, "if maybe I had a better pickup line, *then* would you go out with me?"

Fenny felt she could drown in his oiliness. "Well, it would depend where," she said, "and how dark it was."

The orchestra drummer punctuated Fenny's line with a *ba-dum-bum.*

Once again, Gerry mugged his hurt for the camera, and once again, his expression was closer to his true feelings than the audience would ever know. He was enough of a professional to know that the more laughs a show had, the more successful it was, but if laughs were being counted, he would make damn sure his tally was highest. If guests couldn't understand that equation, he would make sure they paid.

"Okay," he said, looking at the notes on his desk, "I remember you saying—and let me quote you correctly—that you 'pooped in your pants' to get this movie part; what, pray tell, is your encore?"

"I don't know," said Fenny, "maybe a little projectile vomiting?"

Fenny couldn't believe what she had just said, and neither did the audience, who gasped and then burst out laughing.

The sparring between Gerry and Fenny continued, much to the amusement of the audience, until a commercial break.

"Well," whispered Gerry as a long parade of car and telephone commercials scrolled by on the studio monitors, "you're one hot little shit, aren't you?"

"Hey, I'm only giving back what you're—"

"Fortunately, you're funny. That'll excuse even the worst behavior on television." The lights that had been shining on the platform had been dimmed for the duration of the break, and Gerry was allowed to look out at the audience without being seen. "So," he said, not looking at Fenny, "want to grab some dinner after the taping?"

Fortunately the theme music jumped in before Fenny could humiliate Gerry Dale even more. After a clip of *Ike and Inga* was shown, their segment ended, but apparently Gerry hadn't had his fill of Fenny.

"Won't you stay for the rest of the show?" he asked on the air, and, pressured by the audience's applause, Fenny could hardly refuse.

"Great," he said as she shrugged and nodded. "We'll be on opposite teams."

Fenny had no idea what the man was talking about until a curtain opened, revealing a large sandbox divided by a net. Two blond men in shorts gave a quick exposition of beach volleyball, and then they summoned Gerry over, who in turn took Fenny by the hand.

"A little two-on-two?" Gerry asked.

"Sure," said the blonder of the players. "More's the merrier."

Gerry took off his shoes and socks (to his bandleader's rendition of stripper music), mugging and doing a little dance all the while.

"Okay," said Gerry, affecting a surfer's accent. "It's me and the blond dude against the other blond dude and the kinda-blond babe."

As the game began, Fenny wished desperately she had left after her segment. Standing around in a sand pit while Gerry did pratfalls and the two suntanned beach boys struck poses that showed off their well-defined musculature was not her idea of F.A.A.

"So tell me," said Gerry, running back and forth in the sand as if it were hot, "women's beach volleyball is a whole different kind of game, isn't it?"

"It's more a fashion show for them," said one of the blondes after sending the ball over the net. "They play mainly to show off their bodies."

The camera focused on Fenny, whose smile was through clenched teeth.

The match continued, with Fenny gamely trying to touch the ball no one was willing to share. She felt silly and out of place, apparently a combination that cranked up her adrenaline, for when the last serve sailed over, Fenny jumped in front of her teammate and spiked it as hard as she could over the net. She had no target, but the ball found one, and it was Gerry Dale's face.

Immediately after the thud, blood spurted across the sand.

"Jesus H. Christ!" screamed Gerry, whose ability to get a laugh out of every situation did not apply to those in which he suffered bodily injury. "The bitch broke my nose!"

These words of course were edited out of the broadcast when it was aired later that evening, but to a viewer, it was fairly easy to tell what the bloodied talk show host was saying.

Fenny was mortified and ran to help Gerry, but a league of assistants shouldered their way in and encircled the host while his bandleader played "The Party's Over" and the show cut to an unplanned commercial.

Of course, "The B—— Broke My Nose!" was the headline that accompanied hundreds of newspaper photographs of Gerry Dale bringing his hand up to his bloodied proboscis and Fenny standing in the background, looking horrified.

All of the past publicity, along with rearranging Gerry Dale's profile on national television, did wonders for *Ike and Inga*'s first weekend box office, and then word of mouth and excellent reviews kept the theaters full.

"Can you believe it, Harry?" asked his secretary, as she read him *Variety*'s weekend figures. "We beat out *Coed Alien Terminators* for the number one spot!"

"Who'd a thunk it," said Harry, but his voice had lost its resignation and had been replaced by his old ally, wonder.

"The dialogue can be as corny as Nebraska," wrote one reviewer, "the pacing as erratic as a ten-year-old boy at his first dance lesson, but *something*, something in *Ike and Inga* works, and that something is this generation's Colbert & Gable, today's Hepburn & Grant."

Boyd Burch had this review blown up ten times its original size and hung it up in his bedroom, in the center of a grouping of old movie posters.

Harry found some critics' comparisons a bit hyperbolic (he couldn't honestly believe that "*Ike and Inga* has revitalized romance in America"), but he couldn't deny that Fenny and Boyd had energy and vigor and that indefinable chemistry that made people relate to them, made people want to know them, want to *be* them. *Ike and Inga* was a complete love story in that its "lovers" were able to convince audiences across America (and soon across the world, Harry noted) to love them and their story.

That's all it takes, Harry had thought to himself at the premiere as he watched the audience watch the movie. Just let the audience fall in love with the characters and you've got it made. And, too, Harry had had the added benefit of watching the real-life love story of Fenny and Big Bill begin again, and it thrilled his tired soul.

"Remember," Harry said to his secretary now, "I got into the motion picture business for the magic of it."

"But also remember what you've always told me," said his secretary, to whom Harry had often lectured on the importance of the bottom line. " 'What's the use of making a masterpiece if no one's going to see it?' "

Harry laughed, which made his secretary respond in kind. She was so glad to have her Harry back. His easy, playful nature had been blunted by depression, one whose seriousness was marked by Harry leaving his shoes on all day. The return of her boss running around stocking-footed was a sign that a corner had been turned.

As he explained to his secretary, the shooting in Tall Pine had soured him on life in general and movies in particular.

"I knew you were hurting, Harry," said his secretary softly. "And I prayed for you every night."

"Well, I guess someone was listening," said Harry, touched.

His much-needed epiphany had come at the premiere.

As much as people might want to see movie stuntmen blown to pieces in special effects extravaganzas, as much as people might want to watch something that debases and titillates them, they also wanted to see—maybe more than anything—movies where people fell in love.

"Now," he said, leaning back in his office chair, wiggling his freed toes, "if only I could find a love story that didn't have lines like, 'Inga, all the women I've known before you have been crabapples to your Golden Delicious'—well, then I'd *really* be in business."

There were many people who couldn't wait for the principal photography of *Winifred Jones* to be completed so they could meet with the hot new star, but however many offers Marv Gilman was fielding for her, Fenny wasn't interested in catching any of them.

If the Marcy Mincus interview had given her a taste of a public life, her appearance on "Gerry Dale" and the release of *Ike and*

Inga had put her right in the middle of the buffet table, and she did not like it one bit. She couldn't go grocery shopping without people following her down the produce aisle, she couldn't go for a walk along Hollywood Boulevard without tourists stopping her and asking her to pose with them for a picture. She could go no-where as Fenny Ness, regular person, and she felt as trapped as an animal in a cage.

"And that's why I'm going back to Tall Pine," she announced one evening to Bill, Grace, Doug Woo, and Harry. They were pic-nicking in Bronson Canyon Park, by a grouping of huge boulders.

"When?" asked Grace.

"In about two weeks. As soon as I'm done with *Winifred Jones* . . . which I *hope* stays on schedule."

"For how long?" asked Harry, wiping chicken grease off his fingers.

"For good," said Fenny. "I'm tired of being an accidental movie star. I want my own life back."

" 'I'm tired of being an accidental movie star,' " mimicked Grace. She turned to Doug. "Wouldn't you just like to smack her? Here the rest of us would give *anything* to be a movie star, and she wants to walk away from it."

"What'll you do in Tall Pine?" asked Doug.

"Go back to working in Sig's Place and the Bait & Camp, I guess," said Fenny. "Pass me the potato salad, will you, Grace?"

"Well, I hope Hollywood's loss will be your gain," said Harry.

Two horseback riders followed a trail behind the picnickers.

"Hey, there's Fenny Ness," said the man to the woman.

"I love what you did to Gerry Dale!" shouted the woman.

"Thanks," said Fenny weakly.

Harry poured her some more wine and capped off his own glass.

"You know, they shot a lot of westerns up in this canyon," he said conversationally, and then added a rather potent P.S.: "I'm leaving Hollywood, too."

Fenny's announcement hadn't been met with much surprise be-cause everyone had thought it was just a question of time, but Harry—Harry was Mr. Hollywood.

"You're giving up the movies?" Bill asked.

"Oh, no," said Harry. "Can't give up what's in the blood.

Although for a while there I thought it was certainly possible." He held the wine bottle up, the attentive host checking to see if anyone else needed a refill. "No, I've decided to set up shop across the Atlantic—in Italy."

There was a flurry of comments and questions.

"Why Italy?" asked Grace.

"I could say because they've got a thriving movie industry, but the truth, Grace, is I just like the idea. You know, Malcolm Edgely and I talked about it once—he loved Italy—there's just a certain graciousness to life there that appeals to me—especially now."

"What about the language?" asked Doug. "Won't that be a problem for you?"

"Sometimes I think you can only truly miscommunicate with someone who speaks the same language as you do. Besides, practically everyone speaks at least a little English, and I'll learn a little Italian."

"What does Christian think of this?" asked Fenny.

"Christian doesn't need me anymore," said Harry. "If he did, I'm sure he'd hate to see me go, but since he's now *the* hotshot writer/director in Hollywood, he couldn't care less. We had lunch today, and he told me he's weighing two multimillion-dollar offers from Paramount and Twentieth Century Fox."

"I hope he'll keep me in mind for something," said Grace.

"Not me," said Doug Woo. "No offense, Harry, but your nephew wasn't the easiest guy I ever worked for."

"Tell me about it," agreed Harry.

As the sun made its descent, the boulders threw long shadows across the scrubby brown earth and across the picnic blanket.

"Since everyone's making announcements," said Big Bill, stretching his long legs, trying to find a piece of sun, "I guess it's my turn. 'Roar Big Tiger' is number five on the charts, with, as they say, a 'bullet.' "

Congratulations were offered all around.

"So," continued Bill, "that means I'll be going, too."

"To Tall Pine?" said Grace, more an assumption than a question.

"Well, eventually. But first I've agreed to tour for a couple of months with Lorenz Ferré. I leave this weekend."

"Bill's his new keyboardist," said Fenny proudly. "Along with being his hit songwriter."

"Co-writer," corrected Bill.

"This calls for a group toast," suggested Harry, brandishing the wine bottle once again. When every glass was refilled, everyone held them up.

"To Italy," said Grace.

"To Tall Pine," said Harry.

"To songwriting," said Doug.

"To our engagement," said Fenny, clinking Bill's glass.

This announcement caused the appropriate uproar.

"Engagement?"

"Congratulations!"

"When did you decide this?"

"Well," said Fenny, suddenly feeling shy, "I guess we decided it last night, when we were talking about Bill's tour."

"I thought she might want to come with me," said Bill, "but—what was it you said, Fenny?"

Fenny laughed. "I believe my exact words were, 'I cannot stomach any more show business.' "

"That's right," said Bill, taking her hand. "So I said, 'Can you stomach any more of me?' "

"And I said, 'What do you mean?' And Bill said—"

"I said, 'Could you take me as a husband?' "

Fenny laughed again, and as a blush washed over her cheeks, Harry thought she just might be prettier than Ann Sheridan, his all-time favorite.

"And I said, 'Are you asking?' "

Bill raised his eyebrows. "And I said, 'It depends on what you'd answer.' "

"And, of course, I said, 'Probably yes.' "

Grace dabbed her eyes with her napkin. "Why can't we ever be that romantic, Doug?"

"We could," said the cinematographer. He shifted his position until he was on his knees. "Grace, will you marry me?"

The actress, for whom the word *unflappable* was an apt description, was now flapped. She burst into tears and flung her arms around Doug.

"I wonder if that's a yes," said Harry to Bill and Fenny.

The quintet ate a dessert of fresh strawberries and finished the wine as the sun began to paint the edges of the western sky. The air was balmy, the strawberries were sweet, and Harry thought if every day was like this in L.A., he'd never have to leave for Italy to find his gracious living.

Chapter 28

The venues for Lorenz Ferré had been upgraded; he was no longer in seedy supper clubs whose names often appeared in the "Metro" sections of newspapers as the setting for a drug bust or a lover's quarrel turned violent. Now Ferré, thanks to his first hit in almost thirty years, was playing theaters with more status, ones that had been revived as parts of cities' downtown revitalization efforts, or small amphitheaters, weather permitting. He still played the casino lounges; they might not be Carnegie Hall on one's résumé, but they sure paid good. And they paid even better now that he was no longer an "oldies" act, but a current hit-making one.

In Chez Rae's ("Palm Springs' Finest in Entertainment!") Bill had just finished playing "Gone Girl," to tremendous response. He was always a little subdued after playing the song, remembering the loneliness that was its genesis, but Lorenz Ferré never failed to make him stand up and take a bow.

"My collaborator, ladies and gentlemen," he said, "Mr. Big Bill!"

The audience always laughed then, especially when Bill stood up and they saw how true a description the name was.

Bill ducked his head in acknowledgment once, and then twice as the applause continued, and then he smiled and nodded, looking out into the audience, and then the motion of a waitress caught his eye, and then he saw Fenny.

He opened his eyes wide, wanting to make sure he was seeing what he thought he was seeing. The houselights were off, but each table had a candle, so there was some visibility.

Fenny, knowing she had his eye contact, waved her fingers at Bill, who sat back down on the keyboard bench, a loopy smile on his face. She wasn't supposed to have met up with him until Denver, a week away.

After the show, which closed with a reprise of the opening number, "Purr Little Kitty," and an all-stops version of "Roar Big Tiger," fans milled around the stage, hoping to chat with Ferré, who was happy to soak up his regained attention.

There were always several women in the audience who wanted to personally tell Bill how much his music meant to them and he was always very polite, all the while deflecting their invitations to show him how *much* his music meant to them. Tonight, however, he leapt off the stage, rushing over to Fenny's table.

"Hey," he said, taking her in his arms. "You were supposed to be in Tall Pine."

"Well, I was on my way," said Fenny, laughing, returning his hug. "But when I got into Grand Forks, I thought how I'd been in California all those months but never seen Palm Springs. So I bought a ticket and came right back."

Bill kissed her. "I'm glad. How long will you be staying?"

"Just a couple days." Fenny wrapped her arms around Bill. "Just long enough to get my Bill fix, and then I'll have to get back and get things ready in the stores."

The wait staff was busing the room now, blowing out candles and tossing table linens into a pile on the floor.

Ferré had just posed for his last picture of the evening and was autographing a napkin for an unprepared fan.

"Come on," said Bill, pulling Fenny by the hand. "Let me introduce you to Lorenz."

The singer was tickled to meet Fenny.

"So you're the muse behind all Bill's magic!"

"Well, I don't know about that," said Fenny.

"And she blushes, too," said Ferré, poking Bill with his elbow. "So. Where are you planning to tie the knot?"

"I beg your pardon?" said Fenny as Bill said, "What?"

Lorenz patted the back of his neck with a handkerchief he kept in his pocket. He was still sweaty from the show, and the perspiration tended to be the heaviest where his toupee ended and the nape of his neck began.

"Oh, come on, mate. *Ba-dum-da-dum*," sang Ferré, to the tune of "Here Comes the Bride." "Isn't that what this is all about—a romantic wedding on the road?"

Fenny looked at Bill. Bill looked at Fenny.

"I've heard of dumber ideas," said Bill. "I've got our marriage license in my kit bag."

The day after their picnic, along with Grace and Doug, they had gone down to City Hall to get their licenses as a symbol that they were serious.

Big Bill clapped Ferré on the back now. "Thanks for another bright idea, mate."

"Maybe we can write a song about it," said the singer, always looking for ways to continue the roll he was on.

"You work on the lyrics," suggested Bill. He took Fenny by the arm and began leading her out of the club. "We've got other things to attend to."

Lorenz Ferré thought they should go ahead and get married in Palm Springs because he could get a lot of L.A. press coverage on short notice.

"Just what we want," said Fenny. "No, thanks."

"But people would be really interested in this," said Ferré, looking at Bill, hoping to more successfully plead his case. "You're part of a big comeback story, and Fenny's a movie star!"

"Don't remind me," said Fenny.

Ike and Inga was still doing great box office business a month and a half after its release. During its fifth week of release, it had been usurped from its number one position by the sci-fi thriller *Test Tube Killer*, and in its sixth week, it was knocked out of number two by the animated epic *The Marquis De Sade*, but it was still America's third-favorite movie to watch and Fenny was still being noticed far more than she liked.

When the tour bus overheated in the desert town of Joshua Tree, Bill and Fenny and Ferré decided to do a little sightseeing while the bus cooled off, and it was while passing a small wood-sided church that Bill was seized with an idea.

"Look," he said, pointing at a wooden sign mounted on the sparse lawn. "A Lutheran church—just like Benevolent Father's. What do you say, Fenny? Now's the time?"

"Sure," said Fenny, suddenly a little breathless.

They found Pastor Miles W. Walters inside, standing on a stepladder and changing the hymn page numbers on a display board behind the pulpit. When the entourage approached him, he moved a 3 into place and said, "Be my pleasure to marry you folks."

He hustled them over to the parsonage to meet his wife ("Virginia loves things like this!") and she hurriedly picked some of her backyard wild roses, making a bouquet for Fenny and a boutonniere for Bill, who put on a tweed sports coat the minister lent him. It wasn't the best fit, but at least it covered up his Flintstones T-shirt.

The bride felt underdressed in her work shirt and jeans, but then Mrs. Walters, a romantic above and beyond the call of duty, took Fenny by the hand and up the tiled staircase to the spare bedroom, where she shyly took a dress out of her closet and told Fenny she was welcome to wear it.

"It's my wedding dress," she said. "Miles and I both lost our first spouses and were lucky enough to find each other five years ago. I'd be honored if you'd wear it."

Boasting tier after tier of ruffles, the voile dress had sheer sleeves and was dotted with a pale lavender floral print. It was the sort of dress worn by women whose dresser drawers were filled with packets of sachet and who didn't believe in the need for an Equal Rights Amendment because their husbands didn't. It was a dress Fenny wouldn't be caught dead in, but weddings weren't funerals and the gesture was big enough for Fenny to say, "Well, I hope it fits."

She tried it on behind a changing screen in the room that smelled of sunshine and furniture polish, and when the older woman saw it, she put her spotted hands to her cheeks and said, "Oh, my dear Lord, I'm seeing a vision."

Fenny didn't argue there; she felt like a vision, but an entirely different one from the kind Mrs. Walters was probably referring to. She felt like a nut, but a nut of such grand scale that it was almost exciting.

"But my hair," she said. She lifted up a hank of it, as if to show

how its very casualness clashed with the dress, but Virginia Walters was not one to be easily daunted.

"It comes with a hat," she said gleefully.

In the category of outlandish excess, the hat offered the dress stiff competition. It was lavender straw, with a brim that stuck out so far it nearly assumed the proportions of an umbrella. A spray of silk flowers was tucked into the lavender ribbon, which, after encircling the crown, streamed down the back.

When Fenny put it on, she cackled, and Mrs. Walters, misunderstanding the emotion behind the laughter, clapped.

"I agree, it's the crowning glory." She sidled next to Fenny, taking her arm, and together they looked into the full-length oval mirror.

"Oh, my goodness," said the minister's wife, her eyes bright with tears, "you do that dress justice even more than I did."

She raced downstairs, telling Fenny she'd give her a signal when it was time to "make your grand entrance."

Alone in the room, Fenny checked her reflection again, not knowing whether to laugh or cry. She looked hideous; all she needed was a staff to find her lost sheep, and yet there was something about all the flounce and frippery that was right for the occasion.

"I'm getting married!" she said, surprise and happiness coloring her voice. "I'm getting married!"

"You stand over here," directed Mrs. Walters, pulling her husband and the small wedding party toward the bottom of the staircase. "We'll wait here until the bride comes down, and then we'll all go out to the backyard." She patted Bill's arm. "The desert's so pretty this time of year."

They heard Fenny before they saw her.

"Are you all right?" hollered Mrs. Walters after hearing the thud.

"I'm fine," Fenny yelled back. "I just tripped."

The dress's hem ruffle was the culprit, and Fenny held up the skirt with one hand and proceeded to the stair landing.

As soon as Fenny became visible to those below, Mrs. Walters began singing "O Promise Me."

The judge sang along and then Lorenz Ferré began to hum a harmony. Bill was songless.

Relieved that no one had started laughing, Fenny began her way down the stairs. She cradled the roses in the same arm she was using to hold up her dress, oblivious to the thorns that would leave scratch marks from her forearm to her biceps. When she wobbled a bit (nervousness increased her natural clumsiness), she decided to use the banister.

"Steady there, girl," she whispered to herself.

Bill couldn't believe his eyes. He knew Fenny was a lovely woman, but when had her loveliness reached this level of radiance? She was his biggest gift; everything he had ever wanted, everything he had ever needed. A wave of gratitude washed over him and he felt his knees go a little weak.

Why me? he wondered. What did I do to deserve this? And then Fenny smiled at him and he truly felt that he might topple to the floor, unable to support the weight of his feelings.

"Now you follow me," instructed Mrs. Walters, and they did; in a single file, they followed the judge's wife down the hallway and through the kitchen.

"We're having ourselves a little wedding," she explained to the cook, who was on a work-release program through a nearby women's prison. Snapping beans and smoking a Viceroy at the kitchen table, she nodded her congratulations.

Mrs. Walters held the screen door open for everyone, instructing the crew to "follow the path all the way to the gazebo."

The pastor stopped near a wrought-iron bench that stood in the fork of the flagstone path, but his wife said, "No, Miles, over here," and led him to the center of the open-sided wooden building.

"She's the boss," the judge whispered to Ferré, who was right behind him.

"Aren't they all," the singer agreed.

The judge stopped and the wedding party gathered around him.

"A fine spring day," said the judge, smiling, "a fine day to be married."

"I think we should have another song here," said Mrs. Walters, and without waiting for any sort of a vote, she began singing "True Love."

She was not a strong singer, but a fancy one, thinking that her tremolo and high range made up for a slight lack of pitch. Ferré's harmony, however, lent a lot, and he often took over the melody when it seemed she would veer so far off course that she'd never make it back.

Fenny was dry-eyed; despite the surprise and the haste of the wedding, marrying Bill felt exactly the right thing to do. It had been a *long* time since she had made a decision with such certainty, and she was thrilled. She felt the same way she did when she was taking tourists out on the boat and had it at full throttle, skimming it across the water's surface: powerful, in control, and absolutely sure of herself.

Bill, on the other hand, trembled like a brand-new fawn standing for the first time. He was as sure as Fenny in the rightness of what they were doing, but still, he was nervous.

It was the minister's belief that the spontaneity that drove a couple to marry quickly (it wasn't his business, he concluded, whether they were expecting a little one or not) shouldn't be penalized with a cut-and-dried, let's-get-this-over-with sort of service, but honored. In his measured opinion, weddings these days were too extravagant, too much an occasion to show off and get as many presents as possible. His first wedding, he hated to remember, had been such an affair: a year in planning and covered by the society pages of three newspapers ("Mining Heiress to Marry Seminarian"), and he and his bride spending hours debating the price of every present like hagglers at an open market.

Any couple willing to forgo the nuptials rigmarole—the lust for presents, the engraved invitations, the reception dance, the sugared almonds wrapped in netting, and the three-foot cake—was a couple marrying for true love, and by God, he'd give them a service worthy of their selfless love. Especially when the bride was wearing the wedding dress of his beloved Virginia (whom he married simply, at the chapel in the Twentynine Palms Marine Base, where her son was stationed).

Pastor Walters cleared his throat and in the sonorous voice he had often been complimented on, he began to speak.

> *"The fountains mingle with the river,*
> *And the rivers with the ocean;*

The winds of heaven mix forever
With a sweet emotion;
Nothing in the world is single;
All things by a law divine
In one another's being mingle:
Why not I with thine?"

Mrs. Walters sighed. "He loves Shelley," she said, her voice as dreamy as a young girl's describing what attracted her to her first boyfriend.

The minister winked at his wife and continued.

"See the mountains kiss high heaven,
And the waves clasp one another;
No sister flower would be forgiven
If it disdained its brother;
And the sunlight clasps the earth,
And the moonbeams kiss the sea;
What are all these kissings worth,
If thou kiss not me?"

After a brief silence, a songbird chirped, as if asking the same question of its nesting mate, a breeze carried the fragrance of the wild roses, and the beauty of the earth at that particular time in that particular parsonage backyard was so full and ripe that every person there felt in the midst of a sort of divinity.

Bill stopped shaking and stood tall, feeling as if he were a soldier armed with all that was necessary to conquer any foe.

Lorenz Ferré repeated the last words of the poem over and over in his head, thinking what a great song he could write with them.

Pastor Walters looked at the fat white clouds lazing above in a perfect blue sky, wondering if God rewarded poets in the afterlife and wouldn't it be nice if they got a little rain, and his wife looked at Bill, wondering exactly what nationality he was.

Fenny, if asked, couldn't say what she was thinking; her mind seemed empty of thoughts and yet filled with them. She felt like a radio playing a million stations at once, one on top of another.

The minister continued the service then, and when he got to the part about the rings, Fenny was about to remind him that they weren't exchanging rings, but then Bill said, "I changed my mind," and out of his pocket he took two rings. They weren't the standard-issue gold and diamond wedding rings; these were handmade, by Bill, out of the amber beads Fenny never went anywhere without.

"I took them out of your purse while you were getting dressed," he explained.

"I loaned him the needle and thread," confessed the minister.

"I hope you don't mind?" Bill asked, for even as the gesture felt so absolutely right, he couldn't deny the presumptuousness of reconfiguring Fenny's most precious property.

Fenny stared for a moment at the rings in Bill's open hand and then, taking the larger one, she said, "Oh, Bill. That you'll wear them, too—it's . . . it's absolutely perfect." She swallowed hard. "They're courage beads," she explained to the others, her eyes shining, "from a necklace my parents gave me just before they died."

Both Bill and Fenny choked on the words "with this ring I thee wed" as they slipped the circle of beads around their beloved's finger, and after they were declared husband and wife, Fenny looked up at the blue desert sky and, waving her hand, said, "See, Mom? See, Dad? See how brave we are?"

Then Bill waved his hand, too, and shouted, "I'm your new son-in-law!" and the judge figured why not, he could greet the brides' parents wherever they were, and then Virginia waved and and so did Lorenz and then he began singing "I Love You Truly," and Bill finally leaned to kiss his bride, a gesture that took some maneuvering, considering the exaggerated brim of her hat.

Later that night, after officially consummating their marriage, they lay entwined in each other's arms.

"I can't believe you made these, Bill," said Fenny, turning her ring around with the fingers of her other hand. "It made it seem my parents were part of the wedding."

"They are," said Bill. "Somewhere, somehow, they were sitting with my dad, toasting to the union of their beloved children."

"You think?"

"Absolutely. With champagne so bubbly, we can't even comprehend it."

Fenny kissed her husband and adjusted her pillow, which was her purse.

Lorenz Ferré had wanted to spring for a fancy honeymoon suite, saying no couple should spend their wedding night in a room next to rowdy band mates. (Ferré's band was actually as quiet and mild-mannered as a group of CPAs, but Bill knew Lorenz liked to fancy himself a bad boy of rock 'n' roll.) Instead, the couple chose to camp, sans tent, in the Joshua Tree National Monument. It was a surreal campsite, decorated with smooth rocks that rose up out of the ground, high as houses. Growing amid these otherworldly rock formations were the short and scruffy Joshua trees, whose bristled branches were bent and raised to the heavens like their namesake.

Fenny snuggled next to Bill. "For so long, I felt so unlucky. You know, to have Sig and Wally taken away from me so quickly . . . and in such a terrible way . . ."

Bill, his arms already around her, gave Fenny a reassuring squeeze.

"It's only lately that I think, hey, I *was* lucky. Lucky to have them as long as I did."

Bill nodded, his chin bumping the top of Fenny's head. "When I was a little boy—about six years old, I guess—I watched my friend Perry and his dad leaving the apartment complex to go see the Kilauea volcano—Perry's dad was always taking him on these little outings. I was crying as I watched them, then all of a sudden I got this big rush—really, it was a physical sensation—this *knowledge* that my dad and I would have been doing things like that, too, because my dad would have loved me as much as—maybe even more than—Perry's dad. It was such a powerful feeling to know this man really loved me, even though we'd never met and never could." Bill sighed. "I've remembered that feeling all my life, but still, I'd trade it in a second for just one single memory of him."

"Oh, Bill," said Fenny sadly, thinking how, like signs in the road, memories helped you when you started to feel lost. She turned her head then and kissed him, a Band-Aid of comfort against his big wound.

———

Slim, by committee vote, had been promoted from busboy to restaurant manager.

"After all," said Frau Katte, "you know more about za cafe zan anyone."

It was true, Slim hadn't worked side by side with Lee all those mornings without learning a thing or two about the restaurant business.

The menu, the suppliers, and the hours remained the same, but the differences between the new Cup O'Delight and the old were, while not night and day, at least dawn and dusk.

First, of course, there was no Lee and her absence, as Mary Gore said, was "tantamount to San Francisco without its cable cars, New York without its skyscrapers, Texas without its oil wells and cowboy swagger." None of the others, of course, would have put it quite that way, but not seeing Lee, standing behind the counter, one hand on her hip, the other holding a coffeepot, was a loss they all felt every time they came into the Cup O'Delight. Secondary, of course, was the fact that without Lee, there was none of the magical elixir that was the restaurant's namesake.

The last stash of it had gone quickly, drunk down by the regulars in greedy gulps. Then they all took their turns behind the counter, blending different types of coffee, throwing in cinnamon, vanilla, and chocolate, but whatever they poured into a cup, while often tasty, was nowhere near O'Delight.

It still being spring, they hadn't yet had to deal with the disappointment of the summer tourists, many for whom visits to the Cup O'Delight were a vacation highlight. They all hoped that by summer Lee would have returned.

Slim was in contact with her, but only rarely, and only at her choosing. After she had made the financial arrangements for the continued operation of the Cup O'Delight, their once-a-month phone calls were brief. Lee never told him where she was or what she was doing. She wanted to know only two things: how was Slim, and had Bill come back?

To these two questions, Slim always answered, "Fine—I can hardly run a restaurant and freak out at the same time," and,

"Nope." And then, just as he hoped to launch into a full-fledged conversation, Lee would say she had to go, to take care, 'bye.

Slim missed his friend more than he could say; missed her generous spirit and big laugh, missed the talks they had while doing morning prep work in the cafe, or cleaning up after it closed, missed singing duets with her, missed looking into her navy blue eyes and seeing the sun shine on her red hair in little flames of light.

He wanted Lee back in Tall Pine for his sake, but also for hers. He wanted her to see how they hadn't let what had happened destroy them. He wanted her to see the little plaque at the end of the counter that the mayor had made with his wood-burning set, the one that read, "Pete Sat Here." He wanted her to see Miss Penk, and to touch the biceps she was so proud of ("She lifts weights like a maniac," Frau Katte had told Slim. "She could bench-press me"), wanted her to see how Miss Penk danced at Polka Nights in her wheelchair, spinning and twirling it as if it were a compliant partner. Mostly, he wanted her to see a Polka Night, for the very fact they still existed, albeit in a shaggier form, said everything.

One night shortly after Lee had left, Slim had had a terrible nightmare; the same nightmare with the same sights and smells. He woke himself up with his screams and he lay in bed for a moment, panting, feeling like he was going to crawl out of his skin, waiting for Lee to bring the tea and soothing words. Remembering she was gone caused a physical jolt to his body, but then he heard his clock ticking and listened to its beautifully steady rhythm, listened and listened to the minutes passing, and somehow he got through his terror without throwing himself out the window.

He'd had two more nightmares since, but it was as if the volume had been turned down and the color muted; the reception was fuzzier. Both times he was able to calm himself and go back to sleep before dawn broke.

He wanted to joke with Lee, "See, all I needed for my sanity was for you to leave." He also wanted to be serious with her, to confide that in chasing after Marshall Stouffer, an agent of death, he thought he had somehow chased down the bogeyman. He longed to share his progress with her because she, more than anyone, would be so proud and happy.

Now it was almost May, and Slim had lost the bet he had made with himself that Lee would be back by Easter. He had been making bets about Lee's return ever since she had left, and each time he lost, it became clear to him that she might not want to come back at all.

But, surprising everyone, Fenny had, and her return lit another candle of hope for Slim, reminding him that surprises happened, especially when she informed those at the Cup O'Delight that she and Bill had been married.

"Married!" they chorused, and then asked, "When?" and "Where?"

"Actually, I was in the Grand Forks airport, on my way home," Fenny told them, "but then I decided to go back to California—he was playing in Palm Springs—and we were married in this place called Joshua Tree."

"Oh, let's see your ring!" said Frau Katte.

"Bill made them," said Fenny, displaying her finger.

"What's it made out of?" asked Lee.

"Oh, a lot of things," said Fenny shyly.

"Well, we'll just have to give you a shower," said Miss Penk.

"Yes—we'll give you a painting!" Frau Katte clapped her hands with excitement. "You and Bill can come over and take your pick."

"We need to do something to celebrate *now*," said the mayor. "Anyone got any champagne at home?"

The group exchanged looks.

"Dad has whiskey," offered Mary Gore. "But he always says if I touch it, I'm a dead duck."

"I've got an idea," said Heine. "They just got *Ike and Inga* down in Duluth. Let's drive down and see it!"

The crew had a great time watching the movie and eating dinner at a lakeside restaurant until some of the locals recognized Fenny and started pestering her.

"My gosh," said Miss Penk on the drive back home, "those people—'Can I have your autograph?,' 'Do you mind if I take a picture?'—they act like you owe them something."

"Tell me about it," said Fenny. "But at least no one yelled out, 'The bitch broke my nose!' "

"You hear zat a lot?" asked Frau Katte.

"About as much as 'I pooped in my pants'!" said Fenny.

People passing her on the streets often shouted that at her, with as much friendly good cheer as people exchanging good-mornings.

The phrase had become part of the American lexicon, the off-hand quip of those who were asked to explain an achievement or victory.

"Oh, I just pooped in my pants," said a governor-elect, when asked how he had beat his popular incumbent. "I guess I just pooped in my pants," said a swimmer who broke a record thought unbreakable.

"People can be such barbarians," said the mayor, shaking his head.

"Not to change the subject," said Mary Gore, "but how about that Harvest Ball scene? Did you see me? I'm more photogenic than I thought."

"Did you see how mad I looked in the schoolhouse?" asked the mayor. "I guess being in politics all these years helped my acting."

"Well, I thought I looked pretty good up there on those hay bales," said Heine. "And what a kick to hear my accordion in stereo sound!"

"You know," Mary Gore said, "Harry called me and asked me to come to the premiere, seeing as how I had helped rewrite the end of the movie."

"He did?" asked Fenny, surprised. "And you said *no?*"

"Can you believe it? Me, who was all set to have a big screen-writing career? To join Faulkner and Fitzgerald and all the other literary lions who had had their romp in Hollywood?" Mary looked at her hands and laughed, a small laugh. "I was going to go; I had my overnight bag packed and made arrangements for Gloria Murch to look in on Dad, and then, well . . . then I thought, why? I was already out there long enough to know it's not my world, and why waste time pretending it is?"

"Wow," said Fenny, thinking that was the smartest thing she'd ever heard Mary say. "It took me a lot longer to figure out the very same thing."

Everyone but Slim and Fenny begged off a Polka Night.

"We're working on a big contest," explained Frau Katte. " 'What I Look for in Za Perfect Kitchen' in twenty-five words or less."

"If we win, we get a complete kitchen remodeling," explained Miss Penk. "I'd like to have everything lowered a bit to accommodate my chair."

"Last night she told me she'd like to throw it in Tall Pine Lake," whispered Frau Katte to Fenny, "but most of za time she realizes it's what helps her get around. And if Miss wants to do anyzing, it's move forward."

Now alone in the Cup O'Delight, Fenny and Slim shared a pot of coffee.

"So how's business going?" asked Fenny, looking around the cafe.

Slim shrugged. "We still get the thrill-seekers who come in here and ask, 'Is this the place where all those people got shot?' and then those who are looking for you or anyone who worked on the movie."

Fenny shook her head. "What's the draw?"

"If I knew answers to questions like that, I wouldn't have to bark like a dog," said Slim. "Excitement, I guess, something that feeds something that's missing in their lives."

"Speaking of missing," said Fenny, "when do you suppose Lee will call again?"

Slim scratched his head. "Probably near the end of the month. That's when she usually does."

"Well, would you tell her to call me the next time she does?"

Her big love for Bill had filled up a lot of space in her heart, but there was still a vacancy where Lee's friendship used to lodge, and it hurt Fenny that Lee felt no desire to contact her.

"Sure," said Slim, "if I have time. But usually it's a pretty short conversation. She asks me a couple questions and then hangs up."

"What kind of questions?"

"She asks how I'm doing and if I've heard from Bill."

"From Bill?" said Fenny. "She wants to know about Bill but not about me?"

Slim opened his hands in a don't-ask-me gesture.

"Well, now we'll have lots of news for her," said Fenny. "I mean, it's pretty strange to think that Bill and I are married and Lee doesn't even know about it." She took a final sip of her uninspired coffee and leaned over the counter to put the cup in the bus tub tucked underneath. "And she's never said anything about where she is?"

Slim shook his head.

"Well, you can track her down, you know. Right on the phone."

"I figure if she wanted to be tracked down, she'd let me know where she is," said Slim, annoyed. In truth, he had already used the particular phone feature that gave the number of the caller and had written down it and its New Mexico area code. His search didn't go any further; he felt guilty trying to find out something that Lee obviously didn't want him to know.

"Do me a favor. The next time she calls, tell her I want to talk to her."

"You got it," said Slim, lifting the bus tub under the counter. "Take the rags for me, will you?"

Taking the bucket of bleaching rags, Fenny followed him into the back room. She was wringing out rags when Slim, racking up cups, paused as if he were going to tell her something, then fell to the floor in a heap.

Chapter 29

Slim was not a happy patient. When the nurse tried to take his temperature, he growled at her.

She jumped, nearly dropping the thermometer.

"He's a little nervous," explained Fenny, who sat with him in the hospital room.

"Well, even so," said the flustered nurse as she put the thermometer in Slim's mouth. "Even so."

Fenny shook her finger at Slim, but like a mother charmed by her mischievous child, she could not disguise the amusement in her eyes.

The nurse jotted down a figure and took out the thermometer.

"Well, nothing's the matter with your temperature," she said, "nothing that'd make you want to growl at a person."

Slim snarled as she left the room.

"You'd better cut that out," warned Fenny, "or they'll move you to the psych ward."

"Why'd you bring me here?" asked Slim in a tone he'd never before used with her.

"Slim," implored Fenny, "I didn't know what happened to you. You fell to the floor the same way Malcolm did."

"Look at that," said Slim, gesturing toward the electrocardiogram monitor on which were displayed his strong and steady heartbeats. "Now come on, help me with these wires and let's get out of here."

Fortunately Slim's escape was averted by the presence of the doctor, the same doctor who treated the gunshot wound to his foot.

"Mr. Knutson," said the doctor, "what kind of trouble have you gotten yourself in this time?"

"Hey, Doc!" said Slim. "How're you doing?"

"I believe you're supposed to be answering that question for me."

Slim shook his head. "I passed out, that's all. I passed out and my friend here thought it was a medical emergency."

"Any reason why you think you should be passing out?"

"I'm not 'passing out,' Doc, I *passed* out. I felt a little dizzy, and the next thing I know, I'm on the floor and Fenny here is ready to perform CPR."

The doctor turned and smiled. "I thought that was you, Miss Ness. I loved you in *Ike and Inga.*"

"Thank you," said Fenny, who found his remark more annoying than complimentary; couldn't he concentrate on his job and the patient at hand? "So what do you think is the matter with Slim?"

"It's hard to say," said the doctor, "but probably not much of anything. Maybe a little hypoglycemia. In a day or two we'll get some answers from the routine blood tests we took, but all your vital signs are pretty good, so, if it's okay with you, Slim, I think we'll send you home."

Slim shot Fenny such a look of superiority that she almost laughed.

"But if the fainting keeps up, come back and see me."

"Our bass player has low blood sugar and he's always complaining about feeling faint," said Big Bill over the phone after Fenny told him about Slim. "Then he has some orange juice and he's fine."

"He could have hit his head or something," said Fenny. "He could have really hurt himself."

"But he didn't," said Bill. "And you've got other things to worry about besides a hypoglycemic Slim."

"I do?" asked Fenny. "Like what?"

"Like your poor lonely husband who wishes more than anything that you were here next to him in this hotel room."

" 'Husband,' " said Fenny. "I sure like that word."

"Not as much as I like the word 'wife.' So, what do you say, wife— when are you coming back on tour with me?"

"Oh, husband—I'm boycotting show business, remember?"

"But not me?"

"Never you."

"Okay. Then I'll come home—home!" The glee in Bill's voice was palatable. "Do you know how long it's been since I've said 'home' and meant it?"

"Oh, Bill. I'm glad."

"We've got a four-day break before we go to the East Coast. I'll be home in a couple days."

"I can't wait. I'll start cleaning the tent now."

"You'd better. That'll give you a chance to break the news to Mae before I get back."

"Uh-uh," said Fenny, laughing. "That, dear husband, is *your* job."

After Fenny hung up, she thought that while she and Bill had decided they wanted to live in Tall Pine, they had never discussed *where* in Tall Pine. They had joked about setting up housekeeping in Bill's tent under the hostile eye of Mae Little Feather, but nothing had moved beyond the joking stage. They would, no doubt, live in the Ness house, but Fenny occasionally wondered if she and Bill should find a new place to start their new life. She realized that she and Bill hadn't planned much of anything, but rather than scaring her, it excited her. In fact, her life had not gone according to plan since she had agreed to make *Ike and Inga*, and she was beginning to see the beauty of allowing life to make special deliveries, rather than automatically scrawling on the package, "will not accept/did not order." This pleased her mightily, the fact that she had embraced adventure and it hadn't smothered her; maybe those wild Viking genes her parents had thought dormant in Fenny were regenerating after all.

Standing behind the grill flipping pancakes, Slim carefully set down the pancake turner, leaned against the counter, and slumped to the floor.

"*Mein Gott,*" said Frau Katte, who was working the shift with him. "Slim's fainted!"

He fainted again the next day hauling trash out to the back alley and then again during a Polka Night when Mary Gore was reading a poem called "Love Lesions" from the latest edition of *Angel Motors*.

The mayor and Heine pulled him to a booth and Frau Katte ran to get a glass of water.

"Why does everyone run and get a glass of water when someone faints?" Miss Penk asked.

No one knew the answer, but when he came to, Slim accepted the glass and emptied it in one long draw. Slim's hand around the water glass seemed almost translucent to Fenny, the veins dark blue and squiggly underneath. The sight of his hand scared her.

"That's it," said Fenny as he struggled to sit up. "You're going back to the doctor tomorrow."

"No need to," said Slim. "I talked to him yesterday. I know what's wrong with me."

Slim gave Fenny the number he'd written on an "Osterberg Accounting—We'll Figure It Out" memo pad he kept on his phone table. The Polka Night had ended soon after Slim's announcement—no one seemed to be much in the mood for singing or dancing or joke-telling.

"I don't know why you have to bother her," said Slim, but his mild protest convinced Fenny that that was exactly what he wanted, to bother Lee.

With trembling fingers, she finished dialing the number, and when a voice answered, Fenny practically shouted, "Lee?"

"No, this is Sister Margaret," said the voice. "With whom do you wish to speak?"

"She's at a nunnery!" Fenny whispered frantically, her hand cupped over the receiver. Into the phone she said, "Is there a Lee O'Leary there?"

There was a slight pause, and then the voice answered, "Will you hold the line?"

"Of course," said Fenny, and while she waited, she said to Slim, "I can't believe she's in a nunnery."

"You don't know that for sure," said Slim.

"Slim, the woman who answered the phone was *Sister* Margaret."

"Maybe it's some kind of commune," offered Slim. "You know, where everyone's brother and sister . . . or comrade."

"Hello?"

Fenny gasped, hearing Lee's voice.

"Lee? Lee, it's Fenny!"

This time the gasp came from the other line.

"Fenny?" There was joy in her voice, but it was quickly tempered with worry. "What's the matter?"

Fenny, too, felt all sorts of emotions hearing her dear friend's voice. "Lee, I've got so much to tell you, but what I'm calling for is Slim."

"Slim? What's the matter with Slim?"

Fenny smiled at the man who was the topic of conversation, hoping that somehow the muscles pulling up her mouth would strong-arm the rest of her face to look happy, when all she wanted to do was burst into tears.

"He was . . . he, uh —"

Slim took the phone from Fenny.

"I've got cancer, Lee. Leukemia." Slim listened for a little while, shaking his head. "No, Lee. That's not necessary. Lee, really, I —" Slim shrugged at Lee and placed the receiver back on the set. "She hung up on me."

"What'd she say?"

"She said she's coming back, and I said that's not necessary, and she said she'd be there as soon as she could, and then she hung up."

Fenny reached out and wrapped her arms around Slim's broad, bony shoulders and, putting her head on his chest, she yipped like a dog whose master was coming up the steps.

"I'm glad, too, Fenny."

Fenny was hanging a quilt on a wooden display rack when the door to Sig's Place opened. Goose bumps rose on her arm.

"Bill!" she cried, running to him and knocking over the display rack in the process.

They kissed until Dolly, the mayor's wife, came in.

"I heard you two got married," she said. "Congratulations."

"Thanks," said Fenny. "It was pretty spur-of-the-moment."

"I'm all for it. The mayor and I eloped—we were both going to school down in Bemidji, and one warm spring night after we'd been studying in the student union, the mayor slammed his book shut and said, 'I could learn a lot more about chemistry by marrying you.'" Dolly smiled, displaying the dimples her husband was crazy about. "By the next night, we were married."

"Aw," said Fenny, "what a nice story."

"It'll be forty years next week."

"Well, then," said Bill, "congratulations to you."

Dolly made a small curtsy.

"Speaking of weddings," said Dolly, "I need to buy a wedding present." She rolled her eyes, indicating the excitement with which she viewed this task. "Fenny, help me out. What do you think a new bride would like?"

"I don't know," said Fenny. "What's she like?"

"Oh, typical. Young and in love."

Fenny thought for a moment and then took a pair of ceramic candlesticks off a shelf.

"These are kind of expensive," she said, "but look at the craftsmanship. A woman down in New Prague makes these. And, I don't know . . ." Fenny held the candlesticks close together. "Newlyweds always like candlelight, right?"

"I suppose," said Dolly. "I'll take them."

After paying for them, Fenny asked if she wanted them gift-wrapped.

"Yes, please," said Dolly. "In your fanciest paper."

"Too bad about Slim, huh?" said the mayor's wife to Bill as she waited for her package.

"Well," said Bill, "I had a cousin who was diagnosed with leukemia—and that was twenty years and three kids ago."

"That's right," said Dolly. "It's certainly not a death sentence." She crossed her arms as if she were cold. "It's just a piece of news you'd rather not hear."

Fenny handed her the package, wrapped in silver paper with cascades of silver ribbon. "Is this fancy enough?"

"Perfect," said Dolly. She filled out a gift card, tucked it in its tiny envelope, and secured it under a ribbon. "Well, I'm off. Gloria Murch is throwing one of those cosmetic parties, and I like a dummy agreed to go."

She wasn't yet out the door when Fenny realized she had left the package on the counter.

"Dolly—your present!"

The mayor's wife stopped at the doorway. "No, *your* present."

The bell tinkled as she walked out.

" 'To Fenny and Bill,' " said Bill, reading the little card. " 'Happy Marriage. From Dolly and the Mayor.' What a nice thing to do."

"It sure was." Fenny shook the package. "Gee, I wonder what it is."

"I hope candlesticks," said Bill, clasping his hands to his chest. "According to an old Hawaiian legend, if the first present a married couple gets is candlesticks, everything will be spectacular for the rest of their lives."

Fenny tore open the package she had spent so much care on just minutes ago. "Oh, my God, Bill: *it's candlesticks!*"

Laughing, they kissed each other, hard.

"Well, then," said Bill finally, "now that we know everything's going to be spectacular, I guess we might as well go see Mae."

"Oh, Bill, do we have to?"

"Come on," he said, taking her hand. "The sooner we go, the sooner it'll be over. And who knows? Maybe she'll surprise us."

Mae Little Feather did not surprise them; she was livid.

"What? You got married? You got married to her? What were you thinking, Bill?"

She was a flurry of motion, rushing around the kitchen, banging her fist, pot covers, sugar canisters. Fenny stood near the door, ready for a quick exit, while Bill bravely stood by the table in the center of the room.

"Mae, stop that. Quit making so much noise and sit down."

He spoke calmly, but his words had no effect on Mae. She slammed a cupboard door shut. She smacked the side of the refrigerator. She picked up the toaster and banged it on the counter. Bill shrugged at Fenny and sat down, gesturing for her to join him, but she knew the safest place to be in this storm was near the door.

Finally Mae's rage seemed spent, or at least her need to physically abuse appliances was, and she sat down on one of her vinyl kitchen chairs, buried her head in her arms, and began to cry.

Big Bill sat for a moment, slack-jawed. He felt he was witnessing an unnatural phenomenon; to see tears from someone who was so dried up, not just by age but by mean-spiritedness, was not a part of the world as he knew it.

Fenny's compassionate side wanted her to go and comfort the old woman, but the rational part of her brain told her to stay where she was, it was probably a trap.

A huge sob arched Mae's back and tipped her head back.

"Wahhhhhhhh!" she cried, her mouth a black toothless circle. "Wahhhhhh!"

"Mae," said Bill, his stupefaction now turning to alarm. "Mae, please." He moved his chair next to hers and put his arm around her shaking shoulders. Mae was almost obsessive-compulsive in the way she avoided human touch, and that she did not resist him was further testament to her pain.

"Mae," said Bill softly, "Mae, I love Fenny. She is a wonderful person."

Bill's defense of his wife made Mae cry all the harder. Bill looked helplessly at Fenny, who just as helplessly looked back. Bill sat for a few more minutes, his hand patting his aunt's shoulder. Finally he stood up, realizing that maybe the only thing that would comfort Mae was his and Fenny's departure. He was wrong on this account, too, but at least she stopped crying.

"I never had children," she said, wiping her nose with an upward sweep of her palm. "I never had children, and you know why?"

Mae's words stopped Bill and Fenny's exit.

"Why?" asked Bill, turning at the door toward his aunt.

She blew her nose on a paper napkin. "I never had children 'cause I couldn't stand the idea of spreading the pain. Couldn't stand the idea of bringing another Indian into this world that treats them like dogs." So vehemently did Mae believe this now, she had forgotten that what ultimately stopped her from bearing children was her husband Jasper's sterility.

She looked at Fenny now, her swollen eyes little slits. "Couldn't stand if that child grew up and thinned his Indian blood with white poison."

Fenny's mouth dropped open, but Mae's words were a hot blast of air, evaporating any that Fenny might say.

Bill, too, was rendered speechless until he was able to whisper a hoarse "Mae."

"There ain't gonna be any Indians left," said Mae. "Just a bunch of half-breeds who'd rather go shopping than take a walk in the woods. Look at you, Bill. Your dad married some Hawaii girl, and what you know about being an Indian you could put in . . . in this." From the lazy Susan in the center of the table, she picked up the small bottle that held her blood pressure pills. "No, that's too much. You don't know nuthin'."

"I know plenty," said Bill. He had been feeling sorry for his aunt, but his sympathy was quickly becoming a memory. "I know you're a mean old woman who can't stand to see someone happy because you've never been happy yourself."

"Now, when you have children," said Mae, continuing on as if she hadn't heard Bill, "you'll have a bunch of quarter-breeds, and by the time they have kids the Indian blood'll be thin and runny as water. And it might as well be water in our veins, because we're gonna be nothing but a tribe of ghost people, killed off by white-loving traitors like you."

Both Bill and Fenny were shocked by Mae's vitriol, but whereas Fenny was frightened by it, Bill was angry, so angry he felt he could have struck his aunt, and with pleasure.

Instead he said, "I feel sorry for you, Mae," and he opened the door.

"You get your tent and get off my land!" yelled the old woman.

Mae sat at her kitchen table, her wrinkled face in her wrinkled hand, watching her grandnephew walk down the hill, his arm around his wife. She thought of the stories her mother had told her, of the white man who rode into their village and rode out with her mother's sister on the back of his horse, and she cried for that long-ago theft and the theft happening right in her own backyard. Then she saw by the clock that it was time for her soap opera, and she blew her nose and turned on the television.

"Oh, Bill," said Fenny as she drove back to town. "I am so sorry."

Flexing his jaw muscles, Bill shook his head. "I'm the one who's sorry. I wish you didn't have to hear that."

"Well, it would have been nice if she had said, *Welcome to the family!* but in a way I see her point."

"You do?"

"Sure," said Fenny, waving as Pastor Murch, on his pastoral outreach rounds, passed them in the church van. "And in a way I even admire her."

"You *do?*"

"If the government tried to take my culture away, I'd fight to hold on to whatever I could of it, too. The problem is when that thing she wants to hold on to is a person."

"Especially one that doesn't want to be held on to, especially by her."

"The thing that makes me really mad, though, is how could Mae ask for a better Indian woman for you than me? I know how to live in the natural world—I love the natural world—but Mae only sees the white outside—"

"And not the red inside," interjected Bill.

"Exactly. She hurts my feelings talking about 'thinning' the blood—I don't think children of mixed races or cultures are diluted, I think they're . . . they're *enhanced.*" She paused, swallowing a lump that had risen in her throat. "I think our children will be enhanced."

Bill reached across the car seat and brushed Fenny's cheek with his knuckles. "Our children," he said. "Should we pull over and get started on one of them?"

Fenny laughed. "Yeah, and give Pastor Murch the topic for his next sermon: The Power of Lust."

"I'd go listen to that one," said Bill, putting his hand on his wife's knee.

"Come on, Bill, we've got to get back to town and see Slim, remember?"

Bill sighed. "I thought the hard part of this day was over."

Later Fenny would laugh bitterly, thinking how profoundly wrong he was.

Chapter 30

Months earlier, Lee held a funeral for her beloved Bonneville thirty miles south of Santa Fe, New Mexico. The car had been her faithful servant; first it had brought her to Tall Pine, and after all the trouble, it had brought her out of Tall Pine.

After that night with Big Bill in Hinckley, she had driven and driven and driven. Her route was as erratic as a lost child's, full of turns and stops, and it took her as far east as Pennsylvania and as far south as Florida (which, oddly, didn't feel very "southern" to her). She stayed in whatever motel revealed itself when she got tired and she ate whenever she got hungry (a new concept for someone who constantly snacked). She had never before felt so anonymous, so free, and so desperately lonely. It wasn't until two weeks after leaving Minnesota that she didn't cry herself to sleep, and that was only because she'd been too busy killing moths that fluttered out of every drawer, door, or curtain she opened in a motel room outside Akron. Lee's dislike of bugs wasn't as severe as Gloria Murch's worm phobia, but close. She was, however, grateful for the moths' presence because they distracted her from her human problems. She slept until noon the next day, and awoke to the maid's pounding on the door, her moth-swatting towel still clutched in her hand.

Many times Lee thought of pointing the Bonneville back in a northerly direction, but just as she'd put her blinker on to change lanes or get on an exit ramp, her resolve would falter and she would keep driving south or east or west, blinking back the tears that collected in her eyes.

She spent nearly a month in New Orleans, but it was no exploring-the-French-Quarter-listening-to-Dixieland-music-and-eating-Cajun vacation; she barely left her room, in an old-fashioned boardinghouse that let by the week. Originally the mansion had been a single-family dwelling, but its owners had fallen on hard times and there was about it an air of melancholia and defeat that appealed to Lee. She didn't know if Mr. and Mrs. Bix, the elderly couple who ran the boardinghouse, were the owners or hired help; either way, they always seemed on the verge of either tears or outright drunkenness, but they never asked questions or urged Lee to get out and experience what postcards described as the "jewel of the south." They left Lee's meals on tarnished silver trays outside her door or, on the rare occasion when Lee ate in the gloomy, heavy-draped dining room, they served her and the other downcast guests in a silence broken only by hiccups or their humming tunes like "Sweet Adeline" or "Blue Velvet."

Lee left when she realized one morning they didn't seem odd to her, and that fear of not recognizing craziness was enough to make her pack her bag and pay her bill. She felt like a teenager vulnerable to peer pressure; she knew if she stayed around the Bixes much longer, she would begin pouring her meals out of cocktail shakers and prattling on about the kindness of strangers.

She had cousins in Houston, a college roommate in Denver, and acquaintances from Chicago who were now transplanted in cities her driving took her through, but she visited no one. She went for days without ever having anyone call her by name, and when a friendly waitress would ask it, she would stammer and blush and say, "Lee." She would then tip that waitress according to how many times she called her by name, a dollar a "Lee." One chummy waitress in Lexington, Kentucky, pocketed twelve dollars.

It was driving through New Mexico that the Bonneville began to make noises and emit burning rubber, burning oil, and general burning smells, and after a shudder and a bang, it died on a two-lane blacktop.

Lee walked back to a roadside vegetable stand she had passed and a tow truck was called, and when the driver opened the hood and looked inside, he said, "God rest her soul."

Lee laughed and the tow truck driver joined in, happy that someone appreciated his wit, but Lee didn't stop laughing; she laughed herself sick until the driver had chained the car to his truck and asked for her Triple A card.

"You can ride with me into town," he said.

Lee, holding her stomach, asked him how far "town" was.

"Two miles."

"I'll walk," said Lee, and the man tried to temper his smile of relief.

Lee watched as her mustard-colored Bonneville was dragged away and then, bending down, she picked up a handful of gravel from the side of the road and threw it after her car.

"Ashes to ashes," she said solemnly, "dust to dust. You were a great car"—her mind scrambled to come up with a rhyme—"even with your rust."

The Sangre de Cristo Mountains rose up around Lee and the sun was warm, shining in a blue sky. The air was fragrant with sagebrush and Lee felt a lightening in her chest, as if a vent had been opened, allowing in a little breeze of happiness. She even whistled; it was a day that not only called for whistling but demanded it, and when she passed a wooden sign that said "Rest A While Ranch," she had no choice but to follow the dirt road it pointed to.

Both Fenny and Slim were half right in their ideas as to where Lee was; she was in sort of a convent and sort of a commune. The ranch was donated, along with a large amount of cash, in the 1930s to a nurse whose kindness and devout Catholicism had sustained and touched the donor during his lengthy illness. The nurse, a widow with a young daughter, was humbled by the largesse of the gift; she had previously lived in a three-room apartment in Santa Fe, and to go from that to a fifteen-thousand-square-foot house on two hundred acres was intimidating, to say the least.

Then a fellow parishioner mentioned a sister who *was* a Sister, a Sister who needed to take a reflective sabbatical, and the nurse took her in, which led to more referrals of Sisters in flux, and within five years the ranch became not only a retreat for members of religious orders, but a retreat for any woman who was a little lost and needed some time away from all that skewed her navigational skills. The ranch never advertised but was occupied to capacity and sometimes beyond. No one was ever turned down for an inability to pay, but for their room and board they had to work the many jobs required to keep a ranch up and running. Ergo, a schoolteacher might mend fences and a secretary might find herself tending to the small herd of dairy cows or weeding the vegetable gardens.

As it was for many of its tenants, it was the perfect place for Lee to land. Within days she had established herself as head cook, relieving an exhausted former flight attendant who had served hundreds at a time in the skies, but never twenty-seven people on the ground.

"Besides," she said to Lee, showing her around the kitchen, "I didn't come here to cook, I came here to tap my inner maple."

There were those kinds, Lee quickly learned, who were trying to discover their inner trees, inner children, and inner truths; but most of the women at the Rest A While wanted simply to take up the invitation of the ranch's name.

Lee began brewing pots O'Delight in the morning, which endeared her to the tenants and the nurse's daughter, who was now in charge. (The nurse, at ninety years old, still had the mental capabilities to run the ranch, but not the physical ones.)

"I'd like to put you on the payroll," said the nurse's daughter. "I'd like you to be at the Rest A While permanently."

"Oh," said Lee, knowing it was her coffee more than herself that the woman wanted for all time, "I can't make any kind of decision involving permanency right now."

Lee loved the ranch and the tenderness with which she was treated. A former nun who was now a massage therapist gave her back and foot rubs. A former parole officer who helped tend gardens gave Lee little baskets of blackberries.

She loved the big stone fireplace in the meeting area and the songs sung on the porch at twilight, but when all was said and done, the ranch was not the real world and Lee knew ultimately the real world was where she had to live.

As weeks passed into months, it became obvious to Lee that that real world might never again be Tall Pine, but then she got Fenny's call and there was nothing she could do but pack her bag and leave.

Slim needed her.

Bill and Fenny got to the Cup O'Delight after the lunch rush, which actually happened to *be* somewhat of a rush, as the mayor had treated the town council to a meal because their annual "State of the City" meeting had gone so well. Bud Glatte had groused a little that they hadn't gone to the Dog Haus, where he could get a nice steak and a drink, but Bud Glatte groused about everything; it was his first time as a town council member and he didn't know it would involve so much work.

A few early tourists, beating the summer crowds, had been in. Alma Forslund and several women from the church choir came after rehearsing for the upcoming confirmation ceremony, and there were also three movie fans from Breckenridge, so all the booths and counter space had been filled.

There remained in the cafe an after-party atmosphere, a happy exhaustion, the regulars glad there had been lots of customers but even more glad they had all cleared out.

"Big Bill!" said Frau Katte from her perch behind the counter. "Miss, it's Bill!"

All the regulars swarmed around Bill and Fenny, clapping them on the back and congratulating them.

"How does it feel to get the prize of Tall Pine?" asked Heine.

"Frau Katte and I want to throw a party for you," said Miss Penk.

"Did you take any pictures of the wedding?" asked the mayor. "I'd like to run one in the *Tall Pine Register*."

"Keep a journal of these precious moments," advised Mary Gore.

"Are you hungry? We'll make you lunch—on za house!"

Frau Katte didn't even wait for their answer but began making them tuna fish sandwiches.

"Katte," said Miss Penk, "maybe they don't want tuna fish!"

Frau Katte shrugged. "But zere's some left over—I might as well use it up." One thing the Swiss woman added to the running of the Cup O'Delight was practicality; it was she who monitored waste and figured out a way to remedy it.

"Tuna fish'll be fine," said Bill, sitting down. He took Miss Penk's hand. "How are you doing?"

"Oh, I have good days and bad days," said Miss Penk. "But more good than bad—probably sixty-forty. But I know I'd give up everything—even our O'Keeffe—just to get on water skis again."

"She's been working out," said Frau Katte. "Feel her muscles."

Miss Penk didn't need to be asked twice. She flexed her arm and Bill felt her biceps.

"Yikes," he said.

Fenny reached over and felt them, too.

"Wow," she said, remembering a phrase of Grace's, "steel cantaloupes."

Heine poured them coffee. "Now, don't be shocked at this, Bill. We're trying, but it's not a cup O'Delight in any shape or form."

Bill took a sip.

"It's not what Lee made, that's for sure."

"Speaking of Lee," said Fenny, looking at Bill and her friends, "I wanted to surprise you all, but I can't wait any longer. Slim and I talked to Lee! She's coming to Tall Pine!"

"Lee's coming back?" asked Mary Gore.

"When?" asked Miss Penk.

"How is she?" asked Heine.

"Where was she?" asked the mayor.

"She's coming home?" said Frau Katte. "Oh, goody!"

"Oh, goody," said Bill, and there was so much commotion in the restaurant that no one noticed his enthusiasm did not seem at the same level as the others'.

"Hey," said Slim, coming through the swinging doors. "What's going on here? A guy can't even sneak a little nap without everyone making all sorts of noise."

Bill stood and he and Slim hugged one another.

"Congratulations," said Slim, "you got yourself a prize."

"That's just what Heine said." Still holding on to Slim's shoulders, Bill stepped back to look at his friend. "How are you?"

Slim raised his black eyebrows. "Kind of tired, sort of weak, but on the whole . . . not bad." He looked at his friend, who had suddenly quieted. "Boy, talk about bringing down the party."

He looked down at the floor and then suddenly raised his arms and in a dead-on tent show preacher's voice said, "Don't worry about me, folks, I don't plan on crossin' that River Jordan anytime soon . . . and if it's not in my plans, it's not in God's, 'cause me and the big guy are workin' together here. . . ."

Big Bill went to the piano and began playing, punctuating Slim's verbal exclamations with musical ones.

"That's right, that's right," said Slim, striding across the floor, "maybe God has thrown me a little curve—but I've hit curveballs before, I've sent them clear out of the park, and this little curve ain't gonna be no different."

"Tell it!" shouted Miss Penk, clapping her hands.

"Well, I aim to, little sister, I aim to." He looked heavenward, his arms raised, his hands shaking. "And how'm I gonna do that, Lord? You tell me, tell me."

"Ya, you tell us!" said Frau Katte.

Slim nodded his head, as if in conversation with someone. "I see, I see, Lord." He looked at his friends. Bill played three minor chords on the piano.

"What do you see?" asked the mayor.

"I see a need to party!" shouted Slim. He raced over to Miss Penk, his favorite dance partner, and twirled her chair. "I see a *big* need to party!"

Those in the room clapped and shouted and Bill went wild on the keyboard, as if the Holy Spirit itself had taken over possession of his fingers, and Frau Katte grabbed the mayor's hand and Heine, Fenny's. Mary got up partnerless. There was a whirling, swirling motion in the room, accompanied by music and laughs and shouts and "Amens!" and it was into this frenetic late afternoon party that the cafe door opened and in walked Lee.

Miss Penk saw her first and shouted her name, but everyone was hollering and moving and clapping, and so it took several seconds for what she had called out to register, and then when it did, everyone looked at the door except Bill, who still pounded away on the keys until he became aware of the sudden silence. He looked over his shoulder and his hands dropped off the keyboard in a discordant clang.

Near the coatrack Lee stood, her red hair fiery in the afternoon light, her smile wide and hopeful, her hands folded above that which had silenced her closest friends in the world, had frozen them in their tracks, had made their mouths drop open; her hands folded above her huge belly, which stuck out as far as any belly belonging to a woman in her ninth month of pregnancy.

She patted her stomach and in a soft, shy voice announced, "Well, here we are!"

There had been merriment in the Cup O'Delight before, but never this *giddy* merriment; it was a reunion of old friends celebrated in a place that was so important to them, where so much had happened. Added to that already celebratory fuel was the complete surprise of Lee's pregnancy and all it represented: new life, hope, a beginning.

The friends surrounded Lee, who held on to Slim, searching his face with her eyes. As one group, they moved to the counter, everyone insisting that she should sit down, but first, she told them, she had business to attend to.

"When are you due?" asked Miss Penk.

"In two weeks." Lee made a face and rubbed her stomach. "But from the feel of things, any minute. For the past week I've been having these Braxton Hicks—"

"False contractions," Heine informed everyone. "Irene had them with our oldest girl—we went to the hospital at least four times, only to be sent home, and it got so that—"

"Heine," interrupted Frau Katte, "we were talking about *Lee*."

"I know we've all got a lot to talk about," Lee said, "but let's put on the coffee first." She took a brown paper bag out of her purse and gently shook it. "I just happen to have some O'Delight with me," she said, her voice as teasing as a pusher's announcing a new shipment.

She went behind the counter and began to make the coffee, playing to her crowd, using a lot of extravagant gestures as she measured coffee and poured water. She knew the question-and-answer period was coming, but postponing it gave her a tiny sense of control; she was scared to find out about Slim and was scared to have her friends find (more) out about her, but at least she could control *when* all this occurred. She knew the world, at least her world, stopped for O'Delight.

When the coffeemaker began making its industrious brewing sounds, Lee took a deep breath and looked out at her friends. She had thought of these faces so often, dreamed of them, and her gaze landed on the one whose appearance in her thoughts and dreams was the most frequent.

It was then Fenny felt the first twinge of disquiet, but it was so fleeting as to seem nonexistent and she ignored it. She concentrated on Lee, who seemed to be concentrating on Bill.

"First of all," she said, "I can't tell you how good it is to be back. As soon as I started smelling pine, I thought, Ahhh, I'm home." She looked at Slim. "I know you and I will be talking far into the night, but let me just tell you this . . ." Tears came to Lee's eyes and she paused, blinking them back. "You look a lot better than I thought you might, and I'm taking that as a very good sign."

"Hear, hear," said Miss Penk, clapping. "We're all going to help Slim beat this thing."

The group chorused their agreement.

The coffee finished brewing and Lee went down the line, pouring cups.

"Okay," said the mayor, once everyone had been served. "On your mark, get set, go."

They spent a few minutes paying homage to the wonders of O'Delight before Frau Katte got down to business.

"Okay, Lee, why don't you tell us what you've been up to."

Lee looked down as she rubbed her tightening belly, trying to obscure her blushing face. She had rehearsed this moment countless times in her head, but no amount of rehearsal could prepare her for the actual performance.

Standing at the end of the counter, she noticed the wooden plaque and cocked her head to read it.

" 'Pete Sat Here.' "

"I made it," confessed the mayor. "And we hot-glued it to the countertop. We didn't think you'd mind."

"I don't mind at all," said Lee, her voice cracking a little. "I'm glad it's here."

"Ya, we all zought Pete's place should be remembered, seeing as how much time he spent here." Frau Katte held her cup up for more coffee. "But we were talking about you, remember? We're all sitting here waiting very politely to hear your story, and I know zat if you don't tell us right away, I for one am going to explode! How did zis happen? Where's za fazzer? Are you living wiz him now?"

Lee touched the plaque honoring Pete, feeling his name inscribed in the wood. Her knees felt weak and she felt perspiration gathering along her hairline. She cleared her throat at length.

"Well," said Lee, "it happened the usual way, and the father . . ."

She stopped, clearing her throat again, and Fenny looked at Bill, who had the appearance of someone who was standing on deck in some very high seas.

Fenny, feeling a need to break what had all of a sudden become unbearable tension, blurted out, "Lee, guess what?"

"*Fenny*," scolded Miss Penk.

"Ya, wait your turn," said Frau Katte.

"Well," began Lee again, "the father and I haven't been together, but he's, well, he's—"

"Bill and I got married!"

"Bill."

For one horrible moment, Fenny and Lee stared at one another, having heard what the other said but not wanting to believe it. The moment passed and they realized that their desire not to hear something wasn't strong enough to erase it; what had been said was said and, reeling from its ramifications, Fenny ran out of the cafe and Lee ran, as best she could, into the back room.

Bill took off after Fenny, and Slim followed Lee.

Those remaining at the counter were too dazed to move.

"Oh, my," said Miss Penk finally. "And I thought I had troubles."

"As our neighbors to the south say," said Mary Gore. "*Ay caramba.*"

"Poor Fenny," said Frau Katte. "Poor Lee."

"Poor Bill," said Heine.

"That guy," said the mayor, "is up the creek without a paddle."

"Well, he's za one who zrew za paddles away."

"He's the one who got in a boat he never should have gotten into in the first place," said Miss Penk.

"Come on, now, we don't know all the facts," said Heine.

"That's right," said the mayor. "There are probably a lot more sides to this story than we'll ever know."

Frau Katte certainly was not the kind of lesbian whose idyllic vision of the world would be one populated by a Nation of Wymmin; but there were times when the fraternity of men and their need to stick up for each other even when caught red-handed got to be a little much.

"Let's go, Miss," she said, gripping the handles of her friend's wheelchair. "We've got to finish up zat Heath Mattress essay. All entries must be postmarked by midnight tomorrow."

"And I've got to get to the typewriter," said Mary Gore. "The muse has been electrified."

"Well," said Heine after the women left, "I 'spose we'd better close up the place."

"Right," agreed the mayor.

They worked in silence, busing the counter, wiping it down, refilling the condiments.

"Aren't you glad to have your life?" Heine finally asked, and the mayor, understanding completely, nodded his head.

"Yup," he said. "Dolly and I have had our ups and downs, but never all this screwy stuff."

"Same with me and Irene," said Heine. "It's so nice and *normal* with us."

The two friends cleaned what they could, but they left the bus tubs under the counter, not wanting to go into the back room and face whatever was going on in there.

Bill was just fast enough to open the passenger door and scramble into Fenny's car as she struggled to put the key into the ignition.

"Get out!" she screamed. "Get out of my car *now!*"

"Fenny, I can't explain anything."

"You're damn right you can't," said Fenny, but his lack of guile had startled her; it was not what she expected him to say.

She pulled the car out onto Main Street and, taking a left, was startled again, for Slim and Lee had just emerged from the back alley. Seeing Fenny's car, Slim waved Fenny over with such insistence that Fenny felt duty-bound to pull over.

"I think we all need to talk about things," said Slim, opening the back door. He held it open and said to Lee, "Get in."

"Slim, no offense," said Fenny, "but I don't—"

"Shut up. Lee, get in."

No one could argue with an authoritative Slim; no one had ever *met* an authoritative Slim.

"Drive," he ordered when he and Lee were in the back seat.

"Where?" asked Fenny, even as she wanted to tell him to quit bossing her around and get out.

"I don't know. Anywhere." Slim was agitated. He brushed back his thick white hair with his hands and then tapped his knees. "West. Drive west."

Fenny got on the county road and followed the westbound sun, driving for miles in a silence no one seemed able to break.

Her anger was like a living thing, an out-of-control plant that kept growing, that wanted to wrap its heavy, spiky vines around everyone in the car and squeeze. It seemed her anger was squeezing her; she felt robbed of breath and was panting like a bird dog after a chase. Her anger blurred her vision and she had to squint to get a clear picture of the road. She had never been more angry in her life, but a part of her knew that the anger was only dressing covering up her pain.

She didn't need to look over at Bill, slumped over, staring at his hands, to know that he was in pain, too.

Good, she thought; great! He should be tortured by pain, he should think he's dying from pain.

Fenny's fantasies of Bill suffering were interrupted when suddenly a deer leapt out from the bank of trees that lined both sides of the road.

"Jesus Christ!" said Big Bill as Fenny slammed on the brakes.

Her reflexes couldn't have been quicker, but she couldn't control the laws of physics and forward motion, and the deer and the front bumper met in a sickening thump. The deer was catapulted across the road, landing in the tall grasses of the ditch.

"Oh, my God, I hit it!" screamed Fenny. "I hit that deer!"

"Are you okay?" Bill screamed at her, and as she nodded, they both turned around and asked the back-seat passengers the same question.

As Slim and Lee replied in the affirmative, Fenny remembered Lee's condition.

"Oh, my God, Lee. Are you sure you're all right?"

"I'm fine," said Lee. She tugged at her seat belt. "I was buckled up."

Determining everyone's well-being took less than twenty seconds, and then Fenny bolted out of the car and ran to the deer. Bill and Slim were right behind her.

"Oh, look what I've done," moaned Fenny, bending down.

The deer, a doe, lay on her side in the grass, her back leg crumpled and bleeding.

"Is it dead?" whispered Bill.

The deer struggled to rise, flailing its front limbs.

"No," said Fenny sadly.

"But it will be," said Slim. "And the sooner we can help it on its way, the better."

"Oh, geez," said Bill.

One hand cupped around her mouth, Fenny reached out to touch the doe with the other, but this motion only scared her more. The deer flailed again, one hoof nearly making contact with the side of Fenny's head.

Slim touched her shoulder. "You'd better back up."

As she stood, Fenny saw blood was surging from under the deer's tail. Without thinking, she went to Bill, seeking comfort in his arms.

As Fenny stood in the embrace of her husband, Slim hollered to Lee, who had gotten back in the car.

"Lee—you all right?"

Lee, who had hunkered down in the back seat, popped up her head. She rolled down the window a few more inches. "I'm a little . . . I don't want to see what's over there."

"Good, it's not a pretty sight." Turning back to Bill and Fenny, he asked, "How're we going to do this?"

"We could," Bill said hesitantly, "hit it over the head with something. Fenny, you've got a shovel in your trunk, don't you?"

"I did," said Fenny, wiping her eyes with her fingers, "but I took it out to dig the garden. I've got a jack, though."

The trio was debating the efficiency of a jack as a killing tool and who would wield it when a car horn startled them. Pastor Murch pulled his van to the side of the road and he and his passenger got out.

"Welcome home, Fenny, Bill. Gloria told me all about your nuptials—" He saw the deer. "Oh. I thought you had a little car trouble or something." He stepped a little closer to the deer. "She's pretty bad off, isn't she?"

"We were trying to figure out how to put her out of her misery," said Fenny.

The minister looked at his passenger. "Gary?"

The thin, sharp-featured man, whom Fenny did not recognize, shrugged and then walked back to the van.

"Maybe we should get that jack," said Slim.

"No need," said the pastor, and then suddenly Gary was at his side, holding a Winchester rifle. He held it in his arms and fired, and with one quick shot to the head, the deer's suffering ended.

"Nice shot," said Slim.

The man nodded, acknowledging the compliment.

"God bless the beasts," said the pastor, his head bowed in prayer. "Gary's a gunsmith," he said a beat later as he opened his eyes. "Does beautiful restoration work. We just picked up a whole arsenal over at the Loshes'."

"The pastor is kind enough to help me with my pickups and deliveries," said Gary.

"Gary can't drive for a while," said Pastor Murch, patting his friend on the back. "His license was suspended."

"DWI," said the man, nodding.

"It's often when we falter," said the pastor, "that God comes looking for us the hardest."

"Amen," said Gary. "I had to lose my license to find the Lord."

A breeze blew the smell of pine over the small group by the roadside.

"Well, we'd best make tracks," said the pastor. "I've got to get Gary back to Baudette for his AA meeting." He and the man walked back to the van and then the pastor turned and looked at Fenny's car. "Not much of a dent; I've seen deers total cars. You can drive it okay?"

Fenny nodded.

"You got a phone with you?"

"No," said Fenny.

"Well, I do," said the pastor. "I didn't see the need, but Gloria feels more comfortable when I've got a phone on my rounds. I'll call the sheriff and he'll send someone out here to pick up that deer."

After Pastor Murch and his gunsmith drove away, Fenny picked a wildflower and threw it on the doe.

"I'm sorry," she whispered, but Bill, hearing her, said, "There was nothing you could do, Fenny—it ran right in front of you."

"That's right," said Slim, "no sense feeling guilty about something you couldn't help."

Fenny's anger, which had been forgotten in the trauma of hitting the doe, began growing again.

"Okay, Bill," she said softly, remembering her long-ago discussion with him on the subject of guilt. "I guess I feel a clean guilt. But I'm curious. What kind of guilt do you feel about what happened between you and Lee?"

"Oh, Fenny—" said Bill, but he didn't get a chance to say anything more because Slim, who had opened the car door, shouted, "Lee!"

She was sprawled out in the back seat, moaning.

Fenny rushed over to her friend. "Lee, what's happening?"

"My . . . my water broke," said Lee, puffing between each word. "I don't think they're Braxton Hicks anymore."

"And I thought you were just hiding from Pastor Murch," joked Slim. He knew calm needed to be established immediately, or panic—his own, if nobody else's—would reign. He got into the back seat, positioning his rangy frame in the spaces not occupied by Lee.

Fenny jumped into the car on the passenger's side and leaned over the seat to take her friend's hand. "We'll get you to the hospital right away," she said. "Don't worry about a thing."

"I'm not," said Lee, but contradicted her statement with a little yelp.

Bill sat on the driver's side, the only available seat left. Fenny swatted his shoulder.

"Go," she said. "Go, go!"

"Go where?" he asked.

"To the hospital!"

Bill looked dumbly at Fenny. "How?"

"How do you think? Drive!"

Lee moaned again.

"*Drive?*" said Bill. "How?"

"How do you think?" repeated Fenny, her voice shrill with panic and exasperation. "Just do it!"

"I can't drive," said Bill, opening the car door. "Let Slim drive, I'll hitch a ride—"

"Yes, I can drive—" began Slim.

"No!" yelled Lee, gripping both Fenny's hand and Slim's arm. "Stay with me!"

"Yes, we'll stay with you, Lee." Fenny looked at Bill, and there was no room in her voice for negotiation. "Drive, Bill. Now."

Bill felt his heart begin to race. Sweat dampened his neck, his palms, his forehead. He felt faint.

"Now!" said Fenny.

Bill turned the key. The car started up.

"Oh, dear God," moaned Lee.

Bill put his foot on the brake and the gear stick into drive.

He looked into his rearview mirror, and the sight of Lee's anguished face and heaving belly made him light-headed. He moved his foot off the brake and onto the gas pedal and the car went forward. He steered off the shoulder and onto the road.

He wanted to cry out, he wanted to pass out, he wanted to be out of the car, but he kept driving, reciting over and over to himself, "Please help me, please help me, please help me."

"Oh, God!" said Lee, in a voice about two octaves lower than her usual.

"You're doing fine," said Slim, his voice as soothing as an old obstetrician's. "Just breathe."

"That's right," said Fenny, thinking more than anything Lee needed reassurance. "Keep breathing, Lee. You're doing great."

Lee puffed and hissed like a steam engine; she blew her cheeks out and then sucked them in, she pursed her lips, she grimaced, she breathed.

Bill, his knuckles white on the steering wheel, breathed with her. He wasn't as loud as she was, but he mimicked her breathing patterns, responded to Slim's and Fenny's commands as if they were directed at him.

Once Fenny turned away from Lee for a moment and saw Bill,

his posture ramrod-straight, his cheeks puffed out, his mouth moving like a sunfish's.

"It feels like it's coming!" yelled Lee, and Slim said she was doing great, they were almost to the hospital, and Fenny said, just relax, everything'll be fine.

Bill wondered if his heart could beat any faster or if it would just go into a crazed arrhythmia then and there. Salt stung his eyes from the lines of sweat that were dripping from his forehead.

"Fenny," he said quietly, desperately. "Fenny, there's a car coming!"

"What?" said Fenny.

"There's a car coming!"

Fenny turned to look out the front window.

"Bill, it's just a car in the opposite lane. We'll pass each other and it'll be fine."

The cars did pass each other and they were fine, even though Bill thought he might vomit.

"I want to push!" yelled Lee.

Slim and Fenny looked at one another; they weren't experienced midwives, but both knew that this meant things were proceeding at a fast clip.

"Bill, mind speeding it up a little?" asked Slim casually.

"What? I'm going . . ." Bill looked at the speedometer. "I'm going thirty!"

"The speed limit's sixty-five here, Bill," said Fenny. "You can— you *should* go faster."

"Oh, God," said Bill.

"Keep breathing," Fenny instructed him. "You're doing fine."

Bill sped up and was soon approaching Baudette.

"I want to push!" wailed Lee.

"Fenny, where do I go?" asked Bill. "There're cars up ahead, and buildings."

"There's a little hospital up here a ways," said Slim. "About a half mile. Just turn left at the stop sign."

"You want me to make *a left-hand turn?*"

"Bill," said Fenny, "you're doing fine. Keep breathing."

Lee was screaming by the time Bill made his tentative, stop-and-go left-hand turn into the hospital driveway.

"Hey!" Slim yelled at a woman leaning against the building, smoking a cigarette. "Hey, we've got a woman having a baby in here!"

The woman dropped her cigarette and ran inside. She returned moments later with a man and a wheelchair.

"She says she wants to push," said Fenny as they helped Lee out of the car.

"I'll bet she does," said the woman, whose name tag identified her as an RN.

"Don't leave me!" screamed Lee, and Fenny and Slim ran alongside as she was pushed in the wheelchair, and were already in the building when Bill slowly opened the car door, leaned forward, and threw up on the tarred driveway.

He sat there trembling, half in, half out of the car, his feet splayed on the ground, a puddle of vomit between them, not wanting to move ever again, when suddenly he reared his head up. He looked at the hospital door for a moment as if he weren't sure where he was, but then he leapt up and ran, in long fast strides, inside. It was a small hospital, not much bigger than a clinic, and Lee's screams were loud and he found her room just as Fenny, Slim, and the nurse were ordering Lee to push, and he added his own voice to the chorus and less than a minute later his son saw the light of day.

Chapter 31

The next day, Fenny drove along the Minnesota/Canada border, thinking she would head into Manitoba once she was on the west side of Lake of the Woods, but the more she drove, the more a weariness descended upon her and she realized she hadn't the energy for a long drive.

She paid her fee to a ranger and found a campsite within a state park. She set up her tent on the banks of Zippel Bay, as far away from other campers as she could, but as was often the case in state parks, this wasn't far enough.

A family at the campsite to her left seemed to be under the impression that it was National Tease Day and everyone participated, even Mother and Father.

"Come on, lard butt, get those tent stakes out!"

"Mom, Kelly told me I'm adopted and my real mother was a monkey!"

"Dad, Erin says you're gonna leave me here because nobody likes me!"

I can see why! Fenny wanted to yell, but she knew it would do no good to descend to their level. Besides, they were packing up to go, which made their secondhand verbal abuse a little easier to take.

Unfortunately, their spot was filled by a young couple whose first item of business was to set their boom box on the picnic table and turn it up high; fortunately, they turned it up loud enough so even the ranger heard it and promptly paid the couple a visit, lecturing them on common camper courtesy.

Although there was a small canvas pup tent set up on the campsite to the other side of Fenny, there was no action around it; its occupants were either out or sleeping.

After she set up camp, Fenny took a long hike and then got her canoe off its perch on the roof of her car and rowed and rowed as if she were trying to break both speed and distance records. She fished for her supper, catching a nice three-pound northern, and cooked it over a campfire. It was twilight when she washed out her pan and made coffee in the speckled blue tin percolator and she realized she was truly frightened, because she had nothing else to do but sit and think about what had happened.

She sat in her low-to-the-ground camp chair facing the fire and the lake beyond it. The boom box couple had gone to town; she had heard them debating whether they should look for a 3.2 bar or one that served harder liquor.

The boat traffic was still fairly busy, but far enough out on the bay so that she couldn't hear it. Normally a campsite illuminated by a fire and the fading light of a northern sky was enough to bring Fenny into the realm of deep pleasure and contentment, but she felt lost, and that she felt lost in a setting that usually provided her with so much security made her feel even more lost.

"Oh, Bill," she whispered, "what did you do?"

He had tried to talk to her when they were leaving the hospital after the baby's birth. (And what a bizarre scenario that was: Fenny coaching the woman who was giving birth to her husband's baby! And yet she had felt a rush of exhilaration and awe when the baby came out, had felt witness to a miracle.)

"Fenny, we need to talk," said Big Bill, putting his hand on her back.

"That," she said, "is the understatement of the year."

"It was only one night, Fenny, it was right after you'd told me you wanted to break up—"

"Oh, so it fell within a *grace period*, huh?"

"Not really," said Bill, "but sort of . . . I guess. Oh, Fenny, I was so mixed up, so hurting, so—"

"*So what?* Maybe I was hurting, too. Although *I* didn't run out and get pregnant to show you how much."

Slim had walked ahead of them, not wanting to eavesdrop on their conversation, but now, at the car, he had nowhere to go.

"Uh, should I leave?" he asked. "I can hitch a ride back to Tall Pine."

"No, you come with me," said Fenny, opening the car door. "Let Bill hitch the ride."

She gunned the car out of the lot, pretending she didn't see the look on Bill's face.

"Oh, Slim," she had sobbed as soon as she could no longer see her husband in the rearview mirror. "What am I going to do?"

Slim closed his eyes, wanting nothing more than to put his head on a pillow. "A lot of us are asking that same question, Fenny. I know I am." With a sigh, he opened his eyes and looked at her. "And you know what my answer is?"

"What?"

"I'm going to do whatever I have to do."

"Oh, well, isn't *that* deep."

It took Fenny a while to realize Slim was talking about his illness and not her problem, but she was too miserable to feel ashamed and didn't offer the apology she normally would have.

Fenny finished her second cup of coffee. The fire was full strength now, sending up spires of red and yellow flame. She stared into it, wondering where Bill was now, what he was doing. She missed him desperately and yet how could she, when she never wanted to see him again?

"You got an extra cup of that?"

Startled, Fenny looked up. Standing at her side was a man whose face was weathered and wrinkled, mismatched with his strong, compact body. His gray hair was shaved in a brush cut and his posture so erect he looked uncomfortable.

"You shouldn't sneak up on people," she said.

"We Marines are naturally quiet," said the man. "Like jungle cats. But I didn't make less noise or more noise than usual. I just caught you daydreaming."

"I wasn't daydreaming," said Fenny crossly, not liking this intrusion one bit.

"Then you can pour me a cup of coffee."

"If I do, will you leave?"

The man's laugh was like a cough. "Didn't anyone teach you to respect an officer in the United States Marine Corps?"

"Didn't anyone teach you not to sneak up on civilians?"

"Like I said, I didn't make less—"

"All right, all right," said Fenny. "You can have *one* cup of coffee."

The man sat down eagerly and watched as Fenny poured.

"That's my tent," he said, pointing to the old pup tent in the next site. "I brought it home from the Big One."

"Are you talking wars or earthquakes?" said Fenny, bothered by a certainty in his voice that everything he said was interesting.

The old Marine cackled. "Oh, so you're a wisenheimer, eh? I'm talking W.W. Two, where I earned myself a chestful of medals, including two Bronze Stars, one Silver Star, and a Navy Cross. What do you think about that, Miss Wisenheimer-on-the-Snotty-Side?"

Suddenly Fenny felt so overwhelmed by life in general and his ravings in particular, she could do nothing but lay her head on her knees and weep.

The man sat there for a moment, looking not at Fenny but at the fire. "I'm not going to ask you what you're crying about," he said, "because I don't really give a hoot. A woman's tears are a dime a dozen, if you ask me. All I wanted was a cup of coffee."

He took a sip of coffee, making the kind of exaggerated "Ahhh" sound people usually made for O'Delight.

"I will sit here for a while, though. Not that I find myself bad company, but sometimes you just want to sit near someone, even if they are blubbering like a baby."

Fenny lifted her head off the cradle of her arms.

"I . . . am . . . not . . . blubbering . . . like . . . a . . . baby!"

"Sure you are," said the man. "But like I said, it doesn't matter. I can take conversation or I can leave it. It's mostly the coffee I came for."

Fenny sniffed; she had to admire the Marine's honesty, if not his social skills. She sat with her head down, and slowly her jagged little breaths stopped and her breathing returned to normal.

Neither spoke for minutes, but then the old man pulled a harmonica out of his back pocket.

"I hope you don't mind if I play, because I'm going to whether you mind or not. I can't let a good campfire go by without a little music."

Fenny shrugged; not that the man noticed. Closing his eyes, he put the harmonica to his lips and began to play.

Fenny wouldn't have been surprised if the old man had turned out to be Segovia on the blues harp; after all, he had the *attitude*. She was surprised to hear what could only be described as noise.

He played, or tried to, "The Marine's Hymn," and then he destroyed "Ballad of the Green Berets" with notes so wrong and off-key that a military unit, upon hearing them, might decide to join the other side. Fenny laughed at his audacity.

Keeping her head in her arms, she tried to keep her laughter a secret thing; after all, just because he was a jerk didn't mean he wasn't sensitive about his music. But when a loud snort escaped from her nose, she sat up, deciding to come clean.

"I'm sorry," she said, but he was oblivious to what she was apologizing for, continuing to play as if his audience were a rapt one.

Finally someone from another campsite yelled, "Find a key and stick to it!" to which the old man yelled back, "Drop dead!"

"Drop dead yourself!"

The old man blew his bad notes louder and within moments there came the sound of someone stomping through the underbrush, and suddenly there stood by the fire a man dressed only in Bermuda shorts.

Fenny was startled, to say the least. She had planned to spend a quiet evening in depressed reflection; certainly hosting a campsite brawl had not been on her agenda.

The old Marine looked up at his adversary but kept on playing, louder and lousier.

"Hey, gramps, I don't want to start a fight or anything," said the man in Bermuda shorts, "but I will if you don't stop that noise."

The old man's mouth was obscured by his harmonica, but his eyes narrowed as if he were smiling. He kept on playing, this song an excruciating version of "Camptown Races."

"Okay, I've given you plenty of warning," said the man in the Bermuda shorts, raising his fists. But before he stepped forward to deck the man who was interfering with the peace and quiet a harried commercial plumber from Omaha certainly had a right to while on vacation in northern Minnesota, he turned to Fenny.

"I gave him plenty of warning," he told her, as if he wanted to make sure that all parties agreed that, yes, he had given him plenty of warning. He stepped back then, hands on hips, and craned his head forward as if he were seeing a rare specimen at the zoo.

"Fenny? Fenny Ness? My wife and I just saw you in *Ike and Inga*. My God!" He cupped his hands to his mouth and yelled in the direction from whence he had come. "Babs—Babs, guess who I've got over here? Fenny Ness!"

This announcement was finally the one thing that got the nonmusical instrumentalist to stop playing.

Cocking his head, he looked at Fenny, who looked stricken, like a suspect wrongly identified in a lineup.

"Hey, *pal*, that's not Fenny Nest or whoever the hell you think it is. That's my bride—now get out of here and quit disturbing our honeymoon!"

He leapt up, with an agility that belied his age, and lunged. The Bermuda shorts man, who knew when to fight and when to run, ran, bumping into his wife, who had rushed over hearing of a celebrity in their midst.

After the bickering voices of the couple faded, Fenny thanked the man.

"Anytime. So who are you supposed to be?"

"Some movie actress, I guess."

"Movie actress," said the Marine, shaking his head. "You want to impress me, you live on bugs in the jungle while outfoxing the Japs." He tapped the spit out of his harmonica, his eyes locked on Fenny. "You know what tickles me? The pansy believed my story. About us being married, I mean."

"Don't get any ideas," said Fenny, not liking a certain glimmer in the old man's eyes.

"In the Marines I was a colonel," he said. "But most women—and I believe the count is over a thousand, thank you—rank me a general on the love front."

"Whatever a stupid love front *is*," said Fenny, standing up, "you're not going to be on mine. Now please leave my campsite or I'll call the ranger."

"I'm an expert at all hand-to-hand."

"*Now*."

Had the old man been a Marine colonel today, Fenny was certain he would have been court-martialed, probably on harassment charges, if not assault.

"Okay by me," said the man, putting his hands in his pockets as he began to walk away. "You're not my type anyway. I hate crybabies."

Fenny sat by the campfire, shaking, out of both fear and anger. The thought of spending the night next to a crazed former Marine who may or may not decide to launch a sneak attack was one she could not bear, and so she doused the fire and packed up her gear, trying to ignore the sound of the old man's cackles.

Earlier that afternoon, around the time Fenny was working off thousands of calories in her frenzied canoeing, Lee was considering a marriage proposal. It came from Slim, after he had picked up Lee and the baby and brought them back to her apartment. He even got on his knees.

"I know I'm not what you'd call a good catch," he said, "considering the precariousness of both my physical and mental health, but what the hell, you can't have everything, right?"

Lee smiled, touching her dear friend's face.

"I don't know where Bill's going to come in, in all of this," continued Slim, "but it would be my privilege to help you with the baby, Lee, to teach him the essentials . . . how to throw a fastball, how to do long division, how to dodge the draft."

Lee laughed. "I think maybe we should teach him how to sleep through the night first." She looked at the baby, asleep on the coffee table in a wicker laundry basket Lee had lined with a folded bath towel. "I'm going to have to get a bassinet," she said, "although maybe I'll have him sleep in bed with me for a while."

"Lee," said Slim, and he groaned a little as he got off his knees. "You don't have to answer me right away. You can think about it."

"Thanks, Slim. I will."

Slim touched the baby's cheek with his forefinger. "What are you going to name him?"

"I don't know yet," said Lee. "I was thinking of names before he was born and the one I came up with was Sean—it's a good Irish name—but now I don't know if that fits him."

"I guess there's no hurry," said Slim.

"Right," said Lee. "It's not as if he has to answer a roll call."

Lee leaned forward, wincing a little from the pain a newly delivered mother feels, and picked up her baby.

"I know you're not supposed to pick up a sleeping baby," she said, "but how I can resist?"

The infant didn't awaken, but pursed his tiny mouth and crinkled his tiny nose as if he might. He was as bald as Lorenz Ferré without his toupee and his head had the particular point most babies acquire in their travels down the birth canal, but of course to Lee he was the most exquisite thing she had ever seen.

A teardrop splashed on the baby's cheek and he jerked reflexively but still did not wake up.

"I didn't even realize I was crying," said Lee, wiping her eyes. "I just feel so blessed." The only thing intruding upon her euphoria was the pain she felt over hurting Fenny. "Still, I wish things weren't so screwed up."

"Yes," agreed Slim, "life could sure be swell if *life* didn't keep intruding."

When Fenny left Bill outside the hospital in Baudette, he began walking back to Tall Pine. He knew it would be a *long* walk, a forty-mile walk, but he didn't have anything else to do and so he set out. He walked for several hours and then as it grew dark he stopped at a roadside motel called the El-Ray and slept fitfully until morning. He wasn't on the road for more than five minutes when Lars and Trude Larson, on their way home from an overnight visit to his mother in Roseau, intercepted him.

"You want a ride or the exercise?" Lars asked, pulling over in his truck.

"I'll take the ride," said Bill, opening the door.

When the Cup O'Delight had reopened, it had gone back to its closed-on-Sundays policy, but Bill didn't know this. He stood peering into the window for a long time, hoping that, by sheer force of his will, people would appear inside. Not knowing what to do with himself or where to go, he went to the narrow stairwell that led to the apartments and rang Slim's bell, hoping the man would be there and not off visiting Lee. He stood for a long while and then rang Lee's bell, just because he was bored and the bell had a different ringer on it. He rang Slim's bell—a steady buzzing E, and then he rang Lee's bell, which was two short C sharps. He added a little beat by rapping on the door and was about to add to the percussion by giving a little kick when the door opened.

"You're home!" said Bill, surprised.

"And you're a pest," said Slim. "Stop ringing those doorbells—you'll wake up the baby."

"The baby's home?" asked Bill. "Already?"

"They send 'em home early these days," said Slim. He opened the door wider. "Come on in."

Upstairs, Bill knelt by the makeshift bassinet, staring at his son.

"He's a big one, isn't he?"

"Nine pounds, four ounces," said Lee. "Twenty-two inches. Of course, with the two of us, I wouldn't expect anything smaller."

Bill coughed; the reference to the baby's parentage made him uncomfortable.

"Lee," he said, sitting down in the easy chair that faced the coffee table. "Lee, you know I love Fenny."

Lee nodded. "Of course I do."

"And you know I'm going to do everything I can to make sure she'll stay with me, right?"

"Bill," said Slim impatiently, "are you trying to make her feel bad on purpose?"

"He's not making me feel bad, Slim, he's just trying to explain things to me." Lee looked at Bill. "Right?"

"Right. Thank you. That's all I want to do." Bill smiled, his first of the day. "You're such a nice person, Lee. I know you'll make a wonderful mother—it's just that I don't know how much of a father I will be, or want to be . . . at least right now."

"You should have thought of that earlier," snapped Slim in such a way that Lee had to laugh.

"Slim, that's something my mother would have said. And don't be so old-fashioned—I think it's pretty clear that neither one of us was thinking much of anything . . . at the time."

Unconsciously, Bill shook his head. It mortified him, this talk about a night that he had tried so hard (and now would never be able) to forget.

"What are you thinking, Bill?" asked Lee gently. She hated to see him look so miserable.

"I'm just overwhelmed, I guess." Enough so that he was having a hard time not crying. He blew a big gust of air out of his mouth and looked at Lee. "And then I was thinking about contraceptives."

"Fine time!" said Slim.

"Slim!" scolded Lee.

"I was thinking about how great it would be," continued Bill, unfazed by Slim's heckling, "if your body understood when you only wanted to have a good time and released some kind of spermicide. And then when you had sex because you wanted to conceive, no spermicide would be released."

"What if the man was thinking one way and the woman was thinking another?" asked Slim, his voice raised.

"Whoever didn't want a baby would win," said Bill, "because bringing a baby into the world is such a momentous decision, both parties should be in agreement."

"But then that would prevent happy accidents," said Lee. "And this, Bill, is the happiest accident of my life."

"Well . . . you've had nine months to think about it all," said Bill, "and I . . . well, I'll support the baby financially, I just can't promise what I'm going to do, uh . . . emotionally."

"As I told Lee earlier," said Slim tightly, "I'd be happy to do that."

"Slim, I don't know if you're trying to defend my honor or what—but cut it out, okay? And Bill is right, I had nine months to think about this—well, actually six, since I didn't realize I was pregnant until I was in my third month. I was just going through so much trauma, I guess, I didn't miss my periods, but then it dawned on me: Oh, my God, maybe I'm pregnant! I drove into Santa Fe and got a pregnancy test, and I can't tell you what I felt when it turned blue: glee and terror and everything in between. I'd always wanted a child, but I was beginning to think my luck had run out."

From the laundry basket came a faint cry.

"Hey," said Bill, looking at the baby, "he sounds like a kitten."

"Hand him to me, will you, Bill?" asked Lee.

"Me?" But he was already standing, reaching into the basket.

"Remember to support his head," said Slim.

Bill lifted the baby, bundled in a blanket and wrapped like a package. He held it in the crook of his arm, and the baby opened his eyes.

"He's looking at me," he said.

"You're probably kind of blurry to him," said Lee. "He can't really focus yet."

Bill lifted the package until his face was inches away from the baby's.

"Heh-woe," he said. "How's my sweet widdo boy?"

Hungry, the baby mistook the end of Bill's nose for a nipple. Startled, Bill drew back his head. The baby let out a cry.

"Bill, he's trying to nurse," said Lee, laughing.

"You've got some things to learn, little buddy," said Bill, handing him over to Lee.

After the baby had his lunch, he and Lee napped and Slim and Bill decided to take a walk.

"Sorry if I came down hard on you," said Slim. "It's just that I'm so worried about her."

"Worried about Lee? That, Slim, is worry *misspent*."

"No," said Slim, shaking his head. "Raising a kid by yourself is hard work. I *know*. My dad died when I was a boy and my mother nearly lost her mind." He shrugged. "She never *barked*, but she was a nervous wreck."

"My mother raised me by herself, too," said Bill. "She did the best she could, but I know things would have been different—better—if I had a dad."

They were by the river, which was traveling urgently, as if it had to get someplace in a hurry. The crabapple trees were past bloom and with every breeze scattered their pink petals to the ground like flower girls.

"Mind if we sit down?" asked Slim. "I'm a little winded."

There was a bench on the walkway, but Slim chose to sit down on the nearest surface, which was the grass.

Bill looked at his friend. "Hey, with all that's happened, I haven't even been able to talk to you about *you*."

"I asked Lee to marry me."

"You did?" said Bill, surprised. "Why?"

"*Why?* Because I love her and I want to help her."

"I didn't know you loved her *that* way."

"I love Lee any way she wants me to love her. If she loves me as a friend, I'll be her best friend. If she loves me as a husband, why, I'll love, honor, obey, cherish . . . all that stuff."

"What did she say?"

Slim shrugged. "She didn't say—but I take that to be a no."

"I'm sorry."

"Well, the offer's always open, so who knows? She might change her mind in a weak moment."

Laughing, Bill picked up a pebble and threw it. Both men watched as it skittered and hopped and skipped across the water's surface like a flapper on a dance floor.

"So what does the doctor say?" Bill said after a moment.

Slim blew air through his lips in a dismissive sound.

"He says I have leukemia. He says I should probably have a bone-marrow transplant. Beyond that, I don't listen much."

"What do you mean?"

"He gives me percentages and prognoses, but what good are they? How can they predict what's going to happen to *me*?"

"What *is* going to happen to you?"

Compared to Slim's smile, the Cheshire Cat's seemed demure.

"I'll dance on *all* your graves."

The Tall Pine grapevine rivaled any mass communications systems for dispensing information. When Bill and Slim got back to the Cup O'Delight, they were greeted by their friends.

"We heard Lee had her baby!" crowed Frau Katte.

"We ran into Lars and Trude Larson at the Northlands Inn," explained the mayor.

"They like the prime rib, too," said Heine, who every Sunday stood in the buffet line with his wife and the Lambordeauxs. "I wonder why they didn't say anything at church—"

"Well, how could they?" said the mayor. "They were ushering."

"We would have been here earlier," said Heine, "but we had to spend the whole afternoon 'antiquing' with Irene and Dolly—"

"If *that* doesn't make a man wish he were single again," said the mayor.

"We *thought*," said Miss Penk, wanting to get back to the business at hand, "that maybe we'd all carpool over to Baudette to see Lee."

"She's not there," said Bill. "Slim picked her and the baby up."

Mary Gore pointed to the upstairs window. "Madonna and Child are Chez Lee's?"

"Can we see zem?" asked Frau Katte.

"She was sleeping when we left," said Slim. "But I'll tell you what. I'll go up there and if she's awake and *wants* company, I'll let you know. Otherwise you'll have to am-scray."

"What about him?" asked Frau Katte as Big Bill followed Slim up the stairs.

"He's the father," reminded Slim. "He gets extra privileges."

Lee was still sleeping and so was the baby. Slim and Bill stood in the bedroom doorway, looking at the two.

"Madonna and Child are Chez Lee's," said Slim, mimicking Mary Gore. "Well, I guess she's right; if anyone looks like Madonna and Child, it's those two."

Lee slept on her side, one arm under her head, the other circling the baby.

"He won't roll off or anything, will he?" asked Bill.

"I don't think he can roll much yet," said Slim. "Besides, Lee's maternal instinct would probably wake her up before he did anything like that."

"And it is a king-size bed," noted Bill.

Downstairs, Slim told everyone they couldn't come in yet, but he would open the Cup O'Delight if anyone cared to wait.

"I'll make grilled cheeses for supper," said Frau Katte.

"And I'll make strawberry milk shakes," said Mary Gore.

"Make mine chocolate," said the mayor.

"Mine, too," said Miss Penk.

"I'll take vanilla," said Heine.

"Same here," said Frau Katte.

It wasn't yet nine o'clock when Fenny pulled up in front of the Cup O'Delight. The lights were on and she saw her friends, and she sat for a few moments watching them, building up her confidence. Finally, she took a breath that filled up her lungs and went inside.

"Hello, everyone."

She stood in the threshold for a moment and then Bill, his face a mixture of hope and trepidation, went to her. He got the cue he wanted when she held her arms out to him.

Everyone burst into applause.

"Oh, Fenny," said Bill, hugging her. "I'm so glad you came back."

"Came back to you," she whispered.

Bill broke free of their embrace. "Did you hear that, everybody? Did you hear that? Fenny says she came back to me!"

"Zree cheers!" said Frau Katte.

"Hip hip hooray!" chorused the crowd.

Bill took Fenny by the hand and led her to the two booths where everyone had congregated.

"Oh, Lee, can I hold him?"

The baby was gently passed to Fenny.

"Look, he's looking at me."

"Don't get your nose too close to him," advised Slim, "or he'll clamp on to it."

"He's so beautiful," said Fenny, touching his soft cheek. "And his head isn't nearly so pointed anymore."

Lee smiled. "Yeah, it's almost round compared to yesterday."

"I zink he should wear my fez," said Frau Katte. "It's za perfect shape for him."

"Okay, no more head jokes," said Bill. "We don't want him to get a complex."

"Fenny," said Lee, looking at her friend with shining eyes. "I can't tell you how glad I am that you're back."

"And back with me," said Bill, not wanting Fenny to forget what she had told him.

"So why did you?" asked Frau Katte. "Why did you come back to za cad?"

"*Katte*," said Miss Penk.

"Just kidding." She grinned at Bill and Fenny. "Alzough I *am* curious."

Fenny sighed. "As much as I think this is just between *Bill and me*, I know you'll never allow me that luxury."

"Well, we're your friends," said Miss Penk.

"With our words we build bridges," said Mary Gore.

Slim bared his teeth and growled.

Lee playfully swatted Slim. "I thought you were going to kennel the dog for a while."

"Why, I'd be *crazy* to do that." He looked at Fenny. "Can I hold the baby now?"

"We've been passing him around like a football," said Frau Katte. "He hasn't cried once."

As Fenny handed the baby to Slim, Miss Penk said, "Okay, now, so let's hear it."

"Wait," said Frau Katte. "Before you say anyzing, let me just say zat I for one knew zat you wouldn't break up, because true love never dies."

"Maybe not," said Fenny. The mayor slid over, giving her room to sit down in the booth. "But other things can happen to it."

Bill sat facing her, the look on his face like a defendant's waiting for a verdict.

"Things like mistrust," she continued, "or fear, stubbornness—I think all those things can at least *maim* it." She looked into Big Bill's brown eyes, and her heart pounded, thinking how close they had come to crippling their own love. Bill's hand reached for hers and she took it. "I went camping, hoping to get some 'deep insight' "— here her voice had a mocking tone—"but all I got was an old Marine colonel trying to pick me up."

"Really?" asked Slim. "What was his name?"

"He was World War Two," said Fenny. "Before your time." She looked again at Bill, and Lee couldn't help but think she looked at him the way a bride looks while taking her vows.

"Sometimes . . . ," she said, "sometimes we do things that we have no control over—"

"I don't know about zat," interrupted Frau Katte. "Zat makes us sound pretty helpless."

Fenny ignored the Swiss woman. "I just have to think that you and Lee . . . 'getting together' was something you didn't have much mental *or* physical control over. When the terrible stuff happened I . . . I think your bodies decided that, just for a little while, they were going to help you forget about it."

Bill squeezed Fenny's hand, hoping that by his touch she would realize how deeply grateful he was to know and love her.

"Ouch," she said.

Sheepish, Bill released her hand, reminding himself to remember his own strength.

"I'm kidding, Bill," she said, taking his hand back. "Anyway, thinking about all this on the way home, I thought, am I really going to let one brief moment—humor me in thinking it was *brief*," she said dryly, looking at Bill and then Lee. "Anyway, is that one brief moment of losing control going to make me surrender? Surrender the one man who was able to *drive* us all to the hospital?"

"You *drove*, Bill?" asked the mayor.

Bill, near tears, blurted out a laugh. "I was scared stiff."

"Well, I thought it was an act of bravery, Bill," said Fenny, "and then I started thinking how acts of bravery *are* acts of love."

Frau Katte leaned her head on Miss Penk's shoulder, certainly understanding that sentiment.

"And then turn that around: loving is the bravest act of all." Fenny looked at her friends, her smile sheepish. "I know I'm going on and on—but you know how it is when you finally figure something out?"

"Like when I learned how to program za VCR," said Frau Katte. "Remember, Miss? I was so proud, I couldn't shut up about it."

"That's how I feel," said Fenny. "I feel so proud to have figured this stuff out. I thought of all the people who've been too afraid to love—Mae; and your son Alphonse, Miss Penk; and your dad, Frau Katte. I thought about that stupid Marine colonel who was all alone, even though he bragged about being with over one thousand women."

"*One thousand women?*" said Heine.

"I thought about them all and I don't want to be like any of them," continued Fenny. She looked at their joined hands, saw their courage-bead wedding rings. "Remember how we talked about it—joked about it, Bill? About being brave? Well, I want to be brave—*you've* made me be that brave. I'll even take a few hits if I have to . . . because it's worth it."

Silence once again filled the room, but this time it was Mary Gore who broke it. " 'I Was a Soldier on the Battlefield of Love'—will you write that up, Fenny, and let me put it in the next *Angel Motors?*"

Lee laughed, but it wasn't in response to Mary's request.

"I've got it," she said, excitement raising her voice. "I've got it! I'm going to call the baby Fenton! Fenton after you, Fenny. For being so brave."

"Oh, my," said Fenny.

"It's perfect," said Bill.

The baby gurgled, and pursed his mouth in an O.

"Look," said Miss Penk, in whose arms he now rested.

Frau Katte craned her head. "I zink he wants some O'Delight."

Looking at Lee, the mayor, with hope in his voice, said, "Don't we all."

"Hey, it practically took me a half hour to get down here from upstairs—and now you expect *me*—a woman who just gave birth—to get up and make a pot of coffee?"

The answer was a resounding "Yes!"

"The things I do for you," she said, and, planting her palms on the tabletop for support, she slowly rose.

"The zings we do for *you*," countered Frau Katte.

"That's right," said Mary Gore, who couldn't blather so much without occasionally coming up with something that wasn't completely asinine. "That's what friends are for."

And of course, with that lead-in, Bill had no choice but to sit himself down at the piano, and soon the fragrance of brewing O'Delight filled the cafe, and the baby Fenton sat on Miss Penk's lap in the wheelchair and, in his unfocused fashion, witnessed his first Tall Pine Polka.

Epilogue

They all thought they were going to lose Slim at the end of that summer. He lost twenty pounds on a frame that was already ten pounds underweight, and he was too weak to navigate the stairs from his apartment to the Cup O'Delight.

"His only chance is a bone-marrow transplant," his doctor told Lee, and all of the Cup O'Delight regulars submitted to blood tests, hoping they could be Slim's donor.

Bill especially liked the idea of being able to give some of his lifeblood to Slim, because "it would make us brothers, in a way, and since we are sort of co-fathers to Fenton, it would make us seem all the more related."

Unfortunately, no one matched Slim's type, and a call was made throughout the town of Tall Pine and, being the good neighbors they were, almost everyone who was asked agreed to be tested.

The surprise "winner" was Gloria Murch, although when Lee told Slim who his match was, he said in a raspy whisper, "Nope. No way. Nada. No, no, *no.*"

"Hey, it could have been Mary Gore."

"No, I won't accept it. I'd owe her. She'd want me to go to church then and be a deacon or fold programs or head up the youth group."

"Don't be silly, Slim; Gloria's going to give you this gift and you're going to take it."

Gloria, too, was somewhat apprehensive about this sort of gift-giving.

"I know it's better to give than to receive," she said in a small voice to the pastor the night before the procedure, "but it's sure not as much *fun.*"

Slim rallied after the transplant and is still going strong. He hasn't yet become a member of Benevolent Father's, but he leaves the occasional bouquet on Gloria's desk at the church, with a note reading, "You're in my blood," or simply, "Thanks."

He and Lee never married, but they might as well have. They both still live in the upper apartments and spend so much time in each other's that the walls that separate them could well be invisible.

Fenton at four years old is as big as a first-grader. Bill's genes are evident in his black hair and his tawny coloring, but he's got Lee's navy blue eyes.

Long ago, he sorted out all important relationships; Lee was "Mama," Slim was "Papa," Bill was "Daddy," and Fenny was "LaLa." Fenny has no idea where that came from, but she says, "Fenton can call me anything, anytime, and I'll answer."

He's an early riser and helps Lee in the cafe, cracking eggs for the pancake batter and filling the napkin dispensers.

One morning, as she was making the day's O'Delight, he asked her what she was doing.

"Can you keep a secret?"

The boy nodded solemnly. "I can keep a secret."

She hoisted her son up on the edge of the counter and he sat there facing her, his hands folded in his lap.

"Fenton, it's important for you to know that much of God's earth is a great mystery."

"What's a 'mystery'?"

"Oh, lots of things."

"Lots of things like what?"

Lee tilted her head in thought. "Well, love is, I guess."

"Why?"

Lee laughed at her son the inquisitor. "Because . . . because you're surprised when it finds you, I guess. Because it's like the very best present you could ever get and sometimes, if you're lucky, a couple people want to give it to you."

"I'll give it to you, Mama."

"And I'll give it back," said Lee, holding her sweet boy to her chest.

"What else is a mystery?" Fenton asked, prying himself out of his mother's hug.

"Well . . . ," said Lee, and, glancing down, she flexed one of her feet. "How a quiet man could make the most beautiful shoes in the world without anyone ever knowing." Since Pete's death, Lee hadn't worn any shoes other than the ones he made and now had on a pair of rubber-soled taupe lace-ups that she assumed he had meant for her to wear at work.

She sighed and returned to her O'Delight. "Let's see, other mysteries: how the tides follow the moon; how a dog can find its way to its master's new home halfway across the country; how trees know when to bud and when to let their leaves fall." With a sly smile, she held up the small jar holding her secret ingredient. She filled a tablespoon with it and tapped it into the canister of ground coffee. "And how to make a cup O'Delight," she said. "That is a mystery to all but us."

"Why?"

"Because no one can figure out its secret." She put the filter basket into the coffee machine and turned it on. "Sometimes people like not knowing things, Fenton. It gives them a little thrill to think that even if they don't know something now, they might someday. They like the mystery."

"Can I have some chocolate milk?"

Lee laughed. She picked up a small glass and filled it from the stainless-steel dispenser. "White milk's better in the morning."

She regarded her son sitting on the counter, swinging his strong little legs as he drank his milk, and she sent a silent thank-you, up past the red metallic disks, through the ceiling vent, and into the great beyond, to her God who had given her so much.

"Now, this stuff . . . ," she said, pointing to the brewing coffee, "this is our secret, right, Fen?"

"Right, Mama," he answered, and then licked off his little milk mustache. "Our secret."

Alphonse heard about his mother's injury on the news and several weeks later a get-well card arrived in the mail. It bore only his signature, but following letters became chattier and led to phone calls, which led to a visit. After hugging her grown son, Miss Penk tearfully exclaimed that she could now "die happy."

"Well, you could," said Frau Katte. "But don't."

The two women capped their long contest career by winning one hundred thousand dollars in the "Give Us the 'Rand Pianos' Slogan" sweepstakes. ("The Grand Rand—For a Noteworthy Life.") They debated whether to buy a painting (they had extra wall space since giving the Manet to Fenny and Bill for a wedding present) or set up a scholarship fund for disabled students. Altruism won out and their first recipient, a young woman who lost a leg in a powerboat accident, is about to graduate from the University of Minnesota with a degree in music. She brought her French horn to Tall Pine and jammed with everyone on a Polka Night, telling Heine he was a "true folk artist on the accordion." He was tickled by the compliment, but not as tickled as when he heard from a state senator that a bird sanctuary that had been endangered was now saved "because of the efforts of concerned citizens like you."

"See?" Heine told the mayor. "See what a little letter-writing can do? We'll get that gun control yet."

There were several deaths in Tall Pine—Mae's being the one that directly affected Fenny and Bill the most. With the birth of Fenton, an uneasy truce had been forged. The old woman loved holding the baby and decided that "it ain't his fault he's a bunch of different things—I can tell by the way he carries hisself he's mostly Indian." (This she said when the baby couldn't even sit up yet.) Mae hadn't been a soap opera fan all those years for nothing; she appreciated the tangled story of Fenton's parentage. She also appreciated the way Fenny handled the whole thing, how whenever she and Bill brought over the baby, she treated him as if he were hers. Mae, of course, would never tell this to Fenny; there were just so many concessions she could make in one lifetime. She died of a brain aneurysm while watching "All My Children." She bequeathed all her money and property to Fenton, with the understanding that "his dad and Fenny can do what they like with it until you're old enough to take over."

Corby Deele fell asleep out on a frozen lake, in his ice house, and never woke up. Cause of death was carbon monoxide poisoning due to a faulty heater. His children leased the Clip Joint to a barber from Superior, Wisconsin, whose surly attitude and high prices forced him out of business. Currently a barber named Vern occupies the shop and has turned it into a shrine for Dean Martin. The walls are covered with Dean Martin's pictures and movie posters, and only his music is played.

Once the mayor offered to bring in some of his tapes—some Roger Williams or Tennessee Ernie Ford—because, "after all, variety is the spice of life."

Vern crossed himself as if he had just heard blasphemy.

"Dean Martin *is* the spice of life."

Mary Gore's father died of old age, leaving Mary the printing business. She runs it successfully, printing business forms, wedding and graduation invitations, as well as *Angel Motors*, which was recently featured in the *New York Times* in an article about thriving regional publications.

Her charmed collaboration with Christian Freed was not to be repeated; they attempted to work together, but what had clicked in the Northlands Inn didn't click via fax and telephone, and besides, Christian liked the spotlight all to himself.

He has spent plenty of time in it: two Emmys, an Oscar, and a Writers' Guild award sit on his mantelpiece. He writes faster these days, thanks to his vast collection of old movie scripts, which he often mines for ideas. Christian is careful to change names, places, and genres, and no one has accused him of plagiarism yet, although his old "Perky the Puppy" writing partner told him he thought his last picture was "awfully Casablancaesque."

It is a high life that Christian lives in Bel Air, California. Starlets call him for dates; stars call him for parts. He has everything he ever wanted in Hollywood—status, money, power, *and* a personal trainer. It is his Uncle Harry's belief that even though he may never get his comeuppance, he will never learn his lessons, either.

Occasionally Christian sees Doug Woo on a set and the cinematographer always proudly shows off the latest pictures of the twin boys he and Grace Aisles had together. Pregnancy was the one thing that made Grace give up smoking, although in a letter to Fenny she wrote that if anything makes a person want a cigarette, it's twin boys.

Grace and Doug tried to get the L.A.-based cast and crew members of *Ike and Inga* together for "Tall *Palm* Polka Nights," but the idea never panned out. Grace thought it was because no one could figure out exactly what a Polka Night was—a party or a state of mind—and people in Hollywood need a definite reason for their get-togethers. Doug's thought was simpler; sometimes it's just hard to copy an original.

Boyd Burch did show up for the first Polka party, flush from the success of his baseball movie, *Peanuts! Popcorn!* He was sporting dyed black hair and a beard for the leading role in Christian's movie, *Deke York, Bounty Hunter.* He proudly announced he had taken swimming lessons and earned a junior lifeguard badge.

He fired his agent, Mimi Schoals, after she got him twenty million dollars for the third Deke York movie. He had waited until she got him a huge sum of money, because he wanted to give her a commensurate commission.

" 'Commensurate' commission," she had sputtered. "Where'd a dumb cowboy like you find a word like that?"

"The same place I found 'condescending' and 'patronizing,' " said Boyd, who had begun studying a thesaurus nightly. "And I'm tired of you treating me like that. I can be treated like that by my dad—and for free."

Boyd is engaged to be married to a librarian he'd met at the Santa Monica branch who had kindly helped him find self-help books and bring up material from the computer.

"You know, it's something when a critic compares you to Clark Gable," he told Ron Feldman, who had called him from the apple farm he and Bonnie run outside Tacoma, "but when a librarian thinks you're special enough to marry . . . well, that's something *else.*"

Marcy Mincus learned a lot in rehab, most important that it was time for her to give back to the world. She now lives in a Quonset hut in Antarctica, researching the idea that physical cold is conquerable by biofeedback. She has only lost half a toe to frostbite.

In the tradition of Sig and Wally, in the tradition of her Nordic ancestors, Fenny has, along with her husband, been seeing the world. Their first stop was Hawaii.

"You let him know how proud I am of him," Bill's mother, Charlotte, told Fenny as the two women walked a path along the vast pit that was the volcano Kilauea. Bill was far ahead of them, taking pictures like Perry and his father probably did, years ago.

"He says he broke your heart when he was thrown in jail."

"My Bill could have been anything he wanted to be—he was that smart. Two scholarships." She poked out her lower lip and the women walked in silence for a moment. "Yeah, I guess I was plenty hurt, but not to the point of having my heart broken. I save that for the big stuff."

"What was Bill's dad like?"

"You don't fool around, do you?"

Fenny shrugged. "Not when it comes to Bill."

The older woman nodded. "I like that. You always be a tiger for my Bill." She stepped aside as a group of tourists passed. "Well, he sure loved macadamia nuts."

Fenny laughed. "I've already heard that from Bill. Anything else?"

The woman squinted as if trying to see something in the far distance. "If you must know," she said finally, "he didn't want the baby. It's what broke us up. He said, 'You can have the baby, or you can have me.'"

"Oh," said Fenny, as sadness seemed to step beside her on the path. "But what about that picture of you two when you were expecting—I've seen that picture—it's right on the wall in your living room?"

"It was just a pose," said Bill's mother, scratching her eyebrow with her thumbnail. "I was already living back with my mother. It was probably someone saying, 'Smile for the camera'—or who knows, I probably grabbed his hand and put it there. Either way, he was gone the next day for good. Never saw him again."

Fenny folded her arms across her chest, shaking her head in tiny motions.

"We hardly even knew each other before we got married. He

played the steel guitar in a band and had the prettiest voice you'd ever want to hear, and I fell for him the first time I saw him. But the band was a bunch of goof-offs that drank away any money they made. I gave him an ultimatum—you get a real job or you get lost. When he found out I was expecting, he gave me an ultimatum back.

" 'I don't want no baby!' he screamed at me. 'Do you understand—no baby. You can have me or the baby, but not both.' "

Charlotte flicked a graying black braid behind her back. "A couple weeks later was when I heard he got killed. He was working as a day laborer—he'd do that when they couldn't find music jobs—working with a construction crew that was putting up a hotel on Manele Bay." She looked at Fenny. "It's funny Bill's making his living with music now. Like his dad always wanted to."

"Bill's happy," said Fenny. "He's finally found what he wants to do."

"I guess I can see that," said Charlotte. She took her daughter-in-law's hand. "You won't tell Bill any of this, will you?"

"No," Fenny said, and seeing her husband wave to her, she waved back. "No, I won't tell Bill."

And she hadn't. Bill's mother was right in not telling her son the whole truth, for truth wasn't always beauty—truth could be ugly and painful and a killer of dreams. So she kept quiet on their visit to the island Bill grew up on, and swam with Bill in waters the color of jewelry and laughed at his jokes and ate dim sum and laulau and sushi and made love with him on white sand beaches. Once as he slept, she cried long and hard as a Hawaiian moon cast a soft light in their room, cried for Bill's father, who died before he could ever know how wrong he was, before he could meet his boy who could have sung duets with him, who could have played piano to his guitar, who was his father's son.

From Hawaii they left for the South Seas, and it was then Fenny realized that they weren't on a visit, but a journey.

"I finally figured out why I was never so keen on adventure," Fenny told Bill after a morning of snorkeling in Bali. "It's because I didn't have someone to share it with."

Bill was a game and cheerful traveling companion (who was just as happy being a driver as a passenger in the cars they occasionally rented), his only complaint focusing on the lack of quality candy worldwide.

"I hate to be such a nationalist," he told Fenny, "but really, American candy is unsurpassed."

They began their travels three and a half years after *Ike and Inga* was released and two years after *Winifred Jones* was in theaters. (*Winifred Jones* wasn't the colossal hit *Ike and Inga* was, but a hit nevertheless, earning Fenny a Golden Globe nomination and offers, as her former agent said, "up the yazoo," all of which he had to turn down, explaining, "She's out of the business.")

Still, people recognized her in Scotland, in Suriname, and in Shanghai, pressing against her in pubs or pagodas or temples, asking excitedly, "Are you Fenny Ness? Would you mind taking a picture with us?"

She had learned to say no to the first question, and if they insisted she was lying and asked the second, she would answer with a small lecture.

"Yes. I do mind. Look around you! Take a picture of the landscape—or a local—start swimming in waters a little deeper than celebrity!"

"That last line I might use in a song," joked Bill outside the Eiffel Tower, after two American tourists got Fenny's lecture and stomped off, muttering about "star trips" and "ego problems."

Harry Freed left Hollywood and moved to Gaeta, a town in between Rome and Naples. He has become a new force in the art-film world. For his next movie, he plans to travel the globe, filming children in different countries celebrating their seventh birthday.

"The seventh birthday," he says, kissing his fingertips in a Mediterranean gesture, "that's the sweetest. It's when joy and innocence and greed and a sense of selfhood all coalesce."

Lillian will go with him. Lillian is his secretary, and it was on the occasion of his marriage proposal to her that she insisted he call her by her name.

"What are you talking about?" he asked.

"You've called me all sorts of names throughout the years," said his secretary. "And most of them nice. But now I'd just like to be Lillian. Part of 'Harry and Lillian.' "

"What took you so long?" Fenny asked him when she and Bill made Italy a part of their travel itinerary.

"Not all of us are smart at everything," said Harry. "But sometimes we get lucky and wise up."

"I'm glad you finally did," said Lillian, leaning forward to kiss his cheek.

The foursome was sitting out on a terrace that faced the Tyrrhenian Sea, drinking wine and eating antipasto salad out of big wooden bowls.

"Fenny, why don't we just stay here," said Big Bill. He leaned back in his chair and closed his eyes to the sun.

"Okay," said Fenny, tearing a chunk of bread from the round loaf on the table. "How about it, Harry? We'll be your artists in residence."

"You're no artist," teased Harry.

"Well, Bill is."

"He'd better be—I hired him to score my next movie."

Fenny's mouth dropped open and then lifted into a big smile. "When did this happen?"

"When I listened to Ferré's latest CD."

"The one with ten of Bill's songs on it," said Lillian, as if they needed a reminder. "It's wonderful—although I sure hate those dinky little CDs." She smiled and took a sip of wine. "Did I tell you, Bill, my granddaughter says 'Gone Girl' is her all-time favorite song?"

"Well, to your granddaughter," said Bill, raising his glass.

"To music and movies," said Harry, "and making money together."

After a few more toasts, Harry disappeared inside the house for a moment, and when he returned he said, "Speaking of making money, have you seen this?"

He handed Fenny a copy, in Italian, of *An Insider's Look into the Making of Ike and Inga.*

"It's in Italian, too?" asked Fenny, opening up the book. "David's made a killing off this thing."

"He was a good production assistant," said Harry. "Now I hear he's writing a true-crime novel, about that couple that accidentally hired the same hit man to kill off the other one."

Fenny shook her head. "It sounds no more bizarre than the making of *Ike and Inga*."

"So you never think of returning to the silver screen?" asked Harry as Lillian served coffee in little demitasses.

"Never," said Fenny. "Bill's happy to wallow in showbiz, but me, I'd rather wallow—"

"In motherhood?" interjected Lillian.

Fenny blushed. "How did you know?"

"Oh, a certain look you and Bill give each other. You didn't drink any wine and—"

"Are you saying you're pregnant?" asked Harry.

"And so is the doctor we saw in Rome," said Bill.

"Oh, Fenny," said Harry, and his chair was knocked over in his haste to get up and hug her.

"We were going to tell you," said Fenny. "We were just waiting for the perfect time."

"She got a sonogram," said Bill. "It's a *bambina*."

"Oh," said Lillian, clapping her hands. "A girl!"

"Fenton will have a sister," said Fenny.

"And that's why, as much as we know you hate to see us go, we must," said Bill. "We want to get back to our little boy. And Lee. And Slim."

"And Miss Penk—she's on a wheelchair basketball team now," said Fenny. "And Frau Katte."

"Heine and the mayor."

"Mary Gore."

Bill pressed his lips together, not saying anything.

"All right," said Fenny, laughing. "Maybe not so much Mary— we just want to go home." She got up and went to sit on her husband's lap, and together they looked out at the azure sea.

"Oh, you two look so cute," said Lillian. "Let me take your picture."

Cheek to cheek, they smiled for the camera, and the photograph Lillian sent them shows a man with his arms around his wife, his hands resting lightly on her belly. It would be the first picture Bill, as the family documentarian, would paste in their daughter Sigrid's baby book, right next to the envelope holding the remaining courage beads, which, he would one day tell her, represented a legacy not only from her grandparents, but from her parents as well.

For a long time Bill sat looking at the photograph, and although he liked to make up his own captions, for this picture he would cadge the line used by Fenny, his wise wife who knew what was true: "Mom & Dad, *enhanced*."

The Tall Pine Polka

Lorna Landvik

A Reader's Guide

A Conversation with Lorna Landvik

Q: How did you begin this novel? Did a particular character come to you? Did you imagine the town first?

LL: As in the case of my other two books, the title came into my head and right on its tail, one or two of the main characters.

Q: How does the process of writing work for you?

LL: I try to write every day and if I'm at all blocked, I'll take a nap or eat some dessert. At this stage, it's still so much fun, I'm not blocked much. In that case, I find other excuses to eat dessert.

Q: Throughout this novel the best-laid plans seem to go awry. Did this novel end up as you envisioned it when you began writing?

LL: I really never have an ending when I begin writing. It's a big process of discovery for me.

Q: How have your own life experiences—as an actress, comedian, mother, and so forth—shaped this novel?

LL: I lived in L.A. in my twenties, performing comedy and acting, and I know what a heapin' helping of surrealism Hollywood serves up. I've seen people who I thought were out of their league succeed and people who I thought were wonderfully talented move back to their hometowns and take up dental hygiene. I wanted to write about the many paradoxes of Hollywood that I've seen. But motherhood has probably affected my writing the most in that it has opened up my heart.

Q: What inspired you to make the Hollywood invasion of a small town central to the action of this novel?

LL: I just thought it would be fun.

Q: How would you sell *The Tall Pine Polka* to potential book buyers?

LL: My husband's a better salesman than I—he'll corral people at bookstores and say, "Do you want to laugh and cry? Then read this book." I guess that's how I'd sell this book.

Q: How do you go about crafting a distinct voice for each character?

LL: My characters are very nice to me and come into my head fairly well-formed. The little I *don't* know about them, I discover as I write. Sometimes I'm afraid my characters might be a little over the top, but then I'll meet a real, live person whose eccentricities make those of my characters *pale*. In fact, I think all of us are pretty eccentric in our own wonderful ways.

Q: Miss Fenk and Frau Katte are a truly captivating couple. What do you think is their secret to a successful relationship in the face of tremendous obstacles?

LL: They are true to each other and to themselves despite living in a society that would prefer them *not* to be what they are. Love is mighty, and real love can get a person through a lot.

Q: Female friendships, such as that between Fenny and Lee, seem to be at the heart of all your work. Why is this so?

LL: I'm such a fan of women and our ability to make strong friendships. My own friendships have meant a lot to me — in fact, this book is dedicated to my two best friends, one of whom I've known since the seventh grade.

Q: **The characters in this novel seem haunted by their fears, from a fear of driving to a fear of loving. How did this thematic thread become so central?**

LL: I didn't know that it was a central thematic thread; I learn a great deal from my readers. But the longer I live, the more I learn about people and how they may have fears that I never even suspect. What impresses me is that I didn't know that about them. They got over their fears; they prevailed. I like that bravery.

Q: **Why does Pete work so hard to hide his thriving mail-order business from the rest of Tall Pine?**

LL: He's just so shy and unwilling to have any attention shone on him at all. He's even more of an anticelebrity than Fenny.

Q: **If Pete had had a chance to reveal his feelings to Lee, what do you imagine her response would have been?**

LL: She would have been touched and embarrassed — all those things you feel when someone likes you in a way that you can't reciprocate.

Q: **You skillfully skewer artistic pretensions in this novel, perhaps most notably with the characters of Mary Gore and Christian Freed. Were these characters inspired by real people?**

LL: Certainly I've met people who think art is always spelled in capital letters and that as "artists," they are a special breed. I think we're all given our gifts and we should humbly and gratefully use them to bring all of us together rather than using them to separate us.

Q: **I am sure your readers are curious about Fenny's reluctance to embrace her celebrity. Why did you choose to make her such a reluctant star?**

LL: Nowadays it doesn't seem to matter what people are famous for—all that matters is the fame. Fenny knows herself well enough to realize that her life isn't going to be made better by the adoration of people she doesn't know, especially for acting.

Q: **Fenny's interviews with Marcy Mincus and Gerry Dale, which left both hosts incapacitated, are two of the most vivid and hilarious scenes in this novel. So please tell us what you *really* think about the media.**

LL: I think the media is way too intrusive. We don't need to see a victim of a house fire sobbing as family members are carried out. We don't need to know that a president and his mistress play "Twister"! We don't need all this titillation. Titillation is mind- and soul-numbing.

Q: **Do you think small towns such as your fictional Tall Pine are a dying breed?**

LL: I would love to think that small towns are flourishing, but it does seem that they are being abandoned. What I fear is the suburbanization of the entire country.

Q: **Small towns such as Tall Pine seem increasingly dependent upon tourist dollars for survival. Where do you stand on the debate over development and the "quainting up" of small-town America?**

LL: I don't mind "quainting up" if it's done by mom-and-pop businesses rather than franchises. I love doing book tours and visiting places I've never been, but I have been saddened to see that Elvis Presley Boulevard in Memphis looks a lot like Coon Rapids Boulevard in Minneapolis. I yearn for the return of one-of-a-kind places, in both big cities and small towns, that give you a real sense of place.

Q: **Your author bio mentions that you temped at the Playboy Mansion—what was that like?**

LL: The word "strange" comes to mind. I felt like Margaret Mead exploring a secret culture. I typed and catalogued videotapes there in opulent surroundings—a butler served us tea and cookies at 3 P.M.—but the opulence couldn't erase the pervasive feeling that it was an icky place; women were being exploited.

Q: **Did you always plan to become a novelist?**

LL: As a first grader, I had a brief goal of becoming a baton twirler, but I think that I was more drawn to the fringed boots than the actual baton twirling. Since about sixth grade my career plans were very definite: I wanted to be a writer.

Q: **What advice would you give writers struggling to get published?**

LL: Persist! Believe in yourself and don't let someone's "no" be your final answer.

Q: **What writers and works have most influenced you and why?**

LL: Harper Lee, Anne Tyler, Jon Hassler, Amy Tan, Charles

Dickens, Tom Wolfe, Michael Malone, Pat Conroy, John Irving—I prefer character-driven novels, especially when they take you on big, full rides.

Q: **What would you like your readers to take away with them after finishing this novel?**

LL: I would like them to be happy that they took this trip with me, glad to have met the characters. And it would be great if there were an afterglow, some lingering memories.

Q: **Will we hear from any of these characters again?**

LL: Who knows? My characters always let me know when they want a story told; if some of these people want to return, I'm sure they'll harangue me until I let them out.

Q: **What is next for you? Are you working on a new project?**

LL: More books and the once-a-year show I write so I can get on stage.

Q: **And finally, I have to ask, what is the secret ingredient in a cup of O'Delight coffee?**

LL: If I told you, it wouldn't be a secret.

Reading Group Questions and Topics for Discussion

1. Does Tall Pine, Minnesota seem like a place you would like to live, or just visit? Which option would you choose and why?

2. How does Lee end up in Tall Pine from a penthouse apartment on Lake Shore Drive in Chicago? Why does she stay?

3. Slim is plagued by survivor's guilt, among other things, as a result of his war experiences. Discuss the damage he has sustained and how the healing process works for him.

4. Do you think Big Bill leads Lee on in the beginning, since he is aware that she loves him in a very different way than he loves her?

5. Why do Fenny and Big Bill hide their relationship from Lee for so long? What do you think of Frau Katte's decision to tell Lee herself?

6. How do Fenny and Lee overcome their differences? Do you think you could do the same?

7. "She hums when she's at the grill, Bill—did you notice?" says Pete as he is listing off what he loves about Lee. Discuss the things—big and small—that draw us to other people.

8. Do you think Pete would have given Lee the shoes and declared his love, had he not been interrupted by the appearance of her gun-toting ex-husband? Do you think he enjoyed the dream more than the reality of love?

9. Discuss the reasons why so many characters in this novel have a difficult time expressing their love. Why is it sometimes so hard to break through and say, "I love you"?

10. Why is Mae Little Feather opposed to Big Bill and Fenny getting married? Do you think her objections are totally unfounded? Why does she change her mind?

11. "Movie stars are regular people," says Slim. "People just get a kick out of believing they're not." Discuss the culture of celebrity in American society and how it can distort and damage lives.

12. Did the entertainment and media characters in this novel, such as Boyd Burch, Lorenz Ferre, Marcy Mincus, and Gerry Dale, remind you of any real-life figures? If so, who?

13. Fenny is a very reluctant celebrity. How do you think you would handle being thrust into the spotlight as Fenny is?

14. What do you think prompted the ornery director Malcolm Edgely's transformation on the day he died? Would it have lasted if he had not been struck down by a heart attack?

15. How do Fenny and Big Bill's fears—hers of traveling and his of driving—affect their lives? How do they overcome them? Have you ever suffered from such debilitating anxieties?

16. The denizens of Tall Pine and the visitors from Hollywood view each other with mutual distrust and suspicion in the beginning. How do their opinions of each other, once clouded by stereotypes and ignorance, change (or not) over the course of the novel?

17. Who is your favorite character? Why?

18. Why did your group select this novel?

19. How does this work compare with other works your group has read? What will you be reading next?

20. Do you think your reading group offers a kind of self-made community like that found at Lee's café? How was your group formed? Why do you think it has stayed together?

21. What do you think is the secret ingredient in a cup of O'Delight coffee?

"This book is worth reading and rereading. . . . Landvik evokes female bonding and tragedy in a humorous way."
— *The Register-Herald* (West Virginia)

"Funny and romantic . . . Peopled with characters so real, so warm, so funny . . . Readers will be reminded that this is what it is like to live."
— *The Stuart News*

"A cast of characters, funny, sad and real. You can't help but laugh and shed a tear. [It] Has been compared to Fannie Flagg's *Fried Green Tomatoes at the Whistle Stop Cafe*, but for midwesterners it holds a special appeal with a terrific sense of place."
— *BookWomen* (Minnesota)

"Amazingly vivid . . . This novel breezes merrily along, but don't read it without a hankie. This is a winner.
— *Library Journal*

Excerpts from Reviews of Lorna Landvik's *Your Oasis on Flame Lake*

"Hypnotizing . . . readers won't want to leave Flame Lake."
— *Minneapolis Star Tribune*

"Wonderful . . . fun . . . As lovely as anything you're likely to read. . . . A lot of laughs and a little wisdom."
— *Detroit Free Press*

"Captivating . . . This book should delight. . . . Her characters are clever and offbeat, like Garrison Keillor's or Fannie Flagg's."
— *Booklist*

Written with warmth, wit and tart dialogue, the book engages big themes (love, friendship, loyalty, betrayal and the quest for meaning). . . . Landvik's quirky and passionate characters, and her ardent determination to give them dignity, make this a heartwarming story."

—*Publishers Weekly*

"Quirky characters are a dime a dozen, but truly believable, lovable ones are not—a fact that makes Landvik's latest slice of American life a genuine pleasure."

—*Kirkus Reviews*

"A hard-to-put-down novel that finds complexity and intrigue in the simplest of everyday lives and the simple friendships that offer comfort and support. . . . Very clearly character driven, the storyline evolves from the nature and motivations of the people Landvik renders."

—*Middlesex News*

"The novel builds to a well-crafted and suspenseful climax. . . . [It is] a fine, original novel, leavened with humor."

—*Louisville Voice-Tribune*

"The story is freckled with laughter, sadness and life in general. It will often remind you that those small things you take for granted are the ones you will remember fondly in years to come."

—*Rocky Mountain News*

"In *Your Oasis on Flame Lake*, each of the characters tells his/ her own story. Lorna Landvik skillfully weaves each of these stories into one interesting and attention-holding book."

—*Marietta Journal*

"Some writers do comedy really well. Others pen drama best. Luckily for us, some manage to combine true wit and intense conflict in one narrative. Lorna Landvik . . . manages this feat with aplomb in her latest novel."

—*Boston TAB*

About Lorna Landvik

Writing and theater were Lorna Landvik's twin passions when she was growing up in her hometown of Minneapolis, Minnesota. After graduating from high school, she and her best friend traveled in Europe and settled briefly in Bavaria, supporting themselves as hotel chambermaids and English tutors. When she returned to the States, Landvik briefly attended the University of Minnesota before moving to San Francisco, where she performed stand-up and improvisational comedy. Another move took her to Los Angeles, where she worked as a stand-up comic at the Comedy Store and the Improv, then temped at the Playboy Mansion—"I felt like Margaret Mead studying a secret society"—and scouted bands for Atlantic Records.

After six years in California, Landvik married Chuck Gabrielson, whom she first met at a high school dance back in Minneapolis; their first daughter was born a year later. In 1986, the trio walked across the country with the Great Peace March for Global Nuclear Disarmament. "A thousand people started the march on the West Coast, but we were stranded in the desert and a core group of about four hundred decided to go on," Landvik recalls. "It ended nine months later with a candlelight vigil at the reflecting pool in Washington, D.C." After the march, Landvik and her husband decided to go home to Minnesota.

Landvik, who writes her novels in longhand, has continued to nurture her interest in theater since her return to Minneapolis, appearing in several plays, including *Bad Seed, Lunatic Cellmates,* and *Valley of the Dolls.* She also wrote and starred in *Glamour Queen,* a one-woman show, and *On the Lam with Doe and Rae,* a two-woman show. Landvik is also the author of *Patty Jane's House of Curl* and *Your Oasis on Flame Lake.*